Special thanks to the following people for breathing life into the Godsverse when I thought its light had been blown out:

Katrina Roets, Pat Shand, Starr, Ernie Sawyer, I'm a Ninja, Logan Waterman, Matthew Johnson, Gary Phillips, Ramsey Church, Phil, Melissa Hooper, Jean Lau, Eric P. Kurniawan, Peter Anders, Collin David, Nikres. Joshua Bowers, Jeff Lewis, Emerson Kasak, Linda Robinson, Susan Faw, Talinda Willard, Courtney Cannon, Dave Baxter, old_fogey@yahoo com, Nick Smith, Charlotte Organ, Chad Bowden, Jason Crase, John L Vogt, Philip R. Burns. Bloodfists, Death's Head Studio, LLC, Daniel Groves, Rodney Bonner. JF weber, Walter Weiss, Mitch Fittler, Stacey Henline. Stephanie, Kathy Ash, Charlotte Ulla Pleym, Ray, Jason Schroeder, Chris Call, Maximilian Lippl, Andrew Rees, Tawnly Pranger, Minarkhaios, Vincent Fung, Dave Kochbeck, and Bob Jacobs.

ALSO BY
RUSSELL NOHELTY

THE GODVERSE CHRONICLES
And Death Followed Behind Her
And Doom Followed Behind Her
And Ruin Followed Behind Her
And Hell Followed Behind Her
Katrina Hates the Dead
Pixie Dust

OTHER NOVEL WORK
My Father Didn't Kill Himself
Sorry for Existing
Gumshoes: The Case of Madison's Father
The Invasion Saga
The Vessel
Worst Thing in the Universe

OTHER ILLUSTRATED WORK
The Little Bird and the Little Worm
Ichabod Jones: Monster Hunter
Gherkin Boy

www.russellnohelty.com

And Death Followed Behind Her

By
Russell Nohelty

Edited by:
Leah Lederman

Proofread by:
Katrina Roets

Cover by:
Paramita Bhattacharjee

Dedicated to every fan who read the Katrina Hates the Dead graphic novel and hounded me for years to make more stories in this world. You're to blame for all of this.

Book 1

Katrina Hates the Apocalypse

Prologue

Two years ago, the world went through the end of times, the Apocalypse, or whatever the religious types call it. God beamed all the good boys and girls up to some giant orgy in the sky and left the rest of us asking one question: Why not me?

A rift opened in the desert. Hellspawn poured out onto Earth. They ravaged humanity, ripping us apart for their own pleasure, torturing us in the most grotesquely creative ways possible. They looted our towns, raped our bodies, and slaughtered us at will. It was bedlam; Hell on earth. And there was nothing we could do to stop it.

Then, one day, the monsters got bored and opted for a quiet life in the suburbs. They squatted in the homes of the people they once brutally murdered. They were neither pleasant nor polite neighbors. They threw raucous parties late into the night and played their guitars too loud. They shot off fireworks in the dead of night. They lived like frat boys. We lived in constant fear and in a state of perpetual loneliness, expecting to die and scared to live. We tried to get along any way we could, even after we'd lost everything.

Chapter 1

"Stay out of here, man!"

The metal door of my apartment shook and shuddered over and over as a zombie slammed against it. Wooden doors broke too easily. They splintered and sheared during even a light zombie attack. Metal doors lasted forever, if you could find a few suckers willing to lug it up a flight of stairs for you.

The door slammed again. The zombie on the other side wouldn't give up, I had to give him that. "I told you I'm not letting you in, so piss off!"

Zombies were a nuisance more than anything. Their spongy flesh barely held against your fist. They were only intimidating as a horde, and there haven't been zombie hordes for months. At most, you got a few zombies huddled in a group.

As far as monsters went, zombies ranked at the bottom of the Apocalyptic monster scale. There were all sorts of demons around since the Rapture, not to mention ghosts, and minotaurs, and these three-headed dogs, and seven-headed hydras, too. It's a complete mess. It's what you deal with during a full-blown Apocalypse. The kind the Bible warned us about for all those wasted millennia.

Also, most zombies talked, and not just "we eat brains" either. They were lucid just like anybody else on the planet. Well, some of them anyway. If they rose from the grave before their brains rotted, they could speak. Otherwise, they were the shuffling stupid zombies like in old horror movies. But that's just science.

I slammed my weight against the banging door. "Go away!"

"I'm not going anywhere, Katrina!" the zombie shouted back. "I have squatter's rights!"

"Go away!"

This particular zombie might or might not be, but definitely was, my old roommate.

He's a dick. Not because he's a zombie either. That just doesn't help the situation. No, he's a dick because he hasn't paid rent in six months.

I was making headway getting the door actually closed and locked when my phone rang.

Yes, there was still cell phone reception two years into the Apocalypse. No, I didn't know why it still worked, but you don't have to be a genius to figure out that the corporate shills who ran the cell companies weren't churchgoers. Otherwise, they would've been raptured. Weird how that caveat worked; where you could escape damnation just by going to church. Lotta rapists went to church. Lotta good people didn't.

We found all sorts of good men and women God left behind after the Apocalypse began. Men and women who did the Lord's work, even if they didn't go to church or praise his name. God was a vindictive bastard. The Devil was worse, though, for unleashing this Hell upon us.

I flipped open my phone. "What do you want, Ronald?"

Ronald was my boss at the only job I could find after the Apocalypse. Yes, there were still jobs. We're not savages. People gotta make a living. They gotta eat. We're not marauders. Well, some of us were marauders, but not most of us.

"Katie!" Ronald shouted into the phone.

"Don't call me that!" I screamed. I hated when people called me Katie.

His shrill voice pounded against my eardrum. "It's loud over there. Somebody tapping that ass or something?"

The door slammed again. I braced against it with all my weight. "You think I would pick up the phone if I was getting nailed, Ronald?"

"I'd like to think so. I mean, I imagine it often enough, Katie."

"Imagine me ramming my fist through your skull if you ever call me Katie again."

The zombie slammed against the door again. I pressed my ass against it to prevent him from coming in. "Look, Kate. You gotta come in."

"Screw you, man. I've worked for the past three weeks straight. This is my day off."

"Don't know what to tell you, Kat. Gary and Melissa both caught the Plague. They can't come in since they're dying."

"Can't you find somebody else?"

"Who else is there, man? I guess I could pull a couple zomboids off the street. They're always good for a shift."

"No! Do *not* do that. I'll come in, alright? Just do *not* hire any zomboids."

"I knew you would."

"I hate you."

The door slammed again. I'd had enough. I ripped it open and glared at the jaundiced zombie smiling back at me. "Screw off, Barry. I kicked you out two weeks ago."

He scratched his red hair. Flecks of skin fell to the ground. "I know, Katrina, but I just found a copy of *Donald in Mathmagic Land*. I wanna watch it, so I'm gonna need my TV."

"I haven't seen a dime from you in six months. Consider the TV my payment."

"Alright, alright. That's fair. But you know I'm just gonna keep coming back for it, right? I mean, it's not like there's a whole lotta functional TVs left in town, aside from the Black Zone and I ain't crazy enough to go there. I've been salvaging around and looking for one. So, like, you *could* keep it and then you'll have to keep seeing me, or you could let me take it and I'll be outta your hair forever."

I sighed. His zombie logic was sound. "Take the TV and you're outta my life forever, agreed?"

"Scout's honor. Now let me in. I'm freezing my nerps off."

I stepped aside and let Barry into the apartment. "Fine. Grab it and go. I'm late anyway and I gotta shower to get the stench of you off me."

"Fair enough. Hey, can I walk with you? It's not safe out there."

I grumbled to myself on the way to the bathroom. "Fine! Just wait for me out here."

"Thanks, Katie!"

"Don't call me that!"

*

I winced as the cold water hit my shoulder. We haven't had hot water in a year, but my body never acclimated to that moment cold water first hit my naked body.

Hot water was a luxury and we didn't get luxuries anymore. Some businesses still had access to hot water, but only if it was critical to their operation, like water treatment plants.

There wasn't much we could hold on to these days, but clean water was one of them. It was one of the few things that kept us human; one of the few things that kept us going even on the worst days.

On special occasions, I gathered kindling and boiled water the old-fashioned way, but this wasn't a special occasion. This was just a run of the mill Thursday.

I rubbed the remnants of my last bar of soap over my aching shoulder. Trucks didn't deliver soap anymore. Luckily, there was always plenty of human fat to turn into soap, and there was always an industrious person willing to harvest enough to make more, but it took time. Another batch wasn't due for a couple more days.

Scars covered every inch of my body, save for my face. I wore long jackets and pants to cover them up, but as the soap rode against my skin it told the story of every battle I ever fought in Braille, from the first days of the Apocalypse through last night, where I beat back seven zombies with a hatchet. Every scar was a reminder that nowhere was safe.

"Are you almost done in there?" Barry shouted to me.

"No!" I screamed back. "Go away!"

The less civilized zombies still terrorized the countryside. The more docile ones lived in apartments and kept to themselves. The most enterprising demons hired less industrious monsters to flood the streets with terror, and zombies were their weapon of choice. You could go without a zombie attack for days, forget that life was a constant struggle, then face four attacks in an evening. Once the zombies tired us out, the demons would come and finish the job.

Anybody still alive could fend off a zombie attack on their best day, but it's harder to have your wits about you after you've been up for a hundred hours straight. That's where people got slaughtered nowadays. Everybody left was covered in scars, mentally and physically. We could all handle ourselves, but sometimes…you just lost your faculties. Other times, you lost the will to live.

Everybody lost the will sometimes. Hopefully, you got it back before you did anything stupid, cuz there's a mighty crappy price you pay for death.

Hell.

If I died, I went to Hell. There were no ifs, ands, or buts about it. God already beamed the good boys and girls up to some giant orgy in the sky, and I wasn't one of them. Which meant there was only one way out. Hell on Earth was bad enough, but Hell in Hell was an unbearable thought.

I ran the soap over a deep scar across my thigh, received in the first days of the Apocalypse, when Barry was still a human. Back then, and even before the Apocalypse, we were roommates. We met through his sister, Connie, and hit it off well enough. After high school, neither of us wanted to go to college. We just wanted to chill out and smoke weed all day. Barry sold enough dope on the side to make his half of the rent. I worked for mine.

Once the Apocalypse hit, the world erupted into endless flames. If you've ever seen the pictures of a forest fire engulfing Los Angeles, with the Holly Hobby homes in the foreground and the blaze burning inches from it, you know what it looked like.

The entire city of Overbrook caught flame at the same time. Our neighbors ran screaming through the streets. Great demons with swords and scythes indiscriminately hacked down everybody in their path.

That's where I got the scar. I turned a corner and came face to face with a big demon, like Andre the Giant on steroids. It swung its scythe at me and sliced across my thigh.

I bled out on the street, losing consciousness. Barry found me. If he hadn't dragged me to a hospital…let's just say they took good care of me there.

Overbrook hospital did good work until they were overrun with demons. Like the big box stores and malls, they were easy targets for marauders and demons. There weren't hospitals anymore, but clinics existed sporadically around the city. Everything in Overbrook existed haphazardly. There's a doctor over here, a laundry over there, and a restaurant wherever there is room. People found little pockets of safety in the nightmare and hunkered down.

*

I dressed the same every day. I didn't have the energy to agonize over my closet. I needed that brain power to stay alert. Long pants to cover my scars with a white t-shirt and leather jacket.

I rocked workout gloves, too, because they helped me grip poles and other weapons. They are a top five must-have item for any Apocalypse. I've been saved from so many blisters with those gloves. The last thing you want is an open wound when the monsters come out of the woodwork and attack.

I put together my look to be part utilitarian and part badass. I would be lying if I didn't say that part of my schtick was to look the part. People left you alone if you walked with a snarl, combat boots, and workout gloves. Even after two years, there were lots of people who ran away from a fight unless it was necessary, even though we could all handle ourselves. You don't get this far without having some serious survival skills.

I didn't much work out any more, but I didn't need to, either. Just living was enough of a workout. Back before the Apocalypse, Connie and I did Krav Maga with our friends Peter Li and Chad Bowden so we could protect ourselves from her horrible father. It came in handy after the Apocalypse, when I had to break way more than noses. For us at least. Peter and Chad barely lasted a month.

Ironically, you needed those skills less now than you did at the beginning. The monsters were softer now than when the

Apocalypse first started. A function of living on Earth, I suppose. They got a little doughy around the midsection and decided playing video games was better than ripping people apart.

Those that enjoyed the heat and violence of Hell returned to the brimstone to torture billions of new victims. The runty ones remained. They didn't have the same killer instinct. Most of them just wanted to be left alone.

Finally dressed, I walked out of my bathroom, and saw Barry on the couch watching the TV, manspreading like he owned the place, with his hand down his pants. Men never change.

"Let's go!" I shouted to him. "Quit dicking around."

Chapter 2

Barry walked behind me as we made our way through the rusted gate and out of my apartment complex. He'd started banging on my door at twilight. It was dark by the time we left the apartment. Night was the worst time in Overbrook. The dead came out at night.

I don't usually take that long to get ready, but I did drag a little bit. I didn't want to go to work. The job sucked. The people sucked. Not that anybody wanted to work, but slinging moldy pizzas on a Thursday night in Overbrook was bad by any job standard.

Overbrook used to be the nicest little city in the Pacific Northwest, surrounded by trees and cut off from the world's evils. We were content to be left alone. We didn't need much, and we didn't ask for much.

New movies didn't come to Overbrook, except for stuff like *Star Wars* and *Transformers*, and we liked them just fine. Nobody opened trendy new restaurants, but that was okay. Maximillian's had the best pie in Oregon and ice cream sundaes as big as your head. We had a hospital, but most of us just went to the doctor down the street we'd been going to for our whole lives. Mine was Dr. Call. He got raptured up. Deservedly so. One of the few who deserved it by my estimation.

It was the kind of sleepy, little town Norman Rockwell painted. I was perfectly happy living in my quaint little hamlet, working a sleepy, little job, and living a sleepy, little life. It was peaceful in Overbrook.

Main street was the only place in town where it ever hustled or bustled. Most of the shops and restaurants were there. On the Fourth of July, everybody gathered in the square to watch fireworks. Great joy existed there once.

Not anymore.

When Barry and I walked past it now, on cracked and slanted sidewalks, it was a shell of its former self. Mud and soot turned the white-washed buildings an ashy gray; vandals had smashed through the windows years ago. Huge trees grew straight up through the asphalt on the street. Only a ghost town remained.

Years ago, I walked blissfully ignorant through the town square high out of my mind. I remember wandering around after school completely blasted with my friends Dave and Swayze, laughing and joking without a care in the world. That was before they went off and got married, and then dead.

Now, I looked warily around every corner. Streetlights flickered as we ambled through the main drag. The hydroelectric dam still delivered us power, and people manned it at all hours to make sure we had electricity at night. We protected it with our lives. It was the only thing separating us from the creatures living in the darkness.

I probably should have just driven around instead of always walking. After all, there was an abundance of cars in Overbrook. You could have your pick, but cars made noise, and noise attracted monsters. Also, cars are only great until you roll one. Then, they become a liability. Even though I fought too many monsters walking around, it was still less of a gamble than driving. Besides, gas was precious in Overbrook. People fought and died for it. Cabals made their fortunes hoarding it.

I turned up a blind alley at the end of the main drag. Barry huffed and puffed behind me, fumbling his TV with every step. I didn't like using alleys. Alleys were prime spots for an ambush, but this one cut ten blocks off my walk and those ten extra blocks were a harrowing affair. The sooner you got inside at night, the better.

"Wait up!" Barry shouted. "This thing is heavy."

"You're the one who wanted to walk with me," I said. "Remember that?"

"You're a real asshole. You know that? Sound just like my sister."

Connie. She used to be my best friend, until I let Barry die. Since then, she'd been cold as ice. Really, it's a bit of a misnomer to say I let him die. That boy was a glutton for pain and a magnet for misfortune.

"How is she?" I said. "Haven't seen her around for a while."

"She's been avoiding you."

"That'll pass, eventually. She still sacrificing goats to the Dark Lord?"

"I don't think it's goats anymore. I think she moved up to cows."

"Is that an upgrade?"

"I think so. She's still pissed our douchebag dad got blue lighted and not her. Won't stop trying to summon the Dark Lord until he brings her justice."

Blue lighted. It's what we called it when people got raptured up to Heaven. Connie's dad was a real dickhead, but he was a churchgoing dickhead. That seemed to be the only criteria. You could be a child molester, but if you went to church, you'd still get blue lighted.

"Well, that does eat up a lot of time," I said.

"She still finds time for Dennis."

I frowned at her boyfriend's name. "Well, they both need to get over it. Life isn't fair."

"I'll pass on the message. You're all heart, you know."

"Hey, I let you move back in, even though you were a zomboid, didn't I?"

"Yeah, you're a saint, Katie."

"Don't call me that."

"You pitied me and felt guilty for letting me die. It's not like it was out of the goodness of your heart. You coulda just given me a handie and called it a day."

"If I ever touch your dick, it'll be to rip it off."

"See, like I said. Cuun—"

Shook! A five-foot-long stake smashed through the front of the television, shattering glass everywhere, and sliced through Barry's chest. I spun around to see the wooden stake protruding two feet in front of him.

"Aw, come on!" Barry said, looking down at the stake. "Uncool!"

"Relax! You can't feel pain. It's just an inconvenience." I latched onto the stake with both hands. Next time people laughed at me for wearing gloves, I would tell them this story.

"Get it out. Get it out!"

"Hold still, you big baby."

I dug my combat boot into Barry's chest and heaved. With one hearty yank, the stake slid through him and onto the ground. Blood, pus, and mucus spurted from Barry's chest.

"How does it look?" Barry asked.

I knelt to check out his chest. There was a massive hole where his heart should be. "You'll survive."

Zombies didn't need their insides. They didn't seem to need anything, except a functional brain. I was skeptical that one rattled around inside Barry's skull, but if it didn't, then he'd be gone. "You think?"

"I've seen better. I've seen worse. You'll live."

Barry stuck his hand inside the hole. "Gross."

I grabbed his wrist. "Don't touch it."

He slapped my hand away and poked at the hole again. "What do you think that was all about?"

"I don't know, but it can't be good."

Groaning rose from the end of the alleyway. I'd heard it before, dozens of times. A small band of zombies lurched toward us. These weren't zombies like Barry. There were braindead ones, the kind that a demon could easily control. These types of zombies rotted in the ground for years before they dug themselves out.

Unlike zombies in the movies, these ones weren't motivated by brains, and they didn't have some great sense of smell, or sound, or whatever allows for zombies to perfectly track down groups of humans. Mostly, these zombies just stood around, gathering dust, until something found them and took control. It was usually a demon ready to take on a middle management position.

I sighed. "I wish they would just get here already. The longest part is watching them amble over here, you know?"

Three zombies emerged from the darkness. One was tall and lanky, like Keith Richards, except less gaunt. Another looked like a fatter, uglier, Danny DeVito. A third crawled along the ground with its legs missing and looked just like my uncle Ramsey.

"Can we go now?" Barry asked meekly.

"It's just a couple of zomboids, Barry."

Cracking my knuckles, I readied myself, even though I really didn't want to fight. I had tweaked my shoulder last night, and just clenching my fists made the pain vibrate up my right arm. I had intended to ice it but never got the chance.

Like I said, that was how people died. They fought too hard for too long and then a zombie horde found them at the right moment.

"What are you doing?" Barry asked.

"Fighting. What does it look like?"

His head lolled back. "Oh god. We're gonna die!"

"Please. They're the dumbest, slowest monsters on the planet."

The zombies ambled forward.

"They're gonna rip us apart. We should run."

"I'm not running, Barry. Then they'll just terrorize somebody else. I can't let that happen."

"Fine. Fight them. What do I care? Just remember to stab them through the—"

"The brain. I know, Barry. Barry?"

Barry slumped over against a chain link fence, a wooden stake through his left eye. He was dead. For real dead this time. I'd staked enough zombies to know a perfect kill when I saw one.

"That's it!" I shouted. "If anybody was gonna kill that annoying prick, it was gonna be me!"

The legless zombie croaked when I dropkicked it fifty yards into a parked car. It crashed through the windshield, twitched for a moment, and then fell down dead, a piece of glass embedded in its stupid head.

I spun around to pick up Barry's TV and used it to cave in the Danny DeVito looking zombie's skull. He fell on the ground and the television landed on top of him. Blood oozed out from under the TV as the zombie fell silent.

I crouched down in front of Barry. His dead, lifeless eyes looked back at me. "Sorry, buddy."

Pressing my hand against his shoulder, I yanked the stake out of his eye. I clutched it in my hand and thrust it up into the Keith Richards zombie's jaw, sending it shooting out through the back of its skull.

They were all dead. For real dead. They fell within a matter of moments. That's all it took to kill a pack of them on a good day. Last night, it took ten minutes, and I'd almost died four times. Tonight, I was on fire. Every move I made was the right one. But it doesn't always end up like that.

I crawled over the spear that had pierced through Barry's chest. It was still damp with his blood. Poor Barry. He didn't deserve what came to him. He was a good guy to the end, even if he was a deadbeat, and now he died twice, making him the ultimate deadbeat.

Back before we got the lights back on, the night was even more dangerous. Massive minotaurs and three-headed demon dogs roamed through the streets, ripping humans apart. I stupidly refused to stay inside.

I had this grand plan to get out of the city and head to the mountains. Nobody lived in the mountains, and it was cold. Hell monsters didn't like the cold. I tried to convince them all for weeks; Stephanie, Kenny, Linda, John, Emerson, Eric K, and the others whose names faded from memory long ago.

It took two weeks of planning, but we finally loaded up four trucks of survivors and headed out. We were supposed to leave at daybreak, but logistical nightmares forced us to delay until nightfall. Connie told me to wait until the next day, but I didn't listen. I had to get out of Overbrook ASAP.

We didn't get five blocks from our place before a monstrous minotaur smashed into the lead truck and rolled it. Two of the three-headed demon dogs attacked another truck. It was bedlam. I tried to turn them all around. I tried to get back, but demons blocked our exit and forced us to scatter.

Barry and I barely got off the trucks with our lives. We were battered, bruised, and in pain. They wounded Barry the worst. He bled from his forehead and wobbled from a concussion.

I pulled him down an alley with a minotaur rushing after us. Of all the monsters Hell threw at us, the minotaur was the toughest I ever dealt with personally. There were worse ones, like hydras, but not in Overbrook. Demons could be reasoned with, zombies could be killed, ghosts could be evaded, and imps could be punted, but minotaurs never stopped.

We ran until we couldn't run anymore. We turned corners and jumped over fences, but the minotaur just kept coming.

Finally, we reached a dead end. The only way out was a broken picket in the fence. Barry couldn't get through, but I could.

"Go!" he shouted to me.

I wanted to say that I fought him, or at least screamed at him, but I didn't. I left him there. I just left him. In that moment, I knew why I wasn't raptured. No good person would have left Barry to die.

Now I'd let him die a second time.

Clapping echoed from the end of the alleyway. I gripped the spear tightly, feeling Barry's blood ooze over my hand. I gritted my teeth and waited for the son of a bitch who controlled the zombies to show itself.

"Bravo, my dear." I heard from the darkness. "Thank you for disposing of them. They really were the worst mouth breathers I ever had the displeasure of overseeing. Thank you for sending them back to Hell. I doubt they'll be back any time soon."

Out of the darkness came a dapper demon, red as blood, horned, and dressed in an elegant three-piece suit. He was immaculately put together, down to his perfectly polished black shoes that shone like mirrors.

"What are you doing here, Thomas?" I snarled. If there was a demon in the world I hated more than any others, it was Thomas.

"I want you back, my love. You are an exquisite specimen."

I held my spear up to his throat. "You never had me, Thomas. You can't trick somebody into sleeping with you and then get pissed when they wanna cut off your dick."

"Trick? I don't like that word."

"What else would you call it?"

"I don't know. It is my way." Thomas took slow steps toward me, his palms turned up. "I'd call it...Tuesday, I suppose."

"Of course that's how you feel. You have no soul."

"That would be accurate, Katrina, as you well know."

"I'm going to stab you through the throat if you take another step." I shifted into a ready stance.

Thomas grabbed the spear and punctured himself through the throat. He grinned maniacally as blue bile from the wound dripped down his neck. "My dear, I'm not a mortal, or even a zombie. Your weapons have no effect on me. There's nothing you can do to harm me."

I smiled back at him. "Maybe not—" I pressed my combat boot into his groin. A painful moan escaped his lips. "But I'll bet that, horndog as you are, you manipulated your nerve endings so they're concentrated in your cock, just in case I wanted to screw you again."

I pulled the spear out of Thomas's neck and jammed it into the gap between his pants. His confident bravado fell away, and he doubled over. "Now, I'm no expert, but that looks like harm to me. Now, leave me alone or I'll cut your head off. Got that?"

Thomas's blue blood spurted from the fresh tear in his pants onto my jacket as he collapsed onto his side. "Got it."

I looked down at my jacket. Thomas's bile stained the perfect leather. "Man, I love this coat. This stain is never gonna come out."

For good measure, I kicked Thomas in the face as I walked away, because screw him and his beautiful face.

Chapter 3

I shouldn't have slept with Thomas, and I knew that the moment I met him. It eats at me every day. I've made a lot of horrible decisions in my life. I cursed too much, drank too often, and slept with almost anything with a hard body and flashy smile. I wasn't surprised at all when the Good Lord didn't beam me up.

Still, a demon was low, even for me.

After the rapture, things were…the worst. Nothing prepared you for Hell on Earth. You could read about it, think about it, or get lectured about it, but you can't really know how bad it's going to be until you're smack dab in the middle of it. I watched people shoot themselves in the face right in front of me because they couldn't deal with the horror of it all.

That doesn't even account for the psychological baggage of knowing for a fact you aren't good enough for Heaven. Most people thought they were good on the inside and learning that God thought they deserved Hellfire sent them over the edge.

It broke a lot of people. Honest people beat each other for fun. My neighbor Jean looted churches for wine. Straightedge kids shot heroin because nothing mattered anymore. My ex-coworker Jason slaughtered a boy in broad daylight who picked on him at school, laughing hysterically the whole time like a rabid hyena. And people screwed each other. People screwed a lot.

I'm not proud of it, but for those first few months there wasn't a cock I didn't suck or a dick I didn't ride. So, when a strapping, barrel-chested hunk sauntered into my favorite bar, you are goddamn right I pounced on him. I didn't know back then that demons could shapeshift into anything they wanted. I didn't know that his MO was finding tender, human girls, screwing them raw, and ripping them in half from the inside as he came.

I knew it later, though. I knew it when he went from a charming playboy to a demon in front of my eyes. His smile vanished and his pale skin turned bright red. Horns grew out of his forehead and his cock tore me apart from the inside. I screamed and kicked, but that only made him laugh. I pushed him off of me, but he wouldn't move. He was in a trance, and just like a dog with a boner, his dick knotted inside of me. I couldn't get it out.

I wriggled to the edge of the bed. Thomas's eyes glowed yellow and illuminated the whole room with an eerie glow. He chanted under his breath as I screamed in agony. I could see the outline of his throbbing cock through my stomach.

I grabbed for anything that could help me. That's when I felt it sitting on the nightstand; my grandmother's rosary. My mother had given it to me right after the Apocalypse began. She made me swear to keep it close in case I ever needed it.

I reached my arm as far as I could and latched onto it. Then I swung.

Again.

And again.

And again.

Finally, the rosary smacked him across the face and he screamed out in agony. It seared into his flesh. His dick fell fallow inside of me. I pressed my knees against his chest and kicked him as hard as I could. He slid out of me and landed on the ground.

I stood up and ran out into the courtyard stark naked. "Help! Help!"

"You are being dramatic," he shouted after me. "I thought we were having fun."

"Fun? I don't mess around with demons."

"Well," he smiled. "I beg to differ on that front."

The denizens of the apartment complex came out to snicker at me, or to catch a glimpse of my naked body. Even then I was riddled with scars, but at this moment I didn't care.

"You guys get a good look?!" I shouted at them.

"Why don't you come back inside," Thomas said. "And we'll talk about this."

"Get out of here."

Thomas grew a suit around his naked body and wrapped himself in it. "I don't have to do that, Katie."

"Don't call me that! Just get the out of here!"

He dragged his finger across the railing. "Very well. Out of respect for you, I will go. I could rip everybody in this complex apart and not mess one fiber of my suit. But I won't. I'll leave you what dignity you have left, and you will think me magnanimous in that."

"You're a cocksucker."

Thomas laughed as he reached the bottom of my stairs. "Not to make too fine a point on it, but that is a description not out of line in describing you, my dear."

He never took his eyes off me, like I was a pet to be tamed. With one final nod, he turned and strolled out of the complex. I ran back to my room and shut the door. I don't know how long I cried, but the next time I looked up, the bright light of day shone in my eyes.

Thomas violated me. He lied to me. He tricked me. I hated him for that. I still hate him for that. The worst part of it all was that being raped by a demon wasn't even the worst thing that happened to me that week.

Horrible stuff happened all the time. You couldn't get caught up dwelling on it, or it might just get you killed. That's how I would get past Barry's death, too. By compartmentalizing it.

*

I tried to avoid places that hired zombies over humans, but sometimes I couldn't avoid it. There was one minimart, for instance, that supplied the only stain stick in the entire city, and they loved hiring zombies for cheap labor.

A zombie read an old porn mag at the cash register as I stomped into the market. He was a fat one in a ripped blue shirt with a nametag that said "Andrew Rees" on it.

"Welcome to Mickey's Market!" it shouted at me.

From the tremor in his voice, he was only in the ground for a couple of days before he came up. He was still conscious of the world, but just barely. Unlike Barry, who was immediately reanimated, Ole Andy probably missed out on full sentience by a few hours. That's why he was perfect for work in a convenience store. It didn't take much brain power.

I picked up a stain stick and started rubbing it on the blueish green goop that lined my jacket sleeve. "It's not coming off. It's just rubbing it in more!"

"Hey!" the zombie screamed. "You pay! We not charity!"

"Christ."

I grabbed a bag of chips on my way to the front and slammed them on the counter. The zombie took the bag and rang it up. "Bad day?"

"You know I could pop your head like a zit, right?"

"No, please."

There was a spinner rack full of rosaries on the counter. My brain flashed back to Thomas. He would be coming for me, eventually. For some reason, demons hated biblical crap.

That seemed to be the only way to keep him at bay. Maybe other demons, too.

I grabbed a rosary off the spinner rack. "I'll take one of these, too."

"We no sell many."

I threw some money on the counter, wrapped the rosary around my wrist, and walked out. "Can't imagine why."

*

Gary and Melissa lived a couple of blocks from the pizza place. They were usually the people Ronald called in when he didn't have anybody else to cover, and I loved them for that. They were a little too jovial for me, but they both had a twinkle in their eye that never died, even after the Apocalypse took everything from them.

I needed to check on them, and make sure they were alright. They had survived so long that going out by catching the Plague would be an insult to them.

Their apartment was door wide open. Not a good sign. Inside, it smelled of death and decay. Flies buzzed around the kitchen. The swarms intensified as I inched toward the back bedroom. Even for me, who smelled death on the regular, it stank something fierce.

The Plague was the worst disease you could get in the Apocalypse. It came on without warning. People died screaming from the pain in a matter of days, sometimes hours. There were stories of perfectly healthy people puking black bile all over their partners in the middle of dinner and being dead by bedtime. One minute they were smiling and laughing. The next, they had a death sentence.

I knew what to expect before I walked through the bedroom door. Sure enough, there they were, Gary and Melissa, wrapped around each other, black bile spewed all over their bed, their mouths dropped open in a horrible final grimace, their eyes melted inside their skulls.

I was going to miss them.

Soon, the whole complex would pack up and move because the stench was so bad, leaving them to rot forever. One day that would be my fate, too, if I was lucky. Most of us didn't get to die in our beds, surrounded by loved ones. Most of us had no loved ones.

It took me longer than usual to walk the last few blocks to work. I took slow, deliberate steps, thinking about death, and the fickle hand of fate. Seeing a dead body used to get to me. I wouldn't even cut open a dead frog in school because it was too gruesome. Now, it didn't faze me at all.

Ronald didn't really own the pizza place. Nobody really owned anything anymore. He happened to find a restaurant and squatted there. He didn't look like much, but Ronald fought off enough gangs that people left him alone after a while. His place wasn't worth their time, especially so close to the Black Zone.

The Black Zone kept the monsters in the dark where they belonged. Most of them went back to Hell in the years after the Apocalypse, but those who stayed behind would roam around in the dark looking for food.

And that meant us.

Luckily, the nastier the monster, the more it despised the light. When we realized that, it was easy enough to trap them in the darkness. The city turned off all the lights on a five hundred yard stretch right between East and West Overbrook.

That was where the worst monsters lived, those that could not acclimate to Earth and refused to return to Hell. Those that even the demons didn't dare disturb.

I came into the pizza shop through the back entrance and went right into the bathroom to wash the stench of Plague off me. Ronald had left my uniform on the toilet, but I wasn't about to wear it. When I was ready, I walked through the kitchen and into the dining area and saw that it was almost completely empty aside from Ronald and Stacey, the nasty bitch he was always trying to screw, and one gnarly faced customer. I could have stayed home, easily, if they weren't so lazy.

"Are you kidding me?" I shouted. "You called me in to deal with one tragic loser?"

The piece of human garbage eating his pizza looked up. "Hey!"

"That tragic loser is a customer. His name is Bloodfists, and he's worth more to me than you by about a million percent." Ronald replied. "Don't you forget it, or I'll pick some other nothing off the street to do your job. Got it? And would it kill you to wear a uniform for once?"

When he wasn't sweet talking me to come in, Ronald was a real dick. I grumbled back to him. "Yes, it would. It would literally kill me."

Ronald brushed passed me toward the door. "Now that you're here, I'll gonna shove off. Smoke a bowl and screw a hole, you know the routine. Stacey's in charge while I'm gone."

I turned to Stacey once the door closed. "He's got herpes, you know."

Stacey shrugged. "So do I."

"Awesome."

*

The shift went by with the slow, rotting monotony of a root canal, but without the drugs or pain to keep it interesting. Seventeen people came in asking if we had cheese today (we did), thirteen asked if we had pepperoni (we didn't), and seven stormed out in a huff after I told them to get lost (I didn't care). A girl we called Organ and her friend Charlotte came in looking for human intestine, and they looked absolutely devastated when we sent them away. We haven't had fresh meat in months, and intestine was a delicacy, after all. We mostly dealt in Army surplus and whatever we could salvage from the garbage before scavengers ate it.

By midnight, I was over the night, and by two am, I was counting down the minutes until I went home. That's when I heard a loud pop from outside, and looked to see a bright yellow Yugo. I knew the car anywhere. It was Connie's.

I turned to Stacey. "Can I take a break?"

She dangled her feet off the counter in front of her. "Let me think about that. No."

"Why not?"

"Cuz I'm on break. We can't both be on break. It's bad for business."

"You're always on break."

"It's a mindset."

I watched through the broken glass window as Connie flung her boyfriend Dennis over her shoulder. She hadn't changed much in the months since she stopped talking to me. She still dressed in all black, with her bushy hair tied into pigtails on either side of her head. Dennis looked worse for wear, like he'd dropped a hundred pounds. His knees buckled under him as he leaned against Connie and tried to walk.

"Aw man," I said. "Why did they have to come here?"

Connie was the most violent fighter I had ever met, besides me. Of course, in order to be alive still, you had to have some measure of fighting skills. Even Stacey could dismember a zombie with her bare hands.

"They probably figured you'd be off tonight."

I sneered at her. "Shut up, Stacey."

Connie and Dennis walked inside. The bell over the door jingled. Stacey filed her nails. "I'm just sayin'. They asked me yesterday whether you're working today."

"And you're still gonna make me take them, I'll bet?"

Stacey nodded. "That's right, cuz it'll be funny to watch you squirm."

Connie and Dennis slid into a sticky booth in a dark corner of the restaurant and I angry-whispered at Stacey. "I hate you so much. Will you please help me out and cover their table? I can't deal with her tonight. Please. I'll pick up your shifts for a week."

Stacey thought for a second. "Nah. This will be more fun."

I grabbed a lukewarm pizza and hopped over the counter. "I hope your vagina falls off."

"It will."

I didn't want to confront Connie, especially not today. I didn't like the tension between us during the best of times, and now I was going to have to tell her that her brother died. Again. I thought about avoiding the subject and making her find out the old-fashioned way.

That's when you see your loved one's dead body on the side of a road and try to keep your sanity while burying them in a ditch. It was the way of the Apocalypse, but I couldn't do that to her. We had too much history.

I slammed the pizza in front of her and glided into the booth across from her. "I brought you this. It sucks."

Connie pushed the pizza away. "Who said you could sit down?"

"Well, nobody, but it's a free country."

Dennis slumped over in his seat. Connie leaned him against the wall. "I guess that's the truth."

I slid the pizza back over to her. "It's a peace offering, Connie. I figure it's time we buried the hatchet about Barry."

"This ain't about Barry and you know it. It hasn't been about Barry in a long time. It's about you being a selfish bitch who only thinks about herself. And it's a little bit about Barry."

"I let him move back in after he resurrected, didn't I?"

"Yeah, cuz you pitied him. Coulda just offered him a handie and called it a day."

"You really do think like him. Or thought like him. Or think like he thought."

"What are you babbling about?"

I sighed. "Your brother is dead."

Connie didn't even blink. "Because of some fool thing you did, I'm sure."

"It wasn't me. He asked to walk with me."

"Cuz he thought you would keep him safe. He was always an idiot."

I smiled. "That is the truth."

Connie slammed her hand on the table. "Don't you talk about him that way! I can talk about him like that cuz he's my brother, but don't you dare."

Connie flared her nostrils in a death stare. After a moment, I tilted down my eyes toward the pizza. "It's bacon. Rancid bacon, but it's bacon."

"I don't want your moldy bread and rancid meat."

"Then why are you here?"

Dennis spat black bile across the table. It was loud and wet, like phlegm caught in a vacuum.

"Are you alright?" I asked.

"He's fine," Connie said. "Aren't you, baby?"

He nodded. "I'm fine. I'm fine."

He wasn't fine. "I could rustle you up a can of soup, or an ice pack."

Dennis looked down at his napkin, covered in black gunk. We all knew what it meant, but none of us wanted to say it. "No thanks. I lost my appetite."

Connie rubbed his back. "Just leave us alone, alright?"

Stacey yelled over the counter. "Is he sick? Get him out of here if he's sick."

Without another word, Dennis collapsed with a *thunk* on the table. "Dennis!" Connie shook him. "Dennis! Get up baby. Get up!"

"Out of my way," I said, pushing Connie to one side and lifting Dennis onto my shoulder.

"What are you doing?" Connie shouted.

"We've gotta get him to a doctor now."

"Alright," Connie said, helping me lift. "Just be careful. He's all I got left."

"There's a clinic not too far from here but I really wish you'd showed up during daylight hours. Think your car can make it across the Black Zone?"

"It'll make it," Connie said. "It has to."

"Hey," Stacey shouted as we walked out of the door. "Who's gonna clean this up?"

"I don't care," I called over my shoulder as I walked out the door, supporting half of Dennis. "Please don't puke on me, Dennis. Okay?"

It took forever for him to put one foot in front of the other on the way to the car, but we finally got there. I pulled open the back door of the Yugo and Connie dragged him into the car. Then, she crawled over the back seat into the driver's seat.

I went to open the passenger's side door and Connie leapt over to lock it. "What are you doing, Connie?"

She reached over the back seat and locked that door as well. "Screw you! You're not coming!"

"You're a real asshole, you know that?"

She turned the car over, but it wouldn't start. She tried again, and again, and again. "Come on, you bastard! Work!"

"Troubles!?" I walked around the car to the driver's side door.

"It'll work. It'll work. It'll work."

"No, it won't," I said, pointing to the hose sticking out of the gas tank. "Somebody siphoned off all your gas."

I couldn't help but chuckle for a moment. I knew Dennis's condition was serious, but I loved uppity jerks getting what they deserve. Connie didn't get the joke. "This ain't funny!"

"I know, I know. Come on. Help me with him."

She unlocked the back door and when I pulled it open, Dennis oozed out onto the ground. "If you barf on my boots, I'll kick your ass."

He bent over and ralphed black bile over the asphalt. "Help me with him," I said, standing him up and trying to walk toward the darkness of the Black Zone.

"Are you kidding? We can't go in there without a car!"

"I don't see any other choice. There isn't a gas station around for miles. He'd be dead by the time we got back."

"Somebody's gotta have some gas to sell us."

"Maybe, but you got any cash? Cuz I just ducked out on my job to help you. I doubt I'm gonna get paid for a while."

Connie shook her head. "Ain't got no money."

"Well there you go. That leaves us two options. Let him die or take him across the Black Zone ourselves."

"You've gotta know what's waiting in there for us. We'll be dead in a matter of minutes."

"I had a good run. Now, you with me or we leaving him here to die?"

Connie grabbed Dennis's other arm. "We're gonna get mauled to death, aren't we?"

"That's the worst-case scenario. All we have to do is get through five football fields of darkness, surrounded by the worst monsters imaginable. I think we can do it."

Connie took a heavy step with me into the darkness, supporting Dennis's body with her own. "And what if we don't?"

"Then maybe we'll just get horribly disfigured. Besides, we're living in the Apocalypse. It's quite literally Hell on Earth. I mean, how much worse could death be?"

The glowing yellow eyes of the Hell hounds peered at us from the darkness. It would be the only light for five hundred yards. We would never make it, not with a dying Dennis. Not with a frightened Connie. I had just signed my death warrant, but I couldn't let him die. I didn't have much left in the world and I wasn't about to lose Dennis, too.

Not without trying.

Chapter 4

During the first days of the Apocalypse, Overbrook descended into one big Black Zone. The power shut off after the monsters invaded. It took them five days to slaughter their way from Reno to Overbrook. We watched the news every minute—every minute until the monsters arrived at our doorstep. That's when they invaded the hydroelectric dam, and everything went dark.

Without the lights, monsters ruled the night. Three-headed demon dogs rampaged through the streets with reckless abandon. Minotaurs destroyed everything they put their claws on. Clearly, it was an unsustainable lifestyle for us all. To have any chance of survival, we had to turn the lights back on.

My dad was an engineer at the power plant. His supervisor was blue lighted, and monsters mauled the rest of his team, but he survived. Us Clarks survived. We weren't the biggest, fastest, or smartest, but we were definitely the grittiest.

So, with his team and most of the city dead or blue lighted, dad was the only person who could turn the power back on to the town. I didn't try to talk him out of it, but I insisted on going with him. If he was heading into the damp, dark parts of Overbrook, he was gonna need protection. I didn't know about fixing dams, but I did know how to kick skulls, swing a hatchet, and fire a gun. Skills dad never mastered.

Dad recruited five people with a head for math and I recruited five who could fight; Bob, Ray, Courtney, Susan and Phil. I armed them all with guns and ammo, loaded them into two pickup trucks, and headed out to the power plant. Only one of us made it back to tell about it. I'll let you figure out which one.

Before we left on the mission, dad pulled me aside. "I need you to promise me something."

"Anything, dad," I replied.

"If it all goes tits up, and somehow...I die..."

"Don't say that..."

"I'm saying it, kiddo. If something happens…I don't want to live like a zombie. I don't…I need you to kill me."

"I'm not gonna kill you, dad."

"Please," he replied. "I don't want to die, but I don't want to live like one of them. Promise me. You said you would promise me anything."

"I…can't…You ask too much of me."

He nodded. "You're right. I'm sorry. It's probably not going to come up anyway."

I've always wondered whether he knew what would happen, or whether he just wanted to make sure he had his bases covered just in case.

*

The plant sat on a river, five miles outside of town. The city council voted to create the dam back before I was born, and dad was sure that it would keep running forever as long as somebody was there to watch it.

Ray, Courtney and I loaded onto a truck with two of the brains and dad, while Phil, Susan, and Bob loaded the rest of the brains into the second truck in our convoy.

"Water's gonna keep flowing," dad said. "So, the power'll keep going long as somebody sits at the controls."

Back in those days, every city block was a warzone. Demons casually ripped people apart while zombies roamed the woods looking for a meal. Even the newly dead joined in on the fun. Barry later told me how much he regretted the killing.

"I know it's not an excuse," he said. "But I didn't know any better. I was a monster and that's what monsters did."

It was an excuse, and even the best ones stunk like assholes. Still, I never judged him for it. Those excuses calmed him in the worst days. It wasn't easy to live with killing people. I'd killed enough people to know.

It wasn't the zombies, or even the demons, that scared me when we were setting off to the plant. It was the demon dogs. They were extremely hard to kill. Each of their three heads was ungodly strong, and if any of their heads lived, so did the dog. The cujos just kept coming and coming. These were big too, three times as big as a Great Dane and ten times as heavy—like mixing a pit bull with a shark and giving it three heads.

It took all day to battle our way to the edge of town. We started out at daybreak, but by the time we reached the edge of town it was sunset. The demon dogs stayed dormant during the day. They hid in caves and vacant houses until the light faded. I wanted to turn back, or bunker down for the night, but dad wouldn't hear of it.

"That's one more night this whole town will be terrorized," he said. "I won't have it. Not when I can fix it."

I didn't beg or plead. He wouldn't have listened even if I did. "Okay, dad."

We got our first taste of the demon dogs when we reached the border of the town. Three of them jumped out of the darkness and ripped apart a very nice family. Their son Vincent graduated with me. His head lay bloodied on the side of the road as the dogs feasted on his father's organs. The mother, dripping in her family's blood, cowered behind a dumpster. She was next, and she knew it.

I caught her eyes for a horrifying moment. The will to live had drained out of them. I could have saved her but didn't want to waste the bullets. She had lost the will to live, and that meant she'd be dead by daybreak.

We sped toward the power plant. It wasn't long before yellow, glowing eyes glared back at us from the darkness of the woods. Their growls rose from a low roar to a guttural moan before they leapt toward us as a pack.

"Go, go, go!" Dad shouted.

The truck spun forward as the dogs bounded out of the woods. We slammed on the gas and peeled out as fast as we could. From the truck bed, a half-dozen guns riddled the dogs with bullets.

"Reload!" Courtney, our sharpshooter, shouted.

"Cover!" Bob yelled from the other truck.

They were built like Mack trucks and traveled in packs. With every bullet the trucks fired, a half dozen more dogs jumped out of the trees. For all the good our guns did, their sound attracted more dogs to join the fray. That's the problem with guns. They usually attracted more monsters than they destroyed. Swords never had that problem. Knives, spears, and stakes were harder to use, but brought less attention.

Besides, guns made bad melee weapons. If a monster attacked close enough, you couldn't fend it off with the butt of a gun. They worked well from long range, but demon dogs rushed like forces of nature, with no warning. If you didn't have something sharp in your hand, then you were as good as dead.

"I'm out!" Ray screamed from the truck bed.

A demon dog leapt out onto the road in front of my truck. I swerved to miss it and sent Ray off the truck into the ravenous jaws of the Hell beasts. He screamed in agony as I sped off into the distance.

"What are you doing up there?" Courtney spat.

"I'm trying to drive!" I replied. "Shut up and shoot!"

The truck bounced into the air and I latched onto the steering wheel.

"Tom!" Courtney shouted. "We've lost Tom!"

I looked into my rear-view mirror and saw one of the brains on the ground, being ripped to shreds by demon dogs.

As I watched, the other truck crashed into the pack of Hell beasts and flipped over. The dogs chasing lost interest in me and turned toward the fiery truck.

"We have to go back for them!" Courtney screamed.

"There's no time!" I shouted back.

The explosion from the other truck bought us just enough distance to separate us from the dogs. It wouldn't take them long to catch up, but not before we hopped off the truck and ran to the building.

Of course, once we'd locked ourselves inside the plant, a whole different set of problems presented themselves. We couldn't predict what waited there in the darkness.

"How are we gonna get out?" Dad asked as I slid a receptionist's desk in front of the door so the demon dogs couldn't smash through it. "They know where we are."

"Let's worry about that when we need to get back outside, okay?" I responded. "One thing at a time."

I counted the people left. There were four of us. My dad, me, Courtney, and some brain dad had recruited to help turn on the more complicated bits in the sequence. One truck died so we could live. They died, but we made it.

We all knew the risk. We knew why we fought. What we didn't know was how long we were going to last.

"I can never go back," dad said to me as we walked through the plant. "You know that. I'm stuck here forever."

"Don't say that. You'll train these guys and then we can work in shifts."

"You think there are enough people willing to run this place without me?"

I grabbed his shoulder. "We'll find a way, dad. We always find a way."

"She's right, Mister Clark," Courtney replied, clutching her shotgun close. "There's always a way."

Dozens of two-ton metal barrels speckled the massive room in tidy rows, all lit by a red emergency light which flashed down from the ceiling. When the plant functioned, those barrels generated power from the turbines churning underneath the water.

I heard a scream from behind me. The brainiac with us flew into the air and disappeared into the darkness.

"Run!"

Courtney turned and fired her shotgun into the room, then the three of us ran. Dad led the way toward a glass-enclosed room lofted above the rest of the plant.

"The control room is just up ahead! We just have to climb that ladder."

A great roar went up behind us. A minotaur reared its head and charged. I pulled Courtney and dad behind a generator as it galloped passed.

Dad pointed to a ladder. "Right up there."

"Go!" I shouted. "Both of you."

I grabbed the shotgun and fired it into the air. "Hey! Bet you can't catch me."

The minotaur puffed its hot breath on my neck as it chased me down the hall away from Courtney and Dad. I fired the last round of the shotgun at the minotaur, then slid behind a barrel and watched the minotaur skirt past me.

I climbed atop the barrel and looked out into the darkness. Footsteps clanged on the ladder to the control room. The beast must've heard it too, because it let out another roar and galloped toward it.

I couldn't let it hurt my father. I leapt onto it as it charged, landing on the beast's back. I pulled its horns and it reared against me. I used to do well on the bull-riding machines at the Saddle Bar in Ridgeway, but that was nothing in comparison to mounting a minotaur. It bucked me, and I rode it, barely holding on for even a moment. After a few seconds, it shook me off and smashed into the generators by the front door.

The lights flickered on in the control room—Dad and Courtney had made it. They weren't safe, though. The minotaur turned to the newly made light. It was a clear shot from where it stood to the steel beams that held up the loft. If the minotaur charged, it could take down the whole control room. I needed to end it, but I didn't have the strength myself. I needed help.

I bolted toward the front door. If I could get to the entrance, I could use the demon dogs as a distraction to buy Dad more time to get the plant operational. With any luck, the monsters would kill each other and leave us alone. I knew it was a horrible plan, but frankly they were all horrible plans. Even if it worked, we would still have to figure out an escape route. If we could get the plant back online, it would be worth it.

The dogs slammed against the door as I pushed away the reception desk. I wouldn't have time to act if the beast wasn't ready to fight. I had to time it perfectly.

"Hey, monster! I'm over here!"

The minotaur beelined for me. At the last moment, I pulled open the door. Five demon dogs charged through it. The minotaur crashed into them.

They nipped at the minotaur as a pack. In return, the minotaur crushed three of their bodies like zits. In the end, both beast and dog fell onto the ground. Blood from the monsters spewed across the concrete floor.

I loaded the shotgun with the bullets from the truck and ended the misery of what was left of the demon dogs. People said I didn't have a heart. Then, I shot four rounds into the minotaur. I pulled a knife out of my belt and hacked off its head for good measure.

For the first time since we'd left the house, it was quiet.

Too quiet. Something was wrong.

The control room was a blood bath. I climbed the ladder to find three imps taking turns slicing my dad with a knife. Courtney lay on the ground with a blade protruding from her throat.

"Hey!" I shouted to them.

They rushed at me. I grabbed one of their faces and smashed it into the ground repeatedly, then swung my shotgun around and shot the other two in the chest. They flew back against the wall, mangled and bloody.

Dad gagged blood as I knelt next to him. "Dad. Dad! No…please no…"

Blood sputtered on his shirt as he smiled at me. "It's okay. It's okay. I'm okay. You have to start it. You have to—"

I could barely talk through the tears. "How—how can I?"

"I—I—did everything. Just…the lever." He pointed to a lever on the control panel. "Push it up and it'll start."

"Dad. I can't do this."

He smiled at me. "You can. You can survive. Clarks are survivors."

The spark of life left his eyes. He was dead, and it was my fault. I could have prevented it. I shouldn't have let him go. I shouldn't have left him alone. It was the first big loss of the Apocalypse for me. I'd seen others die, but eventually you numb yourself to it. Not this time.

In that moment, I lost the will to live. I wanted to end it there. The shotgun had one more bullet in it. It would have been so easy.

But I couldn't do it. His death had to mean something. I pushed myself up off the ground and gripped the shotgun tightly in my hand.

That's when I heard the moan from dad's body. His leg twitched and his eyes turned jet black. His head jerked up and then to the side. He was alive again.

"Dad?" I asked. "Dad!"

"K-k-k-k-k—"

"Katrina," I said, smiling at him. "I'm Katrina. Do you remember me?"

"K-k-k-k-kill me," he replied.

"What?" I shouted. "I'm not going to kill you!"

"Pleeeeeeease," he whispered. "Can't live...like this."

"What about all that bull that we're survivors," I screamed, tears streaming down my face. "You just said we were survivors!"

Dad grabbed for the shotgun and pulled it up to his forehead. "Pleeeeaasse."

The shotgun trembled in my hand. I couldn't do it. I couldn't kill my father. He could have lived a long life as a zombie. I could have still been happy.

"I'm not going to do it," I shouted. "You want it, you do it yourself."

Dad's hand moved up the trembling shotgun to the trigger. His eyes found mine, and I didn't see that man who birthed me behind his eyes anymore. He was nothing but a hollow shell of my father. My dad might have been somewhere behind the darkness of his cloudy eyes, but I couldn't see him anymore.

I felt his cold hand against my trembling trigger finger. I clutched the gun tightly, but it still wiggled from one side to the other as my body convulsed with tears of pain. I felt my father's face press tightly against the barrels, and his hand push against the trigger.

"Please, don't..." I said through my tears. "Please."

"Save them," he whispered as he forced my hand down on the trigger. The gun blasted him against the wall. His brain shot against the wall behind him, and he was dead for the second time. I would have time to grieve him later, but I needed to fulfill his last wish first.

My motions were mechanical as I stepped through the pool of Dad's blood and made my way to the control panel. I grabbed the lever and pushed. In response, the plant cranked and wheezed to life—lights clicked on, boards lit up, generators hummed to life.

My dad had done it.

*

Once the lights were on, we established a line of communication to Bend, Oregon, which was the closest functional city to ours. Portland, like almost all the big cities, went the way of the dodo some time before. Their destruction was the only thing shielding us from a worse fate. The smaller cities disintegrated, too, as their inhabitants were eaten, murdered, or run out of town. It was only cities like ours that remained, mid-sized cities, away from major population centers, that could surround and protect ourselves.

With the help of the power plant in Bend, we bussed several engineers into town to make sure the power plant stayed stable. They taught our best and brightest how to work the plant. If we could quarantine the beasties into a small area of the city and encircle them with light at all times, then they would stay in a localized area. Thus, the Black Zone was formed. At night, it worked to imprison them. During the day they retreated to the darkness of the apartment complexes.

The Black Zone was designed to keep all the monsters that go bump in the night, in the night forever. They hated the light so much they would do anything to avoid it. You could yell at a demon dog from just one foot inside the light and it wouldn't step a single foot forward to fight you. That was the one advantage we had over them. They were strong, but we were smart.

Okay, not that smart. I was about to willingly set foot inside the Black Zone, carrying a dying man who had no chance of survival, all because I felt guilty that I killed my ex-friend's brother.

"See, Connie," I said. "The Black Zone's a walk in the park."

"Easy for you to say. We've barely gone a hundred feet. Now shut up, unless you want to alert the demon dogs."

Dennis leaned on a car door while he heaved some more. The door whined on its rusted-out hinges and fell to the ground with a crash.

"Or that will do it."

Sure enough, ten demon dogs slammed down from the rooftops all around us.

"Get back into the light," I shrieked. "Quickly!"

I grabbed the car door with all my might and flung it at the biggest dog in the place. One of its necks snapped and lay fallow in front of him. That didn't stop it charging. They never stopped, except when they faced light.

When I was close enough, I threw Dennis into the light. The dogs wanted to attack, but screeched to a halt at the shadow's edge. Playing on their fear had saved me more times than I can count in the early days, and it saved us all when the power plant figured out how to contain them.

"Well, that didn't work," Connie said. "What are we going to do now?"

"I don't know."

Dennis slumped over Connie's shoulder, coughing black bile on her already black shirt. "We gotta figure it out or he's gonna die."

I looked toward the pizza parlor. Stacey was cleaning the black bile off the table wearing a full-scale hazmat suit. A few patrons cowered in the corner, worried that the Plague would infest them too. They were probably right.

Then it hit me. Demon dogs loved rancid meat. The older the better. Their taste for old flesh must have been honed in the pits of Hell, where the dead and enfeebled wasted away. The pizza place had rancid meat in spades.

I ran back toward the pizza place. "I'll be back!"

"Where are you going?" Connie called after me.

"Just keep Dennis alive!"

Stacey turned toward me when I ran inside the shop. "Welcome back. We're gonna have to burn this table, you know."

"That's the price of doing business."

Stacey snapped at me. "It's coming out of your paycheck."

I pulled five moldy pizzas out from under the counter. "Put these on my tab too, then."

"Hey! Those are the last ones we have tonight!"

I ran out the door again. "So?"

Dennis looked horrible when I reached the two of them. Sweat drenched his clothing and his eyes rolled back in his head. Connie fanned him uselessly with her hand. "Where have you been? He's burning up."

"Give me a break. I had to wrestle these away from Stacey."

"Just hurry up whatever you're doing, alright?"

I kneeled in front of Dennis. "Listen, I know that it's hard, but you have to move when I tell you, okay?"

Dennis flopped his head forward. "Is that a yes or a no? Groan if it's a yes."

"Yes," he said, meekly. "It's a yes."

"Good man."

I walked toward the Black Zone again. The dogs chomped their ferocious teeth and slobbered at me as I tilted forward, inches from the light. I felt their hot breath on my arms and legs, and the saliva from their slobbering jaws splattered against my face. "You like this? Do ya? Yeah? Then go fetch!"

I flung the pizzas like frisbees, the dogs chasing after them. "Come on!" I yelled to Connie. "That won't distract them for long!"

Connie pulled Dennis to his feet and we sprinted as fast as we could through the Black Zone.

*

Dennis tried his best, but he couldn't get more than a hundred yards into the blackness before he fell to his knees.

"I can't—I can't do it."

"You gotta!" I said. "They're coming. That pizza's not gonna distract them for long."

"I can't," he said. "I can't."

Connie cradled his face. "It's okay, baby. We can take a break, alright?"

"We can't stop now!" I shouted.

Connie laid Dennis on a pile of rubble. "His heart's gonna explode and then this'll all be in vain."

"It's already in vain, Connie. Don't you get that?"

Connie held back the tears in her eyes. "You can go if you want, but I'm not leaving him."

"Fine." I knelt in front of Dennis. "You still with me, buddy?" Dennis mumbled under his breath. I slapped him across the face. "I *said* are you with me?"

A spark returned to his eyes, just for a moment. "I'm up."

"Good. Now we got another four hundred yards or so to go. You gotta be strong, alright? No more collapsing."

"Okay."

I looked over at Connie. "He's either gonna fall into a coma or a seizure any minute. We need to quit resting and find a doctor *now*."

She nodded. "You're right. Let's go."

Connie wrapped her arms around his shoulder. I looked past her and saw the demon dog I'd injured limping toward us. One of its heads flopped along, weighing it down. "Go! Get to the clinic. I'll hold them off!"

"But—"

"Go! If I die, it better be for something!"

Connie gave me an even stare. "Now we're even."

"We're way more than even."

Connie turned the corner and the dogs were on top of me. Demon dogs were ferocious alone, but, let them surround your position and it's over for you. If you could lead them down a narrow alley, though, then you had a chance.

I pumped my legs fast as I could and sprinted toward the closest alley. The dogs churned at my feet. I couldn't stop now. I couldn't succumb to them. In front of me I saw a wrought-iron ladder leading up to an apartment complex. Below it sat an old, rusted car.

Without breaking stride, I rushed up the side of the car and leapt. I latched onto the ladder with both hands, but it was no use. A demon dog bounded and caught my leg, dragging me down to the ground with it.

The dogs encircled. They snarled and snapped at me. "Easy buddies. Good doggies. Remember who just fed you, huh?"

The injured dog jumped at me. I closed my eyes and waited for my death, but it never came. Instead, the dog whimpered and yelped. I opened my eyes and a great minotaur spun the dog around by another one of its heads and smashed it into an abandoned building.

In his other hand, the minotaur clutched a giant club with a hundred metal spikes on it. He smashed it into the ground and the dogs flew into the air. They crashed into buildings and screeched away into the night.

That's when the minotaur turned its attention to me. I rolled away from his charge at the last moment. He pounded his great club into the ground as I dodged again. I found myself next to the car, with an eyeline to the ladder. I had to time it just right.

The minotaur charged forward again. I leapt onto the car hood, over the minotaur, onto the ladder, and pulled myself up. The minotaur roared, its breast heaving as it charged the wall and crashed its horns into the side of the building again and again. I steadied my hands and gripped the rungs tighter as I climbed.

I reached the roof as the foundation shook below me, the building teetering on the verge of collapse. I only had one chance. I took a running start and leapt toward the building next door. "Please don't die. Please don't die. Please don't die."

The building shook and fell just as I hurtled through the air and rolled onto the building next door. "I made it? How did I manage that?"

I stood up. My sore shoulder throbbed and ached, but I couldn't tend to it now. I looked over the side of the building and saw the lifeless horns of the minotaur under the building's rubble. Demon dogs gathered around to scavenge a meal. They had the last laugh.

*

My friend Talinda lived in the Black Zone, or at least she did back before the Black Zone existed; back before the Apocalypse started.

I didn't know back then that West Overbrook was on the wrong side of the tracks. I just wanted to play in the brownstone tenements with my friend. I wanted to sprint up the stairs and throw spitballs from the roof. I just wanted to be a kid.

Tali had a nice laugh, but all I heard when I thought of her was the bloodcurdling scream she let out as she died.

There were no kids laughing and playing in the city anymore. Most were either blue lighted or dead. Those that remained stayed under lock and key. Nobody dared bring a child into the world now. Pregnant women were easy prey to marauders and monsters alike. The few children left were the most vulnerable. They didn't know the risks. They thought they would live forever. They were a liability.

Anybody you loved was a liability in the Apocalypse. The less you had, the longer you lived. That's why I'd made it this far. I had nothing.

It's also what made Connie and Dennis so amazing. They loved each other more than anything, and somehow survived through it all, together. They shouldn't exist. They shouldn't be alive. Yet, they were. More than that, they were stronger for being together. They looked out for each other. Once the Apocalypse came, I figured their love would fade, but they found solace in each other, even as the world burned around them.

It would have been nice to have somebody looking out for me as I stumbled down the stairwell onto the first floor. I couldn't wait for daylight because the demon dogs slept in the tenements during the day. If they came home, I would be a sitting duck. It was another two hundred yards of full-tilt boogie to the light on the other side.

I crept out of the apartment complex, eyeing a bright shining light from the other side of the Black Zone. The neon sign from the clinic glowed right beyond it. The monsters were busy with their minotaur meal. There would never be a better time.

My legs pumped forward faster than I thought possible. I drove them until they burned. I didn't look back. I didn't look sideways. I just looked ahead. And I didn't stop until I reached the clinic.

I pushed open the door and collapsed on the floor.

Chapter 5

I wanted to live. Like, I really wanted to live. I wanted to live more than anything.

That's the one thing that has always been consistent about me since I was born. It carried me through the darkest days of the Apocalypse.

The only reason I was alive was because I wanted it bad enough. Most people died these days because they lost the will to live. The fire left their souls and the life drained from their bellies. Sometimes it happened moments before they died; other times they walked around like living zombies for years.

I've lost my will to live for a moment here or a minute there, but I always bounced back. My stupid desire to live kept me alive no matter how bad the situation. Even running through the Black Zone, with demon dogs at my back, and the chance of survival nearly zero, I still had the will to keep going.

I didn't say that to brag, either. Frankly, I should want to die. I should want nothing more than to get out of here and see whether I earned my way out of Hell. That was the big question among those of us left behind, whether we could earn our way out of a trip to Hell.

We were probably doomed to Hell regardless, but there was a strong contingent that thought if they prayed enough, if they were good enough, that God's countenance would smile down on them and he would welcome them to Heaven.

It's a moot point, though. Nobody could lead a good life after the Apocalypse. Everybody made sacrifices and committed heinous acts that would have horrified their former selves. Even if they could buy their way into Heaven with good deeds, I didn't know if what we did mattered any more.

I did know one thing…when people gave up the will to live, I certainly didn't blame them. I couldn't do it, though. I couldn't willingly die. If for no other reason than this: if it was bad on Earth, with all the monsters spread out and doing their own thing, and the worst monsters contained inside the Black Zone, how bad would it be in Hell, where they were there for the long haul, and the worst monsters roamed free?

That's the kind of thing that left me clinging to life, if not loving it. No, definitely not loving it. The reality of Hell kept me breathing on the way to that clinic when my heart wanted to give out and my lungs wanted to collapse. But they didn't. I kept going, and I made it. I fell on the floor after I got there, but I made it.

Pressing my hands into the ground, I boosted myself onto my knees and looked into the faces around me. I witnessed the lost hope in their eyes. I scanned the waiting room, looking for Dennis and Connie, but my bleary eyes wouldn't focus. Luckily, a shrill shriek got my attention.

"Katrina!" Connie rushed over to me and reached out to help me. "Come on. Get up."

I pulled myself up. "Don't worry about me. I'm fine, I'm fine. How's our boy?"

She spun me toward a long bench where Dennis had propped himself against the wall, his head leaning against a withered plant. He painted its base black with his heaving. "He's been better."

Connie eased me onto the bench next to him. My shoulder ached terribly, but it wasn't broken or dislocated. I would survive. My health wasn't the concern. Only Dennis mattered. His face was gaunt and hollowed out, his skin sticky and pasty.

"You look terrible," I said.

"Always the charmer," Dennis said, eyes rolling back in his head. "You don't look so great yourself."

"That's why I have you around. I'm an Adonis by comparison."

"Funny. That's why I always had you around, too."

Dozens of moaning families were packed like sardines into the waiting room. There were others with the Plague, for sure, but also some with cuts, scraps, and bruises. Some had broken arms, and the children among them cried and wailed. *That's why you don't have kids*, I thought. *Such a liability.*

"How many people are ahead of you?"

Connie shook her head. "I don't know. They haven't brought anybody else back since we got here. An old woman dragged her motionless husband out of here a while ago. I guess we moved up the list when that happened, so that's something."

I ground my teeth together. "That's completely unacceptable."

"It's life, Katrina. It's not like we're livin' in a fairyland. They'll get to us in time. Either that or he'll die before we get inside. There ain't nothing else we can do."

"That's not good enough." I walked over to where a surly, old woman sat nestled behind the reception desk. She wore a pink medical hat and pinker scrubs. A gruff bitterness shone through the nurse's teeth as a woman pleaded with her. She clutched her daughter's hand tightly. The girl's other arm hung loosely at her side.

"Please," the woman said. "I've been here all day. My daughter's arm is getting infected. Please."

The nurse sighed. "Look, lady—"

"My name is not lady!" She shouted. "My name is Kathy. I'm a person. And this is my daughter, Mariel. She's a spitfire. She's ornery. And she's hurt. She's a person. We are people."

"That was very touching, I'm sure," the nurse said with a disinterested sigh. "But there's nothing I can do. The doctor will see you when he sees you. You're welcome to take the girl home and cut the arm off yourself."

"Cut it off?" she said, shocked. "I couldn't."

"Then sit down and shut up."

The woman bent down to the girl. "It's okay, Mariel. We'll be okay. Let's just go back and sit down."

"But it huuurts!" the girl shouted.

"Life isn't fair, kid." the nurse replied. "If it was, I certainly wouldn't be here."

I stomped up to the counter. The nurse sighed, unimpressed. "And what do you want?"

"What's taking so long?" I demanded. "We've been waiting here forever. My friend—"

"No, you haven't."

"Excuse me?"

She pointed at Dennis. "Your friend, the one that looks like death, he got here less than a half hour ago." She pointed to a fat, old man with his eyes rolling back in his head. "*He's* been waiting forever. I'm surprised he's not dead yet."

"My friend is gonna die and it's all your fault."

She sighed again. "Maybe, but lots of people die. I used to think *everybody* was going to, you know, until my bastard husband blue lighted. He didn't die. He tried to get me into church for years, too. Those guys didn't die. But everybody else," she pointed with her pen to emphasize her point. "You, me, definitely them out there, we're all gonna die. Sooner rather than later, probably."

"That's not good enough."

She crossed her arms over her chest and leaned back. "A thousand people live within walking distance of this clinic, and it's the only one around, 'less you wanna drive across the abyss for a day and take your chances in Bend. Now, I know what you did, dragging him across the Black Zone, and that's admirable, but it's also stupid, cuz we both know he's gonna die. We got one doctor in this place, and he can only see one person at a time. Savvy?"

I slammed my fists on the counter. "I guarantee my friend is the sickest person here."

The nurse looked down at my hands. "Get your hands off my desk. Now."

I grinned. "Make me."

The nurse dug under the table and rose back up with a sawed-off twelve-gauge shotgun. "Sit down or I'll blow off your tits."

"Pull the trigger. I dare you."

She cocked the gun and leveled it at my chest. The barrel of the gun shook. Her arms wobbled, and her finger wiggled on the trigger.

I swerved left and batted the gun toward the ceiling. It exploded in a massive thunder, making asbestos snow down through the clinic. The barrel of the gun sizzled against my fingers as I ripped it from the nurse's hand and smashed it against her face.

Blood from her gushing nose spewed through her fingers when she covered her face. "You broke my nose!"

I leveled the gun at her. My breath was calm, hands steady; I was a stone-cold murderer. I had no problem killing again. "Then it's a good thing you work in a clinic. Now, I'll break more than that if you don't bring us to see a doctor right now."

"You wouldn't. I'm a healer."

"You said it yourself. We all die sometime." I turned to Connie, who wrapped Dennis around her body to shield him from the noise. "Come on, Connie. We're going."

The nurse stood up and walked to the door behind her. "Follow me."

"Watch yourself," I said. "I won't think twice about cracking your skull open and leaving you for the Hell hounds."

The rest of the clinic sat in stunned silence as we walked through the door and locked it behind us.

Chapter 6

The clinic's floorboards were warped and buckled, causing them to creak and moan with our every passing step. The makeshift pressboard walls left gaps between them, so you could see the horrors inside. In one room, a man laid bloated and dead on an exam table while a woman sobbed in the chair next to him. In another, a young child dangled a single leg off the table, his other leg bandaged at the thigh. Cries erupted through every wall.

"How long is the wait once you're inside?" Connie asked.

"It's however long it is," the nurse said, still holding her nose. "The doctor has twenty rooms and two arms. You do the math."

The nurse stopped in front of a wooden door, unfinished and rusted at the hinges. "Here you go."

The vile stench of sick stuck to my tongue when the door swung open. My stomach convulsed, and I fought against the vomit lurching its way up my esophagus.

"Gross," Connie said, heaving under her breath.

"What did you expect," the nurse replied. "Club Med?"

"She's right," I replied, choking back my bile. "It's fine. Everybody inside. You too, nurse."

"I have patients."

I cocked the shotgun. The sound sent shivers up even my spine. Fear was a powerful motivator. If you could harness it right, it was more effective than firing a single bullet. A few cockroaches skittered out of our way as we filed into the room. The walls amplified every horrific shriek from the other rooms.

"Sit," I told the nurse. "Don't make any sudden movements."

She took a seat on an unstable chair near the sink. I noticed her nametag in the glint of the overhead light; Tawnly Pranger. She was a person, too, though not much of one.

The only other furniture in the room was an examination table that was frayed, torn, and covered in dried blood.

"You guys got a towel or anything to clean this up?" Connie asked.

"You'd be lucky if you could find running water in this part of the city," the nurse snapped. "We aren't so lucky as you folks in East Overbrook."

"Lucky," Connie said. "You think we're lucky?"

"Not lucky." The nurse shook her head with a small smile. "Just luckier than us."

Connie sighed and helped Dennis onto the bed. Her feet stuck in a dried pool of Plague bile as she moved. "This is gross."

"We see four hundred people a day, every day. Doctor doesn't sleep. He doesn't eat. All he does is work on patients. Last thing we can do is figure out how to clean this up. One goes out. Another comes in."

Two gunshots rang through the hall and shook our little room. *BLAM! BLAM!*

Dennis shot upwards in a feverish terror. "What was that?"

"Patient care." The nurse shrugged.

We heard a door creak open down the hallway, and the loud stomps coming toward us. I turned my gun to her. "Tell him to come in here. Now."

The nurse cleared her throat. "Doctor. I need to see you. Room Thirteen!"

The footsteps stopped for a moment, then moved toward us in earnest. The exam room door creaked open slowly, and an old man walked through. He wore a bloodied lab coat, spectacles, and a scowl.

"What is all the ruckus, nurse?" He jumped slightly when he realized I had a gun trained on him. "My word! What is going on here?"

"Sorry doc, but we got an emergency. My friend is all sorts of sick. He wasn't gonna last another five minutes out there."

"And if I help you," the doctor said. "what's to stop every desperate person from trying something similar? I'm sorry, but you're on your own. I simply cannot cater to intimidation."

I cocked my gun. "I understand, doc."

"You won't shoot me. I'm the only doctor within a hundred-mile radius. Kill me and only the patients will suffer."

"Got a point, doc."

I swung the shotgun around and blew off the nurse's leg at the kneecap.

"Shit!" she screamed as she fell to the ground.

The doctor grasped for a revolver stuck in his belt. I twisted around and knocked him on the chin with the butt of my shotgun. The gun flew out of his hand.

"You blew off my kneecap!" the nurse screamed.

"I know, bitch. I was there!" I picked the revolver up off the floor. "Now, look my friend over or I'll keep shooting pieces off your nurse joint by joint. So, what'll it be, doc?"

"You haven't given me much of a choice here."

"There's always a choice, doc. Just not always a good one."

The doctor ambled over to Dennis, stepping through his nurse's blood on his way. "Open your mouth."

The bile stuck to Dennis's mouth. The doctor pulled out a thermometer and moved it away. "Stick this under your tongue."

A few seconds later the thermometer beeped with a 105-degree temperature. I didn't have to study medicine to know that wasn't a good sign. Next, he examined Dennis's ears, tapped his knees, and checked his eyes, all in a very deliberate fashion.

"What's wrong with him, doc?"

He turned to me. "I will tell you, but first I want your word that no matter what I say, my nurse and I can leave with no further harm coming to our persons."

"You gotta lotta balls, doc, but no bargaining chips."

"Quit being a dick, Katrina," Connie snapped at me. She turned to the doctor and gave him a strained smile. "Of course you can leave without any more harm. I just wanna know what's wrong with my baby."

The doctor sighed. "Very well. Your friend has the Plague. Pretty advanced stages, too. Frankly, I'm surprised he's still walking. He'll be dead in a day, two at most, if not much sooner."

"No!" Connie shouted. "That's not true. You're screwing with me because of what Katrina did to you. I don't even like her! Tell me it's something else. Anything else."

"This has Plague written all over it. I've seen it enough to know. And unfortunately, there's no cure. My advice is to end his life quickly. Otherwise, he'll suffer an agonizing death."

Connie balled up her fists. "You're lying. You're lying!" She twirled herself around with all the force she could muster and decked the doctor across the face. He fell hard, but she didn't stop there. She leapt on top of his prone body, knocking her fists into any part of him she could find. The doctor held up his hands to protest, but the fury of Connie's punches broke his defenses again and again.

"Connie!" Dennis rasped with what remained of his strength. "Stop!"

"He's lying, baby! He's lying!"

"He's not the enemy!" Dennis croaked.

"He's lying! He has to be! I'm not gonna let you die." Big, ugly tears ran down her face. "We'll get a second opinion."

"You know he's right," Dennis reached out for her. "Katrina knows too. I know you want to help, but if all I have ahead of me is death, please just end it now." He coughed and tried to catch his breath. "I'm begging you. It hurts everywhere."

Connie rolled off the doctor and ran into Dennis's arms. "I can't let you go."

"You have to."

The doctor picked himself up off the floor. His face looked like it went five rounds with a meat tenderizer, but he'd live. "You promised us—"

"Leave. Just leave."

"Stay as long as you need." The doctor took off his lab coat and wrapped it around the nurse's leg. He was frailer than I thought. His bulky lab coat belied the brittle state of his constitution. He scooped the nurse into his arms. "I'll be going now."

"You do that."

Dennis held Connie in his arms. "I know it's hard, baby, but this pain is only going to get worse. I'm gonna die either way, so I want it to be on my terms. Please, Connie. I'm not strong enough."

"What if I'm not strong enough either?"

Dennis smiled. "You're the strongest person I know. You're the only reason I lasted this long. Every day I've had is thanks to you. But I can't die this way."

Connie slowly nodded her head. "Okay. I'll do it." She turned to me. "Give me the revolver."

"Connie, if you need me to—"

"No," she said. "I have to do it."

She placed the gun on Dennis's forehead, both of them sobbing like children. They truly loved each other, and that meant something. Not enough, but it meant something.

"Think I've repented enough?" Dennis said.

"Yes. I think we all have."

"I love you with all my heart."

"And I love you with all of mine. I'm so sorry."

Bang!

And then it was over. Dennis fell off the table onto the floor. His brains splattered on the wall behind him, a reminder that he was alive once.

I placed my hand on Connie's shoulder. "I'm sorry, too."

"I know."

*

I don't know how long we stayed in that room after Dennis died. It could have been five minutes or five hours. Every time we went to leave, the door refused to budge. The weight of the knob was too great. It might have helped if Connie tried to turn it, but she couldn't.

It was too much for Connie to imagine a world without Dennis. He was the only good thing in her life. I'd lost the last good things in my life long ago, but I still remembered the weight of burying my mother, even if I refused to feel the pain.

"I can't go," Connie muttered again and again.

"I'm in no rush," I replied. It was the first time I'd felt like a real friend in long time.

Eventually, she found the strength to turn the knob. We found a gurney in a storage closet and wheeled Dennis out the back door into an alley. In Overbrook, most people simply laid where they died, but Connie refused to let that be Dennis's fate. She insisted on burying him.

By the time we left the clinic, it was light out. The same streets that had been so treacherous last night were mostly empty now, and we pushed the gurney through without any problems. Snarls emanated from the buildings now filled with creatures of the night, but they wouldn't dare show their faces in the sunlight. Once through the Black Zone, we pushed the gurney up to a hill overlooking the city.

The rays of the sun crept over the shops and revealed the truly revolting shanty town Overbrook had become in the two years since the Apocalypse began. No longer did businessmen bustle to and from work along Main Street; no longer were there people who took pride in their homes. Gone were the smiling faces, all replaced by the gaunt dead eyes of people living a waking nightmare.

"This is where we first fell in love," Connie said through her tears. "Right on this hillside overlooking the whole town."

She handed me a shovel, and we dug. My shoulder still throbbed, but the adrenaline quelled the pain. By midday, Dennis was in the ground and my muscles burned. "Do you want to say a few words?"

"Nah, I said it all before. This is nice, though. I'm gonna come back here whenever I need a reminder there's good in the world."

"You should just sleep here then."

Connie chuckled. It was the first laugh I'd heard from her in a long time. "Don't make me laugh, Katie. This is a solemn occasion."

With dad dead, Connie was the only person alive that could call me Katie without getting a fist to the jaw, but I won't lie, it still grated on me. "I know. With so much death it's tough to remember that dying still matters."

She pulled the revolver out of her waist and handed it to me. "Well, it does."

"Don't you think you'll need that?"

She shook her head. "Not anymore. I want to remember the good things about Dennis..." She didn't have to finish her sentence.

I looked out over the horizon. "Screw this whole town. Screw this whole stupid world."

"Katrina, I'm trying to have a moment here."

I threw my hands in the air. "I know, but...we are just so screwed, Connie. Eventually, we're gonna end up like Dennis, caught up with the Plague and a bullet in our heads. Or dinner for some demon. Or ripped apart by a horde of zombies. This is so messed up!"

"Yeah. It sucks." Connie just nodded. "You're right about that."

"Do you know what we should do?" I said. "We should go and tell Satan he can eat a dick. Punch him right in his nose until he bleeds."

Connie pursed her lips. "You know, that's not the worst idea I've heard today."

"I mean it's not fair, right? Nothing about this is fair."

"I just lost the love of my life to a disgusting, horrifying disease that shouldn't even exist." Connie leaned over and started picking up rocks and throwing them toward the city. "That's not fair. None of this is fair. It's not—fair—at—all." She'd run out of rocks to throw and paused to catch her breath. "Nothing's been fair about the past two years."

I gave her a hard look. I was starting to take myself seriously. "Really, though...we should do it. We should totally just get a car, drive to Hell, and kick the piss out of Satan until he agrees to end this Apocalypse once and for all. If we're gonna die, it should be on our terms."

"Yeah, you're right. We should do it."

"Seriously? Cuz I'm just blowing off steam. It's suicidal, what I'm saying."

"We're gonna die anyway. It might as well be by punching Satan in the dick."

"This is stupid."

"So stupid."

I smiled. "I can't wait."

"Me neither."

Chapter 7

It wasn't much work to steal a car. There were cars everywhere in Overbrook, and most of them didn't have drivers anymore. The hardest part was choosing which one you wanted. We chose to drive in style, picking up a red Mustang convertible over the more reliable Prius or some other gas-conscious car. We needed speed to outrun the demon dogs sure to be out along our route, even if we sacrificed fuel economy to get it.

Once we had the car, we needed gas. That was a little bit harder. Gas wasn't cheap or plentiful in Overbrook. It was a precious commodity, and one man hoarded it all. Connie chose to keep her cheap rust bucket specifically because it didn't need much gas. If we were going to make it to Reno, the nearest rift to Hell, we would need to stock up.

That meant a trip to Walter's, the only true gas station in the city. He set up small pop-up shops around town where you could buy a gallon or two of gas, but if you needed to fill up, you had to drive out to him.

I really hated Walter. He was a scummy, greasy, horrible piece of human excrement, and he knew it. He reveled in it. He had something everyone needed and lorded it over all of us. He was the most ruthless bastard in the city, commanding a cruel gang of thugs and extortionists. I was absolutely certain he was responsible for siphoning Connie's gas. Now we would have to buy it back from him at a premium—and thank him for the privilege.

His gas station wasn't even nice. It was a dilapidated building, more like a lean-to, on a burnt-out country road that didn't have another building for five minutes. "Better to see your enemies coming," he told me once. That's the kind of guy he was. Cared more about keeping his money safe than being comfortable.

Walter accepted cash, but he preferred bartering. I stopped home to pick up what I still owned that might be of value: ten boxes of bullets and three kilos of weed Barry paid me for rent six months ago.

I walked into Walter's on a mission. He spun around on his chair and smiled his toothless grin. Even by Apocalypse standards, he was not an attractive man. Still, he'd survived, and I had to give him credit for that. Those of us that survived were a bit like a family, dysfunctional as we were.

"Well, well, well, if it isn't the bitch of Black Street."

"And the bastard of the backwater. Good to see you."

He nodded. "Don't get all sappy on me. What do you want?"

I threw down the boxes of bullets, the shotgun, and the three kilos of weed. Then, I reached into my back pocket and pulled out the revolver. "I need to fill up a tank and get however much gas this buys me. Can you get us to Reno?"

He smiled. "I could, if I had that kinda inventory."

"You've been siphoning off gas for years, asshole. You have it."

"Not anymore. Militia needs most of it. I got a little reserve, but I can't spare it all." He shook his head. "I can get you to Bend. It's the safest town left in Oregon. They'll take care of you."

"Get bent."

He pushed back four boxes of bullets, the shotgun, and two kilos of weed. "That won't get you further than Bend."

I sighed. "I hate Bend."

He smiled again. "You hate everything. That's what I like about you."

"Fine. We'll take it. Can you tell your boys on the wall to let us through?"

He nodded. "You wanna get outta my town, I won't stop ya."

*

The televisions stopped broadcasting a long time ago, except for the dull hum from the emergency broadcast signal. The only way to get news was from a trusted source, who heard it from a trusted source, who heard it from a trusted source. The only source I trusted for information lived at the power plant.

During the day, the drive up was a pleasant one. The last time I'd driven that road everyone with me died, including my father. This time we got to the plant without incident. I banged on the door. Soline answered; a young, bespectacled woman with flaming red hair.

"Oh, thank Christ you're okay," I said, relieved.

She wrapped me in a hug. "Yes. We're okay, for now."

Soline shuffled Connie and I inside the plant and shut the door. "You don't call, you don't write—how am I supposed to know if you're alive or dead?"

"Always assume I'm dead."

"I do!" She fluttered her hands in the air in front of her face, trying to contain herself. "That's why this is so exciting!"

The turbines whirled and spun, the lights flickered and hummed; it was everything my father wanted, and Soline ran it all. She had learned the ins and outs of every machine, then taught it to others who called the plant home. They were all smart, but Soline was a genius.

"Do you want any lunch?" she asked. "It's mostly rat, but I think there's a little dog left."

"No thanks," Connie said. "I don't eat dog."

"Why? Because they're cute?"

Connie shook her head. "No. Just don't like the taste."

"When you are hungry enough, everything tastes good."

"That's fair."

Soline climbed the ladder into the control room. Connie and I followed behind her. "So, what can I do for you, Katie?"

"You know I hate that."

"Your dad called you—"

"You're not my dad."

Soline paused, chin to chest, then nodded solemnly. "I'm sorry, Katrina."

"I need to know what you know about the road to Bend and on to Reno. Is it safe?"

She skimmed through a pile of journals on her desk. "You should probably be okay getting to Bend. Not a lot of activity that way, but once you get down to Sacramento there are more marauders than you can shake a stick at."

"Is Portland still overrun with monsters?"

"Yep. Monsters pretty much run the show in Portland. They congregate in the center of town, though. Not many on the outskirts."

"What about heading east and taking Route 97 instead of Interstate 5?"

"If you want good news about Bend, we don't have it. Haven't heard from them in months. Guy who came through a few weeks ago said they've been without power since the beginning of the year." She raised her eyebrows and whistled. "That's rough."

"I couldn't imagine," Connie said.

"Me either. Luckily we've got power for days." Soline put a hand on my shoulder. "Thanks to your dad."

I shrugged her off. "Anything else you can tell me?"

"Monster activity has been real low for a while now. Most of the monsters seem to be pulling north for some reason, but nobody knows why."

"And yet I keep fighting them."

"Well, you are the special one then, cuz travelers keep saying there's not that many monsters along the way. Not even many marauders. Maybe they fought each other to death."

Connie turned to Soline. "Or maybe they're focused on taking the big cities and leaving the small ones to die off?"

"How many travelers do you see, Soline?" I asked.

"Not that many."

"Maybe that's cuz they got eaten, so they can't talk about it," Connie suggested.

"Maybe, or maybe they have less reason to run."

"Always the optimist." I forced a smile, then clasped her by the hand. "Keep your phone close. I might need you."

"It will always be on for you, Katrina."

*

Six hundred and twenty miles.

That's how long it was from Overbrook to Reno.

There had been a lot of stupid ideas since the Apocalypse, but none as stupid as the one we planned. It was a ten-hour drive from Overbrook to Reno in the best of times, but this wasn't the best of times. The weather-cracked asphalt was crumpled from heavy monster feet.

Of course, we would have to get out of town first, which wasn't a given. There were only three roads out of town, since Walter and his henchmen blew up the rest to make sure undesirables didn't have access. Lots of people wanted to come in because we were one of the most stable cities on the West Coast. With hydroelectric power and the ocean at our back, we were a desirable destination.

The refugees started coming soon after we got the power back on in Overbrook; marauders followed close behind. We kept both at bay using Walter's militia. Once they were gone, Walter and his men took over protection of the border, from both people coming in and those that wanted to get out.

As our population dwindled, people wanted to take their chances in other places along the road. They wanted to try Portland or Seattle, but Walter didn't want to let them go. We always needed more warm bodies, if nothing else. They didn't lock us inside, but it wasn't easy to get out, either.

We hit Walter's roadblock five miles outside of town. It was just wide enough to enclose the power plant and tight enough that it could be manned by a couple dozen men. Thick barbed-wire fencing rose ten feet into the air and wrought iron three inches thick made it impossible to break through.

A skinny boy in a dirty, baseball hat walked out of a guard shack. "State your business."

"Just let us through, Jeff!" Connie shouted from the driver's seat. She'd insisted on driving.

Jeff walked up to the car. He'd been a punk kid back before the Apocalypse, before Walter brainwashed him. Now, he was a nightmare. "You know I can't do that, Connie. We got rules and regulations."

Connie stared bullets at him. "This is the Apocalypse, Jeff. Screw your rules and your regulations. Let me through."

Jeff pulled out a notebook. "Where to?"

"Reno."

Jeff shook his head. "There ain't nothing in Reno, Connie, 'cept a big ole hole."

"You don't think I know that, Jeff? That hole's what I'm goin' for."

"Used to be the biggest little city in America. You know that?"

Connie nodded. "I did. Now it's a hole. Let me through."

Jeff tipped his cap up. "We ain't got the population to just let two fertile girls through here. You know that."

Connie gave Jeff an even stare. "Dennis is dead, Jeff. Even if he wasn't, you think I'd bring a baby into this world?"

"We gotta rebuild, Connie."

"No," I said. "We gotta die out. Don't make me kick your ass, Jeff. Just let us through. Or we're gonna force our way through."

"I gotta ask."

"No, you don't, Jeff," I replied. "Walter already said it's okay."

"I'll have to check that." Jeff lifted the walkie-talkie to his lips. "Hey, Walter. I got Connie and Katrina here at the gate. They wanna go out, but I told 'em fertile women—"

The radio crackled to life. "Let 'em go. Best case, they die on the road."

"What's the worst case?"

"They don't."

*

My cousin Cassandra lived in Bend. I doubted that she was still alive. She wasn't a survivor. She liked fluffy things and creature comforts. Plus, she had three young kids, and kids didn't fare too well when the monsters came. Maybe she'd made her way north, to Canada and the protective cold that kept out most of the worst monsters, but I doubted she lasted a month.

Bend was four hours from Overbrook on good roads, and there weren't any good roads left. People were a little too preoccupied to bother with cleaning up rockslides, so we ended up backtracking through side streets and made our way slowly.

Every few miles, we passed another dead town in another lonely stretch of road. I remembered driving from Overbrook to Bend when I was a kid and stopping along the way to visit fruit stands and gas stations. There was none of that now. The Earth had reclaimed her land.

What surprised me most was the lack of action on the road to Bend. But then, why would monsters live in the middle of nowhere? They preferred the cities, and so the trip to Bend was a quiet, albeit boring one.

That all changed an hour outside of Bend, when our quiet trip was rudely interrupted. Four marauders encircled a truck on a lone highway, shouting profanities at the woman inside. People that liked the structure of a big group tended to join militias or live in cities. Marauders usually traveled in packs of less than ten, and only played nicely when destroying a big target, like Sacramento. Then, they'd split up the spoils and disband. Their disorganization was their biggest weakness.

"We should just keep going," Connie said to me as she put the car in park. "In a few minutes it will all be over. They'll be gone, and we'll be able to keep going."

"That's one way to do it. The other way is to kick their asses and save whatever's in the truck."

"I don't like that plan."

"Me either. Let's do it."

"Ugh. Fine." She slammed the car back into gear and gunned forward while I pulled the shotgun out of the backseat and loaded it with shells. "When I say, swerve."

"I remember."

"Now!"

Connie jerked the wheel and the car spun sideways and skidded toward the marauders. I cocked the shotgun and blew the head off the guy nearest the driver's door. The other three went for their guns. I dropped another one before he could bring up his pistol, and another one as he ran toward his truck.

Connie came to a complete stop and I kicked open the door. "There's only one of you left. Your odds are horrid. I'll let you get outta here if you leave in the next ten seconds. Otherwise, I'll blow your head off."

There was silence for the next several seconds. Then, I watched the last marauder scamper off to his car and speed off.

"You shouldn't have done that," Connie said. "He's going to come back with his friends."

"Yeah, but he'll tell his friends what happened here and by then we'll be gone."

I ambled over to the truck, its hood crumpled in and smoking. Peering in the driver's side door, I saw the airbag deflated against the dash. A middle-aged woman with a black eye leaned against it. She was bleeding badly and barely breathing.

"What happened here?" I asked.

"Marauders," she replied. "Smashed."

Then she passed out. I slung her over my shoulder and walked her to our car.

*

Bend was encircled by a giant gate just like the one in Overbrook. Their defenses mirrored ours, which made sense. After all, we'd worked together to build them. A fat guard waddled out of his guard shack. Three snipers trained their guns on us from the top of their fence.

I remembered coming here on long road trips with my family to see my cousin Cassandra and her family. Back then, it was such a pleasant little town, quaint even. The people were friendly, and the streets were clean. Now, it was a fortress.

"State your business!" the fat guard shouted.

"This woman needs medical attention," I said, pointing to the back seat.

The fat guard looked in the back seat. "Jesus Christ. What did you do to her?"

"What? Nothing. We saved her. She's gotta be one of yours."

He looked at her more closely. "She is. Judith. Where'd you find her?"

"There's a lot of rough road out there," I said. "She's gonna bleed out if you don't let us in."

"We'll take her, but you two are another matter."

I cocked the shotgun and pointed it at Judith. "It's all of us or none of us, I'm afraid. Make your choice."

He motioned for the gate to be opened. Good thing too, because the shotgun wasn't loaded.

Chapter 8

The militia hated that I had threatened one of their citizens. They arrested us immediately and dragged us to the hospital with Judith. I couldn't believe they had an actual hospital, even if it did run on Home Depot generators and Christmas lights illuminated the hallways.

"How did you keep this hospital safe?" I asked as we walked the corridors, flanked by guards.

"It's easy if you have the right priorities," the commander of the unit grunted through a thick mustache. They called him Burns. "Every man, woman, and child in this town has a duty and a place."

We passed Judith's room, and I caught a glimpse of her hooked up to tubes. The sound of a running generator emanated from the corner. "You must use a lot of gas here."

"We do."

"How much time you spend searching for it?"

"Too much, that's for sure."

They shoved me in the room next to Judith's. "If she dies," Commander Burns said, "then we'll assume you shot her and throw you out that window there. These two nice gentlemen will be out front to make sure you don't try to escape."

"That's stupid," Connie said. "Why would we beat somebody up, then bring them to your doorstep?"

He shrugged. "Why does anybody do anything these days? I guess you should hope that she lives, huh?"

He walked out of the room and locked the door behind him. Connie threw her arms up in the air. "This is so stupid!"

They had actual beds in the room. I hadn't slept since Overbrook and the thought of laying on a bed was tempting. This one didn't even have dried blood on it. In fact, the whole place was exceedingly nice compared to the dump where Dennis died.

It had been so long since the one in Overbrook closed, I'd nearly forgotten what hospitals were like. Aside from the smell of gas that permeated every inch, it was spotless. Maybe Dennis would have had a chance in this place.

"Are you listening to me?" Connie shouted.

I sat up. "No."

"What are we gonna do? That poor girl is gonna die and then we're gonna die."

"Relax. I have a plan."

She rolled her eyes. "Of course you do."

I jimmied open the only window in the room. There were no metal bars holding us inside, just the fear of a seven-story fall, and the protection of a tiny ledge which barely fit my hand.

"What are you doing?"

"Just keep shouting like I'm here and not listening, okay?"

"But you aren't listening."

"That's perfect. More of that."

I climbed out onto the ledge and peered toward Judith's room. All that separated me from her room was a large gap—too wide to reach without leaping. Unfortunately, the ledge in front of her window wasn't any bigger than the one in front of mine. If I didn't land on Judith's ledge just right, I would fall and break my neck.

Nothing to it. I took a deep breath and leapt. With my outstretched arms, I managed to latch onto the ledge. My shoulder burned as the weight of my body pulled it down. I gritted my teeth and pulled myself up.

There weren't any guards in the room that I could see when I pressed my nose to the window. Back in our room, I heard Connie pitching a fit at an imaginary me. Or the real me. Whatever. I pushed up the window to Judith's room and shimmied inside.

Judith laid unconscious on the bed. A generator whirled in the corner and connected to her monitors, which beeped slowly and loudly. Those marauders really did a number on her. The thought of coyotes ripping apart their dead bodies brought a smile to my face.

I hated that this poor woman was a pawn in my game, but it didn't make it any less true. She had her role to play, and so did I. I walked over to Judith and yanked off the cords that connected to her heart monitor.

The monitors flatlined and screeched an ungodly beep. A doctor bolted in with a set of defibrillator paddles and a frantic nurse. Behind them, two guards rushed in to see the ruckus.

"What are you doing in here?" one of the guards shouted.

"Isn't it obvious? I'm proving a point."

The doctor moved toward Judith. I held up my hand. "She's fine. I just ripped off her monitor. But that's not all I could do. If I wanted to hurt her, she'd be dead already. Trust that. I know a hundred ways to kill a person."

The guards leveled their guns at me. "Back off!"

The door to our room slammed open. Connie tumbled inside the room through it and beat the living snot out of the guards, leaving us alone with the doctor, his nurse, and two guns.

"Run away," I told the doctor. "Run away and find the commander. Bring him here now. Meanwhile, nurse, plug this back in."

The doctor ran away. I looked up at Connie. "How did you get out?"

"I kicked really, really hard."

It took a couple minutes for the doctor to find the commander. During that time, the nurse reset Judith's heart monitors and Connie tied the guards together with medical tape she found in the cabinet drawers.

Commander Burns walked in with three guards, all training their guns on me. "This is not a good way to prove you aren't trying to harm us."

"Yes, it is. It proves I have no interest in harming you."

"You got a funny way of showing it."

"I could've slit all your throats and run outta here in the three minutes it took to get you here, but I didn't do that. We're all humans, trying to get along in this world. I think I can help, if you do something for me."

He faltered, thinking about what I said. His eyes fell on Connie, then Judith, then back on me. "What do you have that I want?"

"Why, power of course. Enough to set you up for the next hundred years. In return, I want enough gas and food to get us to Reno."

Commander Burns raised an eyebrow. "I'm listening."

*

The Bend power plant didn't run on hydroelectricity. It ran on good ole fashioned coal, and coal wasn't in much supply these days with nobody to mine it. Luckily, I knew a way around that. Commander Burns wasn't convinced. He drilled me with questions until we reached the plant, but I refused to answer them until we were in the control room.

"I really hope you're not messing with us," he said.

"Be pretty stupid if I said all that just to lie to you, wouldn't it?"

He nodded. "Pretty stupid. Also pretty stupid to leave Overbrook. That town's a fortress."

I tilted my head toward Connie. "We got business in Hell."

"Well, one way or another, you'll be there soon."

"Is that a threat?" Connie asked.

"Not a threat, just a fact. I am a man of my word. You do your part for us and we'll do our part for you."

Inside the control room of the power plant, three men sat in chairs. They spun around to us in unison. A man with thick-glasses and halitosis gawked at me. "You the girl?"

"I'm Katrina if that's what you mean."

"We don't care what you call yourself," a bald man said. "Just as long as you help us."

"What's your name?" I asked. "So, I know who I'm going to beat later for being an idiot."

The man gulped. "Collin. Collin David."

"That's a dumb name." I gestured to a road map pinned up on the wall. "By my estimation, half the power lines between here and Overbrook are down, but if you can put together the men to fix them, I can get you power."

The bald man stood up. "Oh, so we just go off your word?"

"Not my word. Soline's word. You remember her?"

The commander nodded. "She's a good woman. Never treated us raw."

"And she won't now. You get her on the phone and tell her I sent you. You'll have your power. Then you'll fulfill your part of the bargain."

He rapped his knuckles on a desk. "You'll have enough gas and weapons to get into Hell and take on a whole army if you get our power back."

Soline and Commander Burns talked for forty-five minutes, until the battery of my phone died, and they had to patch in a new one. Eventually, the commander nodded and turned to me.

"You happy?" I asked him.

He gave a noncommittal shrug. "We're happy. Well, happy as we'll ever be in this hellhole. It's not gonna be easy. Soline agreed to send ten men to fix the power lines between here and Overbrook. We're gonna send an army to protect them. Once we get it all fixed, we'll have power again."

"How long will that take?" I asked.

He shrugged. "Six months. Maybe more. Better late than never. You've done your part. Now it's our turn."

I couldn't leave the city without asking about my cousin first. My memories of visiting her when we were kids were happy ones, and I figured I would never get the chance to see her again. She was the only blood family I had left.

"I have a question for you. You ever heard of a woman named Cassandra Merritt? She used to be from here, before it all went down."

Commander Burns smiled. "Still is. She's got a very special job to do. Come on. I'll show you. It's on the way out of town."

*

Commander Burns drove us through the dark streets of Bend. Connie looked out the windows, waiting for a monster attack. "Aren't you guys scared of what's out there?"

The commander laughed. "We been dealing with the night for a long time and we're not scared of it any more than it's scared of us. We cleared every street out one by one. Not a monster left in this place."

I raised my eyebrows, staring out at the dark roads we were passing. "That's an incredible feat."

"Nothing to it. We were touched by God."

Connie made a face. "What does that mean?"

"You'll see."

In the center of the town, lit with work lights, stood a single massive church. Thousands of people surrounded it. Commander Burns gestured toward the crowd. "These people, their only job's to make God happy. They pray all day and night, every day and night."

Connie chuckled. "That's gotta be the dumbest thing…"

His look stopped her. "It's worked so far. How many monsters you see around here?"

"Fair enough."

He put the car in park outside of the church and we walked inside. The church organ's music filled the room. In the pews, hundreds of men and women sang hymns to the heavens.

"Sandy!" the commander shouted.

A young woman turned to us. She looked familiar, but her face was pale, with dark rings under them.

"Somebody to see you."

"I got work," she said.

"I know, but it'll still be there. Little rest won't hurt."

Sandy walked toward us. Her gaunt arms dangled at her side, thin enough to crack in half. Malnourishment plagued all the churchgoers, but hers was one of the worst. She couldn't have weighed more than ninety pounds, and on her tall frame, it showed.

"You recognize this girl?" the commander asked.

"Of course!" She wrapped her bones around me. "Katrina! It's so good to see you. Oh my god. I was sure you were dead."

I unwrapped her arms from my neck. "It's good to see you too, Cassandra."

"Oh, they don't call me that no more. Not since the Incident."

"What incident? You mean the Apocaly—"

She stuffed her hand against my mouth. "We don't call it that. We call it the Incident."

"Whatever. How's Ben and the kids?"

"We don't talk about them," she whispered. "We don't talk about them at all."

I looked over at Commander Burns, and he gave a nod. "Alright, Sandy. It's time to go back."

"Thank you. Thank you." Sandy shuffled back to her pew and sang her lungs out. She blared over the rest of the women so loudly that her voice cracked.

I couldn't stop staring. "What happened to her?"

Commander Burns led me outside. "Some of 'em can't take it when their families are taken."

"They died?"

He shook his head. "Blue lighted."

"Everybody but her?"

"All of them. Now she can't eat and won't sleep. All she does all day is pray that she can get good enough to join them."

"That is a hell of a thing."

"That's sayin' everything."

Commander Burns brought us to the entrance of the town. His men stuffed our car full with enough food, gas, and guns to get us to Reno. I slid into the driver's seat just as the sun crested over the horizon.

"You should be good with monsters until you hit Reno. The sun will keep them away."

"I know what the sun will do."

"Course. Sure you don't want a better car? I can set you up with a Humvee."

I waved my hand, shaking my head. "We're alright. Thanks, commander."

"You've done a good thing, Katrina." He tipped his head toward us. "Connie."

"We just did a thing. Who knows if it's a good one?" Connie looked out over the dashboard as she spoke. "Maybe you turn out to be sons of bitches and then it would've been a bad thing."

"We weren't blue lighted, so that makes us all sons of bitches."

I had to laugh at that. "Fair enough." The light crested over the hills as I shook hands with him. "I hope things are better for you from now on."

"They won't be," he replied. "but thank you."

Chapter 9

We passed more dead towns the further we drove from Bend. Towns without humans or monsters. Towns abandoned to nature.

Honestly, I didn't expect to see many small towns full of humans on our way down to Reno, but I fully expected to see a couple filled with monsters. After all, there were some peaceful monsters in Overbrook. There was an imp that lived in my apartment complex who just wanted to knit and read. I could see in through the window in his first-floor apartment. Whenever we caused a ruckus he would sigh, put on headphones, and zone out to cross-stitch patterns. He said he wanted to start an art studio; Death Head Studio, he would call it. He was the least awful demon I ever met.

Once, he even made me a nice needlepoint pattern depicting the gates of Hell. He really was quite talented. He would have liked a little town, far away from humans, where he could work. A town like Doyle, near the Nevada line, where we ended up after a full day of driving.

Doyle was a ghost town even in the best of times, but now its crumbling buildings and sun-bleached sidewalks showed how little the Earth cared for humanity. We pulled up in front of the Grocery Hotel. It wasn't much more than an Old West saloon façade slapped onto a five and dime store, but it had beds and a high vantage point, which is what we needed.

Connie and I covered the car with thatch and brought the supplies inside. Not surprisingly, there wasn't anything to eat in the whole place. Whether it was cleaned out by monsters passing through, the last denizens of the sleepy town, or marauders who needed a quick bite didn't matter. It only mattered that the cupboards were empty.

We trotted up the stairs into a small bedroom looking out over the vast emptiness of the town. "You sleep first," I said. "I'll keep watch."

"And I'm supposed to trust you to be the lookout?"

"You don't have to sleep."

Connie was too tired to argue, apparently, and just fell onto the dusty bed. "Wake me up in a couple hours."

I won't lie. I fell asleep. Lookout duty was so boring. You stared out into the dark for hours on end and nothing happened, ever. You forewent sleep on the off chance that in the middle of nowhere, in the dead of night, something was going to occur. Given the circumstances, this was likely, but also, given the circumstances, I was dog tired.

And so, I fell asleep.

And something happened.

I woke up to a jolt. Three men grabbed me by the arms and legs. Two more snatched Connie. We kicked and screamed to no avail. They dragged us out of the hotel and into the light from their trucks. Four more men sat in front of the cars, carrying shotguns.

"Well, well, well," one with a thick Mexican accent and long beard said, turning to the man who held me. "Look what we have here. God smiled on us today, Mitch."

I bit through Mitch's hand until blood spurted out. His skin was briny from weeks in the hot sun. He screamed out in pain.

"God ain't nothing," I said. "He didn't help you. I just messed up."

Mitch fell down screaming, but the man didn't care. Instead, he laughed. "You're right. You did mess up. We ain't seen anything so nice as you in a long time."

Connie glared over at me. A big, hairy palm covered her mouth. "HDSkfj mdsnck hhakljwdlk."

"What?"

Connie bit her attacker until he freed her mouth. "I hate you."

"I know," I replied. "but you should know never to leave me on lookout."

"I did know that!" She threw her head back. "I hate me too."

This wasn't our first time being held at gunpoint by a group of men. It happened, well let's not say a lot, but enough times that it was a thing.

The big man with the thick accent walked up to me holding a shotgun. "You are gonna suck my dick, and I am gonna like it, or I'm gonna bash out your teeth, and you are not gonna like it. Okay?"

I gave him a deadpan stare. "You're gonna lose anything you put in my mouth."

"And you're gonna call me Anansi while you do it," he added with a smile."

The man had a god complex, clearly. I couldn't do anything about that, but he also didn't believe me, and I was gonna make she he regretted it. When he stepped forward, I gave Connie the slightest of nods. Then, I dug my teeth into the man's inner thigh and ripped open his artery. Blood spurted over the men holding me down. In their shock, they loosened their grip.

Connie flipped one of her guards over her knee and snapped his neck. She hadn't lost a step at all. She spun around behind the other, using him as a shield. A shot rang out, and Connie's shield fell to the ground.

I broke free of my attackers and picked up the bleeding marauder's discarded shotgun. I cocked it and fired two shots behind me, blowing away Mitch and his friend who had held me down.

Next, I fired at the truck and shot out one of its headlights. The men fumbled for their guns, but I was on top of them before they could fire. I snapped the neck of a very ugly man with a buck tooth. His revolver fell into my hand and I fired it off into the necks of two more men.

One guard left.

I rose to my knees and fired into his chest, but I was out of bullets. The man looked at me, doe eyed, and pulled his gun.

Bang. Bang. Bang. Blood oozed out of his head and he dropped to the ground. Connie appeared behind him brandishing a smoking gun. "Good thing I didn't stop to take a nap, right?"

The dying men wailed. I stooped down to one of them. "You're going to Hell, you know that, right?"

"I figured as much," Anansi replied, blood spurting from his mouth.

"Was it worth it?"

"Yeah. It was. I got by the best way I could."

"I hear you. We all gotta do what we all gotta do." I stomped him once in the chest before moving on.

*

Connie picked up a map of Nevada from the hotel before we left the marauders to rot in the hot desert sun, but it wasn't any help. As we entered Nevada, the roads ceased to be roads and turned into an endless desert.

"How much further?" I asked from behind the wheel.

"No idea. When I see a huge hole with demons pouring out of it, we'll stop."

"That map has outlived its uselessness. Time to chuck it."

"I'm not gonna chuck it. It's a perfectly good map!"

I reached over and tried to wrestle it away from her. "Then I'll chuck it!"

She ripped it away from me. "No!"

A whistling sound hummed through the air. Our heads snapped up in time to see a giant meteor sailing through the air toward us. Consumed by fire, the giant rock bore down on us as if aimed by Heaven itself.

"Incoming!" I shouted.

The meteor crashed next to us. The sky lit up with a hundred more flaming rocks whizzing toward us. I swerved, zigged, and zagged to avoid them as the molten embers crashed on either side of us. Among the orange flaming rocks was a blue light, streaming through the rocks faster than I could track.

"What is that?" I screamed.

"Who cares? Keep your eyes on the road!"

But it was too late. A flaming boulder sailed in front of us, too close for me to avoid. "Jump!"

We leapt out of the car just as the rock smashed into the windshield, demolishing it on impact. I rolled onto the hot desert sand and hopped to my feet. More molten rocks fell from the sky and exploded around us.

The sky turned black as a fiery rock bore down on us, and Connie gave me a look. "I hate that you're the last thing I'm going to see before I die."

I turned to face the massive boulder. "Me too."

I closed my eyes, ready for death, but once again, death didn't come. Instead, a sharp talon dug into my back and lifted me into the air. Flames licked my shoes, but I wasn't dead. I expected to see a savior when I glanced up, but found my sworn enemy.

"Thomas! Let me go!"

"If I do that, you'll fall a hundred feet to your death. Is that what you want?"

The desert below exploded in fiery embers as we rose higher and higher into the air. I shook my head. "Don't drop me."

Connie was caught in Thomas's other foot. "What is going on?"

"My dear, I'm afraid you've stumbled into a bit of a war zone."

I wanted to fight him. I wanted to hate him, but all I felt in that moment was thankful. "Jesus Christ, Thomas. I never thought I would be happy to see you."

Chapter 10

For all of Thomas's horribleness, he saved me more times than he raped me. That's not saying much, I understand that, and being saved a bunch of times doesn't make up for being violated once, but that was Apocalypse logic. Thomas saved my life three times after he tried to rip me apart from the inside the once.

The first time happened eighteen months ago. Seven demon dogs chased me through the streets of Overbrook, and he vanquished them to Hell with the snap of his fingers. The second time, a hulking minotaur rampaged through my apartment complex and he turned it away before it destroyed my place. The third time, a guy held a shotgun to my head and Thomas ripped him in half.

This whole chivalry thing was an act to make me need him, but, the fact was, he did save me, and when rocks fell from Heaven, there he was again. Still not forgetting the rape, but this was the fourth time he saved me.

Thomas landed us on a hillside overlooking a large encampment. Dozens of tents stretched into the horizon. Demons and imps worked alongside minotaurs and goblins to move swords, axes, hammers, and armor across the camp toward the smoking rift to Hell which crested over the horizon. Massive demons shouted commands to imps and zombies wearing full battle fatigues, who took turns slashing at dummies in front of them.

"Who are you, demon?" Connie said.

"So rude," Thomas said. "Not surprising, though. After all, you're friends with my Katrina."

"I wouldn't say we were friends," Connie replied. "We're putting up with each other at best."

"And I wouldn't say I was your anything," I added.

"Rude."

"This is Thomas," I said to Connie. "I swore if he ever showed his face again, I would kill him in a most unpleasant way."

"*Thomas* Thomas?" Connie said, curling her lip as she looked at him. "I heard a lot about you. All bad."

"Yes." Thomas nodded. "She has a way of embellishing my misdeeds."

"You. Raped. Me!"

"Just the once. And I saved you, what is it—four times now?"

I sneered at him. "We're not even close to being even."

"Maybe not. But we're closer."

I was done talking about it. The whole conversation had already gone over the amount of time I allowed myself to think about the whole thing, so I gestured to the encampment. "What's going on here, anyway? And what are you doing in the middle of the desert with all these monsters? Building an army?"

"In a way," Thomas replied. "But not the way you think."

"So...you're not about to wage war on humanity again?"

Thomas chuckled. "You are thinking too small, my dear."

"Who are you fighting then?"

"The Devil, of course. Or as I like to call him, dear ole Dad. Follow me." He led us down the hill toward the camp. The smell of sulfur overpowered my senses, though Thomas seemed to revel in it. "Welcome to the resistance, my love. These demons have broken my father's control over them."

Hammers smashed against hot lead. Forges burned bright with fire. Thomas strolled past them like a tour guide, without a care in the world. "We hope to gain favor with God by ending this wretched Apocalypse once and for all."

"So, what," Connie said, "by ending the Apocalypse you'll be able to enter Heaven?"

Thomas ducked into a large tent adorned with an inverted cross. "Well, I've never been to Heaven personally, but yes, that's exactly what we expect."

I followed Connie into the tent. Half a dozen demons of various sizes, colors, and shapes smoked hookah and looked over a map of the desert covering the floor. A reproduction of the rift lay right in the middle of it, with hundreds of miniature soldiers on either end.

Connie stepped over the map and trailed Thomas toward the edge of the room, where a tall, bearded demon with soulless, white eyes and long, curled horns sat reading a huge leather-bound book.

"What do you know of demons, Connie?" Thomas asked.

"I know they suck. I've watched demons rip people in half for fun."

Thomas chuckled and waved a hand. "We are not truly like that. There is so much you do not understand. Sit down and become enlightened." He pulled the massive book from the horned, soulless-eyed demon. "These pages are bound in flesh and inked in blood. They tell the true account of biblical events straight from the old man's mouth."

"Sounds like the *Necronomicon*," Connie smirked. "You guys just watched too much *Evil Dead*."

"Yes," Thomas said. "and that is its true name. Sam Raimi was a visionary. Now listen, some of what you know is true, of course. My father was exiled from Heaven even before the dawn of man for plotting a coup against Heaven. He tempted Eve with the first bite of forbidden fruit, though the metaphor was lost on humans." He gave both of us a pointed look. "I'll dispel any notions that she actually ate a fruit and just say they had sex."

I knew it! "Does that mean humans are descended from little demons?"

"No. She didn't get pregnant from him. My dad was very careful. You lot are the inbred disaster from Adam and Eve's children, and some other families that lived around the planet at that time. God sculpted quite a few people out of clay in his time, and he was a subpar craftsman, but that is not the crux of the story."

"What is?" I asked.

"I'll get to that," Thomas said. "Daddy was also responsible for the decadence of Sodom and Gomorrah, though he always believed that their punishment was a bit excessive. A little debauchery was no excuse to turn everybody into stone."

Thomas cleared his throat and leaned forward. "But that is where your religious texts and the truth diverge. For you see, it was actually my father who talked to Moses as the burning bush. And while God convinced Noah to build the Ark, it was my father who drowned the world."

"If that's true," I said. "then why didn't God just set us straight?"

"He tried," Thomas replied. "By incarnating into human flesh, he tried to warn humanity that they had been deceived. But the Devil easily corrupted those in power. And your one true God was slain."

"Wait, wait, time out," Connie said. "That's crazy."

"Yeah!" I added. "Are you really trying to stuff this load of crap down our throats?"

"My love," Thomas replied. "I've spoken to the Dark Lord ad nauseum and heard first-hand accounts of God's glory. You know nothing of the inner workings of the afterlife and claiming otherwise is remarkably ignorant."

"That doesn't make it any less stupid," I mumbled.

Thomas closed the *Necronomicon*. "Very well. I will give you this option. Either have faith in my honesty or go back to the dirt hole you call your city and leave the world saving to the adults. Now, shall I finish?"

I glared. "Yes, but you're on warning. You lie to me and I'll cut off your head."

"Noted." Thomas opened the book again. "Like me, Satan is able to manipulate his form. After the crucifixion, he went to Jesus's apostles and told them a story about the end of the world you know as Revelations. In this tale, the end of times would come after God opened the seven seals and laid judgment on humanity, but that was all a lie set in motion by Satan for his eventual conquest of both Heaven and Earth."

"That did always seem out of alignment with the rest of Jesus's message," Connie said thoughtfully.

"Are we Bible scholars now?" I asked.

"What? I have varied interests. My dad was a zealot, after all."

"Fair enough," I said. "So, if this is all true, why didn't God just set us straight again?"

"After his son's death, God became...disenchanted with humanity. He tried to help repeatedly but you turned your backs on him. He withdrew, then, and prevented all but the worthiest from entering Heaven. That meant sending more to Hell, which gave Satan an even bigger army."

"As the centuries grew on, the Devil's army grew to tremendous proportions while God's dwindled to nothing. Those that passed through the needle's eye were pussies and pansies. Heaven would crumble if Satan ever set his sight on it."

Thomas cleared this throat. "And now, he has. Earth was just a middle ground; a staging area, if you will. Heaven is his prize. It's what he's always coveted, and he's about to take it. God knows that, which is why in a last fit of protection he took the worthy souls up to Heaven. He is still powerful, but his army isn't. And so, I began this rebellion as a last stand against the forces of evil. If we fail, then Heaven will crumble."

"Sounds like mumbo jumbo to me," I replied.

"Every word is the truth, whether you believe it or not. And today we take the battle to Hell itself, with this."

Thomas pulled out a dagger, adorned with a black gem on its hilt, and endcapped by a skull. The blade curved like a sinewy snake from hilt to tip. I chuckled as I looked at it. "Come on, man. A piddly dagger? That's weak sauce. Can you believe this, Connie?"

I looked around, but she was nowhere to be found. "Connie?"

Thomas grabbed my hand. "She is of no consequence."

"What did you do to her?" I shouted.

"What? Nothing! I would never concern myself with a mortal when there are more important matters to attend."

"Yeah, right. Like a little dagger that somehow is going to take down the big bad?"

"Once this dagger is plunged deep into his heart, the Apocalypse will be over, and God will allow us into his kingdom."

A great cheer erupted from the room. "Huzzah. Huzzah. Huzzah!"

I waited until the cheers died. "That's a nice story and all, but how do you know that once the Devil's gone these evil assholes won't just stick around forever, fighting God until there's nothing left in Heaven or Earth?"

"Think about it, Katrina. Evil only exists because of the Devil. He's the reason you have original sin in the first place. He's the reason we are all evil. These demons were once the beautiful voice of God, and then Satan corrupted them. Now they're monsters." He paused to stare out of the tent to the encampment below, gesturing to the demonic minions. "They all want to go home. Once the Devil is dead, he will no longer have control over the Hellspawn. God will see what we have done and open the gates of Heaven to us again. We will return to God's left hand, the evil will vanish from men's hearts, and Earth will become a paradise."

"That sounds like a pipedream, Thomas, but even if there's a chance that it's true, I want to help."

"Me too!" Connie shouted, walking back into the tent.

"Where did you go?" I asked.

Connie sat down next to me with a casual shrug. "I'll tell you later. Don't worry about it."

"I am gonna worry," I replied. "You were just gone for a really long time. What happened?"

"Nothing. Seriously. I mean, something, but it's not important...yet."

I stood up. "Who are you to tell me what's important. We're literally powwowing with a demon here. Everything is important."

"I just went out to get some fresh air. Jesus, Katrina. Not everything is about YOU. This is why we're not friends anymore."

"Cuz I want to know why you're acting weird?"

"No," Connie replied, shaking her head. "Because you can't leave anything ALONE."

I crossed my arms in a huff. "I don't like this."

"Of course you don't, because you have to know EVERYTHING. God forbid somebody keeps something from the great Katrina. How will the world ever go on?"

"I'm trying to help!"

"Then help by leaving me alone!" Connie shouted.

"Fine!" I grumbled. "You're on notice, though."

"Ooooh. I'm scared," Connie snitted.

"Hey!" Thomas screamed. "We're on a bit of a time crunch here."

"Sorry," I replied.

"Connie," Thomas said. "Do you want to know what you just volunteered to do?"

"Nope," Connie replied. "I'm good."

"And you're still in?" Thomas asked, confused as I was at her weirdness.

Connie nodded. "Totally."

Thomas turned to me. "And you're sure you want to help?"

I nodded. "If killing the Devil is gonna get the dickheads and monsters off my planet, I'll plunge the dagger into his heart myself."

Thomas smirked. "I hoped you would say that, because we are about to head into battle and we could use all the manpower we can get."

I folded my arms. "Womenpower. And when is this battle starting?"

"We march into formation in an hour."

"I guess that's convenient for us, then," I scoffed at him.

Thomas smiled. "Not really. Most of my men will fall in this battle and they have supernatural powers. You will have nothing of the sort."

"We'll manage," Connie said.

I nodded. "Yeah, what she said."

Chapter 11

Three hours later, Thomas, Connie, and I stood looking over the battlefield. Thousands of Thomas's demon horde faced off against a legion from Hell that outnumbered us a hundred to one.

The demons of Thomas's army towered over humans, but the legions of Hell made Thomas's horde look like babies. They were stronger, bigger, and meaner than the armies of Earth. I wasn't afraid of much, but they frightened me.

"Why—how are they so *massive*?" Connie asked Thomas.

"The ones who already came up to Earth were smaller, and sick of getting pushed around. These ones here are the ones who were doing the pushing."

"So, you're saying that the ones we're about to fight are bigger and stronger than anything we've fought before, and there's more of them."

"That's what I'm saying."

Thomas turned to his men. Behind the rows of his legions were three dozen catapults full of sulfuric rock. Imps stood with swords at the ready to cut away the rope that bound them and send the boulders flying. Five hundred archers stood with them, ready to light their arrows on fire.

"Soldiers," Thomas began. "This is the final battle. We have trained for this too little and we number too few. Most of you will fall, perhaps all of you. But should you fall, know that your gallantry will be rewarded in Heaven!"

The demons cheered for him. They loved him, and Thomas fed on it. "Your sacrifice today will not be in vain. It will not be squandered. We will succeed. It is our only option!"

The demons cheered again. Thomas pointed his sword toward the catapults and swung it sharply toward the rift. "Fire a volley of molten rock to announce our presence!"

The imps cut through their ropes. The molten rocks sailed into the air and exploded against Satan's multitudes. "Archers! At the ready!"

The archers lit their flaming arrows and let loose a barrage into the sea of Satan's men. A scream arose from our enemies and they charged. Thomas lifted his sword into the heavens. "Attack!"

Thomas's legions charged into battle. The charge kicked dirt and sand high into the air and clouded the sky. Then, armor, weapons, and bodies crashed against each other like deep ocean waves against rock. Shouts rang out from both sides. Once-proud demons screamed like babies as they fell in front of us. Swords, axes, spears, and all manner of weaponry created a haunting orchestra which rang toward the heavens.

The dust cleared long enough for me to see a demon charging at me. I ducked its advance then elbowed it in the stomach and smashed its face with my war hammer. "I think this might've been a mistake!"

Connie ripped the eye out of a demon's skull. "Where's your sense of fun?"

"The fun is in surviving, Connie. What has gotten into you?"

"It will all work out, Katrina." She smiled as she sliced a demon's throat open. "You just gotta have faith."

"Jesus Christ. Have you turned religious on me?"

"He's got nothing to do with it," Connie said. "I just know some things you don't know yet."

She was acting so strange I thought she must have been under an enchantment. However, she didn't have any of the tell-tale signs of being under a spell. She wasn't bleary eyes, nor were there sprinkling bits of dust floating around her, or anything that indicated she wasn't in her right mind. She looked like normal Connie but was talking like an insane person.

"You care to let me in on what you know that I don't?" I slipped under a charging demon and impaled it with its own sword.

"In good time," Connie said. "In good time."

"Great. I'm about to die and you've clearly gone insane."

"I'm not any crazier than you."

The dust cleared again. Thomas fought a massive mace-wielding demon. He managed to dodge the weapon for a few turns, but it finally connected with an uppercut and Thomas flew into the air.

"Oh no you don't!" I shouted, running toward him. "If anybody's killing that demon, it's gonna be me!"

I slid under a pair of demons and sidestepped a half dozen more until I was next to Thomas. The massive demon had his arms raised to deliver a final blow when I embedded my war hammer in his skull. He stumbled back, and I grabbed the crazy, curvy-bladed dagger from Thomas's belt. I jabbed it so deep into the beast's throat that it exploded into a cloud of dust.

"I like this dagger," I said, wiping it clean on my pants. "Can I keep it?"

Thomas rose to his feet. "That would be best, as we are nearing the rift. Once we are inside, only one with full mortal blood can kill the Devil."

"Why is that?"

"Satan is an angel, a fallen angel, one who has tempted humanity since the beginning. Only a human can overcome that pain and convince God they are worthy of redemption, thus, only they can kill the Devil."

"That doesn't make any sense," I said.

Thomas shrugged. "Of course not. You are only mortal after all."

"Wait, if all of that is true, then how can you wield it?"

"Only against other lesser Demons. My mother was Marilyn Monroe."

"That explains a lot."

*

The rest of the battle was, well, a battle. I mean, there was fighting. I killed some demons. Connie knocked a zombie's head clean off with a mallet—coolest game of croquet ever. We got pushed back, then we moved forward, then we got pushed back again, and it went on like that all afternoon.

I haven't been in many big battles, but if you've seen the *Lord of the Rings* movies, just imagine that big battle at the end of the trilogy, except in the desert, and it was that for hours and hours. We started only two hundred yards from the rift. We could stroll over to it in ten minutes on a good day, but in battle it took forever—and thousands of deaths—to move forward even an inch.

You know something else? It stank. Like really stank. When monsters died, they shat, and these monsters didn't just die, they were eviscerated. Their chests caved into their bodies and faces ended up three hundred feet from their skulls. The oppressively hot sun baked their insides and rotted them out in minutes.

Thomas's army didn't stand a chance against the forces of Hell. Decimated bodies dotted the battlefield, cut in half, ripped to shreds, stabbed in the gut…all fighting for a chance at redemption.

I felt bad for them.

They had probably been tormented in Hell and just wanted somewhere they could be free. When the Hell rift opened, they jumped at the chance to swing their big one and cause a little damage of their own. And they were slaughtered fighting beside me, a human, for the right to return to Heaven.

Eventually, Thomas, Connie, and I had killed enough of Satan's forces to find ourselves standing at the edge of the rift. We ducked through monsters and used our own men as shields to make it past them. Thomas really was an outstanding fighter. He was terrible, maybe the singular worst thing I've ever met, but he excelled at killing his kin.

The rift oozed dry heat like an open oven on a hot summer day. My legs turned to jelly just standing next to it for only a moment, and that was where we were headed—into the great maw of the heat's source.

"Okay," I shouted to Thomas. "We're here. Now what?"

"Now we jump!" Thomas shouted.

"Are you crazy? I'm not jumping into the abyss of Hell!" I looked up and down the rift. "Where's the elevator?"

Thomas stared at me, incredulous. "Hell doesn't have an elevator, Katrina."

Even Connie looked at me like I was stupid, but I just hadn't thought about it. I really hadn't thought about the logistics of getting down to Hell once we got to the rift, or how we would navigate Hell to get to the Devil. I just wanted to punch that evil dude in the cock.

"Come up with a better plan!" I screamed.

Thomas was completely exasperated with me. "There isn't one!"

It didn't take long for the forces of Hell to realize we'd snuck past them, and they quickly turned their attention toward us.

A demon swung its broadsword right at my stomach. Again, I braced for death, and again it didn't come. Instead, I felt Thomas's body against mine. A cry escaped his lips, and his face twisted into a gruesome scowl. The broadsword meant for me was embedded in Thomas's side. Warm goo dampened my leg when he heaved blue bile.

"Thomas!" I shouted. "Goddamn it! I was supposed to be the one who killed you!"

Blood spurted out of his mouth. "Sorry to disappoint you."

"I'm used to it by now," I replied. The monsters of Hell marched toward me in greater numbers, snarling and sneering at us.

"Katrina. Go." He pushed me into Connie with a hard shove. I caught her by the arms and the two of us tumbled backwards into the rift. Hundreds of monsters looked down at us, screaming at their dismay. They kicked Thomas's dead body into the pit and it fell next to us.

I spun myself around. The floor of Hell's white-hot chasm was coming up on us quickly—too quickly. The heat boiled my leather jacket until I had to abandon it. "We're going too fast. Hang on!"

I grabbed Connie and yanked her close to me. With my free hand, I pulled out my dagger and dug it into the stone wall. It slowed our descent as we skidded down the side of the rift. At the bottom of the rocky chasm, I swung Connie across the pits of fire and onto a boulder before wrenching the dagger from the wall and leaping over the gorge myself. I came to a stop next to Connie, on the rock. The lava blinded me and scalded my skin, but much to my surprise, I had survived. Again.

"You okay?" I asked, huffing and puffing.

She nodded. "I'm fine."

I looked over at Thomas, who lay twisted on some molten rocks nearby. His dead eyes stared back at me. "At least that's something."

Connie grunted in agreement, then looked around us. "Did we make it? Are we in Hell?"

"Sure smells like Hell."

"Great," Connie replied. "Now we just gotta find the Devil and plunge this dagger deep into his heart without Thomas's help." She stood up and brushed herself off. "Piece of cake."

"Yup, piece of cake." I bit my lip, thinking. "If only I had any clue how to do that."

"Maybe I can help," a friendly voice bellowed from behind a stalagmite. Connie and I whirled around to see a familiar figure crest over the rocks and into the light.

"Barry?" Connie asked, cocking her head. A smile crept onto her face.

Barry just laughed. He hadn't changed at all since I watched him die. He was still a mangled zombie, with green skin, which drooped too much to be considered human. Yet, he was still smiling like an idiot.

"Who else did you expect?"

Chapter 12

Hell sucked.

Not some earth-shattering revelation, but seriously, this place really blew chunks. People said that places were hot as Hell. I compared Nevada to Hell on innumerable occasions. Lots of people said the same thing about Arizona, Texas, and a whole bunch of places.

But we were all wrong.

Nothing was like Hell. Yes, it was hot. It was hotter than the surface of the sun. It would be hot if I were dead, but as a living person, the word blistering came to mind, though I wished it were only blistering.

The hottest day on Earth ever was something like 189 degrees in Iran and would be a pleasant winter day compared to Hell.

Then there was the torture. Each step we took, we heard the pained wails of the condemned echoing off every rock.

Barry diverted us through back alleys, away from the whipping torture and ferocious demons. He turned us away from the wails, but even in the distance they swelled to an overwhelming cacophony.

"So, you've been stuck in Hell this whole time?" I asked Barry.

"Monsters aren't allowed to enter Heaven, not that I thought I had a chance at that anyway. So, yeah. Kinda. It's not so bad."

"Hell…is not so bad."

"If you're a monster it's not."

"That's the dumbest thing I've ever heard," I replied after a deep sigh.

"How did you find us?" Connie asked him, hollering over me.

"Honestly? Dumb luck. I was supposed to be up on the surface, helping some demon terrorize Seattle, but I couldn't kill people. I just can't get into the terrorizing thing. They tried to assign me to some torture squad down here, where I would eat people's brains over and over forever, but it's just not my bag either. It's better than slaughter, but barely."

We climbed higher, away from the molten lava. "What have you been doing down here?"

"Paperwork. I file things. There is a lot of organization in Hell."

"Really? I figured it was kinda freeform."

Barry shook his head. "There's all sorts of bureaucracy. There are ten pits of Hell. Each one has different monsters and condemned souls assigned to it. It may be an eternity of suffering, but the punishment should fit the crime. Or something like that. I don't know. I just started. I'm still getting the lay of the land."

"Sounds horrible."

"It's alright. There's a big city called Dis in the middle, which is cool. I mean it's kind of run down, but they have bars and nightclubs. I rubbed up against a couple of pretty demons in there. Hell's really not so bad if you aren't a damned soul."

"But you're a zombie," Connie said. "How much more damned can a soul get?"

We reached a fork in the path with a tunnel to the right and another to the left. "Very. Technically speaking, I'm a monster. Down here, that gives me the right to do just about anything. I could slit Katrina's throat without a second thought. Wouldn't that be ironic?"

"You could try," I replied. "But I'd toss you into that lava pit so fast your head would spin, right before it melted off."

"Always a charmer," Barry said. "Always."

Barry tapped his feet and scratched his head with one of his undead arms. "I know it's one of these paths."

"What's wrong?" I asked.

"Nothing," he said. "It's just...I've never actually been to Lucifer's palace. I know it's one of these paths, but which one?"

I crossed my arms. "Are you serious?"

"I'll get you there. Don't you worry. We can always double back if I can't figure it out. There's a less confusing way, but it's filled with monsters. This way is unguarded. I come up here to get away sometimes, but I've never gone any further than this."

Connie pointed. "We should go to the right."

I wheeled on her. "How can you know that?"

"No reason. I just do is all." She shrugged, palms up.

"That's not good enough." I stepped in her direction and poked her in the chest. "You've been acting strange lately, trusting in God, telling me to have faith. You're a Satanist, for Christ's sake! Now what is going on with you?"

Connie tripped over a rock and fell on her ass. "Nothing's going on with me. Just chill out." She scooted away from me, toward the edge of a cliff overlooking a river of lava. "The heat's getting to you."

"No," I replied, grabbing her by the collar. "You're acting weird. Tell me what is going on!"

"I can't!" She tried to pull my hands away. "At least—not yet!"

I dragged her toward the edge of the cliff. "Then I'll toss you into the river. Don't be stupid. Tell me what the hell is going on!" She kicked and screamed, trying to break free, but I was stronger than her. "I'm not going to ask you again. What is going on? How do you know where Satan's palace is?"

A blue light flashed behind me. "She knows because of me, Katrina." The light cleared, and a familiar face appeared behind it.

"Dennis? This is too much."

Connie squirmed. "Can you let go of me now?"

*

Dennis materializing out of thin aired cooled me off in more ways than one. Not only did his unexpected appearance quell my immense rage, but he also brought with him a blue light which physically counteracted the effects of Hell. It was as if an industrial strength air conditioner turned on during the hottest day of summer and blew right into my face.

"So, you're an angel, huh?" I asked.

"That's correct."

"But you're in Hell."

"You're two for two."

"So, how is it that you are here, exactly?" I asked, confused.

"I came to Connie when you landed at Thomas's tent." He placed his hand on Connie's lovingly. "Every moment without her was agony."

"No. I mean, how did you get to Heaven in the first place? I get that you're an angel, but what did you do to deserve Heaven?"

Dennis shrugged. "I dunno, honestly. After I died, I just floated up to Heaven."

I blinked. "That is a lame story."

"Yeah, but it's true. I mean, I didn't say it was a great story, or super original, but that's how people have gotten to Heaven for thousands of years. The blue beams of light thing only happened once."

"But what you're saying is that you can get to Heaven if you die during the Apocalypse."

"I'm not saying anything. I don't know how or why it happened, all I can say is that it did. I died. I saw a white light. I ended up in Heaven."

"And why don't you have wings?" I asked.

"I've gotta perform a great deed to earn them."

"A great deed? What are you, George Bailey's angel? You gotta get us to see there is good in the world?"

Dennis laughed. "It's a little more complicated than that. See, Heaven is boring. Have you ever met like a real, die hard Christian? All they do is pray all the time. Now, imagine they were whisked to Heaven, the Christian wet dream. How much do you think they would pray then?"

"Probably a lot."

"Literally all the time. I thought my mother praying the rosary three times a day was bad. When I saw her in Heaven, she wouldn't even look up at me. She just kept praying."

Connie, Barry, and I all made faces, trying to imagine this. "That sounds horrible," I said.

"It is, but at least I got to punch Connie's deadbeat dad."

"You punched that old fogey?"

"Right in the mouth," Dennis nodded. "I laid him out good."

"And I thank you for that," Connie said, squeezing him tighter. She'd attached herself to him since the moment he appeared, nibbling on his neck and draping herself around his shoulders. "Did you ever figure out how people like that got into Heaven in the first place?"

Dennis shook his head. "They don't really tell you stuff like that. You just know you got in. I did get accosted by a rather large angel for fighting, though. He told me that if I did it again, it would seriously damage my continued relationship with Heaven."

"Does that mean you'd be kicked out?"

"I guess, but I don't know. Thing is, besides praying, there's nothing to do. They have shuffleboard, and knitting, and you can watch all the PG movies you want. I guess that's fine for some people, but I hated it."

"Poor you," Barry said. "I've been stuck down here in the bowels of Hell and you're complaining about Heaven? Asshole."

"I'm sorry, but it's true," Dennis said, emphatically. "Heaven is dull. The only people who have any fun are the archangels. Total badasses! They protect Heaven from invaders and get sent out on missions around the universe. They're also the only angels with wings. They kind of lord it over everybody else."

"And you want to be one of them?" I asked.

"Yeah, I do. Those dudes are friggin' sweet. But to get wings, you gotta perform a hella awesome deed. I mean, think about the archangels…"

"Are you sure you should be cursing?" Connie asked, looking at Dennis doe-eyed. "I mean you are an angel. Won't they get pissed? I don't want you to get in trouble."

"God has bigger problems than me cursing. Besides, I literally can't curse in Heaven. They just don't allow it. I have been aching to curse since I died. It feels so good."

"Can we get back to the problem at hand, love birds?" I asked.

"Sorry," Dennis replied, smiling like a fool at Connie. "Where was I?"

"Archangels," I said, shaking my head.

"Right. Well, they are the biggest badasses in Heaven." Dennis took a deep breath in and I knew I was in for some sort of sports fan drive-in totals. "Gabriel impregnated Mary with God's seed. Raphael evicted Adam and Eve from the Garden of Eden. Uriel saved John the Baptist from the Egyptians. Michael kicked the piss out of Lucifer and sent him down to Hell. Samael is the angel of death."

Dennis paused to catch his breath and then grinned. "You don't have to know who they are to know those are feats of awesome."

"Sure, sure. Point conceded." I scratched my neck and tried to sound interested. "And now you wanna do something totally badass to earn your wings too?"

"Yup." Dennis looked smug. "Something...like ending the Apocalypse."

I clucked my tongue. "Glomming onto my glory, then."

"Hey," Connie shouted. "*Our* glory."

"Fine," I replied with an eye roll. "Our glory."

"Thanks a lot, guys." Barry was picking a zombie booger when we looked at him. "What?"

"Yeah, alright," Dennis said. "I want some of that sweet, sweet glory, okay? The only thing I enjoyed doing in Heaven was watching Connie. I saw you plan on ending the Apocalypse and figured that would be a huge enough deed to make me an archangel, so I snuck down here. They say God's omniscient, but trust me, he's got plenty of blind spots if you know where to look."

"I would never say that about him," I replied.

"Tell her how you already helped us, baby," Connie said. She squeezed his face and kissed him on the cheek.

"Well, I protected you from those fireballs in the desert, for one."

"You mean...the ones that nearly killed us?"

"I did the best I could. You would've been destroyed way sooner had I not come, but there were too many. I was so pissed when that demon jerk got to act like the big hero."

"Aw, baby," Connie said, smooching his cheeks again. "That's so sweet."

"Yeah, yeah. You have one of the great love stories of all time. Get on with it."

"Well, I followed you until Thomas revealed his plan. I knew you'd never succeed without me."

"Why? You don't think we're tough enough?"

"No, it's because you're mortals. Mortals can't survive in Hell for long. At least, not without a cooling agent."

"So, you're going to earn your wings by being a walking air conditioner?" I replied.

Dennis glared at me, pursing his lips. "I appeared to Connie and have been watching out for you ever since. I made sure you were okay on the battlefield, blowing away the dust in time to make sure you could foil any attack. Then, I followed you through Hell until you flipped out, and that brings us up to just now."

I yawned loudly and stretched. "I'm bored. If Heaven is half as dull as that story, I feel really sorry for you, brother."

"Trust me, it's worse. That's why I'm trying to help you."

"Does that mean you're going to lead us to the Devil now?"

"Yes. I studied the path before leaving Heaven, but—"

"Fantastic, cuz if I don't kill something soon, I'm gonna die of boredom."

Dennis turned to Connie and Barry. "You weren't wrong. She really is still like this."

They both nodded. Connie said, "Told you."

"Hey!" I shouted. "Shut your faces."

"I gotta warn you, it's not an easy road ahead." Dennis walked down the path to the right. "Follow me."

Chapter 13

Dennis led us to the top of a craggy rock path. It was an hour hike to the top of the sheer cliff. Every muscle in my body ached by the time we reached it, but my adrenaline kept me going. I could taste the sulfur in the air from the Devil's castle. It was so close.

Dennis stopped us behind a massive rock formation that jutted a hundred feet into the sky. "We'll see the Devil's castle just up ahead…after we get past the first obstacle."

I peered around the formation. A thin rock bridge traversed a hundred-foot gorge carved by the lava river flowing below. A wolf monster, adorned with golden bracers, chest plate, and helmet like he was right out of an Egyptian hieroglyph, spanned the bridge's entire width as it paced back and force.

This wolf looked unlike anything I'd ever seen on the surface. It carried itself as more human than animal. In its eyes, I saw more than the vicious idiocy of the demon dogs. It marched on its back legs along its well-worn path, a golden staff eternally clutched in its paw.

"This protector is left over from the old guard," Dennis said.

"The old guard?"

"Before the Devil. You really think Lucifer was the first Devil?"

"Don't you?"

"Well, not anymore."

"Why not?"

"Because I read the history books in Heaven and I know what I read on the map. These guys are left over from days of the first Devil. I don't know any more than that."

I sighed. "Fine. And it's the only one?"

"One is enough."

"We'll see about that." I gave a wry smile.

"Be careful. Demons in Hell are more powerful than they are on Earth."

"I heard."

The wolf paced in our direction. When it reached the end of the bridge, it turned on its heels and marched back down the small path. There wasn't enough room to fight, but it was enough to make one surprise attack. I snuck toward the wolf until I was close enough to smell the sweaty musk of his backside.

The wolf reached the end of the bridge. When it turned, its weight shifted off balance just for a moment. I leapt onto his neck and spun him around, then kicked him off the bridge. The monster fell into the abyss, howling.

I dusted off my hands and looked back at Dennis and the others. "Easy peasy."

We walked across the bridge toward a great black gate. I could see the Devil's castle in the distance now, surrounded by a moat of lava. The obsidian castle struck a fearsome image, its sheer size overpowering the rest of the landscape.

Dennis pointed over the rock bridge to a trail below us. Demons marched thousands of zombies past a boiling lava lake toward their next assignment.

"If we'd taken the left path back where I showed up, it would have led us down there, into the pits of Hell. We would have come face to face with all those zombies."

I shrugged. "Zombies are easy and dumb."

"Hey!" Barry whined. Connie smacked him in the arm.

"Maybe one, but thousands? Even you'd get tired from that."

*

The wails never ended in Hell. Strong men wept like little girls. Young women bleated out in incredible agony. Old men howled as their feet burned in lava. No matter where I turned, the piteous cries overwhelmed me.

I hoped against hope that my mother wasn't caught in the great expanse of Hell. If Dennis could earn his way into Heaven, so could my mother. She was the sweetest woman I'd ever known. She swaddled me as a baby, overfed me as a child, and protected me as an adult. Whenever I had a bad day, she was there. Everything she had, she gave freely.

The fact she wasn't blue lighted pissed me off something fierce. She just wanted to love, and she would do anything to make sure that those she loved were happy.

That became exceedingly tough after the Apocalypse began. Everybody she loved was rightfully miserable and died in horrible ways. It was in those days that my mother's strength came though the most. She never cried. She never wavered. She accepted strays into her house. She fed us all and kept us smiling. My parents' house became a base of sorts for hundreds of frightened people.

No offense to Dennis, but my mother was a better person than him. Dennis looked after Connie, sure, but my mother looked after everybody. The thought of her being torn apart for the rest of eternity was too much to bear.

"We're here," Dennis said, crouching behind a large rock.

I tilted my head around the corner. A massive demon dog snoozed in front of a thousand-foot-high black gate.

"More dogs? How original."

"It's effective. I couldn't find any way to scale this gate or get around it. The angels of Heaven have never breached its walls. The only way through is past Cerberus."

"Cerberus? Like the Greek dog?"

"Exactly like her. Those demon dogs on the surface—this is their mother. She's an ornery little bitch with a voracious appetite. Nothing gets through that gate and into Satan's palace without her approval."

I thought a for a moment. "Not a problem. I'm sure she's as dumb as her children. Come here, Barry."

"Huh?"

I grabbed Barry's right arm and ripped it from its socket. The flesh peeled apart like a warm, dinner biscuit. Barry howled. "What are you doing?"

"*Shhh*! You'll spook her."

Cerberus lifted her heads and took a giant whiff of the air. Slobber pooled on either side of her mouths. She could smell the meat, and grumbled under her breath, curious.

I walked toward the cliff with Barry's arm outstretched in my hand. "Come here, girl. Yeah, you like that? You like the smell of rotten flesh, don't you?"

Cerberus barked and howled for a moment. When she noticed Barry's arm, her mood changed from angry to excited, like a puppy with a ball. She leapt into the air and wagged her tail furiously, yanking at her heavy chain.

"Yeah. That's a good girl. Come on." I waved the arm some more. Barry muttered and rubbed his empty shoulder socket.

Cerberus had worked herself into a lather, her three gigantic heads chomping at the bit. She pulled and jumped, and when I threw the arm off the cliff, the old bitch lost her mind.

"Go get it!"

Cerberus lurched forward and ripped her chain from the wall. It streamed behind her as she leapt off the ledge and into the lava lake.

Connie, Barry, and Dennis walked to the ledge and peered over, speechless.

"What's next?" I asked.

Dennis looked over at me. "Twenty angelic legions couldn't get past her."

Connie nodded, eyes wide. "Girl, you're single-handedly destroying Hell."

"Because Hell is stupid," I spat back.

Barry just picked at his arm hole.

"I've said it before and I'll say it again, guys. I'm better than twenty legions of angels. Now, how many more of these challenges are left?"

I turned and walked through the huge hole in the rock wall Cerberus had left when she'd wrenched the chain free. The others followed behind me.

In front of us was the massive black castle with endless spires and towers, surrounded by another huge lake of lava. There were no bridges to cross. There was no way into the castle without swimming though miles of molten liquid.

"Just one," Dennis said. "But it's pretty much impossible."

I smiled. "Bring it on."

Chapter 14

I stomped down the dirt road from Cerberus's gate toward the lake of fire that separated us from the Devil's castle. Even the cool breeze from Dennis's blue glow couldn't prevent me from dripping sweat. The heat wouldn't stop me, though, even as it sapped all of my energy. The end-goal was in sight, and I wasn't about to stop now.

"The last challenge is getting over the lake of fire," Dennis told me.

"Cool," I replied. "Can you fly us over?"

"No. I can fly myself, but, without wings, I'm not strong enough to carry anybody else, at least not for that long."

"Fine. What other options do we have?"

"Unfortunately, there's only one, and it's a boat."

"That doesn't sound too hard. I can row."

Dennis shook his head. "No. There is only one boat, and one oar to row it. And only Charon's allowed to carry the gondolier's oar. It's enchanted—the boat, too—so they don't burn up in the lake."

"So…I guess that's a 'no' to swimming across…?"

Dennis exhaled sharply. "Can you swim in lava, Katrina? Have some sort of super power I don't know about?"

I shook my head. "No. Can you swim across?"

"The lake probably wouldn't hurt me or Barry, but we'd still disintegrate before we reached the other side. Maybe we could do it in bursts, if we had a way to break."

Barry put up a hand. "I vote for *not* swimming in lava. Who's with me?" Connie smacked his hand down and looked back at me.

"You're not giving me much of a choice, Dennis. I guess I'll just pay the sumbitch. How much does it cost, like five bucks?" I started patting my pockets for loose change.

"It's not that easy. He only brings across souls personally invited by Satan himself, and nobody has been invited in years."

"*Pfft.* That sounds stupid."

I needed that boat, and if Charon wasn't going to give me a ride, I would take one. I didn't exactly know how, but I was going to get across that lake. No stupid gondolier was going to stop that.

When we reached the bottom of the hill, the gondola waited for us, tied to the dock. On the boat was a cloaked figure, holding a large, black oar. Only two glowing eyes escaped the blackness under his purple robe.

"Who requests passage to the Dark Lord?" Charon asked.

I stepped forward. "I do. And I guess them, too."

"No bodies may pass."

"I'm not just anybody. I'm Katrina, and these are my friends."

"Only souls of the underworld may pass on to Lucifer's dwelling. Bodies may not pass."

"I don't like your attitude."

I pulled the dagger out of my belt and used it to stab Charon through the chest. He evaporated into a big ball of light, leaving nothing behind but his cloak, which I threw into the river.

"What did you just do?" Connie said.

"We'll never get to the castle now!" Dennis threw his hands in the air. "Only Charon could wield the gondolier's oar!"

"Relax," I said, smiling. "I have a plan."

Barry looked down, scared. "I don't want to know."

"Tough. Cuz you're a big part of it."

"Oh, man…" Barry said.

"Yup. Dennis, you said you and Barry could swim in bursts if you had a place to stop, right?"

"Yeah." Dennis chuckled nervously. "Why?"

I smiled. "You are our new oars."

*

Dennis and Barry rowed us across the river, bitching and moaning the whole way, but eventually we crossed the river to the castle. I didn't care about their whining. I was about to give Satan a piece of my mind. As we tied the boat to the dock at the castle's steps, my stomach fluttered. I was so close.

"Alright," I said. "Up the staircase, kill the Devil, end the Apocalypse, go home and have a sandwich. Couldn't be easier, right?"

Barry blew out the smoldering embers on his remaining arm. "If I ever get my arm back, I'm beating you to death with it."

"I'm right there with you, buddy," Dennis added.

"That's a nice dream. Never gonna happen, but a nice dream none the less," I said, climbing the stairs. "Now stop complaining. We're about to kill the Devil. Then, Dennis will get his fairy wings. Connie will get a nap. Barry can go back to doing whatever Barry does, and I won't ever have to talk to any of you ever again."

"That's a nice thought," Connie sighed.

"Isn't it?"

"I don't really get anything out of this," Barry said. "Why did I even help you?"

"I'll tell you what. I promise not to rip anything else off you today. How about that?"

Barry wiped at his eyes and sniffed. "That's the nicest thing you've ever said to me."

"Don't mention it."

I looked up at the imposing castle in front of me. For some reason, I couldn't stop thinking about He-Man when I stared at it, then it came to me. Lucifer's castle was a dead ringer for Skeletor's. I mean, it was black obsidian instead of green rock, and Lucifer used bones instead of wood, but it looked just like it, down to the creepy skull whose mouth acted as a doorway.

I leaned my weight against the heavy bone door and pushed with every ounce of energy I could muster. I felt the dusty, old bones give under my weight, and heard a ribcage snap under my pressure. The heavy door creaked on its hinges. When it finally groaned open, light streamed into a long corridor and we crept inside, single file.

Moans emanated from the end of the hall. These weren't the pained groans of the tortured, though. These were different. This was the first time I'd heard crying in Hell; the first time I'd heard sadness. Sadness was a dull emotion. You feel it in the absence of pain. It cut against you in the silent moments. It took shape over days, weeks, even years sometimes, but physical agony drowns it out. The tortured souls in Hell didn't have time to cultivate sadness over the screams of their anguish.

The cries led us down a hallway, where Gothic paintings of dead bodies lined the walls, framed in bits of bone. Bones crunched on the obsidian floor beneath our feet and culminated in a massive pile, atop which sat a throne, where the Devil was perched.

There was no power in him. No swagger. Just a fat, old, goat-legged demon, in shorts and a stained wife beater. He looked…pathetic.

"There he is!" Barry shouted triumphantly, his remaining arm raised into the air.

"No duh," I replied. "It's time to end this."

My feet crunched on the bones as I made my way up to the throne. The Devil looked up, his glowing, yellow eyes peering into my soul. "Well, well, well. If it isn't the distinct smell of humanity." He sneered at Dennis. "And an angel. How very interesting. God sent a peon to communicate with me."

The Devil rose to his feet. "You think I would have earned more respect after two hundred millennia of service."

I crossed my arms in defiance. "We're here to stop your rampage on the world."

The Devil chuckled. "Oh, that's rich. What are you babbling about? The Apocalypse?"

"That's right!" Connie yelled. "The Apocalypse you started!"

The Devil descended the bone pile. "Whoever told you that fairy tale was sorely mistaken, or simply lying to you."

"Your head games won't work on us, Satan!" Connie said. "We know the truth."

He stopped and eyed her with an amused look. "And what truth is that?"

"We know that if we kill you, the Apocalypse will end and there will be Heaven on Earth!"

He chuckled again. "My dear, if you kill me there won't even be Heaven in Heaven. God doesn't care about you. He doesn't care about any of this. He's no better than an absentee landlord. Do you know what that is?"

Barry raised his hand. "I don't, if that means anything."

"It means that he can't be bothered with the whole lot of you. Ever since you killed his son, he could care less if any of you humans entered the kingdom of Heaven."

"Then why did he let some people in with all the blue lights?" I asked.

"I don't know. I'm not him. He clearly thought some of you deserved it, like those that followed him without question. But from the beginning of time, I've toyed with your head, manipulated your minds, and destroyed your souls. Has he ever once tried to stop me?"

"Yes," Dennis said. "But you had Jesus killed."

Lucifer guffawed. "Is that what you really believe? Humanity destroyed Jesus on their own. I didn't need to be involved. And once you killed him, God deserted you for the last two thousand years, so he could sulk, leaving you with nothing but his greatest joke."

"Oh yeah," Connie said. "and what's that?"

"Free will, of course. He granted every person the ability to ignore his teachings, yet eternally punished those that chose not to follow him blindly. What kind of ego trip is that?"

"It's a big one," I said. "But I'm not here to talk about God's ego. I'm here to use my free will to jam this dagger through your heart!"

Lucifer spread his arms wide. "I won't stop you. God has forsaken me. All I wanted was to see the Elysian Fields one more time. Maybe in my next life, I'll be a simple apple farmer."

True to his word, he didn't fight me. I rammed the dagger deep into Lucifer's chest. He didn't scream. He didn't whimper. He just fell to the ground, blood oozing from his wound.

"Wow," Barry said, walking over to me. "He fell like a sack of potatoes, huh?"

"Didn't put up a fight or nothin'," Connie added.

"So...does that mean it's over then?" Dennis asked, peering at the Dark Lord's corpse.

A voice boomed from the rafters. "Not quite!"

I turned to see Thomas, flawlessly quaffed and dressed in a perfectly tailored suit. He sauntered down a flight of stairs toward us. "Appreciate you finishing off Daddy for me, though. I do so hate dirtying my hands."

"You...were dead," I said, stammering.

"Silly girl. That is what I wanted you to believe because it furthered my ends. Did you really think you would have made it this far if it weren't my bidding?"

"Obviously," I said.

"You realized the ease of your path couldn't have been an accident, of course." He studied my face. "No? Do you not understand how I manipulated the marauders to chase you down to boost your resolve, or how I protected you through the battle and in your descent to Hell? Did you not guess that I died at just the right moment to push you that last step of the way?"

"So, everything you told me was a lie?"

My jaw dropped as Thomas continued, a polite hand covering his mouth for a moment. "Oh my yes. Every word since the moment we met. You really didn't know. You truly do have simple minds. I've been planning this from the moment the Apocalypse began. I just needed the perfect mortal. One with the drive and skill to follow my plan through with single-minded focus. Somebody who would take care of my father while I shifted his focus to my resistance. I've tried so many women before, my dear, and you were superior to all of them." He stepped toward me, his arms out for an embrace. "Now, my love, join me in ruling Hell and I will give you everything."

Thomas pulled me close. I struggled against him, but he was too strong. My mind flashed back to the day he raped me. Then, too, I was absolutely helpless against him. But as it played through in my head, haunting me, I remembered something.

I remembered a rosary had burned him once before.

And I remembered I had one in my back pocket. I'd purchased it for precisely this moment. With my free hand, I wrapped my fingers around the chain and swung it at his face. It sizzled against his skin.

"I don't think so!" I shouted. "I hate all dead shit, but you're at the top of my list."

Thomas was hunched over, holding his face in his hands. "You fool. We could have ruled Hell together!"

"No thanks. This place is the pits."

Thomas rose again, a crucifix mark singed onto his check. "No matter. It doesn't affect my plans."

"I don't get it," Barry said, counting the fingers on his remaining hand. "Why get anybody to kill your father?"

"Because I desired control of Hell, of course. And dear old Daddy wanted me to be content with middle management. I don't sully my genius with trivial day to day tasks."

Barry gulped. "I guess we can kiss paradise on Earth goodbye, then."

"I'm afraid so. Now that I've taken control, a whole new era of carnage will commence." Thomas held his hands at his lapels, proudly.

"That doesn't sound good for you guys," Dennis said to Katrina and Connie.

"That doesn't sound good for anybody," Connie added.

Orange tendrils of light snaked out of Lucifer's dead body and settled in the air, hovering listlessly. Then, in one swift action, they beelined for Thomas's body and shot through him. He flew backwards into a stone pillar. Moments later he rose from the rubble, throbbing and animated. Orange light pulsated out of every orifice.

"The power!" he shouted. "The absolute power!"

He looked down at his glowing arms. "Yes! Yes! The old way of doing things is finished! Prepare for a new reign which will topple Heaven itself!"

I wanted to fight, to rail against him. I wanted to end Thomas right there, but I couldn't move. I became one with the void. All I could do was watch as I faded into the white light.

Chapter 15

I tasted maraschino cherry. Not fresh cherry like the kind you pick off a tree. No. This was the kind you get on the top of an ice cream sundae, like the one they loaded up for you at Oscar's Diner. The kind that melted into the whipped cream as you devoured the scoops of cold goodness underneath. Then, in the last moment, once all the ice cream was gone and you couldn't eat another bite, you bit down on the cherry stem and squished the sugary juice into your mouth. The final taste of perfection.

That's what I tasted in my mouth when the world went white. I thought I'd had a stroke. I should have had a stroke. It was a lot to take in, after all, this idea that the Devil, for all his evil, wasn't much of a big bad at all.

Far from being evil, he was, if anything, pathetic.

He didn't have some grand plan, except to sit in his castle and sulk. He was merely surrounded by evil. Of course, if you are surrounded by evil, and complicit in evil, that kinda makes you evil by default. Didn't seem like he enjoyed it, though.

I quickly discounted the idea that I was having a stroke, mainly because I was cogently thinking the whole time the world faded away. Once that thought knocked out of my head, then I was sure I had died.

After all, Thomas stated that his new reign would topple Heaven itself and killing me would be a good first step. Wiping out me, Connie, Barry, and everybody else for who knows how many miles, seemed like a good enough first step to enacting an evil plan.

I stayed in the white light for longer than was comfortable. There was nothing to do in the void except float. For the last few days I had been running through the world with a purpose, and I didn't like the sudden, still silence. I tried to keep my mind busy to avoid it. In the silence, pains made themselves known. I remembered all those I'd lost: Dad, Barry...Mom.

Mom's death was the worst of them all. It came eight months after the Apocalypse began. We'd watched how the other cities defended themselves. Los Angeles used tanks with lackluster results. San Francisco dropped a dirty bomb on Ghirardelli Square. Sacramento carpet-bombed their own citizens.

Nothing worked.

At best, cities fended off the monsters for a time. In San Antonio, the military held for ten months. In Washington, they managed to keep a functioning government almost eighteen months, but eventually it devolved, like these things do, into a power grab for territory.

All that remained were small towns fighting for themselves. Places like Overbrook, where the monsters ripped through homes with the speed and power of a bulldozer. Mom and I kept the resistance going longer than we thought possible, given our resources. It's one of the reasons Walter respects me even a little, because he and I fended off monsters at our gates together, more times that I could count. But it couldn't last forever. Eventually the monsters came for us, too.

We made night runs in those days. Night runs were more dangerous, which meant fewer neighbors were stupid enough to risk their lives doing them. Our house was ill defended in the night when we were out. Monsters hadn't trekked through our neighborhood yet, so we thought it was safe. Oh, how wrong we were. When they came for our house, it was a bloodbath.

Mom and I returned from a food run later than usual. I turned the corner in our overstuffed, cargo van and watched two minotaurs plow into the house, knocking it loose from its foundation. Dozens of people fell to the ground as it toppled. Zombies and demon dogs devoured those that didn't die in the fall.

"We have to go to them!" Mom shouted as I slammed the van into reverse and peeled away.

"If we go back, we die."

She pulled the wheel toward the house. "But those people!"

I spun the wheel away from her too hard. The unbalanced van teetered and collapsed. It careened into the side of a big, beautiful Tudor house and flipped over.

Blood pooled in my eye socket when I came back to consciousness. I hazily looked out the window and saw Mom stumbling toward the house. I pulled myself out of the van and crawled toward her.

"Mom!" I shouted. "Mom!"

She turned to me. "Those people!"

I staggered toward her. "They're already dead. Don't you get that?"

"They wouldn't be if we helped them!"

I latched onto her hand and pulled her away. "Yes, they would, and we'd be dead too!"

I pulled Mom down the cul de sac against her will. Around a bend, Connie slammed into me, her eyes petrified in horror, a pack of demon dogs at her heels. Dennis fought them off with a lead pipe as they lurched toward him.

"Run!" Connie shouted.

The dogs chased us through the woods and into the heart of town. Every time I looked back there were more of them. We looked for any open door. Anything to save us from the demon dogs. Then it happened. My mom tripped.

"Come on, Mom. Get up!"

She huffed and puffed. "I can't—I can't—"

I saw it in her eyes. I've seen many times before and since, but it never broke me like it did with her. She'd lost the will to live.

"Go on, Katrina—get out of here!"

Dennis shouted to me. "Come on! Let's go!"

The dogs closed in on us.

"KATRINA JEAN CLARK! GET OUT OF HERE!"

I let go of her hand and ran. The dogs, so close on my tail, lurched to a stop around my mother. I heard the crunch of bone, the squish of flesh, and the final, garbled screams of my mother as she died.

Dennis screamed at me from an open door. "We found one!"

I wanted to lay down and die with her, but my body wouldn't allow it. Mom had lost the will to live, but I hadn't.

I slipped into the door right behind Dennis, collapsed, and cried for the last time. My parents were gone. All I had left were Dennis, Barry, and Connie. They would be gone too, soon enough.

The scene in front of me faded. I wanted to cry, but I couldn't. All the tears were gone, burned away. There wasn't time for that anyway. Now was time for action.

Resolve came back into my belly. The white faded from my eyes and I could see again. I stood on an enormous platform, surrounded by clouds. Connie kneeled on one side of me. Dennis and Barry to the other.

"Did we all just stroke out?" I asked.

"No, my child," a booming voice said. "This is Heaven."

In front of me sat a bearded man in a white robe, serenely floating in space. To his right was a pissed off man with long flowing robes and wings. I gathered he was an angel. On the other side of the floating man was the recently eviscerated Lucifer, healed and reclined comfortably on an old couch.

"If this is Heaven," I said. "then you must be God."

The old man smiled. "That I am."

Dennis muttered under his breath. "I'm so screwed."

The angel stepped forward. "You're right about that, Dennis. What right did you have leading these chippies into Hell?"

Barry scratched his head. "What's a chippy?"

The angel groaned. "How stupid can you idiots be?"

God cleared his throat. "Calm yourself, Michael. They know not what they unleashed upon us."

"Of course they don't," Michael said. "They're idiots."

I walked past Michael until I was face to face with God. "So, you're the big man, huh?"

"I am not a man. I am the all-powerful, all-knowing, and all-benevolent God of scripture."

"I call bullsham on that. Bullsham. Why the flork can't I curse?"

"Because the almighty wishes you don't," Michael said. "And he is all-powerful."

"That's where he draws the line? Naughty words? I definitely call bullsham on that. I call bullsham on all of this."

"Excuse me?" God said. "I'm quite sure I am the almighty."

"No. I believe you're God, but I can't square up that other stuff about you being those three things you said. There's way too much bad crap that's gone down in my life to make me believe you are even one of them, truth be told. If you were…then I wouldn't have watched my mother be torn apart by a bunch of three-headed dogs, and you certainly wouldn't have made me relive it again just now."

"How dare you talk to the Almighty like that!" Michael hissed.

"Why not? If he's really all good he won't care what the hell I say to him, will he?" I turned to the Devil, still clad in a wife beater. "And you are the Devil. I see that you haven't changed at all."

"Well, you did only kill me a little while ago." Lucifer stretched his arms out on his couch. "And please, call me Lou. You murdered me in cold blood. If you haven't earned the right to call me by my first name, nobody has."

I nodded. "I appreciate that, Lou. You seem less nutty than the last time I saw you."

"Yes, several millennia in Hell will do that to you."

"I'll bet. I was only there for a little while and it was awful. Who's this other jerk barking orders at me?"

"I am Michael," the angel scoffed. "The archangel. The most powerful of all the archangels."

Lucifer chucked. "You. The most powerful archangel. *Pfft.* Maybe second to me."

"Ha!" Michael said. "You're a fat sack of garbage that got murdered by a mortal."

"In a moment of weakness, and I didn't even put up a fight." He looked at me with pleading eyes. "Go on, tell him I didn't put up a fight."

"He didn't put up a fight," I said.

Michael flicked his hair. "And that's why you could never be the most powerful."

"Boys! Enough!" I shouted. "Whip it out and compare or shut up. And while you're at it, why don't you tell me what I'm doing here?"

"I'll handle that," God said. The other two immediately shut up. "Look over the edge, Katrina."

I gave him the side eye. "Are you gonna push me over?"

God chuckled. "If I wanted you dead, I wouldn't have brought you here. I would have let Thomas have his way with you, or snapped my fingers and evaporated you into nothingness. Still could, too."

"Fair enough." I walked over to the edge of the platform. It was bedlam. The monsters of Hell tore apart the people of Heaven. Angels screamed and bawled across the Elysian Fields. They were unprepared for slaughter, thinking they would just live the rest of their lives in cushy perfectness.

God help me, but I smiled a little. The little snowflakes that got raptured up to Heaven before the Apocalypse were now getting a taste. I wondered how many times they looked down and thanked their stars they weren't down with us, slumming it up with the monsters.

"There is a war raging, Katrina," God said. "A war you began."

"It's such a cop out to blame me. I didn't have anything to do with this stuff. I just killed the Devil a little bit."

"Exactly. You're not the one waging this war," Lucifer agreed. "But you did put my son in charge. Moments after I died, Thomas took control of Hell and began an all-out attack on Heaven."

"Truth be told, Heaven is filled with cowards," Michael said. "Do you have any idea the litany of infractions a person can't commit to pass through the needle's eye? The meek couldn't swing a sword if their afterlife depended on it."

"And it clearly does," I replied.

"Once our army was the grandest in the universe, but now…it won't last another hour of this onslaught. We need your help. You've survived for two years on an Earth filled with the worst monsters imaginable." God studied me closely. "You are our best hope. And besides that, Thomas seems to have an affinity toward you—one I will never understand."

"I might help," I said. "But not until you answer a question for me."

Michael's angelic jaw dropped. "Who are you to demand anything from God Almighty?"

"I'm his creation. The one that's been suffering down there for years. Who's watched her loved ones get taken away from her, one by one. Who's bled, and wept, and cursed the heavens. I'm who he made me."

"We don't have time for this!" Michael shouted.

"Relax, Michael," God said. "We created Katrina to be inquisitive, and I will acquiesce to her demands."

I scoffed. "Suck it, jerk."

I turned to God, who smiled at me and said, "You wish to know why the Apocalypse began."

"Yes, of course I do. But more importantly, I wanna know who's responsible. You? Thomas? Lucifer? It's all really confusing."

"Very well," God said. "The Apocalypse was the inevitable eventuality of a fatal flaw in the human condition that I, as your creator, am responsible for."

"What?" Connie said. "Can you speak English?"

"Yeah," I replied. "Quit with the flowery language. Who opened the Hell rift and unleashed the monsters on Earth?"

"That is a long and complicated explanation. I ask that you trust it was the only possible solution to an impossible problem."

"Trust you? I've been fighting off monsters for two years. Everybody I've ever cared about is either dead or hates me. So no, I don't trust you, not one iota. Now, tell me everything or I'm not lifting a finger to help you."

God sighed. "Lucifer was not the first Devil of Hell. Did you know that?"

I shook my head. "No. I didn't."

"He was the fourth, and the least qualified."

"Hey!" Lucifer said. "Not cool."

"I took pity on him when I realized he was in over his head, and made him an offer. If he could keep Hell running for three hundred millennia, I would let him back in to Heaven, and lift his burden as the Devil."

"It wasn't so much a deal as an ultimatum," Lucifer said. "I had just waged a coup on Heaven, after all, and I wasn't in a good position to bargain. It's not like I had a lot of choice in the matter."

"You always had a choice," God replied. "It just might not have been a good one."

"Right," I scoffed. "Either agree to your terms or suffer in Hell for eternity."

God smiled. "That is a choice."

"Doesn't seem like much of a choice to me," I said.

"Me either," Lucifer said. "That's why I accepted, and for the first few millennia things were swell. Not great, but not terrible either. Life expectancy was low. Infant mortality was high. People feared God and generally couldn't commit that many horrible acts before they died."

"But after the invention of cars, planes, and the internet, humanity could do and see things their ancestors never even imagined. Have you ever seen a donkey show? That's six mortal sins in under an hour."

"I'll take your word on it," I said.

"Combine that with the fact penicillin and other drugs made it possible for people to live forever and all their sins added up to an eternity in Hell. It got incredibly crowded and I couldn't keep order anymore."

God chimed in. "And so, being the benevolent God I am, I began the Apocalypse to ease his burden. He was my oldest friend, after all, even if he did betray me."

"Just the once!" Lucifer scoffed.

"You treat your friends horribly," I mumbled.

"That is your opinion." God replied. "Besides, it's not like you humans were making much use out of Earth anyway. Destroying the ozone, waging endless wars, fighting over the pettiest things like who marries who. At least the Apocalypse brought your priorities back in order."

"Back in—what? Survival? Scaring us out of our minds? Those are priorities to you?"

"Family. Loyalty. Courage. Comradery. Cherishing every day like it was your last. Those are good things, Katrina. Think about how selfish you were before the Apocalypse, and how much good you've done since it began."

I turned to look God square in the face. "Let me get this straight. *You* unleashed Hell on Earth, not the Devil, and you did it because there were too many people in Hell."

"Correct. The bonus being that humanity might see the error of their ways and atone for their sins."

"Uh huh. And how'd that work out for you?"

"For some people it worked out great. Look at Dennis. He's a perfect model of self-improvement."

"And what about my mother? Did she make better of herself?"

God looked down. "Your mother did not make the cut. Your father either, since he killed himself."

"Yeah," I replied. "After he turned into a zombie. Before that, he died saving my whole town!"

"Still," God replied without a hint of emotion. "Rules are rules."

"Are you kidding? They were better than the whole lot of us."

"You are entitled to your opinion," God said.

Lucifer leaned over on the couch so I would look at him. "Pretty messed up, right?"

"That's *exactly* what I was thinking! Man, now I'm a little sorry I killed you."

Lucifer smiled and bowed his head slightly. "Well, I appreciate that."

I sighed. "You answered my question, so I guess I'll help you. I hate you though, for what you've done."

"Loving me is not a prerequisite to helping me," God replied.

"Good. Is there any way to suck those creepy crawlies back to Hell?"

God shook his head. "No. Unfortunately, that is a decision that can only be made by the Devil."

"So…you can't just vanquish them all?"

"No. The Devil is an autonomous position. I have no power to control it.

"That is so stupid," I said. "There is no way you are all knowing. How could you be so stupid?"

"He assumed I would be there to carry out his orders until time stopped," Lucifer said. "or he could find another sucker to replace me."

"It's a little more complicated than all that." God smiled. "Still, Lucifer was a loyal subject until the very end. He understood the delicate balance between Heaven and Hell, and that one could not exist without the other."

"You're a better man than me, Lou," I said. "I would've gone postal and kamikazed Heaven eons ago."

"Probably why I was such a powerful ally," Lucifer replied.

"This Thomas, however," Michael chimed in. "is a plague. He was trouble from the start. I begged God to let me lop off his head years ago. Now it's too late. Since Thomas became the Devil, he's gathered every pitiful soul in Hell to march against our ranks."

"And that's why you need me."

"Like God said, he has a special affinity to you." Michael looked over at God while he brown-nosed. "Since we can't approach him, you've got to get close and kill this Devil."

"Sounds easy."

"It won't be. Are you sure you are willing?"

"Yes. I hate you, that's for sure. But no matter how big a dick God is, and he's a huge dick, Thomas is worse. He sent zombies to kill Barry, tricked me into killing Lucifer, manipulated me into sleeping with him, and now he's destroying Heaven. He's gotta die."

Michael nodded point by point with my laundry list of why I hated Thomas. "Fair enough. He sits at the back of the battle, in his throne made of bones, watching Heaven crumble."

I walked to the end of the platform, and a series of stairs appeared out of the side, hovering in thin air. "Great. One head of Thomas, coming right up."

"Wait!" Lucifer shouted. "You can't kill the Devil without an enchanted weapon."

"Duh. I've gotta find that dagger again."

"Thomas threw it into the molten lava of Hell." He paused, cocking his head. "In hindsight, I should have done that eons ago."

"Fantastic. How am I gonna kill him, then?"

God snapped his fingers. A great flaming sword, adorned with runes, appeared in the middle of the platform, sunk into a raised stone. Michael walked over toward it. "With this, the Sword of Damocles, the most powerful object in the galaxy. Only the worthy can wield it."

I cracked my fingers and spit into my hands. I'd seen the King Arthur cartoon. I knew what to do. "Alright. Here goes nothing."

I placed my hands upon the sword, took a deep breath, and pulled. I expected resistance, but it loosened from the hilt like butter and swung into the air without any effort at all. The blade was longer than me, yet lighter than air. It glowed with an orange flame, but it was cool to the touch.

"This is awesome," I said.

"It will make short work of the demons and monsters on your way to Thomas," God said. "Be sure to cut off his head. He can regenerate everywhere else, but if you cut off his head this blade will cauterize it immediately, and Thomas will die."

"Got it. Come on everybody. Let's go kill a Devil."

Michael put a hand on Dennis's chest to stop him. "Oh no. I'm not letting these dummies anywhere near that battle. They'll just bungle it up."

"Okay, how about just Connie then?"

Michael sighed. "Fine. You can have her."

"Cool, then let's go, Connie."

Connie turned to Dennis and squeezed him tight. "I promise this is the last time you'll ever have to hug me goodbye."

"We don't have all day!" Michael shouted.

"Okay, okay, sheesh," Connie said, loosening her grip on Dennis. "Hey, don't I get a sword or something?"

I pulled the rosary out of my pocket. "Here. You can have this."

"I'd rather have a demon gun."

"I wish I was home in bed. We all have our cross to bear."

Chapter 16

Michael wasn't lying. God's sword really did cut through Hellbeasts like butter. Whether it was demons, three-headed dogs, imps, zombies, or any manner of disgusting baddie, with one slice from my sword they were gone. The sword didn't just rip them in half, it evaporated them from existence. Connie managed to arm herself with a war hammer discarded by a fallen demon, and could swing it like a pro. She was handy like that.

The plains of Heaven were unlike Earth or Hell. The ground wasn't hard and rocky. Heaven was like fighting on a trampoline covered in pillows. Every time you got a good stance, it fell out from under you. More than once, I went to cut a monster in half and fell on my ass. Luckily, I was a trampoline ace in my youth, and that's a learned skill you never forget.

Thomas's throne towered in the air hundreds of feet over Heaven. In front of him, spanning into the horizon in every direction, a reserve army of monsters waited for their chance to enter the battle.

We were bouncing our way toward the reserve army, when a massive swinging head pitched forward and slammed into us. We didn't even see it until it was on top of us. I rose to greet the biggest monster I'd ever seen, the seven-headed Hydra.

They'd never come to Overbrook. Only big cities satiated their massive appetites. I watched whole army battalions go up against them on the news and not inflict any damage at all. Even when they managed to destroy one head, two more came to take its place. The crazy lizard things were unstoppable. Or so I thought. None of those armies had a flaming sword bestowed on them by God, though.

The monster's seven heads screamed at us. I should have been petrified, but gripping the sword in my hand, I felt empowered. The heads lunged at me one after another. I bounced and avoided them.

One of its heads dove past me. I saw my chance and sliced through its neck. The flaming sword left the neck sizzling. It cauterized the wound and prevented another head from growing.

The Hydra was aggressive and cocky. It had no fear of losing heads, and that was my advantage. I stuck my sword through another head and it fell limp. Connie smashed her hammer against another head, and I jumped to slice it the rest of the way off. We worked in tandem like a choreographed dance.

"Three heads down. Piece of cake."

Still, they lurched forward. I bounced high above the monster, spun my sword around and chucked it through the air. It cut through two more heads in the process and embedded itself into a third.

"Keep the last one busy!" I shouted.

I leapt across the stumps as the last one chomped at Connie. I pulled my sword out of the Hydra and ran up its spine just as it tried to bite Connie in half. It never had the chance. I sliced off its final head in one fell swoop of my blade, and it slumped over, dead.

I slid down from the Hydra's body like a slide. "Well that was a fun little warm up," I said to Connie.

She rolled her eyes but smiled. "You're a moron."

*

After the Hydra, nothing of consequence stood between us and the reserve army of Hell. Some monsters tried to stop us, but we cut them down with ease. Eventually, we stood face to face with the army of demons.

A big hulking giant of a demon stepped out to meet me; twice as tall as the others and rippling with muscles, but not the cute, hot, attractive muscles. No. These were the kind a body builder gets after years of steroids. Gross muscles. He carried an enormous ax over his shoulder, its blade as long as my body.

"Turn back now, mortal," the hulking demon said.

"Save it. I'm here to see Thomas."

"There is no Thomas here, little girl."

I sighed impatiently. "The Devil, alright? Let me though to see the Devil."

The demon stood in place, unmoving. "Leave, before I rip you apart."

Connie pulled at my shoulder. Even though I wasn't scared about anything anymore, that didn't mean Connie wasn't terrified. "This is a bad idea."

"Don't be a baby." I stepped toward the demon. "You're pretty cocky. I'll tell you what, how about I rip you in half and find him myself?"

The big demon chuckled. "I'd like to see you try."

I swung the sword across my body and cut the demon in half. His legion clamored around me, then. They tightened around us and raised their weapons.

"Maybe this wasn't my best idea," I said.

"You think?" Connie replied.

"WAIT!" Thomas's voice boomed from the back of the garrison. "Let them through."

The monsters grudgingly separated. They created a path to a great palanquin at the rear of their ranks. It rose into the heavens like the great Empire State building. Atop the palanquin, Thomas's voice quaked the ground. "No one is to hurt them without my approval."

"Maybe it wasn't a bad idea," Connie said.

"At least it got their attention."

I whispered to Connie as she trailed me across the plains of Heaven toward the great stairs which led to Thomas's throne. "I need you to follow my lead, okay? We got all the way here and we don't have a plan. I need you to just go with it."

"Go with it?"

"Yeah. When I say 'now,' you just go with it. Okay?"

"That sounds like it's gonna get me killed."

"Well yeah, but so will just about any other plan I come up with in the next five seconds."

"Fair enough."

"My dear, I'm so glad you've come," Thomas said as we climbed the stairs. "When you disappeared, I feared the worst.

I thought the 'Good Lord' might've punished you for killing one of his loyal disciples."

"Nope," I replied. "God just wanted to have a little chat, you know. Woman to omniscient being."

"Isn't that funny to call him omniscient—when he couldn't even see I was coming?"

"Yes, very, but let's talk. I came a long way to see you."

I stopped in my tracks when I hit the top of the stairs. Gone was the beautiful, suave Thomas I knew. In his place was a gnarled meat patty of a demon, a disgusting amalgamation of muscle, double the size of the biggest demon on the battlefield. His horns had lengthened to triple their original size. The only thing I recognized about him were his eyes. They were just as dead and evil as I remember.

"Come now, Katrina," he said. "Don't make that face. Are you not happy to see me?"

"Oh, I am. I am. You're just kind of…gross is all."

"Yes, I know. But as a war general I must exude a sense of power and prestige." He stood. Black goop wrapped around him. When he broke free of it, he was no longer a demon, but the gorgeous man with long, flowing hair and the kind eyes I remembered from the bar the first time we met.

"Rest assured, once Heaven is mine, I can become anything you want." He reached down and kissed my hand. "Tell me, what do you want?"

I snatched my hand away from him and rubbed it against my jacket. "The only thing I want is for you to drop dead."

"Then you'll have to kill me."

"That I can do… *Now, Connie!*"

Connie swung her hammer, but she was too slow. Thomas dodged the attacked and wrapped himself back into his black cocoon. He emerged again in his monstrous war general form.

"Fools!" He swung his meat hooks and knocked us into the air. Connie and I sailed a hundred yards across Heaven and collided into the ground at full force, bouncing across the clouds.

I rose to my knees, beaten and bruised, but I wasn't broken. Connie wasn't so lucky. She had cushioned my fall and took the brunt of the punishment. Both of her arms were snapped the wrong way, and her ribs poked through her skin. She gurgled through her breaths.

"Connie. Connie, come on. Connie. Get up."

She vomited blood onto my shirt and looked at me with half a smile. "I always knew you were going to get me killed." Her eyes lost their twinkle. She went limp. She was dead.

I hadn't cried since my mother died, but thick, wet tears filled my eyes now. I unwrapped the rosary she clutched around her hand and squeezed it tightly. "I won't let him win."

"Win?" Thomas said. "But I've already won. Heaven is mine. Your friend is dead. You don't even have your sword anymore."

He was right. I looked over at my sword dug into the ground a hundred feet away, equidistant between Thomas and me.

Rage filled me as I looked back at him. I spoke through clenched teeth. "I can still beat you."

"I should have known you would betray me. I've been so blind. Consumed with love and lust."

My hand twitched. My body quaked. "And you underestimated me."

"I did, at that, but I won't again. You look frightened, and you should be. You'll never reach your sword before I reach you."

"That sounds like a challenge."

I took a running leap and bounced into the air. Monsters lined up to block my path. I found a patch of monsterless Heaven and bounced again. Thomas's hulking brute force barreled through the plains of Heaven, too heavy to bounce along with me.

"Don't touch the mortal," he bellowed. "Leave her for me!"

I landed again, the sword inches within my grasp. My fingers wrapped around it, but I couldn't pull it free before the monstrous claw of Thomas seized me at the waist and moved me toward him.

"Aw, and you were so close." He threw back his head and laughed. I struggled and kicked against him, but his strength was too much. "Unfortunately, close just isn't good enough. Now, I will absorb you into myself and we will be together forever. You will never betray me again. Say your prayers, little one."

Thomas unhinged his jaw and brought me up to his mouth. I unfurled the rosary and tossed it into his mouth. "Great idea."

He choked back the rosary and keeled over like he'd eaten a bad burrito. "What have you done to me?"

I strolled over to my sword. The monsters backed away from me—for the first time, they were as scared as I was confident. "Isn't it obvious? I beat you."

"Please, Katrina," he coughed. "Spare me."

I gripped the hilt of the sword. "Spare you? After all this time, you want me to be merciful. Why would I do that?"

"Because I love you."

I lifted the sword over my head. "No, you don't. You lusted for me. You saw me as your plaything, maybe even a doll to protect, but you never loved me. I was just a thing to you. And now, you are a thing to me. A thing I'm going to kill."

I brought the sword down and sliced through Thomas's neck in one motion. The monsters scattered into the ether as thick orange plumes escaped out of Thomas's body and drifted into the air. They had nowhere to go, until they turned to me.

"Crap."

That's when I understood God's plan for me. I had been too dense and consumed with revenge to see it before. He needed a patsy. Somebody he could manipulate, and, as the fire filled my lungs, I knew he'd chosen me, and he'd chosen well.

God's voice boomed through Heaven. "The monsters of Hell are now yours to command."

"Yeah?" I yelled. "I want them back in Hell, where they belong."

"Thank you, my child. You have done wonderfully."

Humanity's long nightmare was over, and we were once again safe. The rifts around the world sucked the monsters back to Hell where they belonged. The rift in the desert closed forever.

Everybody was happy.

*

After the dust settled, things went back to normal on Earth. Humanity rebuilt itself slowly but surely. People found love and married. They had children. They thanked God for saving them, as if he had anything to do with it.

Overbrook became one of the most important cities in the new world order. It was one of the few left with a functioning community. They worked with Bend to drive marauders out of Portland, Seattle, and the entirety of the West Coast. Things weren't perfect, but they got on for a time.

Soon enough, people forgot about the Apocalypse. As the years went on, truth turned to memory, which turned to myth, which turned to legend, which turned to fiction. People laughed when their great-grandparents talked about the Apocalypse, as if it had never happened.

But we know the truth. We who were there.

For his service, God allowed Barry to live out the rest of his life in human form. He lasted a year before electrocuting himself in the bathtub.

Even though she died, things worked out alright for Connie. She was reunited with Dennis in Heaven. Michael thought so highly of Dennis that he promoted him to archangel. Now Dennis gets to have all the fun—when he's not with Connie, of course.

Yes, everybody made out in this deal except for me, the new Devil. I'm stuck here in Hell with everything I hate most for three hundred millennia. That's what you get for being a hero, kids. Never again.

Although, maybe I shouldn't say that. After all, three hundred millennia was a very long time.

Book 2
Katrina Hates the Gods

Prologue

Ten thousand years ago, God raptured all the good boys and girls up to some giant orgy in the sky. The rest of us were left on Earth, wondering "why not me?"

A rift opened in the desert. Demons, zombies, minotaurs, and all manner of Hell beasts poured out onto Earth and roamed the land. They ripped apart everybody they could find and tortured us to the brink of extinction. Then one day, they got bored, and opted for a quiet life in the suburbs.

They squatted in the homes of the people they once brutally murdered, stole our jobs, ate our food, and made our lives a living Hell. We thought the rampant destruction was bad, but that was nothing compared to the torture of listening to a demon poorly play his guitar all night or having a zombie for your cashier.

They took everything and left us quivering in the shadows, shells of our former selves. Two years of that was more than I could take. I snapped and realized the only thing that could give me back my life was the Devil, so I set out to kill him.

I brought my best frenemy Connie and we traveled across the desert to the Hell rift that had engulfed Reno, Nevada. Along the way, we met up with my ex-lover and demon-jackass Thomas, who convinced me to join his rebellion against the Devil. Bad idea.

Before long, we came face to face with ole Lucifer himself, and I stabbed him through the heart. His death didn't change anything though. In fact, it made things worse, as Thomas used me to take the power of Hell for himself.

With Hell under his control, Thomas waged war on Heaven. He would have won too, if God didn't call me to his aid. He gave me a flaming sword and sent me off to kill Thomas, which I did.

He didn't tell me that by killing Thomas I became the new Devil. TL;DR – I'm the devil now and it sucks.

Chapter 1

"Did I ever tell you how much I hate Hell?" I asked my impish assistant Carl as we walked across the heat-cracked canyons of Hell to my next meeting. Fire and brimstone erupted on either side of me. Since becoming the Devil, I had become accustomed to the heat, but I would never become accustomed to imps like Carl.

His Hell-given name wasn't Carl, of course. I think his real name was K'hal'el, but, I got it wrong so many times, he just asked me to call him Carl.

He waddled behind me, tail dragging on the ground. "You've mentioned it once or twice over the millennia, madam."

I stared out into the grand, burning chasm of Hell. "Good. Cuz I really hate it."

When I inherited Hell, there was a bit of an overcrowding problem.

No.

There was a massive overcrowding problem.

We lived ass-to-ankles in Hell. Trillions of damned souls crowded every inch of the place. God, in all his infinite wisdom, made it nigh impossible to pass through the eye of the needle, which meant nearly every human ended up in Hell. On top of humans, millions of demons, bureaucrats, and imps, populated Hell. It was just a mess.

When I took over from Lucifer, I immediately started expansion plans. I kept the worst of the worst in the lowest pits of Hell. They deserved their Hellfire. These were your Hitlers, Stalins, Attilas, and Trumps, among others, but they only made up one percent of all damned souls.

Most of Hell was filled with slightly horrible people who, yes, had done more bad than good, but they'd never raped a baby or even robbed a bank. They'd lived mediocre lives, the same kind of life that I lived before the Apocalypse. They didn't deserve Hellfire. They just needed a place to chill out.

That's why I annexed Pluto and Neptune for the less terrible damned souls. After that, I annexed Mars and Venus for the quite awful, but not as awful as Hitler types. These were your murderers, rapists, thieves, and other jackasses that died without an ounce of repentance in their souls. While my best torturers stayed on Earth, I sent my gentlest monsters to Neptune and Pluto. Mars and Venus received my middle management enforcers. These baddies weren't tortured every day, but there were plenty of opportunities to beat the bad out of them.

Setting all this up didn't happen overnight, but over my first millennia in charge, we really got Hell in order. Now things ran smooth as butter.

There was only one issue.

A lot of the damned souls in Hell didn't deserve to be there at all. I mean suffering an eternity of torture simply because you cheated on your taxes wasn't fair. How long is a lifetime? A few decades? And how long is eternity, like a billion years?

That is not fair.

That's why my crowning achievement was about to be approved by God today, a system by which people—damned souls—could earn their way out of Hell.

The plan equipped every soul with a timer when they entered Hell. Based on the severity of their crimes, the clock counted down exactly how long remained until they could enter Heaven. If they became a shining example of morality, they earned bonus points. If they messed up, the device added more time. Once their timer ran out, my team sent them to Heaven.

God wasn't keen on the idea, but I've been very persistent. His rules were way too strict. Seriously, like .001 percent of people lived a good enough life to enter Heaven during their lifetime, so Heaven was a wasteland. I couldn't expand Hell any more without exiting the solar system or creating new planets, so the man upstairs just had to approve my proposal.

Sometimes, against all logic, I missed the old days when it was as simple as "see a monster, kill a monster." I never thought I would long for the good old days when it was just the Biblical rapture.

"When do I leave, Carl?" I shouted to my imp.

Carl flipped open his notepad. "The portal opens in five minutes, my liege."

A heavenly portal wouldn't open for you without an invite. No matter how often I tried, God never opened the heavenly plains to me. Instead, we corresponded exclusively through the archangels, who acted as the voices of God but were truly nothing more than revered messenger pigeons. But today, he had invited me up, which meant good things for my plan.

"Do you know what today means, Carl?"

"Uhm...that you can finally get rid of a lot of these people and make them Heaven's problem?"

I nodded. "That's right, Carl. Look at this mess. Starting tomorrow, most of them will be Heaven's mess."

"I do not want to be a bother, mistress, but perhaps you shouldn't count your chickens before they hatch. After all, they could delay..."

Fire flickered in my eyes. Not metaphorical fire, either. Like actual fire. One of the great benefits of being the Devil was access to supernatural powers galore. "Why would you say that, Carl? Why would you jinx me?"

"I'm sorry, mistress. It's just that I know how disappointed you get."

"Just shut up, Carl."

Frankly, he had reason to worry. Heaven put off ruling on my proposal eleven hundred times over the ten millennia I've governed Hell, but this time Gabriel swore that God would make a decision. He was so serious that he even called me up to Heaven. I hadn't been there in ten thousand years, not since the Apocalypse ended by my hand.

"This time is going to be different, Carl. I can feel it. I have a good feeling."

Carl didn't look so enthusiastic. "Yes, mistress."

"Don't you have a good feeling, Carl?"

"Yes, mistress."

It didn't matter what Carl thought. I was about to go to Heaven. God would see how well I managed the underworld, he'd approve my plan, and then, for Christ's sake maybe he'd let me out of managing Hell once and for all.

After all, I'd made Hell so efficient even a trained monkey could run it. I often took vacations to Dis and let Carl run the show for weeks at a time. He was a moron, but even he didn't bungle it. I'd created so many systems that even my systems had systems.

A beam of light appeared in front of us. I'd know it anywhere: It was the soothing, blue light of Heaven.

"It's time, mistress," Carl said.

I took a deep breath. I'd prayed for an invite from Heaven for eons. I had remembered it fondly since the last time I was invited, during the war Thomas waged against Heaven. Even then, in the midst of battle, the serenity of Heaven was the only time I'd felt at peace in the last ten thousand years. Even at its most awful, Heaven was more pleasant than Hell on a good day.

I stepped into the beam. It tasted like Maraschino cherries, just like I remembered. I turned to Carl. I hoped to never see his ugly face again.

Thousands of years ago...

Velaska sat on her throne, fire licking the feet of her subjects. They were all evil, she told herself, not worthy of redemption, and not worthy of a second thought. After Hades left, she had kept watch over the suffering of the damned; she had been the queen of Hell for thirteen thousand years.

It would be lying to say there wasn't a piece of her that didn't love the suffering. After all, it was what drew her to the job in the first place. Hades told her she would have dominion over the suffering of all the denizens in Hell; she had absolute power to deny the will of Zeus. But he didn't tell her she couldn't leave Hell until she found a replacement. That would've been a nice thing to mention.

If she had known that, she might not have taken the gig, even with all its benefits. When her appetite for suffering waned, she tried to get out of the gig, but nobody wanted to take her place. The other gods weren't as sadistic as she was, it turned out.

"Sorry," Zeus told her. "Until you can find a successor, there's nothing I can do."

She waited, and she waited...and she waited. And then one day a brash, young angel came along, angry at God's management of Earth. Lucifer was God's envoy to Hell and one of his most trusted angels, but he had a wild side, and he didn't like taking orders.

Velaska convinced him to revolt against God, build an army, and take back the Heavens for himself.

Admittedly, she was bored and thought it would be fun to watch Heaven tumble, even if the idea was riddled with flaws and had little chance of succeeding.

However, he didn't know that, so he accepted, and set out to topple Heaven. She kept him hidden as best she could while he built an army, but even with her help, Lucifer's attack lasted less than a day. He was only an angel after all.

God was kind, though, which was unlike him.

Instead of vanquishing Lucifer outright, God simply turned his angel into a hideous demon, and sent him back to Hell, broken and hideous.

"Velaska," he said, stumbling into my castle. His beautiful face gnarled into that of a hideous demon, with huge, ugly horns and feet shaped like those of goats. "Velaska, look what they have done to me."

She pouted her lips, though she really wanted to smile. "Poor baby."

"I did everything you said, and still my war against the Heavens failed in less than a day. What can I do now? The denizens of Hell demand my head. I cannot fight them off forever. No longer done the fear of my angelic nature to keep them at bay. I cannot rest. I am doomed."

Velaska stood, careful to conceal her glee. "Well, my dear. There is one thing you could do, but—"

Lucifer kneeled. "Anything, my queen. The other gods have all abandoned Earth to oversee Zeus's next planet. There is nobody left to help me but you."

"Do you know the power of Hell, Lucifer? Its true power?"

"No, my queen."

"It does not rely on the rules of Heaven to govern it. Down here, we have complete control. Absolute power. If you were, for instance, to take my crown, then you would be equal to Heaven itself. The Hell beasts could not touch you, for you would have the power of the Devil, which is rivaled only by that of the gods themselves."

Lucifer stepped back. "My queen. I could never…this kingdom has always been ruled by a god. I am but a lowly angel. How could I—"

"First, you're a demon now, not an angel. And second, what are you saying, are you saying you don't want it?"

"No, no, no. It's not that. It's just that…I'm not worthy to accept such a grand role."

Velaska snickered as she reeled in her prey. She couldn't pull too hard or the angel would turn away, but if she stroked his ego, he would be putty in her hands. Men were so easily corrupted. "It's governing the damned, Lucifer. You are overqualified. But if you don't want to escape God's wrath, or that of the demon horde, then I understand. Good day."

"No, no—I do! I would do anything to escape it."

"Then listen to me. Take my crown and become the Devil incarnate, and in return, you will be given absolute power in Hell. Even god cannot touch you."

Lucifer thought about it for a moment, before he bowed his head. "I accept."

She snapped her fingers. A spherical golden necklace appeared in front of Lucifer. An infinity symbol spun slowly at its center. Lucifer poked it with his finger, and the symbol spun faster, creating a powder blue glow.

"Put it on. You work for me now. Should you ever need to call me, this necklace will be your beacon."

Just like that, Velaska was free from the torment of the underworld. She'd found a successor, and, in doing so, freed herself. As she vanished from the Earth for the last time, all she thought was "Wasn't that easy?"

Chapter 2

I didn't know blue had a taste until Heaven beamed me up for the first time. I never forgot it. I tasted the same flavor again now, and my mouth lit up in ecstasy. A lot had happened in ten thousand years, but that flavor had managed to swirl around in my mouth every day for the last ten thousand years.

Maraschino cherries. The kind I used to top sundaes with back at Oscar's in Overbrook. Back before the Apocalypse, when I lived on Earth.

The blinding white light faded, and I regained my eyesight. There I was, standing at the gates of Heaven. Honestly, it was a bit underwhelming. When I took over as Devil, I erected giant apartments to house my workers and constructed massive highways in order to help things become more efficient. Luckily, Hell is full of slave labor.

Heaven, on the other hand, looked the same as it had my last visit. It was still cluttered with fluffy clouds and harp music. It looked like a 1960's love fest, but brighter. The angels still wore white robes. Okay, it was different in that they'd cleaned up after the battle—it had been stained with blood after Thomas unleashed his army on the Elysian Fields. They weren't prepared for battle, then. They weren't even prepared for a light breeze.

I guess when you have everything you'll ever desire, there's no need to innovate. God should have learned his lesson since the last attack and overhauled some things, but clearly, he thought me as much of a sucker as Lucifer.

Lucifer may have been a fallen angel, but he was still an angel. He still felt allegiance to God Almighty, and wanted to please him. So, after he led his failed coup and took control of Hell from the previous Devil, Velaska, Lucifer took a deal God offered him, which would allow Lucifer to reenter Heaven and wipe his debt clean. If the Morningstar could hold Hell together for three hundred millennia without cracking under the pressure or starting another war with Heaven, God's countenance would shine down on him once more.

Frankly, Lucifer was a horrible ruler of Hell in a time when ruling horribly was acceptable. For most of Lou's reign, life expectancy was low, so people couldn't commit enough sins by the time they died to warrant eternal torment. But when life expectancy went through the roof, so did sinners, and the population of Hell ballooned.

What did an archangel know about management? They don't know anything but fighting and…well, that's about the long and the short of it. Ask Michael or Samael a logic problem or discuss the intricacies of supply chain logistics, and they'll fall apart. Gabriel was the only one with half a brain in the whole lot of them.

Lucifer was no different. He was made for a single purpose. To fight. I was made as a human with high reasoning power. Surviving for two years in the Apocalypse made me scrappy and gave me certain powers of deduction. Plus, living alongside humans—living and dead—and monsters gave me a keen insight on how to improve relations among them.

"I'm sorry, are you Katrina?" a little voice said to me.

I turned to see a spry, young man, no older than ten, smiling at me. "Yes, I am."

I didn't spit the same vitriol to her as I did to Carl and his ilk. In fact, I didn't have any vitriol. I was, for the first time in centuries, calm.

"I'm Rodney Bowers. Please follow me."

Glistening, gilded gates guarded the entrance to Heaven. They rose three hundred feet high and connected to the only non-cloud structure around, a three-hundred-foot-high marble wall which stretched into the horizon in every direction. In front of it, thousands, millions of people, stood in line awaiting Saint Peter's judgment.

"We have a bit of a backlog," Rodney said, nodding his head towards the line of people.

Centuries ago, God agreed to use his people to help judge the dead. Previously, that burden fell completely on Petrus, guardian of the Gates of Abnegation, and our team of monster bureaucrats, but as the population ballooned exponentially, our backlog worsened until the line for judgement was several millennia long. Even with Saint Peter carrying half the burden, it was impossible to keep up with the massive number of souls that died every day. My plan helped solve this burden by bringing in AI automation into the soul judging process.

"I've noticed."

Most of the line would find their eternal end in Hell with me. How many hopeful idiots thought they would see beyond the pearly gates, only to be licked by Hellfire? It's not fair that they saw Heaven before sentencing, some for a thousand years, before it was ripped away from them for the rest of eternity. The bliss of Heaven was sacred, and the longing for it tortured the damned more than anything I could do to them.

Saint Peter, the protector of Heaven, stood in front of the gate, proclaiming the fate of each person as they stepped up to his pulpit. "Mister Nick Smith," he said. "I'm sorry, but you are damned to Hell for eternity."

The clouds opened below him, and Nick fell screaming into the pits of Hell. My minions would be there to greet him. It would not be pleasant.

"How many people get into Heaven these days?" I asked Rodney.

"Oh, that's over my pay grade, Devil."

"Katrina."

"Devil Katrina."

As I passed in front of Saint Peter, groans erupted from the dead. I turned to the line with fire in my eyes and flames on my arms, and the line shrunk back in fear.

"That's what I thought."

Rodney stopped in front of Saint Peter. "I bring Devil Katrina into Heaven for a meeting with God. I believe she has an appointment."

Saint Peter looked down at his sheet. "Ah, yes. I see her scheduled here. Open the gates!"

A calming light burst from behind the gate and the sound of a choir of angels flooded my ears. The men and women waiting in line openly wept at the sight of it.

"I don't understand," I said, pointing to the joyous crowd. "What's going on there?"

"They've never seen the gates open for anyone but an angel," Peter responded.

"Seriously? How many people do you let into Heaven?"

Saint Peter looked down at his sheet. I peered over it with him. He flipped the pages in his notebook. Every name for five hundred pages was condemned to Hell. There wasn't one Heaven in the bunch. "It's sad. I can't remember the last time."

"That explains a lot."

*

Walking through Heaven wasn't like walking on Earth or through Hell. The clouds that made up the floor of Heaven were meant for sleeping and sitting, not for walking. The ground wasn't solid, and it moved like fluffy pillows, so walking around was more like bouncing.

"I'm sorry," Rodney said. "I usually fly. I didn't realize it was such a long walk."

"That's okay. It's nice to be away from the sulfuric stench of Hell for a moment."

"Yes, it must be horrible down there."

I didn't mind Hell as much as I let on. It wasn't that bad after the first thousand years or so. It's not like Earth smelled so great either. It reeked of sweaty flesh like Hell smelled of burning flesh. Heaven didn't smell like anything, except the gentle wisp of a cherry cordial.

"We ran millions of tests and found that everybody in Heaven enjoyed cherry pie, so we use that smell for everything." Rodney smiled at me. Tiny wings fluttered out from underneath his robe. Everything was so white in Heaven I hadn't noticed them before.

"I thought only archangels got wings," I said to her.

"Oh, that all changed some time ago. God started giving them to anybody who asked. I guess he figured what's Heaven if you can't do what you want, you know?"

I smiled despite myself. "Yeah, I guess that's true."

If God had granted wings to angels back ten thousand years ago, I never would have become the Devil. A big reason that I succeeded in killing Thomas was because of the help of

Dennis, boyfriend to my old bestie-frenemy Connie. Plague killed him after the Apocalypse, but he returned to Earth to help me take down the Devil, so he become an archangel and received his wings.

If they gave out wings to everybody, Dennis wouldn't have met us in Hell after he died. He wouldn't have saved us from Thomas's flaming catapults. He never would have even left Heaven in the first place. My journey with Connie would have been over before it started, likely with our inevitable deaths. One thing was for sure, I never would have been forced to become the Devil.

"Ah, there we are," Rodney said sweetly, pointing into the distance.

I recognized the structure from my last time in Heaven: a hovering platform, replete with pillars at its base and a spiraling staircase up its side that attached to nothing. It was the place that God brought me the last time I visited Heaven, ten thousand years ago.

"Great. Let's go."

The angel held up his hand. "Oh, not yet. God is very busy, and he's running behind."

"How behind?"

The boy looked at his schedule. "Shouldn't be more than a hundred years or so. Thank you for your patience."

"A hundred years! What the fudgecake do you mean a hundred years? Flapjack—curry powder—why can't I curse?"

"Oh silly, you can't curse here. It's Heaven."

"Oh right. I forgot about that."

The angel flapped his wings and took off. "And I'm sorry for the inconvenience, but I promise we will be with you as soon as possible. Buh-bye."

My rage flooded back upon me. I remembered that Heaven wasn't perfect. God certainly didn't know what was best. He couldn't even predict that Thomas would rise to power. On top of it all, he was kind of a dick.

I'd seen too many good people rotting in Hell for eternity, pleading for God's mercy that never came, to be impressed by him. I'd held babies who died too young, unbaptized, that would be punished unmercifully even though they would never understand why. I'd let the beauty of Heaven cloud my judgment for a moment, but I was back in control of my faculties in that moment and the rage filled me again.

"Holy shit, is that Katrina?" I heard behind me. It wasn't angry vitriol, per se, but it wasn't the welcoming dulcet tone of a friend, either. I knew immediately who it was, even after ten thousand years. Connie.

"What are you doing here, bitch?" she said, strolling up to me.

"How the frogcake can you curse and I can't?" I replied, uncomfortably accepting her warm hug.

"I'm dead and in Heaven. I can do whatever I want. They don't want people like you ruining Heaven for the rest of us."

"Yeah, I can see that. I am a bad influence."

"Man, that's the truth. How's the Devil business?"

I sighed. "Got more evil people than I know what to do with. Annexed Pluto, Neptune, Venus, and Mars, but they just keep coming."

"Yeah, Dennis told me a little bit about that. I'm actually here to wait for him now."

"So, that's still a thing."

Connie smiled brightly, and a twinkle filled her eyes. "Ten millennia and still kickin' like it was the first date."

"That's some soulmate level stuff right there."

"Tell me about it," Connie said with a big smile. "I'm headed over to God's podium to welcome him back from his latest trip. Come on."

Connie loved Dennis more than anything. In the middle of the Apocalypse, we'd dragged him across the monster-filled "Black Zone" of Overbrook to the only doctor in town, with the hope that we could find a cure. We knew it was hopeless, but she held out hope Dennis might get better. He wouldn't. Dennis put a gun in Connie's hand and asked her to pull the trigger. And then they met again, when Dennis came back from Heaven to help me. After Connie died fighting Thomas, they reunited in Heaven, and I guess they've been together ever since.

Connie floated toward God's podium and I bounced along behind her, trying to take myself seriously. "Do you like it here?"

"What's not to like?" Connie replied. "It's Heaven."

"Yeah, but it's oppressively dull, isn't it?"

She smiled. "You haven't been to the orgy pits yet, huh?"

"Say what?"

"Dude, you can do literally anything you want up here, aside from straight-up sucking the soul out of people and draining their essence."

"Yeah, right. You can just straight-up murder somebody?"

"I guess, but nobody up here would wanna do that. That's kinda the whole point of how we got in here. It's all good people who just wanna mess around, get baked, and watch cartoons. My brother would've loved it. How's he doing down there, anyway?"

Her brother Barry was the reason Connie and I hated each other. Or to be fair, why Connie hated me. I still liked her just fine. Barry was my roommate before the Apocalypse. He died saving me, and when he came back to life, I watched him die again by the hands of Thomas. After I saved the world, God gave Barry back his body, which he promptly lost again in a bathtub electrocution incident. He's been helping me in Hell ever since.

"He's actually pretty competent at making sure Pluto runs effectively. It took two thousand years to train him, but he's not doing too bad at the end of the day."

"Is he happy?"

"It's Hell, Connie. Nobody is happy."

A great gust blew from the podium. Three iron-clad angels hovered in front of us: Samael, the Angel of Death, dressed in his iconic black hood, Michael, commander of the archangels, and Dennis, who must've been working out over the eons because he looked deliciously beefy.

"Baby!" Dennis shouted. He flapped his enormous wings over to Connie, wrapping her up in a massive hug as they soared upward into the sky. I watched them fly for a moment before I felt a tap on my shoulder.

"So, you're here, huh?" Michael said to me.

"It looks that way."

Michael had never liked me. He thought it was foolhardy to kill the Devil, and Michael could not be impressed by foolhardiness. Luckily, I'd never tried to impress him.

"He's never going to say yes, you know."

"Why do you always have to be so negative? Seriously, what is your problem?"

Michael sneered at me. "My problem is that you're a reckless nobody that nearly got Heaven destroyed."

"Yeah, and in case you haven't noticed, I've been paying for that the last ten thousand years, and doing a good job of it, if I do say so myself."

Michael scoffed. "You are doing adequate at best."

"Yeah, then why am I standing here, if I'm only doing an adequate job?"

Michael snarled his teeth, bit his lip, and clenched his fists. He wanted to swing, but Samael placed a hand on his chest and calmed him down.

"You will destroy us all before the end," Michael finally said.

"Well, I saved you once, so I guess if I destroy you I'll just be even with the universe, now won't I?"

Another gust of wind blew forward and Dennis stood next to us, flushed and smiling. "You're here. Why are you here?"

"I'm trying to get my merit system passed," I replied. "They said he'd have an answer today."

"Right…right," Dennis paused. "Can I talk to you for a second?"

Dennis pulled me aside, away from Michael's prying ears. "Listen, they're just jerking you around, man. There's no chance they're going to soil Heaven with your people."

I clenched my fists. "What do you mean, 'my people?'"

"Dude, chill out. Those are their words, not mine. Lou went to bat for you, God is stubborn, you know. He still hasn't forgotten the smell of the damned the last time they rode on Heaven, and he doesn't want anything like that to happen again. When you think about it, he kind of has a point."

"He has a point! He has a point?" I shouted, waving my hands in the air. "Are you kidding me? I sit with those tortured souls every single day and let me tell you, none of them deserve eternal damnation."

Dennis held up his arms. "Look, I don't know about you, and I don't know what's going on down there, but from what I've seen, they don't deserve Heaven either."

"From what I've seen, Heaven ain't so great, and if God's gonna screw me around, he can tell me straight to my face."

I pushed past Dennis and bounced toward God's podium. Samael flew up and landed in front of me, followed by Michael and Dennis.

"Where do you think you're going?" Michael said.

"Get out of my way, Michael. I'm going to see the big man."

Michael stopped me with his fat hand. "I can't let you do that."

"You can't let me do what? I am the Devil. Do you not understand my power?" Fire grew in my belly and sparked out of my eyes. "I have allowed you to lord over me out of respect for this place but block my path and I will show you my true power."

Michael drew his sword. "I have fought your power before, and I will fight it again."

I snorted. "You will lose."

Dennis drew his long sword as well. "It doesn't have to be like this, Katrina. It took Thomas an entire army to get through us. You don't stand a chance."

My size doubled in seconds. It doubled again in a few more. "I've had ten thousand years to master my power, angel. Thomas had less than a day. I don't need the forces of Hell to take you down."

Michael and Dennis confronted me from the front like idiots and I swatted off their attacks like flies. Samael flew around my back. I grabbed him in my hand and tossed him against God's podium. The façade shattered against the force of my strength.

Michael flew at me again, striking my foot with his flaming sword. I balled up my fist and drove him deep into the clouds until they collapsed over him. Only Dennis remained. He flew up to my face.

"We don't have to do this, Katrina!"

Blue flames shot out of my eyes and entangled Dennis, licking his face. "You're right! Just let me pass and I'll send you back to your Connie in one piece."

"I can't do that."

"I didn't start this fight, but I'm gonna finish it."

I flung Dennis, tired and singed, across the clouded plains until he skidded to a stop in front of Connie. Satisfied, I shrunk back down to my human form.

"You're a real dick, you know that?" Connie said, looking down at Dennis and then back at me. "I guess ten thousand years in Hell hasn't changed you at all!"

I looked down at my smoking hands, then at the three archangels I had just dispatched like they were nothing.

"Oh yes, it has. It's made me much, much worse."

Chapter 3

It seemed like every Devil was tricked into taking their position. Anubis tricked Hades, who tricked Velaska, who tricked Lucifer. The only Devil who wanted the position was Thomas, but he didn't truly want to be the Devil, he wanted the power to topple Heaven, like a vengeful child. God tricked me into doing his dirty work by convincing me to battle Thomas (of course, I won), and then banished me to Hell for ten millennia. If I was going to do God's bidding, then he would have to look me in the eyes before he screwed me.

Samael groaned as I stepped over him and onto the winding stairs toward God's podium. A battalion of archangels flew in from the east. They would be too late to interfere. With every step, the fury coursing through my veins grew stronger and the fire in my belly blazed more intently. I was ready to burn God.

I looked out onto the podium, into the great expanse, and saw two chairs. On one sat God, his white beard sagging to the floor as he moved his knight across a chess board hovering between him and Lucifer, who sat across from him.

"Knight to queen six," God said.

"You sunk my battleship," Lucifer whined.

Lucifer was a slovenly Devil. He still wore the same stained wife beater from the first time I met him, and his beer belly had only widened over the years.

God inhaled slowly with a perplexed look on his face. "I don't think we're playing the same game."

"We never were."

"Are you kidding me?" I shouted, flames shooting out of my mouth and eyes as I stomped across the platform. "You had me wait downstairs, said you were one hundred years behind, and you're playing chess! And you're not even doing it right!"

I wanted God to stand up and apologize. I wanted him to admit he was an asshole. Nothing else would do, but he didn't budge.

"I'm sorry, Katrina, but some things are important, and I must have my mind right before I deal with the issues of the day. Chess calms me."

He didn't even glance up from his game. He didn't think enough of me to look at me when he insulted me.

In the middle of the podium, embedded in stone, sat the flaming Sword of Damocles. It was one of only a few weapons in the solar system that could kill the Devil. The last time I used it, the Devil Thomas lost his head. It was massive, five feet long, and flamed brilliantly orange when held. I missed the feel of it in my hand. I wondered if it could kill God as easily as it could kill the Devil...

"No, it couldn't," God said. "It could kill a god, don't get me wrong, just not as easily as it could kill the Devil. Killing gods is tricky, tricky business."

Lucifer moved his bishop across the board. "Check."

Pieces flew everywhere when I kicked over the board. "Then how about I just end your stupid game, huh?"

Lucifer looked up at me. "Uh oh. I think she's pissed. I remember that fire in my eyes. I don't miss it."

God sighed. "Don't worry. I know where we left off." His blue eyes sparked lightning when he looked over at me. "Very well, Katrina. You've captured my attention with your temper tantrum. What can I do for you?"

He leaned forward in his chair and I caught a whiff of sweet wine on his breath. Dozens of metal wine carafes speckled the podium, some full and others cast aside, empty. Lucifer grabbed one and guzzled from it, an ocean of wine spilling down his shirt. He didn't seem to care one bit. A golden, spherical necklace dangled from his neck. At its center lay an infinity symbol which spun slowly around the base, almost hypnotically.

"It was given to me by my predecessor," Lucifer said, following my eyes. "Should I ever need her, this will call her."

"That's stupid," I said absently, trying to count the empty carafes of wine. "Are you *drunk*?"

God wobbled on his chair and listed to the right. "God doesn't get drunk, Katrina. God is as sober as he needs to be."

"You are! You're hammered. You made me wait down there while you got hammered with Lucifer."

"Call me Lou, baby," Lucifer shouted over his shoulder.

"I'm not calling you that," I snapped. I stepped up to God. "As for you, explain yourself."

God smiled. A purple hue stained his teeth from the red wine. "No."

"Excuse me?"

"I'm God. I don't have to explain myself to anybody."

I gestured towards Earth. "What about all the people down there that pray to you?"

He shrugged. "That's the benefit of being God."

Flames shot out of my fists. "You are unbelievable. All this time I thought you were some sort of infallible God thing and now I find out you're just a drunk. What happened to the old God? The one I met before."

"Acting!" He shot his arm in the air. "Acting!"

Lucifer clapped and the two of them burst into a fit of giggles. Fire shot out of my nostrils. "What about my proposal? What about the merit system? The thing I've been patiently waiting on for seven thousand years? The thing you promised me I'd have an answer for today?"

"Ah yes, the proposal." God snapped his fingers. A stack of papers appeared in front of him. "A little long, don't you think?"

I pounded my fingers on my palm so hard it stung. "It outlines, in detail, a rock solid three-thousand-point plan to fix our massively broken system. So yeah, it's long!"

God read through the document very slowly. "Still...seems a little long." He leaned back on his chair towards Lucifer, nearly falling over. "Doesn't it, Lou? You never sent me anything this long."

"Seems a little long to me," Lucifer replied. "I would never have sent you anything that long."

"Stay out of this," I said with a glare. "And I know he never sent you anything this long—he was a horrible Devil."

"Hey!"

"You were the Devil for a few measly millennia and God had to start an Apocalypse just to ease your stress. I've been down there ten thousand years with literally zero help and things are running smooth as silk. So, objectively, you suck compared to me."

Lou returned to his drink. "Still. That hurts."

I looked back over at God. "Look, it's a solid plan. I have the foundations in place. All I need is your stamp of approval. I've crossed every 'T' and dotted every 'I.' My people have looked it over. Your people have looked it over. All we need is your sign-off and we can make this happen."

God pondered for a moment before giving a shrug. "No. I'm gonna have to pass."

"Excuse me? What do you mean pass?"

"I mean, it looks good and all, but that would mean a lot more people up here and frankly, we're kind of at capacity."

"Are you kidding me? There are *zero* people around! I had to annex four planets to create enough space in Hell, and you won't even take on a few worthy people?"

The god of the universe leaned unsteadily on his elbow and slurred. "Yeah, but what does 'worthy' even mean, really?"

"That's literally the first three thousand pages of the document! I outline in detail what being 'worthy' means!"

God snapped his fingers and another cask of wine appeared in his hand. "I wish you had gotten this to me sooner. Then you wouldn't have wasted your time."

"Are you kidding me?"

Heaven quaked in that moment. The sky turned black, and a thunderous screech erupted from the sky. I thought for a second that I'd broken Heaven, and I couldn't have been happier.

Massive clouds swirled and rumbled, then lightning streaked out across the Elysian Fields. In its wake, three figures emerged. The tallest had a chiseled body and wore a red breast plate adorned with a yellow sun, gilded shoulder armor, and a flowing golden robe. With every step, his muscles rippled from his pecs to his shins.

Behind him sauntered a tall, golden-haired woman with a gilded crown resting upon her perfectly coifed head. Blood-red lipstick popped against her milky white skin and golden bracelets adorned her otherwise naked arms.

Next to her, a fierce, dark-haired woman strung an arrow into her bow and pointed it at God. She stood out from the others for her squat physique. As opposed to the other woman, who looked like a super model, this one resembled a weightlifter who deadlifted cars for fun. Her breastplates weren't designed to accentuate her beauty. They were designed for war and covered with thick leather.

"Bacchus, you fat, sniveling lush," the chiseled man said in a booming voice. "Get down here and face us!"

All the color escaped God's face. His drunken smile faded and left him looking every bit his ancient age. He trembled in place while Lucifer, ever the friend, rushed to his side.

"It's okay," Lucifer said. "It's going to be okay."

God crumbled to the ground. "It's not. They can't—they can't be here. They can't."

Lucifer wrapped his meaty paws around him. "It's okay. We're going to be okay."

When God looked up, big, sopping tears filled his eyes. His voice trembled. "How?"

I kneeled next to God and Lucifer. "Do you wanna tell me what is going on?"

Lucifer shot me a glare. "Show some respect. The man is going through some stuff."

"Bacchus!" the armored man shouted again. "I know you are here. I smell your cowardice in every step I take!"

"No, no, no, no," God repeated. He rocked back and forth against his knees. "They can't be here."

"Who are they?" I asked. "And why do they keep calling you Bacchus?"

God was speechless at this point, and Lucifer answered for him. "Because that's his name."

"Like the Greek god who drank everything in sight?"

Lucifer nodded. "That's the one."

"This makes all the sense now. And you're scared of the people that just came out of the sky and are walking up here?"

"Uh huh," God replied.

"They give you nargals all in your belly?"

"Yes. Yes, they do."

"And the last thing you want is for them to find you?"

"Katrina," Lucifer said, grabbing my wrist. "Don't."

Blue flame blazed from my wrist where he held it and licked Lucifer's hand. He was used to the pain, so he lasted longer than most, but eventually he relented, his hand charred black when he retracted it. All he could do was look piteously as I stood and walked to the edge of the podium.

"Hey! The one you're looking for is up here!" I turned back to Bacchus. "You are a very bad god. Did you know that?"

God looked up at me. "I know. I did the best I could with what I had. I could do better with more. If I just had *more* I would do better."

"No, you wouldn't." I bent down on one knee, so I was face to face with him. "Now, who are we talking to here? Who's coming up these stairs?"

Bacchus sniveled like a sick child as he peered up at me. "The one, that voice, is Apollo. How many others are there?"

I looked down over the ledge. Apollo stormed up the curved steps toward us, while the two others stood on the clouds, waiting and muttering to each other. "There's a very tall, pretty older lady with gold hair, and a short, body-builder type holding an arrow to my head."

He stared down on the ground, contrite. "That's Hera and Artemis."

"The old gods are coming home," Lucifer added, solemn.

I'd fought minotaurs, hydras, Cerberus dogs, and worked with a dozen more Greek monsters down in Hell, but I will admit that I didn't believe in the gods. Yet here I was, staring at three gods, from time immortal, directly in front of me.

The vibrations from Apollo's steps crescendoed as he appeared before us. "Ah, brother. Look at you, exactly as I left you. Drunk and pathetic."

Something in my belly didn't sit right about Apollo. He was an outsider, coming to Heaven and insulting the only god I've ever known. Yes, he was a lush, and an idiot, but he was ours.

"That's not very nice," I said. "I can say that about him because he's my god, but you're nobody, so back off."

"I am Apollo, god of the sun. A thousand times I have watched humanity rise from the primordial ooze, and hobble onto two feet," he scoffed as he looked me up and down, unimpressed. "I am a god among gods. Who are you?"

"I'm Katrina. The Devil."

"What happened to Velaska?"

Lucifer stood. "I took over for her before she abdicated her throne. Katrina took over from me."

Apollo stared at the two of us for a moment before bursting into laughter and pointing at Bacchus. "You chose a cherub and a mortal to control your underworld kingdom? It's no wonder Zeus summoned me here."

Bacchus wept big, ugly tears. "What did our father command?"

"What do you think, dear brother?" Apollo stepped over to him. "You started an Apocalypse, appointed a mortal to be your Devil, and made this...*Heaven*, which allows mortals to entreat with the gods once they died. It's an abomination. Humanity should never consort on Olympus, Bacchus. You know this and still flouted it. Even one mortal is too many, and there are many more than that here."

"Excuse me," I said. "There aren't enough people up here. That's the whole reason I came."

Apollo snapped his fingers and my lips fell mute. I couldn't speak. I couldn't scream out. All I could do was stand there in silence.

"Quiet, mortal. I didn't travel across the universe to listen to you squawk. I'll release you if you promise to behave."

I raised a middle finger to him. Then, the other. Apollo stared at them for a moment, and then let out a loud laugh.

"Ha! That's very funny, mortal. I like you." He snapped his fingers and released me. "Speak out of turn again and I will rip the skin from your body."

Apollo turned to Bacchus. "Little brother. How could you muddle this up so completely? This was such an easy post. Far in the nether reaches of the galaxy."

"I tried," Bacchus said, meekly. "I really tried."

"And you failed. Miserably. Now, you must face your judgment. Hera! Artemis! It's time. Bacchus, you are under arrest for the high crimes of incompetence, inciting an Apocalypse, and on a personal note, being the worst god I've ever seen."

"Thank you!" I shouted.

Apollo grabbed Bacchus by the throat. "Hera! Artemis! To me!"

In a flash of light, Artemis and Hera appeared before Apollo. "It is by the decree of Zeus himself that no planet may exist without a God to oversee it. Therefore, since we have arrested Bacchus and he must await a trial for which he is assuredly guilty, this quadrant of the solar system will be moved into our temporary repository in universe 4239 until a suitable replacement can be found. Should no appointment be made, this sector shall be abandoned by the gods and left to rot in another dimension forever."

Apollo snapped his fingers with his free hand, and then he was gone, along with Bacchus, Artemis, and Hera. Complete blackness fell across Heaven. The sun pulsated slowly and faded from yellow to red and then to a dull orange, before condensing into a tiny, white ball and exploding out across the galaxy in a brilliance of every color imaginable.

A black hole opened where the sun once reigned; the skies screamed and howled as the whole of the solar system moved toward it. I watched Mercury and Venus dissolve into nothingness as the Earth inched closer to this new, dark center of the galaxy. In a matter of moments, Earth would be gone as well, and Heaven along with it.

No matter how hard I fought, the force from the black
hole pulled me. I worried it would turn me inside out. Lucifer
was struggling behind me. With every ounce of energy I had
left, I turned my head toward him and watched him claw his
way toward the Sword of Damocles and lift himself onto the
hilt, before he pulled it from its stone. "Follow me!"

"What is that gonna do?" I shouted.

Dennis appeared on top of the podium. Connie clung to
his side as he struggled to remain upright, flapping his wings
against the pull of the black hole. "What have you done?"

"I didn't do anything!"

"We can argue later!" Lucifer screamed.

I could barely hear him over the sound of the black hole
sucking us and everything toward it with ever-increasing
force. Lucifer closed his eyes and swung the sword. In front
of him, the sky ripped in half. On either side of the celestial
incision was a distressed Heaven and earth, but directly within
it, a craggy cave appeared, surrounded by glowing embers of
every color.

"Get inside!" Lucifer shouted.

"What is that?" I replied.

"Get in or you'll be swallowed alive!"

"To hell with this," Connie shouted, releasing her tight
grip around Dennis. "I'm in."

Connie disappeared into the void. I looked back at
Lucifer, then at the black hole sucking everything toward its
gaping maw.

Lucifer shouted over the screaming sky. "In a few seconds
you won't be able to jump forward, and you'll be lost
forever!"

"Screw this!" I jumped into the void.

Meanwhile, on Earth...

Rebecca Lobdell stood outside her 3,256[th] floor apartment, staring at what used to be known as Los Angeles, and now was known as Thebos. Of course, she didn't know that Los Angeles was a city that existed ten thousand years before, any more than somebody in the twentieth century could name a town from the settlers ten thousand years before.

Most people didn't like living above the cloud cover, but Rebecca enjoyed it. She enjoyed her tea, and the quiet. She enjoyed watching the sun fade into nothing and turn into a giant black hole.

Wait. That wasn't right.

The sun wasn't supposed to do that. Rebecca turned to run but her feet were stuck in place. She tried to scream but the screeches from the black hole drowned her out. It pulled Mercury and Venus into its clutches, and then reached for Earth with voracious winds.

The top of her apartment ripped off first, followed by the sliding door that led to her charming patio. Before long, she was floating in the sky. Around her were thousands, millions of vehicles, trees, houses, and people sailing toward their impending doom.

Rebecca knew in her bones that it was all over, but she was a human, and humans fought against their demise, even when it was no use. She struggled in vain until the atmosphere fell out from under her and she descended into darkness behind the veil of the Black Hole. She couldn't see or feel a thing. Then, her door hit her in the head and she blacked out. It was the last thing she felt.

Chapter 4

We fell through space and time. All around me stars, planets, galaxies whizzed past us as we floated through the cosmos. A clear, elastic membrane was all that separated us from the vacuum of the intergalactic void.

In front of me, the craggy rocks of a brand-new planet came into view. Behind me, the faint glare of our solar system blinked out of existence as Apollo's black hole sucked everything I ever knew into another universe, from Venus, Earth to Mars, Neptune, and even poor Pluto. Ten thousand years later, and humans still can't agree if it's a planet.

Now it was all gone. I had spent ten thousand years building it up, and it was taken from me in the blink of an eye, but I was going to do everything in my power to get it back.

"Watch your head," Lucifer said next to me. "The landings'll kill you."

"Good thing I'm immortal then."

"Nothing is immortal, Katrina, not even the gods."

"What does that mean?" Connie asked. "Can you kill a god?"

Lucifer smiled. "Anything can be killed, given the right circumstances. Now, we're going at the speed of light, so duck and roll."

The uneven rocks in front of us grew from tiny specks to towering behemoths in a moment. The giant rocks were part of an island, and that island sat in the middle of a turbulent sea, with water crashing violently against its shore.

I fell through the cool chill of the atmosphere until *wham*, I smacked full force into the rock formation and slid down its scratchy face until the ground halted my fall. If I wasn't the ruler of Hell, I would have splattered into a thousand pieces. That was the first moment I felt lucky to be the Devil.

I brushed myself off and stood up, breathing in the smell of salt water. I'd always liked the rocky shore of Scotland, and the island reminded me of it. It was a massive rock formation, set out in the middle of a giant, cold ocean with water as black as the meanest heart in Hell.

I craned my neck up to the dark sky. Millions of stars filled up every corner, like I had never seen before. "Where are we?"

Lucifer pointed to an empty quadrant of the sky. "See that dark spot right there? That's what you'll see in a few million years when the light stops shining. We're looking into the past here, Katrina. Here, your world is still alive. Look."

Lou turned my attention to a bright shining part of the galaxy. "See right there? In that clump of stars, that's Earth, way before you arrived. Back when the dinosaurs roamed free. You still have a whole lifetime to live out there, before Apollo destroys your planet. Take comfort in that."

And I did. I took great comfort in it, actually.

"There's nothing else on this whole planet except water and this rock cave," Lucifer said, looking around. "They didn't want him to communicate with anybody or anything."

"Who is 'they?' What is he? Where are we?" I asked.

Dennis floated down from the sky with Connie in his arms. His landing was as perfect as his chiseled jaw. His wings curled back into his body with the grace only a heavenly body could manage. "That was quite the adventure! What's next?"

"The only way to get back our planet is to find Bacchus," Lucifer said. "The only way to do that is to find Zeus. The only way to find Zeus is to talk with Cronus."

"Like, the Titan Cronus?" Connie asked. "The one Zeus killed after Cronus ate him and all his siblings?"

"Well, that's the story Zeus tells, though I doubt Cronus would agree with his rendition. But yes, that's the Cronus we're talking about here."

I balled up my fists, ready for battle. "Awesome. What are we gonna find in there? Demons? Angels? Zombies? Hydras? Some sort of Sphinxian-direwolf hybrid?"

Lucifer shook his head. "There aren't any beasts guarding Cronus. He'd turn them to do his bidding. No, in there, all you're going to find are crazy mind tricks meant to drive you crazy. Only a strong mind will get you through this puzzle and on to Cronus's prison."

"Then I'll have no problem," I said. "If I can deal with the pits of Hell, I can deal with anything."

Lucifer turned to Dennis and Connie. "You don't need to come. I can open a portal to anywhere in the galaxy and you can rest easy for the remainder of eternity."

Dennis shook his head. "No way. These gods destroyed my home planet."

"And everybody we know," Connie added. "Except for Katrina and you, of course, the two jackholes we could've never seen again and been thrilled about it. We're going in."

Lucifer white-knuckled the flaming sword in his hands. "Then in we go. Remember, nothing you see inside these walls is real. They're meant to trip up a god and turn them stark raving mad, so stay on your toes. You've gotta be ready for anything."

*

The cave lit up red like a nasty, sex dungeon in Holland. Skittering and scattering sounds echoed across the rocks and shadows danced along the walls.

"This is a pathetic attempt, Lucifer. Like my dad trying to scare us at Halloween."

And *bam,* I was there.

Six years old. Halloween night. Dressed as Tinkerbell. My mom hand-stitched the frayed green dress herself. I'd never worn stockings before, but I begged and begged and begged for a pair of white stockings until she relented. She put my hair up in a bun and placed a tiara on top of my head. I swear to Christ, that costume, that moment, was as real to me now as the night I'd worn it.

Mom was diligent and kind. She spoke softly and rarely, but when she did, it meant something. "I love you," she told me under her breath. And she did. I loved her too. She was the last person I ever loved, honestly.

Mom grabbed my hand and led me into the kitchen. "Dad's making pumpkins." Dad's back was toward us when we walked in. Pumpkin juice splattered over the walls, except that it was red, not orange.

"Do you like what I've done with them?" Dad turned into the light, a maniacal look in his hollow eyes. On the table weren't pumpkins, but human heads. My cousin, Cassandra, eyeless, her tongue falling out of her mouth. My grandmother, a bloody frown carved into her face.

Dad held up the bloody knife. "You're next!"

"Mom!" I screamed. "Help!"

Mom wasn't protecting me now. She walked over to the table, pulled the scalp off my grandmother, and ate a piece of her brain.

She wiped some blood off her chin and grinned. "Tastes like chicken." Mom plucked another piece of brain and leaned toward me. "It's delicious. Wanna try a bite?"

I turned to run, but my stockings on my feet slipped on the floor. I fell on my ass and crawled toward the door, but it just kept moving further from me. The harder I kicked my legs, the further the door slid away.

Dad loomed over me with the knife in his hands. He pulled back the knife to strike, when I felt a sting in my face. I rubbed my cheek. In place of my dad's face was Lucifer's.

"Snap out of it, Katrina. Snap out of it!"

I was back in the cave. I was back under control.

"The others aren't doing any better," Lucifer said.

Connie's mouth frothed as she kicked the air. Dennis flopped across the ground with his eyes rolled back in his head.

"You can fight this," Lucifer said. "You have the Devil in you, and that power can conquer any madness. Connie and Dennis had it too good for too long in Heaven, but you know how to defeat this place. You know the madness of Hell. Fight this."

I balanced myself with Lucifer's shoulder. "How do you know all this, Lou?"

"I was an angel much longer that I was the Devil," he says. "I was there when it all began. I fought with Zeus when he battled Cronus. I know everything."

I grabbed Connie under her armpits and carried her. Foamy spit ran down her chin while she mumbled incoherently to herself.

"Stop…Off! Hate!"

"Wake up, girl!" Lucifer shouted, shaking her violently.

Connie swung her fist and clocked Lucifer across the jaw. Then, she swung at me. I blocked her fist punch, but she caught me in the gut.

I admit that I lost myself. My hands lit on fire and I uppercut Connie in the jaw. I swung back my fist, but Lucifer jumped between us. "Stop! Both of you!"

I sneered at him but couldn't deny that he was right. I looked down to see my hand on fire. Connie's hair smoldered as she patted it down.

"I-I-I'm sorry," I said, with a low voice.

Connie looked at me quizzically. She was back in the cave, but her emotions still swarmed under the surface. "What happened?"

I stood. "Nothing. Let's just get going."

"Where's Dennis?" Connie asked.

"I already carried him through the cave. It was easy once I knocked him out. Don't make me do the same for the two of you." Lucifer pointed at us. "Are you done killing each other yet?"

I nodded, rubbing my chest. My breath heaved in my chest. I knew it was all a memory, but it felt so real. "You still throw quite a punch."

Connie gingerly touched her chin as she nodded back. "You, too."

"Yes, yes," Lucifer said. "You are both vicious. Now will you come on? We've got a lot of work to do."

Chapter 5

Nine hundred years after the Apocalypse, I built up the nerve to find my parents. I'd wanted to see them before that, but I knew what Hell did to people, and there was very little I could do to ease their suffering. Though their death was the product of an old Devil, I knew they would blame me for their agony.

That broke my heart. The idea that my parents would suffer for all eternity under my rule was too much to bear. It's almost too much to bear now, but eventually your heart becomes callused when you're the Devil, even to the suffering of your parents.

And I must remain callused. I couldn't cry in front of them. There was little room for me to break down and cry during the Apocalypse, and I couldn't cry as the Devil for any reason. Crying is weakness, and it can destroy the fragile emotional state of the suffering. Showing any emotion gives them hope that their torture might be reprieved, and that simply isn't fair.

Most people would disagree, but I thought myself a fair Devil. It's very hard to make the punishment fit the crime and make sure people weren't enduring more than their own fair share of suffering. I wrote and distributed a fifty-thousand-page instruction manual on best practice when it came to torture, and forced every monster in Hell to read it, take a class, and pass a test before they could torture any of my wards. If that's not fair, I don't know the meaning of the word.

I gave denizens of Hell the most lenient punishments possible. I demanded enough space so they weren't mushed in ass to ankles. I tried my best to make them comfortable, even in their torture, but I also had a job to do, and that job was to ensure their suffering. Their unending suffering.

I never used any of the other medieval tortures that stemmed from Velaska and Hades' obscene methods. I even tried to give breaks to the tortured, but found those breaks made it even harder to restart the torture again, so I ceased them. That might seem cruel to you, but I know it was an act of mercy.

I found my father quickly enough. He was a monster after all, having become a zombie before he killed himself, which meant he worked in Hell instead of being tortured in it.

Lucifer assigned him to work in the third pit, supervising an eternal treadmill, a punishment for the slovenly. He even made a friend in one of the other zombies, Joshua Bowers, from Connecticut. They both liked to talk about Star Trek.

The minute I saw him, my callused heart turned to mush, and we held each other in a tearful embrace for almost an hour. With him safe, I moved him into my castle where I could keep a watchful eye over him. Then, I went to rescue my mother.

She'd been assigned to the sixth pit, far from the outskirts of Dis, the biggest metropolis in Hell. Most demons and Hell beasts lived inside its walls and commuted to their jobs by way of the inter-Hell highway I commissioned in the second century of my reign. Dis was a lot like any city on Earth, full of coffee shops, pool halls, and restaurants where a monster could kick back and unwind.

Mom's torture was one of the worst in Hell. She was disemboweled every day, and her entrails were eaten by crows. Every night she would regenerate her bowels and restart the process anew. Her overseer was a chilled-out demon who didn't like his work. Even in Hell there are levels of sadism, from needlessly cruel to almost kind, and his methods were as kind as possible, given the circumstances.

Knots formed in my stomach the entire ride out to my mother's torture site. I was thankful, for once, for the rough terrain of Hell. It took my mind off my impending meeting with my mother, as every bump knocked me out of my grisly daydream.

The putrid stench of rotting flesh, sizzling in the scorching heat of Hell and decomposing, caught me immediately when I stepped out of the car. I had grown accustomed to the smells of Hell, but this was rank by even my standards.

"What ho, Jason!" I shouted to a fat green orc monitoring a field of squawking crows in a pit beneath him.

"Good morning, ma'am. I'm surprised to see you."

"Didn't Carl tell you I was coming?"

"Yes, ma'am. Still surprised to see you though. It isn't going to be easy seeing your mom, you know, and I just figured—"

"I appreciate the concern, Jason, but I am the literal Devil. It's my job to oversee every horrible torture in Hell. I've seen things that would make your eyes melt and brain ooze out your nose. I think I can handle this."

"Yes, ma'am."

Concern was something you wouldn't imagine coming from a demon, but, in my term as Devil, I have learned that there are demons I kinda like. I've had drinks with them, dined with them, and even partied with them at my castle. I don't know if I had Stockholm syndrome, or they were simply kissing up to their boss, but honestly, some of them were downright cool.

A long, craggy staircase descended from Jason's watch station into the pit itself. The narrow stairs were broken in multiple places. The closer I got to the bottom, the louder the screams and the slower I took the stairs, until I was barely crawling down them.

When I stepped into the torture pit, the stickiness of the floors locked me in place for a moment. The entrails oozed a goo that stuck to the bottom of my Keds and made a sharp clomping sound when I moved. The wretched moans of the tortured souls drowned out the cawing of the birds, who gleefully choked down bites of large intestine.

Oddly, the look on the sufferers' faces wasn't one of pain, but resignation. They'd come to terms with their eternal torture, and their dead eyes showed no hope of salvation. It was there that I first realized the stupidity of eternal torture. It did nothing but overcrowd Hell with people who quickly grew numb to it. There was no repentance.

"Mom!" I shouted over the din. "Mom!"

The dank pit consumed all light, so I lit a fire in my hand and brought it up to my face. I crouched down and looked at the contorted faces of the damned, trying to place my mother.

"Mom!"

Finally, I found her, in the back of the pit, staring blankly into the darkness. The skin on her face was cracked from screaming, but aside from her gray complexion, she looked as I remembered her.

"Mom!" I rushed over to her. "Mom…Mom? Mom! Get off her!" I brushed the birds away, but they returned in force. "Jason! Get these birds off me!"

Jason turned a dial, and the birds turned away, flapping at the top of the pit, awaiting further instructions.

"Mom, look at me."

Her dead eyes rolled in her head until they met mine. She caught my gaze, but there was no recognition there.

"Can you hear me?"

"Uuuhhhh…" she moaned, but there was nothing else; nothing except the wounded groans of relentless death.

"What did you do to her?" I shouted to Jason.

Jason glared at me. "My job, ma'am! And I do a damn good job of it!"

It was true. Jason was doing his job, just like an electrician, or a plumber, or a mechanic. His job was to torture these poor souls within an inch of their lives, every day, for eternity.

"How long has this batch been down here?"

"Few hundred years or so."

"What are they in for?"

He shrugged. "They don't tell me these things. Sloth, I guess, or not being pious enough. Maybe not going to church. I don't remember. I just push the buttons."

I scooped my mother up in my arms. "Are you saying all these people are here because they didn't worship God hard enough for the few measly years they were on Earth?"

"Maybe. I guess they could've raped babies or something, but I think they stick your cock into an eternal meat grinder for that."

I carried my mother's torso, divorced from her legs, toward the stairs of the pit. "Shut it down, Jason. Shut it all down."

"What do you mean?"

I climbed the stairs, wobbling my mother's body over the cracked stairs. Her entrails slapped against the rock face. "I mean until you hear from me, no more torture of these people. Got it?"

The nipping of the crows grew as I reached Jason, along with their incessant flapping. They were hungry, and I'd stolen their food. Their cold black eyes shimmered in the fires of Hell. I knew what they were thinking. With one push of Jason's button, they would be on me.

"Can you just take her like that?" Jason asked as I passed him.

"I guess we'll find out," I replied.

I looked down in the pit one last time. For the first time in countless years, those poor souls weren't being pecked at, yet instead of jubilant celebration their groans grew into shrieks of terror.

"What's happening?" I asked.

"They're waking up, and realizing the pain they are in."

"Will it pass?"

"I don't know."

I looked up at the crows. I sighed. There was no pity in Hell. "Let them feed."

I didn't want them to, but it was the humane thing to do. I couldn't leave my mother with them, though. She screamed and moaned all the way to the car as her guts leaked sticky viscera all over my hands.

"It'll be okay. I promise." I placed her in the passenger's seat and strapped her in. "Don't worry, Mom. You don't have to worry about anything anymore."

As I drove, another slap brought me back to consciousness. It was Lucifer for the third time. "Wake up!"

I shook off my daze. "I'm going to murder you if you slap me again."

"You won't have to, we're out of the woods."

I sat at the opening to a massive cave. A low groan shook us from below. Connie and Dennis shivered in each other's arms, recovering from their experience.

"You got us out," Connie said to Lucifer.

"No thanks to you," Lucifer said. "Where were you this last time?"

"With my mom…the moment I decided to change Hell's incessant, eternal suffering policy."

"Yeah, that always bothered me, too."

"Then why didn't you change it?"

"I don't know. I guess I had nobody to change it for." Lucifer sat down on his goatish hind legs. He sighed loudly and his voice dropped to a whisper. "You have to understand, Katrina. It was a job for me."

"It's a job for me too."

"Maybe, but Earth isn't my home. It isn't anything for me. It's just another planet where I've worked."

"What does that mean?" I asked.

The groaning underneath us rose to a thunderous roar. "I think it will be better if I let him explain it to you. Come on." Lucifer grabbed his sword and reached out a hand to help Dennis stand.

"Wait, what do you mean, *him*?" I asked.

"You'll see," he replied. He walked toward the edge of the chasm and started down the stairs.

Meanwhile, on Hera's planet...

Hera hated the prison population on her home planet. Zeus sentenced her to house all the criminals and riff raff from across the universe in one location, and it smelled terrible. Hera liked beautiful palaces and pretty things, but her planet had neither. It was a barren wasteland filled with screaming and moaning prisoners.

"Please, Hera," Bacchus begged as Apollo dragged him through the dank walls of her prison. "You don't have to do this. I'll behave. I'll do anything you ask."

Hera never much liked Bacchus, or any of Zeus's bastard children, except for Apollo. She loved Apollo more than Ares and Hephaestus combined, and they were her blood. The lying whore who birthed him did one thing right, and that was to create a god chiseled from marble.

She tolerated Artemis, too, as she was Apollo's twin, and he loved her. She would give Apollo anything, and he wanted Artemis by his side. It was his one flaw.

To Hera, Artemis was nothing but a byproduct of a pregnancy, the remnants of chiseled marble so easily discarded. Nobody asked to see the leftover materials after a great masterpiece was constructed, and yet Hera was reminded of it every day. Artemis was a worthy and true shot, which made her valuable, but Apollo was a real god, one who never embarrassed her. Besides, Artemis loyally worked for Zeus before she came under Hera's employ, which drove the queen up a wall.

"Shut up," Apollo said, knocking Bacchus on the head.

Hera smiled. There was no compassion in Apollo, just cold, rational logic. She saw herself in Apollo, whereas Bacchus received all the slovenly irrationality of his father and the whore he fathered him with so many eons ago. It's not that Hera hated Zeus, but she did hate much about him, not the least of which that he put his dick into anything that moved, family or no. She did hate the children he conceived out of wedlock, each one a slap in her regal face.

Apollo dragged Bacchus around a sharp corner and into a massive holding cell, thousands of feet high. The tortured screams of gods and demons alike rattled the cages around them.

"Please, merciful Hera, save me!" Caerus, spirit of opportunity, shouted. He must not have known Hera at all, because mercy was not something she carried in her heart.

"Stop, Apollo," Hera said, walking up to Caerus's cell. She peered in at him. "You were useful once, yes?"

"I was useful, goddess. I can be again. I can be anything you want."

"I want nothing but for you to act like the sprite we molded you to be."

Others called Hera cold, but that wasn't it. She just demanded a level of perfection that none could meet. Millions lined her jail, all having committed offenses against the gods over the millennia. They waited judgment from Zeus, who never came to collect them.

That was the deal when Hera began her prison. She ran it, and Zeus cast judgment over the prisoners. Hera did her job, and she did it well. She captured every lone god who had evaded the law, sending their worlds into black holes throughout the universe, but the resolution Zeus had promised never materialized.

Sometimes, Hera worried that the sheer volume of black holes would consume the universe whole, sucking everything through it into nothingness, but that was not her problem to handle. In fact, she didn't know if it would be a problem at all. This world, this universe, was a tedious place, filled with beings who never lived up to her expectations. Perhaps she could find more worthy beings beyond the void.

Apollo threw Bacchus against a wall. "Stay."

Artemis drew her bow and aimed it at Bacchus's heart as Apollo opened the creaky metal gate to a cell and threw him inside.

"You will rot in here, brother, until Zeus sees fit to condemn you himself."

"How long will that be?"

Hera looked around at the countless prisoners. "At least ten thousand years, but upwards of a million. Maybe more. Enough human lifetimes for you to contemplate your failure."

Bacchus dropped to his knees. "Please, Hera. This is heartless. I only tried to please you."

"Then you have failed, and that sin is unforgiveable."

Chapter 6

Deep, guttural heaves quaked the walls of the cave as we descended into its depths. I lit myself ablaze, and Dennis did the same. His blue aura licked at my orange one, and together we made enough light to see in front of us.

"I warn you," Lucifer said. "what I'm about to show you has only been seen by a handful of beings in the entire universe, most of them gods, none of them humans."

"Why are you being so secretive?" I asked. "Just tell us what we're in for."

Lucifer turned back to Connie. "Alright, you seem to know a little bit about the Titans—"

"You mean the Greek Titans?" Connie said. "Like Rhea and Cronus and all them?"

Lucifer snapped his fingers. "Exactly."

Connie rolled her eyes. "Uhm, I might know a thing or two."

"When did you get to be a Greek scholar?" I asked.

"I got a life outside of you, Katie. It has been ten thousand years, you know. People learn things."

I grumbled at her. "I hate when you call me that."

Connie scoffed. "I hate when you question my knowledge."

"Fair enough," I said, throwing my hands in the air. "I guess we got a Greek scholar on our hands."

"Shut up, both of you," Lucifer said. "I can't handle any more of your arguing. It's giving me a migraine. Now, Connie. Tell me about Cronus."

"Cronus…right. Well, after he ate up all the Greek gods, Zeus cut open his stomach, chained him up, and imprisoned him in Tartarus."

Lucifer made a sweeping gesture with his hand. "Well, if that's true, then welcome to Tartarus."

The earth grumbled beneath our feet. "Of course, that is not true."

Two luminous slits opened in the darkness. Yellow light poured out of them as the tiny beams grew into giant round orbs a quarter mile wide. Beneath them, a knobby nose and craggy mouth peeked out. "But, of course, you knew that, Lucifer."

Lucifer's back stiffened and his voice sounded different when he spoke. "Yes, great Cronus. I do know as much."

"After all, you were there."

Every syllable Cronus spoke shook the cave. We struggled to keep our balance as the ground quaked and rocks tumbled from the walls. Lucifer reached the bottom of the stairs and bowed again. "What ho, Cronus? It is good to see you again."

"Mmm. I wish I could say the same for you. The Usurper is not with you this time?"

"He is not. I come to find him."

"And you bring these," he sniffed the air, disgusted. "These *things* with you. They are unworthy to be in my presence."

"Hey!" I shouted.

Cronus's saucer eyes turned bright red. "You dare raise your voice to me, insolent cur? Have you no idea who I am?"

"Me specifically, or us as a group? Because me specifically—no idea."

His eyes glowed redder for a moment, then a throaty bellow came from his mouth, shaking the earth until stalagmites toppled. "Ha! Very good, you insignificant thing. You are quite funny. I have not laughed in ages."

I tapped Lucifer on the shoulder. "Does he know I'm serious?"

Lucifer didn't answer. Instead he genuflected further. "Great Cronus, can you help us find the Usurper, so we can end him once and for all?"

"I have helped dozens of gods meet their final end at his hand. And now, you, lesser beings all, come to parlay with me. If I were to help, it would be a death sentence." The rock face wrinkled into a thoughtful expression. "I don't disdain you *that* much."

Connie stepped forward. "Yeah, well it's our death sentence to have!"

"Another feisty one."

"That's humanity for you," Lucifer replied. "They never listen."

Dennis stepped forward to join her. "Zeus and the other gods stole our home and sent it through a black hole. The only way to get it back is to find our God and free him. If that means dying, so be it, but we're not stopping until we're dead."

"*Do not* speak his name!"

Dennis shrunk back slightly. "My bad."

Cronus's nose crinkled on his rock-like face as he turned back to Lucifer. "Tell me about this...humanity. They are very different than gods."

"They are one of the Usurper's creations, which came to be billions of years ago. With these ones, he decided they should...evolve."

"What is this...evolve?"

"Instead of coming into the world fully formed as humans, as most animals had before, these ones mutate from little single-celled organisms to fish to reptiles to mammals and finally, to humans."

Cronus pushed his nose closer to Connie and Dennis, who squeezed each other's hands. "These little things were fish, too?"

"They have been every creature during their cycles."

Cronus tilted his head. "Fascinating. Finally, an interesting use of my essence. It only took billions of years and thousands of failures."

"Excuse me," I said. "But what do you mean, essence?"

"You'll have to accept my apology for these humans," Lucifer said. "One of their biggest flaws is unceasing inquisitiveness. It's an infuriating quality."

Cronus pondered for a second. His massive face collapsed onto itself. His eyes beaded, his nose creased, and his mouth curled as he stared at me. "Yes, I do see it. It's faint, but I see my essence. It's just a glimmer, a single cell in all the cosmos of their body, but I see it there. Amazing. You truly are…me."

"What do you mean by that?" Connie asked.

"Do you truly wish to know, weird humaninny thing? Then I will tell you, since you are my children and deserve to know the truth."

"Yes," I said. "That's what we've been saying."

"Very well. It started at the dawn of time. My parents, Uranus and Gaia, created the spark that led to this universe. They shaped the stars, and the planets, and everything you see. They loved each other more than you will ever know, in a way that you can never comprehend. The universe bored them, though. They wanted more. They wanted to create life—to create another one of themselves.

"I won't bore you with the combinations they tried, but they all failed. You must remember, they were children then, barely more than toddlers in the universe's standards, and they have had to learn everything on their own.

"Finally, after eons of trying, they created me. For a time, again, we were happy. My father created others like me. My brothers, Oceanus, Hyperion, Coeus, Crius, and Iapetus, and my sisters Mnemosyne, Tethys, Theia, Phoebe, Rhea, and Themis.

"Neither of my parents had any true love for us. They thought us mere playthings for their curiosity. How could they think any different? While they had created the universe, they were not part of it."

"Like when a kid gets sick of playing with Legos," Dennis said.

"I don't know any of those words," Cronus responded. "But their fascination soon turned into malice. They crashed galaxies into each other for fun, they destroyed planets and stars, and they stopped creating new things, which was the most magical part about them.

"And then I discovered that Uranus and Gaia had tired of this universe and would soon destroy it. I couldn't have that. I begged them to save us, to allow me to take it over, but they refused. I was nothing but a speck to them; an oddity. How dare I even speak to them?"

The cave rumbled as Cronus recalled his parents. "That's when I banded my brothers and sisters together in a battle against my mother and father. It raged for thousands of years, but eventually, in one last heroic stand, Rhea and I defeated Uranus. We took massive losses. All but a few of my brothers and sisters died, but I had something new. My father's allspark. The ability to create life from nothing.

"I created whole planets and beautiful galaxies, but they never survived when I left their immediate vicinity. I needed help. That's when I created the pantheon of gods you know today: Hera, Poseidon, Hades, Hestia, Demeter, and the traitorous one.

"We worked together to foster life across the galaxy. I created life and they watched over it, from the smallest bloom to the largest monster. We nurtured it until the world could survive on its own. Once the world was fully realized, we would leave for another planet."

"This is the same method Zeus uses today," Lucifer said.

Cronus's eyes lit red fire. "I told you never to say that name."

Lucifer bowed his head. "I'm sorry, your grace. Continue."

"I do not need your permission," he growled. "For a time, the system worked, but every system has its flaw, and mine was Zeus. He didn't like being ordered around, and he had other plans. He wanted to make dozens of planets at once and scale the entire galaxy into a habitable ecosystem. My life force wasn't strong enough to do that, and even if it was, we would need too many gods to sustain it. I didn't want to create a fighting force for him to use against me."

"Unfortunately, it didn't matter. Zeus didn't like that he wasn't the man in charge, so he set about changing it. He turned all my children against me, and they went to war with me. They locked my wife Rhea in another dimension before turning their sights on me."

"It was a long, hard battle and many gods died, but eventually Zeus, Hera, and Hades got the better of me. I thought I would be killed, but Zeus had other plans. He saw how creating life drained me and didn't want to be weakened in the same way, so he kept me alive, and drained my life force on an as-needed basis. Every millennium or so he comes to this cave and weakens me further, then leaves me to regain my strength until the next time my essence is required."

Cronus's eyes sunk down. "In this way, Zeus is always strong, stronger than any other god, and he leaves me too weak to fight back."

I stepped up in front of him. "I'll be honest with you. I only half listened to that story. It was very long, and quite boring, but I heard enough to know that Zeus is your enemy, and if he is your enemy, then he is my enemy, too. If fighting him will make you help us, then let us fight for you."

"That is very kind, but Zeus has learned much in his day. He has enough children to quell any uprising. A few with Hera, yes, but most with women and gods from around the cosmos, who are all willing to do his bidding."

"There's always a way, Cronus. We need to start with finding Bacchus, our god, the one that governed over my Earth. Can you help us do that?"

Cronus shook his head. "No. I can't, but I can tell you the last place Zeus created life. First, though, you must do something for me."

"What is it?"

"I am so hungry. I haven't eaten in ten million years. One of you must sacrifice yourself to me, so that I may eat."

Connie put up her hands. "We are *not* doing that."

"Then I cannot help you."

"Be reasonable," Lucifer said.

"Do not tell me about reason! This is a very reasonable request. You have asked of me a great favor, and I, in return, ask a small one."

Lucifer stared into the Mad Titan's eyes. "Then you will have it from me."

He turned and handed me his sword. "This sword will take you wherever Cronus tells you to go. All you have to do is picture the coordinates in your mind's eye and swipe the blade downwards."

He removed the spherical necklace that hung around his neck and placed it around mine. "Don't lose this. It's very special to me. It was given to me by my predecessor, Velaska. I thought it was lost to time, but Bacchus gave it back to me. He gave me my life back. He...and you."

I shook my head. As much as I didn't like Captain Sweatstain, I didn't want to see him get eaten. "Don't do this."

Lucifer smiled as he turned back to Cronus. He spread his arms wide and tilted back his head. "Here I am, Cronus. I give myself to you freely in exchange for—"

"NO!" I screamed. "I will not let this happen!"

I gripped the sword in both hands. My whole body lit on fire at once, glowing red and orange in equal measure. "I have lost everything today, and I won't lose you, too."

Cronus sighed. "While I appreciate your moxie, it took a pantheon of gods to defeat me last time. You have no chance here."

"I've never had a chance," I responded. "And that's never stopped me before."

"Can you just be cool for one second?" Connie whispered to me. "Lucifer is willingly giving himself up. Just chill out."

"I've never been chill, not for one second, in the last ten thousand years. I'm not gonna start now."

I charged forward and slashed at the Mad Titan's jaw. The sword bounced off with a reverberating *thud* as I fell against the ground. "I told you," Cronus said. "This course of action is foolish."

I ran forward again and stabbed at his chest, but again my sword did nothing except bounce off the Titan's stone hide. A guttural laugh came from inside Cronus's belly. "You are a funny thing, human. I have never seen such fire before. I have never seen such...spunk. I am inclined to let you win, just for the sheer fun of watching you fight Zeus."

"Tell me where he is, and I will destroy him."

"Feed me, and I will."

His eyes narrowed on me, and I saw an opening. His eyes were the only place not covered in craggily rock. I took a running leap and boosted myself into the air with a burst of flame. The fire carried me twenty feet, and with a great slice, I cut across the Mad Titan's eye. He bellowed in pain.

"How dare you hurt me, human!"

I latched onto the bottom of his eye lid and made a second thrust. Effluvia spurt out on me. I saw the back of his eye, where I could enter his brain and light it on fire if he didn't tell me what I wanted to know.

"Tell me what I want to know, and I will end this."

"Katrina!" Connie shouted. "Stop!"

But my fire only burned brighter, until Cronus's rocky hand blotted out the cave light and pulled me from his eye socket.

"Katrina…Foolish human. Now I will destroy everything you hold dear."

I struggled against Cronus's stony hand, but it was too strong for me. There was nothing I could do but watch as his other hand rose to smash Connie, Dennis, and Lucifer.

"Wait!" I shouted. "This was all me—they've done nothing wrong. Don't blame them." I paused for a moment, realizing the implications of what I was about to say. "Take me instead."

Cronus rolled me around his palm. "Hmm, that is an interesting proposition. Your seething anger would make for a delicious meal. However, I believe you are the only person here with the force of will to defeat Zeus, and he is the meal I truly want."

Cronus' damaged eye repaired itself. He looked at the assorted group around me with both eyes. "I'm going to make you a deal. I will not eat any of you today, but I will keep one as my…guest. Should this 'Katrina' bring back Zeus to me, you will be free to go. However, should she fail me, I will eat you alive."

Lucifer stepped forward. "That sounds like a fair compromise, my lord. I will accept the task of being your prisoner."

Another chuckle came from the Mad Titan. "Nobody cares enough about you to fight to save you." Cronus looked past Lucifer and saw the undying love between Connie and Dennis. They were so cute it was almost sickening. "The girl. She is the one I want."

Dennis pushed Connie behind him and spread his wings. "Never!"

"I could kill you all now, if you would prefer. You and Lucifer are archangels. Katrina is a Devil. You can fight. This little one. She is nothing. She is just another one of the countless dead."

"Alright, I'll do it," Connie said, turning to Dennis. "It's okay, honey. You'll come back for me. I know you will. Just don't get dead."

"No! I won't risk your life over mine."

"It's not your choice to make," Connie said. "It's mine." She wrapped her arms around Dennis and squeezed him tight.

"Do we have a deal?" Cronus asked.

Connie nodded. "Yes."

The Mad Titan opened his palm and dropped me to the floor. Connie grabbed my hand and pulled me to my feet, smiling. "I always knew you would get me killed. I just didn't know how many times."

"I'm sorry."

"Don't apologize, Katie. Just come back, okay?"

"Your life is in my hands and you're calling me Katie?" I gave her a half smile. "I'll come back."

I walked over to Lucifer and Dennis. Dennis's fury was pouring off him. He couldn't even look at me. I knew he was angry, but there wasn't anything I could do, except find Zeus and bring him back to save Connie. If I did that, I could fix everything.

Chapter 7

Connie was the first friend I ever made in Overbrook. I was
an adorable, little first grader with short, cropped hair and a
terrible attitude even back then. I was garbage at making
friends. I had a temper and would rather knock the teeth out of
somebody than play with them. I guess that never changed
much.

When I walked into school that first day, I swear there
was a record playing because it screeched to a halt the second
I walked inside. The romper I was wearing accentuated just
how out of touch I was with fashion, and my wild bangs jutted
out from underneath a pink hat adorned with a unicorn. I was
a disaster. My knee-high socks and Doc Martens immediately
caught snickers, but there was one girl who didn't snicker.
She was tall and thin, with crazy hair and bright-white
sneakers. She didn't say anything to me then, but I could see
the laughing pissed her off something fierce.

At lunch, I brought my homemade sandwich in a brown
paper bag into the cafeteria, ready to conquer my fears and
find a place to sit in the crowded room. You couldn't just sit
in the corner and eat alone. If you did that, you would be left a
pariah. And you couldn't just presume somebody would let
you sit near them because, if denied, you would be mocked.
Forever. That was the conundrum I faced walking into the
cafeteria and hearing my second record skip of the day. I
closed my eyes for a moment and muttered a prayer to myself.

"Please God, just let me get through this in one piece."

I would love to say that, after that, somebody beckoned
me over, but that isn't what happened. Of course, it wasn't.
The gods are shit weasels. I passed through every table in that
cafeteria and watched as people scooted around and moved
chairs so that I wouldn't have a place to sit. At one, Daniel
Groves called me ugly. At another, Dave Kochbeck threw a
spitball at me. Children are the worst. Finally, I found a table
at the end of the cafeteria, away from everybody.

I was halfway through my bologna sandwich when the girl in the white sneakers sat down across from me. I would like to say she was the most popular girl in school, but she wasn't.

"You mind if I sit here?"

I swallowed a big bite of my sandwich. "You sure you want to? There's a lot of other places."

She looked around, clearly disgusted with what she saw. "Yeah. I'm sure."

"Be my guest."

She tossed down her tray and took a seat. The food on her plate looked less appetizing than what I brought, but she ate it without wincing. "Can I tell you something about this place?"

"If you want."

"It's full of jerks," she said with a mouth full of mystery meat. "All of 'em. Every single one, including me. If you wanna survive, you gotta be a jerk too."

"I'm not much for that."

"Don't worry. I'll teach you, if you want."

I smiled. "I'm Katrina."

"Connie."

We were best friends from that moment. She showed me how to navigate the world: how to talk to boys, the right clothes to wear, and even what teams to join. By the end of middle school, I was a hot, confident woman ready to take on the world. By the end of high school, I could kick some serious ass after Connie dragged me to Krav Maga. She's the reason I survived this long.

And how have I thanked her? Watched her brother die twice, lugged Dennis across the Black Zone so Connie could shoot him in the face, dragged her into Hell, then into my war with Heaven, watched her get killed, and now left her to rot with Cronus. I was a terrible friend, and she had every reason to hate me. So did Dennis.

I'd watched their pained faces as they said goodbye to each other in Cronus's cave. The last words she whispered to him during their final embrace were, "Come back for me."

She could have been scared, but there was no hesitation in her voice. She knew he would come back, just like he had a thousand times before. As I tumbled through space, I realized that I would never believe anything as much as she believed Dennis would return for her. I certainly didn't have that much faith. I hoped we could defeat Zeus, but also knew that nobody had before.

There must have been other uprisings against him before, led by beings much more exciting and powerful than me, Dennis, and Lucifer. The difference was that I was bold enough to expect to win; bold enough to risk Connie's life to prove it. I hoped I was right. I'd watched her die once. I couldn't bear the thought of it happening again.

I caught my last glimpse of Connie as the portal collapsed upon itself, her head tilted toward the floor, waiting for her savior to return. I rolled out of the portal into a lush, green field. Across the field, Lucifer and Dennis wiped grass off themselves.

I couldn't shake the feeling of déjà vu. Everything looked like Earth. The blue sky was filled with fluffy, white clouds. A fresh, summer breeze flowed through the green grass. Butterflies flapped their wings across dewy flowers.

"I know what you're thinking, Katrina," Lucifer said. "It's like this because the gods are a combination of unimaginative and vain. They want worlds that look familiar and pleasant to them. The clouds, and the trees, and the flowers…the gods are pleased by these things, so the humans they create are pleased by them, too."

"Does every inhabitable world look like Earth?"

Lucifer chuckled. "Not every one. Sometimes, life grows without the gods' knowledge and outside their purview. Those planets can evolve to be anything—and do, until Zeus puts them down. The ones controlled by the gods, though, they're filled with things the gods want to see. They want to see more things like them."

The rolling hills of flowers carried on into the distance where the sunset reflected off the rooftops of a town, making it shine like a beacon. Lucifer pointed to it. "There. That's where we'll find more information on the planet."

I turned to Dennis as we walked. "I'm sorry about—"

"Just don't, Katrina. Let's just focus on the mission at hand."

"Do you remember the last time I saw you, Dennis. Alive at least?"

"Yeah. You watched Connie shoot me in the head."

"No. Before that. Do you remember when I carried you across the Black Zone after Connie's car broke down? Or when I let you escape those demon dogs by leading them away from you? How about the minotaur that knocked down a building as I tried to escape and almost killed me? Do you remember any of that?"

"I remember everything, Katrina. That's the curse of being an angel. Perfect memory."

"Then maybe you can remember I tried to save your life because I love you and Connie. Sometimes I was a real dick about it, but I never stopped loving you guys. She was the best friend I ever had. I would do anything to help her...and you. So just remember *that*, okay?"

I ran forward toward Lucifer. I didn't look back to see if my words landed, but I hoped they had. Dennis and Connie were the two closest things to family I had left.

"So how will this town help us? Are we gonna smash through it until the gods come for us?"

"You're funny, Katie. Has anybody ever told you you're funny?"

"Please don't call me Katie, and yeah, I've been laughed at before."

"Well, Katrina, have you ever been to Greece or Rome or Egypt before?"

"No."

"Seen pictures?"

"Sure."

"Then what can you tell me about every city you passed in the ancient world?"

"They had a ton of columns?"

"Well, yes, but I mean the temples. Hell, what do you see in every city *now?* Lots of churches, right?"

"So many churches. You know, Satanists started worshiping me after you left."

Lucifer shuddered. "Ugh, they are an annoying bunch. Always sacrificing pigs and goats. As if I needed more goats."

"Tell me about it. What am I gonna do with a goat?"

"But that's the point, isn't it? Every single city is filled with churches, synagogues, mosques—places of worship, right? And they're all devoted to Bacchus, aren't they?"

"Well, they didn't *know* it was Bacchus, but sure."

"The old gods worked the same way. Their cities built temples to them. We're going to find out who this city worships."

"What if it's unfriendly?"

"Then we keep walking until we find a city with a god that can get us into Mount Olympus."

"I know that place. It's where the gods lived on Earth."

"Heaven is just a retooled Mount Olympus, as it will be on this planet, but you can't get in without approval from a god, just like on Earth. Heaven is home to the gods, and that's why Hell is the default for everybody."

"Is that why Apollo was so pissed off in Heaven? Because humans were around?"

"Yes. Bacchus's Heaven is a bastardization of what the gods want. They want a closed-off space where the gods and humans never interact."

"Then why did they screw so many humans? Both screw with them and literally have sex with them?"

"That's different. Gods want to interact with humans when the humans have no choice in the matter. Let humans into Heaven, though…now it's a two-way street. More importantly, if you let humans into Mount Olympus, they attain a certain level of godhood." He waved a hand towards Dennis. "Take a look at this guy. Take a normal human, let him into Heaven, and *boom!* He's an archangel. To any self-respecting god that is a no-no. Humans are below gods, not equal to them in any way."

"What about me becoming a Devil? Is that a no-no, too?"

"Yes, as was me taking over for Velaska." Lucifer sighed. "Can we talk about something else?"

"Suit yourself."

And so, we were silent, each of us contemplating our own burden, and the task in front of us. Lucifer looked up into the heavens; Dennis down at the Earth, and I looked straight ahead at the small town in the distance.

It looked like the pictures I'd seen in textbooks of ancient Athens or Rome. The thatched roofs evoked a feeling of history and the columned marble, a sense of wonder. It was like stepping into a time machine.

We exited the meadow onto a small, dirt path that led to town. Farmers pushed donkeys full of merchandise, and other horse-drawn buggies lined the path. On either side of the road, piles of horse manure were stacked high.

"Watch out, Dennis," I called over my shoulder, but it was too late. He'd soiled his perfect boots with a big mound of manure. I couldn't help but laugh as he hopped around trying to wipe it off.

"Thanks for the warning!" he growled.

"Anything for you, buddy."

He levitated off the ground. "Enough of this. I'm flying."

As we neared the town, the whispers began. People stopped their animals to watch us pass. It wasn't hard to see why. While I maintained my devilishly good looks, Lucifer was half goat, half monster and Dennis floated over the streets with his massive wings.

The mumbling continued as we approached the gates of the town. A crowd dressed in gilded togas surrounded a plump, smiling, red-faced man, the kind of red-faced you get after drinking a ton of red wine over several decades. He waved a fat hand at us.

"What ho, good travelers! Welcome to Brunatai."

"What ho!" Lucifer replied, waving. "Thank you for the fine greeting."

"Of course. We always welcome parlays with the gods. How can we be of service?"

I stepped forward. "We aren't gods. We are...we're gods. We are requesting that we might be granted... to...entreat... with the god of this town." Fancy talk didn't come easy.

The plump man smiled. "Absolutely. She welcomes those that pay her respect. Have you brought an offering?"

Dennis spoke up. "What kind of offering?"

Lucifer slapped himself in the head. "No way."

It took me another moment to see what Lucifer saw—a thirty-foot tall, marble statue dedicated to a beautiful woman with long thick hair and a crown atop her head. "What is it?"

"Velaska."

"Ah," the fat man said. "You know of our goddess. Very good. Then you know what it takes to entreat with her."

"I do."

"And you have it?"

Lucifer turned toward me. "May I please have the necklace?"

I pulled off the spherical necklace from around my neck and handed it over. He held the necklace up in front of the plump man and the entire congregation dropped to their knees. "I am Lucifer. I took over as Devil for Velaska on a planet not unlike this one. I offer this necklace, a sworn symbol of my devotion to her, as proof of my worthiness."

"I am Helobrius, good Devil." He pulled an identical necklace from inside his toga. "You have proved your worth. Come and entreat with us."

Meanwhile, on Hera's planet...

Apollo and Artemis followed as Hera made her way through the moaning chorus of the dismal jail. Eventually, she reached a gilded door which stood three stories tall and rested at the end of a twisted corridor. A Cyclops tugged at a gilt chain and the large door inched open at a glacial pace. She walked through the golden barrier separating the jail from her castle, ready for a relaxing nap after a long day of doing Zeus's bidding.

The inside of her castle was as ostentatious as the prison was dreary. Her footsteps on the shiny marble floors echoed against the walls and gilded pillars. Oil paintings of herself hung from every wall. Painted reliefs of Hera's great deeds adorned even the ceilings, accented with Apollo's conquests through the universe.

The hallway from the prison dead-ended at the throne room—all of them did, by Hera's design. Every hallway was a spoke in the great castle, and all of them led to her, just as it should be.

The sparkling throne, fit only for Hera, raised thirty feet above the rest of the room, with a smaller throne on either side for Apollo and Artemis. Hera didn't want a place for Artemis, but Apollo insisted. His infatuation with a god far below his standing exasperated Hera, but her love for Apollo outweighed her anger. It was his only flaw.

"Goddess, Goddess, Goddess!" Urania screamed at her as she entered the throne room. "I have news."

Urania was a minor god, far below Hera's station to deal with normally, but she was a wiz with telescopes and astronomy, which helped Hera to police every inch of space.

"Can it wait, Urania? I'm very tired."

"Unfortunately not, ma'am. You asked me to alert you if ever somebody entered Cronus's cave that wasn't Zeus, right?"

Hera's ears perked up. "That's correct."

"Well, twenty minutes after you picked up Bacchus, four beings entered the cave."

Urania handed Hera a set of pictures that clearly showed Lucifer, Katrina, Connie, and Dennis entering the cave. "Poor, poor unfortunate souls. They won't last three minutes in the cave of madness."

Urania looked away, scared.

"What is it, Urania?"

The little goddess sighed. "We found them again, just a couple minutes ago. They appeared again on Aphrodite's planet."

Hera fumed. Her face turned beet red and she raised her hand in the air to strike Urania, who cowered in fear. "How did this happen?"

"I'm sorry, ma'am, but I don't know. I am just in charge of the telescopes, not figuring out what to do with the information they give me. That's way above my class."

Hera found Urania's pathetic humility pleasing, and she collected herself. "You're right, Urania. Do you have the coordinates?"

Urania handed Hera a piece of paper. "Yes, ma'am."

Hera turned to Artemis. "Do something with this. I don't want to hear of this nuisance again."

Artemis nodded. "May the other gods have mercy on their souls, for I shall not."

Chapter 8

The townsfolk sang hymns as we walked through the bazaar. Hundreds of peasants stopped their haggling and sang with the group. They abandoned their copper kettles and porcelain statues to watch us pass. With each step, their chorus grew.

Velaska Velaska
Your mercy knows no bounds
Your perfection knows no equal
You are everything
Our savior
Velaska Velaska
Your mercy knows no bounds
Your perfection knows no equal
You are everything
Our savior
Forever.

Lucifer waved at the crowd, smiling. He loved the attention. "It's impolite not to make a scene, Katrina. These people think you're a god."

"But we're not gods and this is stupid."

I looked back at Dennis. He spread his wings and floated above the ground, much to the thrill of the crowd. "The bigger a scene you make, the more likely Velaska will take an interest."

"If that's true, then I don't want to 'entreat' with her."

"Oh. I'm sorry," Dennis said. "I thought you would do anything to help Connie. Didn't you just say that like twenty seconds ago?"

I sighed. "Fine."

I knew just the trick.

A cascade of fire lit my whole body. It started with a light red and grew into a flaming, blue ball. I sent fireballs into the air as we passed through the streets, which delighted and horrified the crowd. At the apex of their flight, the fireballs cracked into fireworks and exploded through the air. The eyes of the crowd stood affixed to the sky, and, when the explosions were finished, the people collectively shouted, "Again! Again!"

I indulged them with another show, each explosion more magical than the last. The cheers and screams swelled as we reached the entrance to the temple. The building was ornately trimmed with gold and replete with colorfully painted statues of large men whose giant penises flanked the front entrance.

"That's a, uh, nice statue you got there." I tried not to giggle.

"Yes," Helobrius said. "They were commissioned by Velaska herself. I find them slightly revealing for my tastes, but who am I to argue with a god?"

"You are nobody." I could get used to talking to people like I was a god.

"Yes." Helobrius cleared his throat. "Quite. Please quell your fire and we will continue on into the summoning chambers."

I turned off my flame as we stepped into the temple. Inside, the chamber was as grand as the outside. Massive pillars, hundreds of feet high, held up a ceiling mosaiced with glorious reliefs of Velaska and her various dealings over the centuries.

"Velaska is a master of manipulation," Lucifer said. "Each of these images shows another innocent she tricked. See that one." He pointed to the mosaic of an angel kneeling in front of Velaska as she snapped her fingers. "That one's me."

"Not necessarily. There's lots of angels."

"It's me. I know it is. She's particularly proud of deceiving me."

"Fair enough, Lou. I didn't know you were so touchy about these sorts of things."

Dennis brushed past us, heading further into the temple. "Let's just find this god and be done with it. The sooner we're out of here, the better."

We entered a room painted like the bluest sky of my childhood. Hundreds of candles bathed the room in a dull glow and shimmered against the surface of the reflecting pool that filled most of the room. A grinning statue of Velaska stood against the far wall. Paintings of the goddess hung on every surface and a chorus hummed of her greatness.

Velaska Velaska
Your endless beauty is unmatched
Your kindness is unparalleled
You are everything
Our savior
Velaska, Velaska

"Oh brother," Lucifer said under his breath. "It's everything she ever wanted."

*

Helobrius climbed onto a marble podium overlooking the reflecting pool. "Now, we shall call upon the great goddess to bestow her countenance upon us. Please, will you join me?"

Helobrius gestured to Lucifer, who plodded up to the podium. "You have the blessing of Velaska upon you, and she will hear our prayers if we both chant together."

"I don't know about that."

I gave Lucifer the "are you crazy?" eyeballs.

The priest caught his tone, too, and asked, "Do you not wish to entreat with the great goddess?"

A muscle in Lucifer's jaw twitched. "No, no...we do."

"Then chant."

Velaska Velaska
Your endless beauty is unmatched
Your kindness is unparalleled
You are everything
Our savior
Velaska, Velaska

Lucifer joined in on the second verse, reluctantly. His teeth gnashed the words out the side of his mouth.

Velaska Velaska
Your mercy knows no bounds
Your perfection knows no equal
You are everything
Our savior
Forever.

The necklaces around Lucifer and Helobrius's necks glowed and vibrated. Helobrius pattered his feet and waved his arms in excitement. "It's working, it's working! Come to us, Velaska. We implore you to grace us with your presence."

A sharp wind blew out the candles. The walls shook, and a column of water rose from the middle of the reflecting pool and shot into the air. It splattered onto the ground and rose again as a beautiful woman with flowing yellow hair. Her crown glowed the same blue as the medallions Lucifer and Helobrius wore.

"It is I, Velaska. Mother of the moon and stars, and—oh, no." Her eyes fell on Lucifer. "What do *you* want?"

"What ho, Velaska," Lucifer said. "It's been a long time."

Velaska floated toward Lucifer, dripping a trail of water behind her. Yet, she didn't look wet. "You are looking well. I like the horns. It's a good look."

"Bacchus did this to me after my coup failed, so thank you very much for the suggestion."

Velaska threw her head back and cackled. "Bacchus did that to you? He really is quite a vengeful bastard. No wonder that whole planet went downhill."

"I suppose you heard, then?"

Velaska floated up the podium stairs. "About Earth and all the planets around it being sucked into the void? We've all heard, honey. It's a small universe."

"Great Velaska," Helobrius said. "It is a great hon—"

"Shut up, Helobrius. Grownups are talking."

"Of course, your grace. It's just that—"

Velaska snapped her fingers. A spout of water comported into a needle and thread, then sewed Helobrius's lips together. "Now, Lucifer. Why have you summoned me? I hope it was just to catch up."

"It was not. If it were up to me, I'd only summon you to destroy you."

Velaska ran her fingers playfully across Lucifer's chest. "Please, Lou. Why do you foist such venom on me? We made a deal, and I honored my side of it, did I not?"

"At what cost to me?"

"Ah ah ah." She wagged her finger. "You should have read the fine print. Now, my question was, did I honor our agreement? Did I give you the means to end your bondage and be set free?"

"Yes. You did."

"And was it my fault that you failed in your service to me and were turned into this…" she gave him a concerned, appraising look, "…thing?"

"It was—"

"Not. I will answer that for you. It was *not* my fault."

"You only gave me this power so that you could escape Earth."

"Of course, that's true, idiot. I was the queen of Hell. Do you know how popular that made me? Zero popular! And now look at me—people build shrines to me here. They love me! Why would I not want that? But that's not the point. The point is that I fulfilled my commitment to you."

Lucifer groaned. "I suppose so."

"And yet you are still bitter. Now, is that fair?" Velaska snapped her fingers. The stitches on Helobrius's mouth vanished. "Tell me, fat one, is that fair to your god?"

Helobrius shook his head. "No, my queen. It's not fair."

Velaska nodded. "I didn't think so, either. What's the deal then, Lou? Why are you here?"

I stepped up, sick of listening to Velaska's crap. "We're here to kick Zeus's ass."

Velaska turned to me with her lip curled. "I smell Hell on you."

"Yeah. Well that's where I've been for the past ten thousand years. It doesn't wash off easy."

Velaska floated over to me. "Are you a damned soul? My goodness. They keep you in very fine shape these days. My souls were always so ragged and haggard."

"I'm not a damned soul. I'm the Devil. Or at least I was until Apollo plunged Earth into a black hole."

Velaska laughed. "Oh my god, Lou. You tricked this poor girl into taking over for you? *That's* rich. And you think I'm bad. You, my love, have no room to judge me."

"I didn't trick her...Bacchus did." Lucifer was straight-up pouting at this.

Velaska roared. "That old drunk tricked you? Oh, that's too good. And what happened to you, Lou? How did you get out of it?"

"Katrina...killed me." With his chin tucked into his chest and his shoulders hunched, he thumbed in my direction.

"Killed? By a mortal?" Velaska put her hands to her chest and took a few melodramatic steps backward. "This is too rich! I can't possibly finish it. My dear, dear Katrina. You must tell me all about it."

Velaska grabbed my hand, but I pulled it away from her. "We don't have time. We've got to find Zeus and bring him back to Cronus. Now."

Velaska's smile turned into a pout. "You are no fun."

"That's what I hear. Can you get us into Mount Olympus or not?"

"And very blunt. That won't get you far with the gods, missy. We like being wined, dined, and adored. It's part of the whole experience. Look at this place. These people have lavished me with gifts and they would never dare seek Olympus. Why would you be so bold as to ask?"

I lit myself aflame. "Because they can't kick your ass. I can."

Helobrius jumped in front of Velaska. "How dare you speak that way to our goddess! In her own temple, no less!"

Velaska pushed Helobrius aside. "Thanks, pal. I can fight my own battles."

I popped a fireball into the air. "Is that what you want? You want me to kick your ass?"

Velaska clicked her tongue. "You remind me of a headstrong fairy I once knew. Or was it a pixie? She was ornery and willful as well, but she bent the knee eventually, when I offered her something she wanted."

"You want to make a deal with me?"

"Not with you. With him." Velaska turned to Dennis. "I've seen my share of cherubs in my life, but this is the most strapping specimen I've ever come across."

"I'm not for sale," Dennis snorted.

Velaska caressed his chest. "Everything is for sale, honey, for the right price. I smell love on you. It has an intoxicating smell. You never forget it. Tell me, where is the woman you love?"

"She's locked in Cronus's cave as his prisoner."

"And do you want her back?"

"More than anything."

"Tell me, what would you do to see her again?"

"Conquer the heavens."

"Seems so droll. I was thinking of something a bit more…" Velaska squeezed Dennis's crotch. "…fun."

Dennis jumped back. "Never!"

"Oh please. In all these years with a human sewer rat girlfriend you never once thought about shacking up with a god? Even for a night? I mean, what is one night in the balance of eternity?" She came in closer once more. "I'm very good."

"I couldn't—"

"This isn't about his pecker, Velaska," Lou said. "This is about his purity. He's loved the same woman for ten thousand years, never straying from her side, and you want to corrupt that, as you've already corrupted me. Tainting purity has always been your sick drug, and the only pure being in this whole temple is Dennis."

Velaska turned away from Dennis. "That's true. You take all the fun out of it, Lou."

"I have let you have your fun for the last thirty thousand years, give or take, and now I come to ask for a favor. You owe me that after what you did to me. Tell us where Zeus is and help us take him down."

Velaska grinned. "You have a favor to ask, but nothing to bargain with. My answer is no. Come back to me when you aren't so ill prepared."

Velaska snapped her fingers and she was gone. A puddle of water remained in her place.

"What just happened?" I shouted. "What did you do?"

Lucifer threw his hands in the air. "I didn't do anything!"

"Untrue!" Helobrius shouted. "You are nonbelievers, unworthy of the great Velaska, and she showed you the door. I have brought great shame on my people by allowing you to come here and speak with her. Now be gone! I banish you from this city!"

With that, an arrow shot into Helobrius's heart and he fell, dead. I whirled around to see Artemis's hulking figure staring back at me, brandishing a bow pointed at Lucifer's heart. "He talked too much."

"Artemis," Lucifer said. "It's so good to see you again."

"Why have you come here? Why were you within the sanctum of Cronus? Why have you defied the gods?"

"Those are all very good questions, and they deserve answers, they truly do. And I do have answers for you." Lucifer bent down and picked the necklace off of Helobrius's dead body. "However, the simple fact is that I don't think you will like them."

"It is not I who you must convince. Hera demands your heads."

Lucifer walked toward her, unimpressed by her giant bow that tracked his every step. "Of course. Hera. She is a demanding boss, isn't she?"

"She is not my boss."

"And yet you work for her, doing her bidding. Do you not?"

"I work at the behest of Zeus, to further the gods' mission in the universe."

Lucifer placed the necklace into my hand but didn't take his eyes off Artemis. "Of course. Of course. And how does stealing Bacchus further your place in the universe, exactly?"

"Bacchus was a fool. His actions made us all look bad." Artemis drew her bow. "Now stop stalling."

I whipped the necklace over my head and the spiral medallion glowed blue like the one around Lucifer's neck.

Lucifer turned to Dennis. "Hold her off. Don't let her destroy the temple." He pulled me into the reflecting pool, humming Velaska's hymn under his breath. An arrow sailed over my head just as I sank under the water. I clawed against him, but Lucifer squeezed me tighter and dragged me down until a blue light washed over us.

The water spat us out onto a lush field of bright green. In front of us, Velaska was stretched out on a long chair being fanned and fed grapes by two naked men. When she saw us, she sat up. Grapes and penises scattered everywhere. "What the—" she shouted. "Oh. It's you. I thought we were done. No means no, Lucifer."

"The situation—" Lucifer panted. "—has changed. Take a look."

"Ugh." Velaska rolled her eyes in disgust but clapped her hands so that the water pooled into a giant television screen, projecting a great battle between Artemis and Dennis. Dennis ducked and dove between the town's marble buildings, avoiding every one of Artemis's arrows.

"That boy is impressive. I've never seen anything move so fast before. I wonder if he has the stamina to last where it counts."

I tried not to curl my lip. "Your town is being destroyed."

Right then, Dennis slammed through a marble column and it collapsed atop Artemis. Moments later, she sprang forth without a scratch.

Velaska popped a grape into her mouth. "There are other towns."

"Yes, but what do you think will happen to the other towns who rely on you for protection when they hear of this? Do you think they will move to a new god…a *stronger* god?"

Velaska spat out her grape. "You have my attention."

"I propose a deal," Lucifer said. "If we can rid this town of Artemis, you take us to Olympus."

"Or I could take care of this myself."

"You could, but we both know you don't like getting your hands dirty. Especially against Artemis. What if she beats you? How would that reflect on you?"

"Poorly."

"Exactly. Now, if you send in your champions to fight her, and they win, you get to take all the credit. And if we lose, we get all the blame. It's a win-win. In return, we just ask a small favor."

Velaska sniffed. "Getting into Mount Olympus is no small favor."

"Maybe not, but ask yourself, is the juice worth the squeeze?"

Velaska thought for a moment. "Okay, Lucifer. You have a deal. If you can defeat Artemis, then I will take you to Mount Olympus. But if you fail, then you leave this planet forever, in disgrace, and return to the void from whence you were banished."

I stuck out my hand. "You have a deal."

Velaska snapped her fingers. "Decisive. I like that."

The medallions on our necklaces glowed blue again as we dematerialized on our way back to the city.

"Did you..." I tilted my head, trying to place Lucifer's words. "Did you just quote *The Girls Next Door* to her?"

"What?" Lucifer said. "I liked that movie."

Chapter 9

The reflecting pool spat us out in the middle of a war zone. Arrows flung past at incredible speeds and embedded in the walls of buildings. Fire spread wildly across the floor. Dennis zig zagged through the temple, barely avoiding Artemis's arrows.

"About time you showed back up!" Dennis shouted as he sped past in a blur.

"I thought I told you not to let her destroy the temple!" Lucifer motioned at the wreckage. "Why are you here?"

"It was either this or have her kill about a thousand people outside. I figured this was better."

"Boys! What's done is done. Let's just take care of her now!"

I pulled out my sword and Lucifer unleashed his claws, but he was too out of shape to make a difference with his fists. Just walking into town, he was moaning and grunting. I handed him the sword. "Here. You need this more than I do."

"What will you use?"

I lit myself on fire. "I've always been good with my hands. Keep her distracted."

I rushed toward Artemis, dodging her arrows, and slid under her planted feet. Lucifer followed behind me and landed a crushing blow to her armor, lodging his sword in her rib cage.

Artemis howled in pain, but lost no time pulling a knife from a sheath on her leg and lashing madly at Lucifer. I knocked my flaming fists into her ribs repeatedly.

She swung around and swiped at me, which gave Lucifer just enough time to dislodge his sword. Her pink blood spurted everywhere. Artemis looked down at it, and Dennis smashed into her at full speed. They jetted through the pillars of the agora and into the meadow where we first landed.

"She's outside of town," I said. "Now we just gotta get her off the planet."

"I have an idea." Lucifer grinned. "Follow me."

We sprinted to the meadow, where Dennis and Artemis were engaged in brutal hand to hand combat. They exchanged blows that left them both bloody and weary, but Dennis received the worst of it. He was strong and fast, but he couldn't take on a god, not even a wounded one.

"You don't have to do this, Artemis," Lucifer shouted at her. "We aren't here to hurt you."

Artemis connected another fist with Dennis's jaw. "You are here to change the natural order and free our prisoner. That is an affront to Zeus and must be stopped."

"He's not gonna be able to take much more of this," I shouted at Lucifer.

"You know what to do."

I ran up to Artemis and blocked her next blow with my arm. Still, the force of her fist sent me flying into a nearby tree. I pushed myself up, bloody and broken. I couldn't believe Dennis was still standing after so much abuse. "Hey! Is that all you got?"

"It is enough." Artemis picked up Dennis by the neck and held him in the air.

I intensified my flame and shot it at Artemis. It knocked her backward into the woods beyond the field. She dropped Dennis to the ground as she sailed through the sky. "Get out of here!" I yelled to Dennis.

"I'm not leaving the fight," he replied, wobbling.

"You've got nothing left."

Dennis stubbornly stood up, knock-kneed and swaying. "More than you," he said with a bloody grin. "You can't take her on your own."

I eyeballed Lucifer at the other end of the field. He nodded at me. "Alright, when she comes back, you just follow my lead."

Artemis jumped high into the sky and landed with a shockwave in front of us.

"Not bad." I unloaded everything I had on her, my flames kicking her back across the plains. "Get outta here!"

"Katrina!" Lucifer shouted. He spun his sword and cut a hole in the universe. "Now."

"Smack her back, Dennis!"

Dennis took a running lunge and flew into the air at top speed. I held my flame against her until the last moment. When Dennis closed in, I cut off my fire. Artemis didn't have time to recover from my blast before she saw Dennis's boot in her face. She flew backward into the void, and the portal closed behind her.

I ran up to Lucifer. "Where did you send her?"

"The only coordinates I remembered. Cronus's pit."

"Are you crazy?" Dennis shouted. "You locked Connie in with her!"

"No. I locked her in with Cronus. He does not like gods and despises shills for Zeus. I promise you, Connie will be fine. Cronus will make sure no harm comes to her. I cannot say the same for Artemis."

Dennis stuck his finger in Lucifer's chest. "You better be right."

"I am."

*

A combination of anger, fright, and elation met us as we re-entered the town. We'd saved them from the gods, but, in doing so, destroyed everything. Velaska, their god, stood in the middle of them all.

"And I have found three champions who will carry out my bidding." She noticed us across the square. "Ah, here they are now. What good news have you brought us, heroes?"

Lucifer took the lead. "Artemis is vanquished, goddess."

Velaska turned back to the townspeople with a smarmy smile. "You see, your goddess provides for you in all her wisdom and glory."

"What about our town?" one shouted. "It's ruined!"

"And the fires in the fields!" another screamed.

Velaska looked out into the fields where my fires raged. "Oh, that." She snapped her fingers and a thousand gallons of water fell on the ground, extinguishing the flames. "Done."

"As for the town, it can be rebuilt, but I help those that help themselves."

"I'll bet Hercules wouldn't make us rebuild ourselves," an old woman muttered.

"Yeah!" screamed another. "He would be right here with us. Maybe we rebuild the temple to honor him instead!"

Velaska backpedaled. "No, no, no. Don't be silly. He's not wise or kind."

"But he's strong. With him we'd never have to worry about our city being destroyed again."

I couldn't believe it, but I felt bad for the old hag. She retreated through the agora as the townsfolk inched toward her.

And so, I came to the rescue. I held up my arms and used my "god" voice to get their attention. "He would make you bow to him in servitude. Do you think you could ever speak to Hercules in such a disrespectful manner?"

"Well—"

"Of course not!" I shouted. "He would rip out your spine! And yet, here is Velaska, trying to help. It wasn't her fault your city was destroyed—that was Artemis! Velaska sent her champions to defeat the evil, and we did. Rebuilding your own city is a small price to pay for her grace." I lit myself on fire. They ate it up. "And if you don't believe me, you can watch what happens when you lose her good fortune."

The townsfolk screamed and ran away to fix their battered homes.

"Thank you for that," Velaska said. "I do so want to do a good job. I would hate to be given Hell duty again."

"Yeah," I said. "Hell is the worst."

"Tell me about it. It's one thing when it's ruled by monsters, like Lucifer—no offense, dear!" She gave him an ingratiating smile, and he just shrugged.

"But when such ravishing damsels like us are forced to rule it, well, it's a crime against nature is what it is. I am much happier with the love of a people. And that heat killed my complexion."

I forced a smile. "That's all well and good, but really I just want you to take us to Heaven now."

"It's called Mount Olympus here," Lucifer corrected.

"Yes, yes. Of course," Velaska said, hesitant. "A deal is a deal." She shifted her eyes left and right and hopped from one leg to the other. She snapped her fingers, but we didn't vanish. Instead, a nervous grin escaped her lips.

"So, are we gonna go?" I asked.

"Of course. It's just that...I'm not really a god."

"What?"

Velaska pushed us into her temple. "I'm not quite a god, at least in the traditional sense. I do have powers, that is true, but I am not part of the pantheon."

"The panthe-what?"

"The pantheon are the gods who live on Mount Olympus. They have complete access to it at all times. They snap their fingers and poof, they can enter Mount Olympus at will. I have petitioned 254 times to be included in the pantheon and been rejected 254 times. So, I can't really bring you to Mount Olympus, *but* I can get you in with the person who can."

"*Pfft.* And who is that?"

She snapped her fingers and we appeared outside of a massive arena. Thunderous applause boomed from thousands of voices inside its gates. "You might laugh." Velaska walked toward the front entrance. "Come now. Follow me. Let's hope this is painless."

"Please tell me this isn't what I think it is, Velaska," Lucifer said.

"Well, I hope you don't think it's Hercules's arena, because if you do, you'll be sorely disappointed."

"Isn't there another god we can parlay with?"

"Yes, of course. If you can find one, but when they're not off diddling sheep or tricking mortals, they pretty much stick to themselves on Olympus. This is the only one who regularly visits Earth to be among his people. Sure, he's violent, cruel, and crude, but if you get past that, it's kind of noble, really— being among your people, instead of governing from afar." Another roar went up from the arena and Velaska winced. "Admittedly, it's really hard to get past the violence."

"I'm okay with violence," I said. "I want to commit some right now as a matter of fact. On you."

"Take it out in the arena, dear. In the arena." Velaska led us up to the gates.

Two beefy men with chiseled abs and horse legs crossed their lances in front of her. They were centaurs, though I had never seen one in person before. "Pass?"

"Please, boys," Velaska said with a twirl. "Don't you know who I am?"

"Oh, we know who you are, ma'am. And we were specifically told not to let you in without a pass."

"Well, isn't that rude! I'll tell you what, if you look the other way, I'll grant you each a wish of your choice. No strings attached."

A bellowing voice boomed from the top of the stadium. "There is always a string, Velaska. If I know one thing about you, it's that there is always a string."

Velaska gazed up at a great bearded behemoth staring down at her, five stories tall and rippling with sweaty muscles. "Oh please, Herc. Name one time that was the case."

"Do you see my guards? There weren't always centaurs. I asked they be as fast as bucking broncos, and that was the result."

"Oh, come on. That's the old me, and they were asking for it. It won't happen this time, honest to goodness. I'm a straight shooter now."

"And what brought about this change in your black, black soul?" Hercules snorted.

Velaska turned to us. "These nice folks, Herc. They need your kindness. They assisted me in a bit of a pickle. I promised them a favor, and I need you to help me deliver."

Hercules looked at us and guffawed. "You promised them entrance into Olympus, didn't you?"

"Only a little."

"When will you stop with—"

"This is the last time. Come on, Herc. Help a girl out."

"You know the rules and the stakes. These friends of yours reek of death. They have all been claimed by another. You know my rules about bargaining with the dead. Without a fresh, unclaimed soul there will be no bargain."

Velaska snapped her fingers and I stepped forward. "No, Herc. Not this one. This one still has a fresh soul. You never died, did you dear?"

"No. I didn't. How did you know that? To be fair, neither has Lucifer."

"Tut tut tut," Velaska said, covering my mouth. "This is about you, not him. Angels don't have souls, honey. That's what he's after."

"I can smell it all over you, doll," Hercules said. "Your soul reeks like old cheese."

Velaska grabbed my face and turned it up to Hercules. "See, this one. She's still got an intact soul, unclaimed by any god. I wager to bet she'll wager it on a bet."

Hercules took a bite out of a big piece of mutton. The blood dripped off his lips. "Is that true girl, are you willing to risk your immortal soul to see the gods?"

I looked back at Dennis. I saw the pain behind his eyes. I couldn't let him down. "I need to rescue Bacchus from wherever Hera took him, and I need to find Zeus. I will do anything necessary to those two ends."

Hercules smiled a greasy smile. "I cannot help you find Zeus, but I can get you into Olympus. If you complete my challenges."

Of course. "What are they?"

"Well that would be cheating, wouldn't it? I can tell you there are three labors total, and they will all take place inside this arena."

"I'll be fighting, then?"

Hercules laughed. "Oh, yes! I will wager entrance into Mount Olympus against your soul. Come here, girl!" Hercules pulled a chain around his arm. A dark-skinned woman with emerald eyes nudged herself into view over the ledge. "I tire of this concubine and need another. You look feisty enough to entertain me for a spell. What say you?"

I took a deep breath and turned to Velaska. "I'm going to murder you later."

"That's what they all say."

I looked to Hercules. "Alright. I'll take your wager, so long as I get to pick my weapons and armor."

"That would only be fair." He sucked his teeth. "Then a bargain is struck. Centaurs, let them inside. Have the satyrs bring the girl to my dungeon. The others can watch from my private balcony."

The centaurs parted their lances and let us pass.

"Yup," I told Velaska. "I'm definitely going to kill you later."

For the first time since I met her, Velaska looked noticeably scared. "I have faith in you, dear."

Meanwhile, on Earth...

The first thought that passed through Rebecca Lobdell's head when she woke was surprise—surprise that she was still alive. Her bloody head rested on a broken rock. A piece of glass dug deep into her back. There was blood dripping down onto the cracked road beneath her.

Rebecca had never felt asphalt before, growing up a thousand feet above the streets where Los Angeles used to be. The sticky asphalt was rough against her skin. She only felt it, and she didn't like it. She had never seen the road, either and she still couldn't see it now, even right underneath her. Everything was pitch black.

"Come now, my little minions," a heavenly voice said. "Search for survivors."

More and more lights flickered on. Gigantic leathery wings flapped atop the lights, which were clasped tightly by dark black talons.

"We don't have much time, my dears. You know how humans are. Fragile." Orange glowing eyes scanned the horizon and lit the pointed nose and thin lips beneath them.

The eyes stopped on Rebecca. "Oh, hello, my dear. How are you feeling?"

"Uhm…"

"Not great, I assume. After all, you did just fall through dimensions. It's not a fun ride, and it does have its perils. I know your soft bones can't much handle interdimensional travel. Well, let's have a look at you."

The eyes came over and scanned her body. "Doesn't look like any broken bones. Turn over, love."

Rebecca complied, revealing the blood oozing down her back.

"No, no. That just won't do."

A snap of fingers and the glass dislodged from Rebecca's back. She felt a quick sting and the wound cauterized itself.

"There now. It looks like you'll be alright, my dear. We'll see if we can find you a doctor in all this mess. Considering what you've been through, you're just a little worse for wear."

"Where am I?"

"Hmmm… Well, it's probably easier to tell you where we aren't. We aren't in your universe anymore. We are in another place, another time. A different dimension. And unfortunately, I've found this to be a one-way door. No going through the other way, no sir. We are stuck in this dimension."

Rebecca looked around in every direction, trying to get a sense of place, but found none. "What is this dimension?"

"I don't know, fully, but it's not all bad. The Bat things, they make decent companions. I do wish I'd been able to create a more luminous universe, but Cronus is really the one with the gift for creation. He taught me a thing or two. I think I did okay, though, given what nothing I had to work with. They look ugly, but they are truly dear. Not unlike your garden-variety demons, at the end."

"Demons are evil, aren't they?"

"Oh, they can be, surely. But nothing is good or evil dear, except when their actions make them so."

"Who are you?" Rebecca asked.

"Where are my manners? I am Rhea, mother of the universe, the gods, and everything. And what is your name, deary?"

Maybe it was the blood loss, or the knock on the head, or meeting a Titan, or being sucked through a dimension, but that was the moment Rebecca Lobdell fainted again.

Chapter 10

Four satyrs led me inside the arena where a ruckus crowd screamed bloody murder and two muscular gladiators, clad in thick chain mail armor and armed with broadswords, fought a bear.

It was hardly a fight. The bear swatted them about like rag dolls. I heard the snap of a gladiator's neck and the audience went wild. As we descended the stairs into the dungeon, another scream rose from the audience and the bear roared again.

Hercules rose from his seat. "Two more souls for my army! Well fought, men. You are worthy of my legion."

Apparently, the men who failed in the arena went into Hercules's legion while the women became his concubines. I wasn't surprised by the rampant sexism. After all, the Greek gods were obscenely sexist. There were hundreds of stories involving gods like Zeus tricking women into sleeping with them.

It was a stupid policy, that's for sure, one that wasted a lot of potential. Women can kick some serious ass. I've kicked ass across the whole universe, destroyed countless monsters, become a Devil, and fought a god. If Hercules was smart, he would put me at the front of an army, instead of using me as his play thing.

Underneath the stadium, the floor rocked with shouts of fans watching the gore. A rusted iron door led out into the arena. In front of me, on a wooden table, lay every weapon imaginable, from a flailed mace to a double-edged lance, and dozens of armor choices in every type from leather to thick chain mail. If you wanted spry, then you could take the bow and arrow, and if you wanted tank, then you could suit up in metal armor and carry a heavy ax. I didn't want any of it, though. I had other plans.

"You have ten minutes to ready yourself," one of the satyrs told me. "Then, your trials begin."

"Can I ask you a question?" I replied.

"You can do anything you want...for the next ten minutes."

"What is your name, satyr?" I asked.

"Sully."

"Not a very majestic name, Sully."

"It's short for Sullivantrix, which means full-headed."

"Well, that's slightly better, I guess," I said. "How many people have beaten Hercules's trials?"

The satyr smiled. "None."

"Zero. Seriously? How is that fun for the crowd if there's not even a chance?"

"They all want to see how far you'll get."

"And how far will I get?"

"Only two hundred men have ever passed the first test. Only three have passed the second."

"So, my odds aren't very good."

"They are impossible."

"Great. Thanks."

"Don't you want a weapon or armor?"

"I'll get around to it."

I sat down to wait my fate. The satyrs mumbled to each other for a moment, then fell silent. The next ten minutes were my own, and I used them to sit mutely and think about my life, about all the times I was tricked into doing something ridiculous. You would think that I could smell deception better after Bacchus deceived me into becoming the Devil, and after Thomas fooled me into killing Lucifer.

You would think, but then Velaska tricked me again. Well, no more.

*

Ten minutes later, a rhythmic, impatient stomping thundered above me. The crowd was ready for me. The satyrs turned to me. "It's time."

I stood and faced them. "I'm ready."

The great gate in front of me rose, and the satyrs led me through a tunnel and into the center of the stadium. Two centaurs passed us on the way, dragging a dead gladiator off the pitch while two small nymphs followed behind, covering the blood with dust. The screams of "Kill her!" ripped through the stands. The blood lust was palpable. Even the tortured souls of Hell didn't spit vitriol as brutal as this.

The satyrs forced me to kneel. Hercules wiped the bloody turkey leg off his mouth and grinned at me. "Poor woman, you have chosen to die without any weapons or armor. A foolish choice."

"Actually," I said. "I just didn't have access to them before. I choose the archangel Dennis's armor and Lucifer's sword."

Hercules huffed. "I can't allow that. You only get your choice of the weapons available under the arena."

"That was not our deal. You told me I could have my choice of weapons and armor. That was my price for entrance. Are you not a man of your word?"

Hercules scowled. "You are correct. That was our deal, and it is a deal I will honor. Just know I don't take kindly to trickery."

"And I don't take kindly to people trying to kill me."

Hercules waved his arm. Dennis flew down from the stands with Lucifer, who handed me his sword and said, "This is a pretty ballsy thing you are doing. I hope it works out for you."

"Yeah, me too," I said.

He took a step back and watched me as I stuck the sword in the ground and turned to Dennis, who unhooked his breast plate. "I haven't taken this off in a long time—I mean, years. A few thousand of them."

"You're telling me it might stink? Don't worry, I promise to give it back after this."

"In one piece. Usually people say they'll give it back in one piece."

"I wouldn't count on it. I have no idea what's going to happen in here, Dennis. I have all the confidence in the world, but I've never gone up against a god by myself before. And what are these challenges going to be?"

Dennis snapped the breast plate into place around my thin shoulders. "You'll be fine."

"Do you want to know a secret?"

"Sure."

"I never think I'm gonna get out of these things. That's why I can fight so hard, for so long. I always assume I'm going to die."

Dennis clasped a leg plate around my shin. "Don't die."

"Thanks." I tried to tighten the guard around my leg.

When I was finished, I could barely move. The armor was too big for me by several dozen sizes. Lucifer was still staring at me with a sad expression.

Hercules looked down and laughed. "A good choice indeed."

Dennis smiled and spoke out of the corner of his mouth. "Just wait."

The armor shined bright like the morning sun. Rays of arresting light shot in every direction and blinded me for a moment. I felt the armor meld to my body. The breastplate shrank to perfectly cover my shoulders. My leg guards tightened to allow me a complete range of motion.

When it finished contorting to my body, the armor didn't shine gold at all. It was black and tough, filled with jagged spikes and a howling demon dog snapping its three jaws on the breast plate. Thick black thorns grew out of my arm bracers. I'm not going to lie, it was awesome.

Lucifer hugged me. It surprised me for sure, but it had been a while since I felt a warm body pressed against me, and it was nice. Dennis wrapped his arms around me as well and the three of us shared a little moment. It wasn't too awkward.

"Enough of that!" Hercules shouted. "This isn't a brothel. Not yet at least."

They flew away without another word. It was time for me to start. I'd faced death many times in my long life, but never when the stakes were so high. I could deal with death; I could even deal with Hell. But I could not deal with Hercules's sweaty paws touching me.

"Very well, Katrina," Hercules said, silencing the crowd. "You are here to fight for the favor of the gods. Should you win, you will be brought to Mount Olympus. Should you lose, you will be my eternal paramour. Do you accept these terms?"

"I accept."

"Then we begin. I had chosen your feats already, but given your new armor and weapons, I think they will be too easy for you. Therefore, I will up the ante, as they say. If you can play tricks like a god, let us see if you can fight like one. These trials are all from my personal conquests. Your first feat of bravery shall be to defeat the Stymphalian Birds."

The crowd cheered as Hercules continued, "These massive carnivorous birds terrorized your ancient world until I was able to tame them. No mortal can stand up to their power. Their razor sharp, bronze feathers can cut through any material. Good luck, challenger." He waved a hand. "Open the gate!"

I could hear the hideous squawking of the birds begin before the gate rose. They smashed against the doors of their cage until the satyrs pulled them open, and then the three massive birds swallowed the satyrs whole as they flew into the arena.

Once free, the bronze birds flew toward the sky to escape, but Hercules blew a great whistle from his mouth and pointed at me. The birds locked their eyes on me and barreled forward at breakneck speeds. I dodged them on a first pass, and a second. They turned around for what I thought would be a third pass, but then stopped in midair.

They expanded their wings as wide as the stadium, shimmering in the light. Their feathers forked into a massive set of knives, the blades shooting out of their wings and sticking in the ground and posts around me. I ran as fast as I could away from the razor feathers.

"You can only run so far, little one!" Hercules shouted.

He was right, there was only so far to run, but he was wrong that I was little, or more accurately, that I had to be little. Planting my feet into the ground, I closed my eyes. I grew twenty feet in the air in a second, and my armor grew with me.

The birds were now half my size, and their feathers barely put pinpricks in my shoes. I grabbed one of them around its scrawny neck and turned it against the others. It impaled the other two birds with a dozen, razor sharp feathers and they both collapsed to the ground, dead. I flung the third bird onto the ground and shrunk myself to a normal size. I grabbed my sword and cut off its head. It convulsed frantically before falling dead.

The crowd fell silent for a moment, then erupted in thunderous applause. The "kill her" chants turned to "Katrina!" and the stadium shook with cheers.

"Silence!" Hercules shouted. The crowd hushed obediently. "You are stronger than I thought, Katrina."

"Oh, did I forget to mention she was a Devil?" Velaska muttered with a sly grin.

Hercules clenched his fists, ready to strike. "Yes, you failed to mention that."

"Oops. My mistake."

He took a deep breath. "No matter. Now that I'm aware of your powers, I have a challenge worthy of a Devil. The first of my epic trials saw me fight the Nemean lion! Completely impervious to all weapons, with claws strong enough to cut through any armor, the Nemean lion is unbeatable…unless you are me, that is."

Hercules waved his arms. A layer of blue sparks spread across the area five feet over my head. "And just to make sure the lovely Katrina cannot stomp the lion to death, this barrier will prevent her from growing, lest she wants to be cut into little bits. Now, open the gates!"

The hulking lion smashed out of its cage and burst toward me. I rolled to avoid the lumbering beast, but it slashed at my arm and cut a deep gash into Dennis's armor. I bowled backwards, sword in hand. I took a swing, but it bounced off the impervious hide. The lion swiped at my sword with its immense claws and cut it in half. The pieces fell out of my hands as I ran to avoid its meaty maw.

The lion followed close behind me and pounced. I bicycle-kicked it skyward into the barrier above me. There was a sizzling sound, and I thought maybe I'd managed to wound it, but the thing fell back to the ground without a scratch. It roared and charged me again.

This time I was ready. I jumped into the air and latched onto the lion's mane, swinging myself onto its back. I pulled at its golden fur, trying to steer, but the lion was immoveable. At full speed, the great cat rolled onto its back. I leapt off just before it crushed me under its hideous bulk.

I rose to my feet and stared down the lion. Things did not look good for me. It was impenetrable, vicious, and violent—and it had no "off" switch. The lion rushed toward me again, and this time I couldn't avoid it. It tackled me to the ground, tearing deep gashes into my armor as I ducked its paws.

I grabbed on to one of them and drove it back into its body. The lion yelped and jumped backward. It staggered slightly when it came to its feet, and there was blood on the dirt floor beneath it. I saw the great paw covered in blood, and I immediately knew what to do.

This time I rushed the beast, slamming into it and forcing it to the ground. It spun over onto its back, swiping furiously at my face. I caught its front paws and used them to slash open its stomach.

Blood gushed from the lion's belly. I rolled away from its gory body and grabbed the hilt of my sword. It was broken, but the tip was still jagged and sharp. I jammed the sword through the lion's open wound, deep into its exposed insides. The great cat went limp.

Again, the crowd screamed with excitement. The arena shook so loudly it felt like the walls would come crashing down. My armor fell off of me, ripped to shreds. My weapon was destroyed, but I was still alive to see the third task.

Hercules leaned forward, eyeballing me from his place of honor on the balcony. "You have proven yourself a great warrior, Katrina, possibly the rival of myself. But you are broken, bruised, and battered. You have no strength left. The third task will most certainly kill you. Since you have fought heroically, I will give you one chance to avoid death. Walk away now, and I will return your soul to you. You will forfeit your right to Mount Olympus, but you will leave with your life and your soul."

I wiped some sweat and blood from my face and sniffed before answering. "My soul never meant much to me, Hercules. It hasn't in ten thousand years. And if you take me as your concubine, I will rip off your dick and feed it to you. Bring on the third trial."

A quiet gasp went through the crowd, and I saw Lucifer slap Dennis on the back with a hearty chuckle. Then he gave me a thumbs-up. Hercules just smiled.

"Very well. For my second labor, I defeated the Lernaean Hydra. This nine-headed hydra regenerates its heads when severed." As Hercules spoke, the barrier rose fifty feet in the air. "For every head you cut off, two return in its place. On top of that, this beast has one immortal head which cannot be defeated! This test was so great I couldn't even do it alone, and I am a god! Open the gates and let the hydra feast!"

I picked up the hilt of my sword. This wasn't the first hydra I'd come across, and I'd managed to kill the last one. I lunged at the beast as it snapped at me, slicing off the first head in moments. It fell without issue and I sent a fire blast to cauterize the head, so it wouldn't grow back. Easy enough. The crowd exploded while I flipped between the other eight other heads lunging at me. I hacked off each one until there was only one left, the immortal head.

This is where it got tricky. The immortal head chomped at me like an oversized, ugly Pez dispenser. I skipped and rolled around the arena, trying to come up with a plan while I dodged it. I knew I couldn't cut off the head, but Hercules hadn't said anything about the body being immortal. I jumped onto the back of the beast and sliced through to the spine, severing the head from its body. I remembered what Lucifer told Connie. *Anything can be killed, given the right circumstances.*

The immortal head flopped around the arena, gnashing its teeth. I quadrupled in size until I could pick up the head with ease. The barrier meant to contain me buzzed over my head. I pulled back my arm and flung the head through the barrier, which flayed the head into a million pieces.

I had won. I bested the three labors of Hercules.

Hercules clapped for me. "Very impressive, Katrina. I dare say you are the greatest champion I've ever seen. Of course, most of our challengers don't have godly weapons or a Devil's pedigree, but even so, you performed admirably."

"I only care about you honoring your deal. Your words mean nothing without action."

"And you shall have it, but you came across your victory rather easily, and I can't help modifying the rules, just one little bit."

"You can't do that!"

"No? You are in *my* arena! I can do anything, or have you forgotten that I am a god?"

"For this last challenge, you must defeat…" Hercules jumped off his chair and into the arena. "me."

"That's impossible. You're a god."

"We all have our gifts."

"I thought you were an honorable god, one who found justice in the ring." I turned and raised my arms, addressing the crowd. "Is this justice?"

The crowd booed. "No!"

"Am I not your champion? Have I not performed bravely?" I tried to remember the lines from *Gladiator.*

The crowd cheered for me, making the stadium foundations tremble with their voices and applause. "And what of Hercules, this god who beset me with three impossible challenges, which I defeated, then tricked me into a fourth. What say you of him?"

The people booed and stuck their thumbs down toward the earth.

Hercules couldn't believe it. He stomped his foot. "I am your god! Stop booing me!"

"You are only a god as long as the people believe in you, as long as they worship you. The second that goes away, you're just a sniveling worm. Once they abandon you, there's nothing left but shame. You'll have to go build another town, and who's going to love you once they've found what you've done, and how unfair your justice really is?"

The booing continued, and I took a step closer to Hercules, who was glaring at the people in the stands but listening closely.

"Now, I will give you one chance to do the right thing. End this, fulfill your agreement, and you can keep your pathetic arena. Or kill me, satisfy your bloodlust, and lose it all."

Hercules took one last look around at the people in the stands and then fell to one knee. "Very well. You have defeated me. Take your victory."

I smiled at him. "I will."

Meanwhile, in Cronus's pit...

Connie sat in the corner of Cronus's pit, absentmindedly drawing penises in the dirt. She had nothing more to say to the Mad Titan. She'd asked everything she could think of and he returned depressing, horrible answers that bummed her out. So now she just wanted to keep her mouth shut and bide her time until Dennis returned.

A tear in the universe opened and Connie's heart skipped. Dennis hadn't been gone even a day and already he was back to save her. She figured she'd be stuck in the cave for months or even years. She stood up with a big smile, ready to welcome Dennis with open arms. Except it wasn't Dennis who came through the rift, it was Artemis.

"Who are you?" Connie asked. "And what did you do with Dennis?"

Artemis readied her bow. "Where are the cretins that knocked me through that portal? Send me back to them now!"

"I don't know how!" Connie shouted. "Otherwise, I wouldn't be stuck here, would I?"

Artemis laughed. "They left you here to rot while they traipsed around the universe? That's rich."

"They're coming back for me!"

"Do you really think so? When?"

"Once they get that old, crusty bag of rot, Zeus, and bring him back here!"

Artemis laughed again. "That is never going to happen!"

Cronus's saucer eyes lit up in the darkness. "Ah, Artemis. Loyal to Zeus until the end, I see."

The goddess trained her arrow on him. "Cronus. I hoped I would get the chance to kill you again."

Cronus's eyes softened. "I always liked you, Artemis. Truly I did. I wish you would have come to visit your grandfather more. We could have been fast friends had you freed me."

"If I had done that, you would have ended the universe."

"And created a new one out of nothing. You could have ruled it with me."

"What would have happened to all the others?"

"Whatever happens to all playthings when you are done with them. You grow tired of them and they drift into memory."

"I couldn't do that."

"I know. And the fact you still favor Zeus says a lot about your character. I always thought better of you."

Artemis drew her bow back with a sneer. "Sorry to disappoint you."

Cronus grabbed Artemis and lifted her into the air. "Not at all. You can still serve a purpose." He tossed her into his mouth and swallowed, then turned conversationally to Connie. "It has been so long since I've had a meal. Your friends delivered a very nice appetizer. I hope they can deliver the main course, for your sake."

Cronus picked at his rock butte teeth, then spit out Artemis's bow and arrows onto the ground. "Yuck. Those would give me terrible indigestion."

Cronus closed his eyes and drifted off. Connie scooped up the bow and arrows. If Dennis didn't come back for her, she would need them, either to end Cronus's life or her own.

Chapter 11

Dennis looked down at his destroyed armor laying on the oaken table in the dungeon under the stadium. He put his hand over his mouth and shook his head. Lucifer sat in the corner, holding the shards of Bacchus's flaming sword with the same look on his face.

"I can't believe you destroyed it," Dennis said.

"This sword lasted since time immemorial," Lucifer added.

"I really think you two are making too much of this," I said.

Dennis spun to me. "I kept that armor pristine for ten thousand years! Do you know how long that is?"

"Yeah, I do!" I shouted. "I've been the Devil for exactly that long, so I know every bit how long that is!"

"And you destroyed it in one day?"

I threw up my hands. "Armor is supposed to protect people, and that's just what it did. I'm alive because of it. Isn't that something?"

"Yeah," Lucifer said, standing. "It is, and we're happy for that. It's just...do you have to destroy *everything* you touch?"

"Right!" Dennis added. "I loved that armor."

"And I loved my life. Thank you both for helping me keep it."

"It can still be repaired," Hercules said, walking in the room. "The armor and the sword."

"How?" Lucifer and Dennis said at the same time.

"Hephaestus forged both that sword and the armor himself." Hercules threw a cloth bag at Dennis. "If you bring him every piece, he will make them whole again. Now, quit being women and hurry yourselves."

"Does Hephaestus still brew the best mead on Olympus?" Lucifer asked.

"Yes, but there is no time to waste. Katrina, with me."

I walked over to Hercules. "We're going to have to work on this misogynistic bullshit, Herc. Otherwise, I'm gonna rip off your cock and stuff it in your mouth."

"My apologies, Katrina. I've never met a woman as...spirited as you. I am an old man set in my ways."

"I don't care what you are, cut it out."

"I will try," Hercules said. "Now to the matter at hand. Even as my guests on Olympus, you will not be welcome. You must let me lead you through the Elysian Fields to one of Hephaestus's workshops, then on to Aphrodite, the regent in charge of this sector. No deviations. Understood?"

"Whatever you say, Herc."

Hercules turned back to Dennis and Lucifer, who were busy packing the last of the sword and armor into the cloth bag. "Come now. No time to lose."

*

We were following Hercules into a meadow outside of the arena when Velaska approached us. "About time, kiddos. I was starting to think you abandoned me."

"Unfortunately, you are part of this deal, too," Hercules said.

"I would hope so," Velaska replied. "I'm the one that put this whole thing together."

"Just let me do the talking up there, okay?" Hercules looked at each one of us while he talked. "That goes for everybody. I speak. You listen. Please don't get me into trouble."

I chuckled suddenly. "Oh my god, Herc. Are you scared of Mount Olympus?"

Hercules shook his head. "I'm not scared of anything. I just don't much like it up there."

He closed his eyes then and chanted under his breath. A bright blue light emanated from the sky. It reminded me of the blue beam of light that took me from Hell to Heaven. This one didn't taste like cherries though. It tasted more like blueberry pie.

We vaporized and reappeared on Mount Olympus in an instant. The fluffy clouds were familiar, but the similarities ended there. Instead of the vacant landscape of Heaven, Mount Olympus bustled with liveliness. Hundreds of cherubs and gods walked along paths built around thatched roof homes and Romanesque columns. It looked just like Helobrius's town, but with a cloudy touch.

"Come," Hercules said. "Hephaestus's workshop is right ahead. He is one of the few gods I can stand. He's quiet, thoughtful, and works with his hands, like me!"

Velaska made a face. "When was the last time you worked with your hands?"

"Just last night, in fact." Hercules grinned and elbowed Lucifer, who grimaced.

"What did I say about that crap?" I growled.

Hercules stayed silent for the rest of the way to Hephaestus's shop. Everybody scowled with our passing. They pointed and stared. It felt like a fluffy high school.

Hephaestus's stables dwarfed everything else in the surrounding area. Outside, dozens of winged horses twirled in the sky. Massive purple buffalos grazed in the yard. The sound of hammering metal arose from a half mile away and deafened my eardrums as we entered the shop. Inside, a great, bearded man stood in front of a fiery furnace hammering a great sword on his anvil. I'd never seen a god like him. Most gods were beautiful, perfect, and shapely. Hephaestus was not. He looked like somebody played his face like a drum. Strong for sure, but also portly. Dark, black soot covered his body from his long beard to his thick, hairy legs.

He looked up from his iron when the bell over the door rang. "Hercules, my friend! It's good to see you!" He pulled the work goggles off his eyes and wrapped Hercules in a big hug.

Hercules, in return, slapped Hephaestus on the back. "It's been too long."

"I thought you were on Earth for the duration."

Hercules glanced back at us. "Things changed. Besides, I missed my oldest friend."

Hephaestus smiled. "And Velaska. Always a pleasure. Come to make your case to the pantheon again?"

Velaska backed away as Hephaestus charged forward to greet her. "No offense, but this is a brand-new dress."

"Of course, of course!" He didn't seem offended. I suppose he was used to it. "And who are these fine people?"

"You probably remember Lucifer, but it's been quite a while."

"From Bacchus's Earth? My, you've changed."

Lucifer smiled, taking Hephaestus's outstretched paw. "Many things change over the generations. Except you, my friend. Still the same as ever."

"These two," Hercules continued. "are new. This is the archangel Dennis, and the Devil Katrina."

"My, my," Hephaestus said, openly admiring me. "You are prettiest Devil I've seen."

"Hey!" Velaska shouted. "What about me?"

"I stand by what I said." Hephaestus winked at me. "Do you have time for a drink?" he asked, turning back to his forge. "I just brewed a new batch of mead. It's particularly good, if I do say so myself. This time I used apricots. I've never done that before. Splendid."

"Another time, my friend. I have a favor." Hercules gestured to Dennis and Lucifer, who dumped their cloth bags on a nearby work bench.

"These are important relics, fallen in battle. They have your mark. Can you fix them?"

Hephaestus examined the weapons and armor. "Hmmm, yes, yes. I remember these." He picked up the breast plate. "It looks like an epic battle."

"The Nemean Lion," I said proudly.

"Yes, that was one of Hercules's favorites."

"It fought bravely and died in combat."

"A brave death for a brave animal." Hephaestus weighed a shard of the blade in his gnarled hand. "Well, luckily these seem like clean breaks in the sword, and the armor can be worked out. I think I can mend this for you. How does one hundred and twenty years sound?"

Hercules let out a nervous chuckle. "I think that's a little long for us, buddy. Can you speed it up? Maybe put us in the front of the queue, for an old friend?"

Hephaestus thought for a moment. "I have a project for Zeus, very hush hush. I probably shouldn't have even said that…but I suppose he can wait a bit longer. Very well, my friend."

Hephaestus and Hercules embraced and said their goodbyes. "Thank you, old friend. I will return for the mead and the company. Count on it."

*

Hercules led us out of the forge and across Mount Olympus. His chest burst forth, proudly. I laughed at him as we walked. "I can't believe you have a friend, like an honest to goodness friend. Not one you had to coerce into friendship, or whose soul you had to steal."

"I'm not much different than you, Katrina. You have very few friends, those who you keep close, who've watched your back repeatedly. I am the same. Come, let us away."

I looked back at Lucifer and Dennis, and more importantly at the empty spot where Connie should be. My heart ripped.

Looking around at Mount Olympus, I was again struck by how different it was than Heaven. It wasn't just a luxury spa like on Earth. There weren't people lounging around all day.

Everybody seemed to know their place here on Mount Olympus and had a job to do. There were blacksmiths, cobblers, haberdashers, and tailors. Even the gods worked, like Hephaestus. Artemis, for all her faults, had a job protecting Zeus's jail, just like Apollo had a job arresting gods. It all seemed so normal, honestly, like any other hamlet I watched in old movies, replete with a small castle in the distance. Hercules pointed to it on the horizon as we passed a cart full of wine casks.

"Aphrodite is the most beautiful goddess in all the cosmos. She radiates love, kindness, and energy—but don't let that fool you. She is as ruthless as she is beautiful, and as vengeful as she is loving. Her emotions turn on a dime. Zeus isn't an idiot, though. There's a reason she's been tasked with running this place in his stead."

"Like the reason he chose Bacchus to run Earth?" I replied.

"Exactly like that. Earth was a podunk, little backwater on the edge of the universe. It's structurally insignificant. We almost left an angel in charge of it, except that we needed to be rid of Bacchus. He was a lush, holding us back and fouling everything up. We needed to offload him somewhere and figured he couldn't do much damage there, at the end of the day. I mean, what kind of idiot would start an Apocalypse?"

"Glad to see you think so highly of us," Dennis said.

"We enjoyed making your Earth," Velaska said. "Not that I had much to do with it, but I doubt anyone would say it was the best planet we've ever constructed. It certainly wasn't the worst, and at least it is gods sanctioned."

"Gods sanctioned?"

"You were built by the gods, unlike some life in this forsaken universe," Lucifer said.

"I thought only Cronus, and by extension Zeus, could make life?" Dennis said.

"Technically," Velaska said. "But Zeus, let's just say he can't contain it as well as Cronus could. After all, it's not really his power, is it?

"It is not," Hercules butted in. "So, when he creates a planet, there's all this ancillary radiation which spreads out and sometimes, it creates other life. We try to stamp it out as best we can, but, well, sometimes it grows. Life has a funny way of doing that."

"Aliens?" I asked.

Hercules walked up the steps to the castle. "Sometimes they're insects, or lizards, or rats, but they're not humans, and that's not good. After all, what would happen if they ever attained godhood? It would be an affront against the natural order."

"How can something become a god?" Dennis said.

Hercules pushed open the front door of the castle. "Oh, there are a few ways. None you need to concern yourself with, but the easiest way is to kill a god. Once you kill a god, all that power has to transfer somewhere. I hear you know that better than most, Katrina, having gotten your powers from killing a Devil."

"Yeah," I replied, following him through the door. "But he wasn't a god."

"It's the same principle. Devil or god, everything dies if you hit it hard enough, Katie. When it does, the power has to go somewhere."

I sighed. "Don't call me Katie."

"Very well, Katrina. I hope you are ready to parlay with a god."

Chapter 12

Tapestries of the various gods hung below every stained-glass window inside Aphrodite's ostentatious castle. The stained-glass itself featured depictions of Aphrodite's visage, which literally shone like a well-constructed cliché. Along with the tapestries and stained glass, large mirrors hung on the walls at regular intervals.

Our feet echoed against the rock walls as we passed cherub guards on the way to the throne at the end of a long hallway, each one adorned in beautiful, golden armor and gripping a long spear with a flaming blade. The guards looked forward without flinching. Dennis looked down, missing his shimmering armor.

"Don't fret, pretty one." Velaska sidled up to him and lay a warm hand on his shoulder.

Dennis shook in his angelic skin. "Don't...talk to me."

At the end of the hallway, a large window shone light on a gilded, ornate throne where a breathtaking woman sat in flowing, golden robes, replete with golden hair and a golden crown. Her hair and robes flowed as if teased by a perfect gust of wind.

"What ho, good Aphrodite!" Hercules said, waving across the hall.

She gave him a haughty look. "You have no appointment, Hercules, and I have no time to deal with you today."

"Come now, Aphrodite. I enter Heaven so rarely these days. Have you no time for me, truly?"

"I have time for you. I have no time for your favors." She tossed a few tresses of hair over her shoulder and I watched her gaze into one of the many mirrors around her before Hercules spoke again.

"Aphrodite, please. You have so little faith in me."

"You do realize I too am a god? I know what you have done, sullying our home with unworthy intruders."

The blood boiled in my face at the implication we were unworthy, but I dared not speak. Even I knew my place on

Mount Olympus. I would be dead in a moment, along with everybody else, if I opened my mouth.

"Don't be like that, Dite. This woman bested my challenges, which proves her worth."

"To you, and only to you. Your judgment means nothing to me."

Hercules sighed. "I'm sorry to disappoint you, sister."

"You cannot disappoint me anymore, Hercules. I've long since lost the last ounce of respect I had for you."

I couldn't believe I felt bad for Hercules. The wanton, brazen, horrific Neanderthal quivered his lip in shame and said, "Then I will be brief. My guests have a favor to ask you."

"Yes," Velaska replied. "I would like to again lodge a formal request to join the pantheon."

"Hmmm," Aphrodite thought for a moment. "Your request is noted. Expect a response in one thousand, five hundred and twenty-one years. Next!"

"What are you doing?" I shouted to Velaska. "That's not what we wanted!"

"It's not?" Velaska replied, slyly. "It's what I wanted."

I turned back to Aphrodite. "Queen Aphrodite. That is not our request."

"Funny. I noted it as such. Next!" she hollered over our heads. "Guards, come take these people away."

"No, no, no! We have to find Hera's prison planet. All we need are the coordinates." I was talking fast. "Can't you void that request and make a new one? Just this once?"

Aphrodite held out her hand. "That's not how it works here, dear. There is only one god who keeps the location of that planet. The only person who would need it, actually."

"And who is that," Lucifer asked. "so that we might entreat with him?"

"You should know him well, Devil. His is your patron. My uncle, Hades, of course."

"Ah crap," I said. "So that means…"

"You can travel to Hell and find him. I hear Tartarus is particularly lovely this time of year."

I sighed. "You've gotta be kidding me."

Aphrodite smiled. "I never kid. Three of you have the stink of Hell on you, so it should be a nice, pleasant homecoming."

"No way," Lucifer said. "I ain't going back there."

"Me either," Velaska said. "That's how I got into this mess in the first place. I'm quite happy where I am."

I sighed. "Fine, you big pussies. I'll go myself." I turned back to Aphrodite. "Give me a moment, please. I need to collect myself."

"Take all the time you need. I'm immortal." Aphrodite shifted in her throne to examine herself in one of the mirrors again.

I walked over to Dennis. "Make sure the weapons and armor are ready, so we get out of here when I'm done."

Dennis nodded. "Will do."

I turned back to Aphrodite. "Alright, queen. So how do we do this thing?"

Aphrodite waved her hand without bothering to look at us. "It is done."

*

The stink of Hell never changed, apparently. Frying flesh and sweaty ass filled my nostrils the moment I reappeared in Hades's domain. It reminded me of home. I'm surprised I missed it so much. When you live in a place for ten thousand years, it becomes a little piece of you, I guess.

Aphrodite's blue light teleported me directly to Hades's palace, which looked remarkably like mine. Here was that template again. The contractors painted by the numbers every time. How much creativity did Zeus really have at the end of the day? He'd only managed to come up with a weaker version of himself.

I wondered, as I walked through the castle, if the reason Cronus had the spark of life in him was because only he had any creativity. After all, Zeus just continued on with Cronus's plan. He followed the same exact blueprint for millions of years. Cronus, however, tired of his creation and longed for something new, like any good creative. True creativity isn't about making the same thing over and over again. It's about making new things. Or at least new slants on old things.

Hades, I could tell right away, reveled in the muck and the mire. He featured thirty-foot demonic sculptures in his walkway, and his stained glass dealt with the hellish conditions of his world. His sculptures showed pride in the condemnation of his subjects, and in their fall to Hell. He was dressed in a three-piece suit sitting at the end of a long red carpet, on a gnarled, black, obsidian throne. A devilish smile was plastered across his face. He reminded me of Thomas, the great trickster demon who convinced me to kill Lucifer, so he could take on Heaven and topple God—or, well, Bacchus.

There was one difference between Thomas and Hades though. While Thomas always looked anxious, like a duck on the ocean, kicking its legs vigorously below the surface, Hades came across serene and peaceful, like he lived for the chaos around him.

"You must be Katrina," he said in a smooth voice, standing up. "I've heard so much about you."

I smiled. "All bad, I hope."

"I hear you've taken over for me on Earth's Hell."

"I've tried."

"And how have you done?" He asked the question like a boss at a review. I half expected him to whip out some paperwork with my stats on it.

"Well, there isn't an Earth anymore, so I couldn't have done very well."

"Ah, but that is not your concern. It wasn't you that started the Apocalypse."

"No, that was our idiot god."

"Bacchus was never good at management." Hades waved a hand, dismissing the idea of Bacchus altogether.

"I suppose it wasn't you that left him there?"

"I voted to destroy Earth eons ago. It wasn't our best effort, truth be told. We all wanted to be closer to the action at the center of the universe, but Zeus insisted we needed to populate the whole universe, and your sector is part of the universe, after all."

"Well, I suppose I'm glad you didn't get your way."

"If you enjoy existence, then I suppose not. Do you, though, Katrina? Do you enjoy existence?"

"I don't know anything else."

He studied me, stroking his pointed chin. "That wasn't my question. You know, I have asked that question to countless humans over countless galaxies, and none of them have ever answered yes."

"It's not surprising to see why," I said, folding my arms across my chest. "If they could be blinked out of existence instead of being tortured, it would seem everybody would choose that."

"But they don't," Hades replied, wagging his finger. "That's the fun part. Because I asked that, you see. I asked whether they would rather me just destroy them right then and there, and not one of them said yes. Do you know why?" Hades gave me an expectant look, waiting for an answer.

I gave him a deadpan look. "I'm sure you'll tell me."

He was happy to. He clapped his hands together and said, "It's because they don't know what will come next. You humans put so much emphasis on this thing here, you have no desire to know what comes before or after."

I scoffed at him. "And you do?"

"Of course not," he said, waving his hand. "I am the first to admit that I enjoy the tedium though. I truly enjoy every piece of it. I enjoyed designing the pits of Tartarus on every planet and finding the perfect god to take over for me as I turn my chaos to the next planet."

I furrowed my eyebrow. "Gods like Velaska."

"Wasn't she the perfect choice? No heart, no loyalty. She only wants her own aims, and her own power, and her quest for power ended as it does for so many others, in the pits of Hell."

"But what happens when she chooses somebody unfit, like Lucifer, to take over?"

He shrugged, taking slow steps around me. "You can't win them all. Besides, sometimes it ends with a delicious surprise."

"Like an Apocalypse?"

"No," he shook his head. "Like you."

My hand involuntarily went to my chest as I chuckled. "Me?"

Hades leaned close and smelled my hair. I jumped back from him. "Yes. You. I smell Hell on you. Deep into your pores. You have been the Devil for a long time, and yet you have never waged war on Heaven, gone crazy, or destroyed yourself with power. On top of all that, you have never bargained away your right to rule. Do you know how uncommon that is?"

I brushed him away and stepped back. "Actually, I didn't know I could bargain away my power."

"I don't believe that." He raised an eyebrow. "Honestly? I think you like Hell."

"I don't like the torture."

Hades spun his finger in a tight circle. "But you know that's not the end goal, is it? That's not the true end game of Hell. It never was."

"Then what is it that we're doing down here?"

"Preparing."

I cocked my head, confused. "For what?"

"For the end, of course," Hades replied, giddy and smiling. "This whole thing, it's a holding cell. It's just a way to get people ready for the next thing, which is what makes it so exciting."

"What's the next thing?"

"Come, Katrina. You've seen Cronus." Hades walked back toward his throne. "You know his power is a fraction of what it once was. That is because creation, at its core, is finite. At some point, we must all return to the Source to replenish creation. But, but, *but...* " He held a finger in the air. "creation is pure, Katrina. It's as pure as the driven snow. There can't be even a hint of impurity. Not even one little piece, or it could corrupt the whole system, and that would be chaos. That would destroy everything."

"You know I designed a way for people to earn their way out of Hell."

"Yes, Katrina," Hades said, stroking the arm of his throne. "I know everything that happens in every world I help manage. It's a clever idea, but there is one flaw in your design."

I stared up at him, excited for some actual feedback from someone. "What? What is it? Tell me."

"Heaven isn't the end goal," he said, sitting down again. "That's not where people go next. Heaven is just our home, just like your home is Hell. The real place they all go, everybody goes at the end, is back to the source."

"So...what? Eventually you just kill them?"

Hades laughed. "No. Eventually they *choose* to go. That's the last step. That's when the impurity is cleansed, Katrina. When they choose to go back to the source. All of this, all of this torture, is only so that they can choose to go back to the Source, uncorrupted as a perfect beam of light. Bacchus corrupted that. He made Heaven the end goal when it never was, which is why he was arrested."

"So, Bacchus changed the rules of the game, and you don't like the game changed, right?"

"It's not about the game—"

"Sure it is. You have a way of doing things that hasn't changed in a million billion years and you don't like anybody messing with the system. Who cares if you can't create any more planets? That's such arbitrary garbage."

"Bacchus upset the natural order. I thought you understood that. The natural order is everything. Without it, everything would collapse. Your feelings for your god are corrupting your judgment."

"I don't care about Bacchus, Hades. I don't much like him, but I need Bacchus to bring back my people. I need to return my world to this universe."

Hades sighed. "I had such high hopes for you. I thought we understood each other, Katie."

"Don't call me that. And I don't know why you would think we have anything in common."

"We both prefer Hell to Mount Olympus. That takes a very special kind."

"All I want are the coordinates to Hera's home world. I don't want a new friend. I don't want to bond. I just want to get Bacchus and go home. Will you help me or not?"

Hades leaned forward on his throne. "I will give you the coordinates you seek. Bacchus is held within Hera's castle, which you already know, but the prison is a dark labyrinth. Navigating it will be impossible without the help of Hephaestus."

"Why him?"

"He designed the castle and built all its nooks and crannies. Ask him for my key, the one I left with him so many ages ago." He motioned toward me. "Come to me."

I walked up to Hades. Something compelled me to kneel before him. "Yes?"

He placed his hands on my head and kissed my forehead. "The coordinates are inside you now."

"Why are you helping me, if I am such a disappointment?"

"You will learn, Katrina. And that means everything. Do not attempt to fight Hera. Bargain with her first. My sister is cunning, but she is wise. Only fight if it is absolutely necessary, for if you fight...you will lose."

And with that, Hades snapped his fingers and I was gone. The other flashes of light tasted like delicious dessert, but Hades's tasted like a grilled steak. I wondered if the gods got to pick their flavors, or if they were chosen for them. Either way, Hades's flash of light suited him, as did the grilled steak, and it returned me to the front of Hephaestus's blacksmith shop. Laughter bubbled from inside. I walked in to see Dennis, Lucifer, Hephaestus, and Hercules drunk over a jug of mead.

"And then, he swung the pig into an active volcano," Hephaestus said, pointing at Hercules. "It smelled of burnt swine for a month!"

"BACON!" Hercules bellowed.

Everybody burst out laughing until they heard the door creak open. They turned to me with eager, curious faces.

Dennis stood up, wobbling. "Katrina! That didn't take long. We thought you would be gone longer."

"I guess I'm more persuasive than I thought. What happened to Velaska?"

"Once Aphrodite denied her request, again," Lucifer said with a bellow. "she vanished. If I never see her again, it will be too soon."

"Good riddance," I replied.

Hercules stood. "Is it time to go, then?"

I looked around at the happy group. "No. We have some time. Pass me that jug of mead."

A great huzzah erupted from all of them when I sat down and poured myself a cup of mead. They patted me on the back like old friends. It had been a long time since I had friends, old or new, and, if only for a moment, I let myself get lost in the sensation. Who knew if I would ever have a chance to be with old friends again.

Meanwhile, on Earth...

Rebecca Lobdell sat on the ground and gazed at the black hole spinning about her. Light from the flying bats ebbed and flowed as they changed elevations. Electricity stopped working almost immediately, since neither solar nor wind power worked in the dark stillness of this weird dimension.

She had found peace with her new life. It had been a long time since she had pulled herself from the wreckage of the city and relocated herself into meadows with the other survivors. She savored the crisp softness of the grass under her feet as she walked. Rebecca hadn't realized how much she loved the ground until feeling it under her fingers and between her toes.

Long ago, she'd heard stories about meadows, brimming fields of flowers, but she had only ever seen them on the holographic projectors, or in old movies. She never dreamed she would touch them, nor did she have any desire to do so. However, running her feet and hands through a field of daisies, she wondered how she could have lived without knowing such a simple, exquisite pleasure.

"Subjects," Rhea's voice boomed. "It is a new, glorious day. I have provided for you a new life. Would you not agree?"

"Yes, we would," everybody responded in unison. Rebecca understood that it was a little culty, but she really did believe it. Her life had never felt more complete.

"And do you love your new goddess?"

"Yes, my queen," everybody responded again.

"Then, now is the time to prove your love!"

"And how would we do that, great Rhea?" Rebecca asked, echoing the rest of the group who responded in kind.

"I demand a sacrifice. I have long forgotten the taste of man flesh and need to regain my strength for the long road ahead. I have already lost much of my strength saving you, and I cannot maintain my protection without sustenance."

"Excuse me," Rebecca said. "But are you saying you want to eat one of us?"

"No," Rhea replied. "I am saying that I must. You may choose amongst yourselves, but a choice must be made, or I will make it myself."

Rebecca turned to the people she'd lived with in peace, just moments before, and realized one of them was about to die. More than that, she knew this ultimatum wouldn't be a one-time thing. Human sacrifice was part of the new normal.

Chapter 13

I woke up the next morning with a vicious hangover. I didn't remember anything after the third flagon of mead, and honestly the first couple flagons weren't too clear, either. There was a lot of laughing, some dancing, and a little bit of fighting, all smashed together in a hazy daze of debauchery. I've not had a night like that in over a hundred centuries.

I pressed my forehead into the cold ground. For a moment, it relieved my throbbing headache. Then, I heard the booming laughing of Hercules.

"And don't forget the net you made that allowed me to capture the great Sphinx."

"How could I forget?" Hephaestus replied. "You destroyed it three times."

"That's not my fault. That was shoddy craftsmanship."

"It's a poor craftsman who blames his tools, my friend."

They both had a hearty laugh as I walked over to them. "Did you ever go to bed?"

Hercules turned to me. "Gods don't need bed. It's only purpose is to lay with women, am I right, Heph?"

Hephaestus pulled at his beard. "Um, no. That's not the only reason, I guess. Sleeping is probably important..."

Hercules slapped Hephaestus on the back. "You'll have to excuse my friend. He's just a little rusty when it comes to women."

I groaned. "Honestly, I don't care enough right now. I'll beat you both later. Do you have coffee or aspirin?"

"They don't use that here," Lucifer said, walking in from outside. He was already fully dressed in a suit of black armor like the one I'd worn in the arena, except his had a minotaur on the breast plate instead of a demon dog.

"I told you that you were too puny to handle the mead of the gods," Hercules said.

Hephaestus walked to his forge. "It's a strong brew. For somebody that isn't a god, it'll knock you for a loop if you're not careful."

Hephaestus pulled a bottle of yellow goop out of the forge. He poured the thick gelatin into a flagon and handed it to me. "Watch out. It's a little hot."

Steam plumed from the container. I took a sip. The putrid, yellow ooze dripped down my throat and I retched. "What is this stuff?"

"My hangover cure. Pure Phoenix eggs. I pay a pretty penny to Hermes every time I need more. He's the only one quick enough to steal them. Drink up. I promise it will work."

"Yes, yes," Hercules chimed in. "Tilt your head back and finish the cup, puny one."

Hephaestus lifted another cup in Lucifer's direction. "Would you like one, too?"

Lucifer shook his head. "I've partied with enough gods to know how to handle my liquor. Seriously, those Phoenix eggs are no joke. I needed them a few times in the early days."

I plugged my nose and downed the entire cup. I didn't have a chance to swallow the last of it before the swelling in my brain subsided. I felt better than I had for years, millennia even.

"The nectar of the gods," Hephaestus said.

"I thought that was ambrosia," Dennis replied, groggily, as he entered the room.

Hercules flexed, showing off his rippling muscles. "Ha! Ambrosia is for wimps and women. Mead is the only true drink worthy of my lips."

"Whatever," Dennis said. "Do you have any more of that stuff?"

Hephaestus walked back to his forge. "You are destroying my whole supply. Hermes will be most pleased. He demands a king's ransom for his talents."

He handed the flagon to Dennis. "Thank you. I appreciate it."

"Of course, my friend. That is what we do."

"Do you have everything we need to defeat Hera and take on Zeus?" I asked.

He nodded. "I have repaired your sword and the suit of armor and here is Hades' key. It will open every lock in

Hera's dungeon. Do you know the terror you bring upon yourself by using it?"

I shrugged. "I know that Bacchus and Hera are there, and that if I cause a ruckus, Zeus will come running. That's enough for me right now."

"Then I wish you the gods' speed. I urge you diplomacy at all costs."

I turned to Dennis, Lucifer, and Hercules. "Are you ready?"

Hercules looked down at his feet. "I…am not coming with you."

"Excuse me? If diplomacy fails, there will be a great battle. You live for battles."

"I have no chance of winning this battle, Katrina, and neither do you. A good battle is one that you can win. Otherwise, there is no glory. Despite what you might hear, there is no glory in death."

I stepped toward him. "You're a chicken, then?"

Dennis jumped between us. "Thank you for all you have done for us, Hercules. We will never forget it."

Hercules shook Dennis's hand. "If Hera denies your request, you will be dead long before you have a chance to forget it, but I hope I am wrong, and that you live long enough to forget everything that happened here." He frowned, repeating his words under his breath to figure out if what he'd said made any sense.

"I will never forget you, friend," Dennis replied.

Hephaestus handed me a tattered scroll. "This map will get you through the dungeon. I hope you do not need it. Go to the guard tower first. Ask to entreat with Hera. She does not like to parlay, but she will do so. She is a stickler for the rules, as you can imagine."

"I will try not to piss her off."

"Indeed. For all his belittling, Hercules is right. You cannot win this. If you fail to parlay with Hera, your only choice will be bloodshed. Her army is strong. Even if you somehow get out of the dungeon, you will be on the run forever. You will never be able to rest, anywhere in the universe ever again."

"I know."

"Then why are you doing it?"

I looked over at Dennis. "We made a promise, Heph, and I'm not breaking it."

Hephaestus nodded gravely. "Understood."

I placed my hand on his gnarled hand. "I knew you would."

"You should know, Katrina, that I made your blade sharper than before. It can slice through a god in one go."

"Really?" I turned to Hercules. "Can I test it out on you?"

"He's not worth it," Hephaestus said, waving a hand. "Did you know this is the Sword of Damocles?"

I shrugged. "It sounds vaguely familiar. Should that mean something to me?"

"It means that if you cut through a god with it, they won't be able to regenerate. They will die, forever, assuming the blade is sharp enough to do the job, of course, and I have taken care of that. Use it wisely, Katrina. This is a dangerous game you are playing."

I smiled. "Wise has never been my strong suit."

"And you, Dennis," Hephaestus said, walking over to him. "This armor is strong enough to survive a blow from Apollo with nary a scratch. That's the god you should worry about the most. Hera is a wicked and evil queen, but she is weak. Her strength lies in her forked tongue and legion of minions. If you can avoid falling under her spell, you can capture her. Apollo, on the other hand, is strong—but his weakness is his strength. He believes it will save him always. If you can get him to succumb to his strength until it becomes his undoing, you can beat him."

"Understood," Dennis said.

Hephaestus stood in front of his forge. "One more thing. Katrina, I know that you do not like armor, so I made you this."

Hephaestus held up a leather jacket, just like the one I once wore. This one was black, with dark red patches on either sleeve. "It's not quite as strong as Dennis's, but it will take quite a beating before it's destroyed. Wear it well."

It slid on perfectly and fit like a glove. "Thank you. Thank you both. Dennis, we should go."

Dennis nodded. "Until we meet again."

"Until then," Hercules said. "Just know that Hera is a difficult woman. She will not take kindly to your intrusion."

"Nobody ever does."

*

Dennis, Lucifer, and I wore our fears on our faces as we walked out into the Elysian Fields. It wasn't easy to go to our deaths, and even all my swagger couldn't alleviate the gut ghost in my soul. "Are you ready?"

Dennis looked up at me. His soft eyes shimmered in the sun. "No."

"No?"

"I know we have to do it, but I'm not ready for it."

I squeezed his hand. "Me either."

I pictured the coordinates Hades gave me. I rubbed the key in my pocket. Then, I slashed a hole in the sky. Through it, I saw a planet devoid of life, swallowed by darkness. A dismal castle rose up in the midst of a desolate landscape.

"It's time."

Dennis flapped his wings toward the rift. He gave me a knowing look before disappearing into the void. Lucifer followed him, not before patting me on the back. I led them both to their doom, and by doing so, sentenced Connie to an eternity with Cronus. I took one last look at the blacksmith shop where I had my first good evening in ten thousand years and stepped into the void.

Chapter 14

The universe flashed before me. It was quite beautiful, even magical, to behold, if I could stop thinking about the future and the past and live in the moment. I'd never figured out how to quiet my mind. I usually wanted to look ten steps ahead.

But there, in that moment, I let go and witnessed the universe pass below me. Thousands of white lights flew under my feet, and dozens of multi-colored nebulas danced around them. I wondered how many other worlds the gods had created before ours. I wondered how many they would create before the end. Mostly, I wondered how there could be so much beauty in the world, even when we didn't see it. And then, it was gone, as the universe fell away and all I saw was Hera's bleak planet before me.

I rolled out of the rift onto the cracked, flaked desert in front of Hera's prison. It stood a thousand feet high, covered in thick, rock walls on every side. There was nothing in any direction except the expanding horizon.

I had no flair for diplomacy, but I wasn't an idiot. I knew that invading Hera's dungeons half-cocked was a fool's errand. I would try diplomacy—although it didn't come naturally to me—and if that didn't work, I was ready for battle, even if it would surely be a losing one.

We trudged up to the door of the castle; a high, wooden drawbridge that rose into the heavens. A minotaur guarded the gate, armed with a two-sided axe. As we approached, he spoke. "What is your purpose?"

"I am here to entreat with Hera and Apollo," I said. "They have the god of my world and I seek to release him."

"We do not recognize your right to speak with the queen."

"I don't need you to recognize it. I just need you to let me inside."

"No."

I white-knuckled the hilt of my sword, ready to strike, but Lucifer held my shoulder. He took a turn. "I believe that the rules of diplomacy state that any devil, angel, or god can entreat with Hera to make a case for their world. Do you know the rules of which I speak?"

"I do."

"Then, let us pass."

The minotaur snarled, "Lower the drawbridge!"

The drawbridge lowered with a thud. The minotaur walked across it and gestured with his axe. "Follow me."

We marched across the wooden drawbridge. A crushing feeling of hopelessness overwhelmed me. Even in Hades's lair, I'd never felt such a powerful feeling of bleakness. In Hades, the people were tortured, but Hades truly believed he was trying to save their souls so that they might return to the source as pure as the driven snow. There was honor in it; dignity. Hera's dungeon had none of that. There was no torture, but neither was there redemption, or even a purpose. There were only millions of monsters howling as we passed.

"Do not stray from the middle of the path," the minotaur called over his shoulder, though he sounded like he didn't really care whether we followed his advice. "The monsters are hungry. They haven't eaten in thousands of years and will rip the flesh from your face."

"I'd like to see them try," I replied.

*

The minotaur led us for hours, down corridor after corridor, until we finally dead-ended at a shining, gilded door a hundred feet tall which stood out from the black, dingy hopelessness all around it. "Wait here."

He walked up toward the Cyclops guarding the door. Its knuckles dragged along the ground as it bent down to talk with the minotaur.

I turned to Lucifer. "There is nothing that prevents them from slicing off our faces right now, is there?"

"Nothing except the flimsiest of diplomatic policies, and even those accords deal with planets that still exist in our dimension, not ones that have been swallowed into the void."

"So, we're boned?"

"Not yet, exactly. Right now, we're both boned and not boned. Schrödinger would be pleased. It all depends on what the Cyclops says."

After several minutes, the minotaur walked back toward us. "You will have five minutes to entreat with the queen. If she approves your proposal, then go with the gods. If not, then you are at her mercy, and she is not merciful."

The Cyclops ambled toward a giant, golden chain and pulled with all its might. Every winded heave inched the gilded doors open a bit more. Satisfied that his part in our sorry charade was concluded, the minotaur pointed us forward with a grunt and disappeared the way we'd came.

Past the doors were the gold-plated hallways and mosaics I expected from a god's castle. The drudgery of Hera's prison transitioned into the most gorgeous palace I've ever seen.

A long, ornate, red cape flew behind Hera as she walked down the steps of her throne to meet us. She oozed regality out of every pore. Her feet glided sensually on the air and her golden tresses blew in the wind. Here in her throne room, with the lighting perfectly aligned to accentuate her body, Hera shone like the goddess she was.

"I hear you have something to discuss with me." The words dripped off her tongue like honey.

I gripped the hilt of my sword tightly. I remembered Hercules's words. She has a forked tongue. If I avoided her cunning, I could beat her. "Yes, ma'am. I come to ask for the release of our god, Bacchus, and the return of our solar system into the universe."

"Hmmm, yes. I know your plea. I have heard it all over the universe. Do you know that I am aware of everything, Katrina? I watched when you rolled out of the rift into Cronus's cave. I saw when you made a pact with Velaska, when you fought my best warrior, brave Artemis, and sent her to a horrible death. I saw you when you beat Hercules, more brawn than brains. I saw when you entreated with Aphrodite, and Hades, and finally, when you came here. I know everything about you, and your plans."

"Then you are one up on me. I don't even know my plan, except to find Bacchus and defeat Zeus, both of which you can help me with. The rest, I'm just winging it."

"Yes, I'm sure it looks that way to you."

"If you know what I'm going to do, then why even agree to see me? After all, you already know if I succeed."

"I wanted to meet you, of course. I have been around a long time and have rarely seen one being that annoyed the gods so much."

"Yes," I agreed. "I am good at that."

"That you are. And all for a drunk? Tell me, is it really worth it, to save him?"

"No, but it's not about him. This is about my planet. It's about my whole solar system. Keep Bacchus if you want, honestly, but bring my solar system back from the abyss."

Hera smiled. "Ah, therein lies the problem. I can't do that. Not even if I wanted to do it, which I don't. A sector without a regent is open to invasion or innovation, both of which are equally heinous, and give others grand ideas. There are rules, Katrina. Rules that have stood for millions of years. Rules that you have repeatedly and brazenly broken with your impetuousness."

"I admit to being hot headed, but everything I do is for the good of my people."

"Yes, which is the only reason you are still alive. You do have a good heart—a stupid one, but a good one, full of misguided bravery."

"I appreciate the backhanded compliment, but I am here for one purpose, which is to get back my solar system."

Hera walked toward her throne in the middle of the room. "Ah, but that is not true. It was true for a time, but now your plans are much grander. Now, you plan to capture Zeus and bring him to Cronus."

"How do you know that?" I asked in astonishment.

"I told you, I know everything. And that is where I can help you, I believe. You see, my husband, for all his glory, is a sniveling idiot who will screw anything that moves. He has made a fool of me for long enough, so I will make a deal with you. If you can, in fact, destroy my husband, then I will return your world to you. Fail me, and you shall never see your planet again."

"How do I know you will be true to your word?"

"You don't." She raised a haughty eyebrow. "That's the beauty of having power over somebody. You have to trust me."

"That's never been my strong suit."

"I have faith you can learn it. I've watched you traipse all over this galaxy doing the bidding of the gods. One more favor won't kill you, especially if it finally achieves your ends." Her eyes dropped and along with it, the simpering act. Her next words were sharp. "Urania! Come here!"

From the darkness of a nearby hallway, a small woman scooted forward. "Yes, my queen?"

"Is it ready?"

"Yes, my queen."

Hera pointed down a long hallway. "Follow me."

*

She led us down a great hallway that dead-ended in two metal doors, which she flung open with a melodramatic flourish and led us inside a giant observatory. Dozens of beautiful women watched a bevy of monitors, arranged in a semi-circle around a gigantic telescope set up in the center of the room. A smug Apollo leaned against the telescope as if it were his own personal toy.

"Don't lean on that!" The demure, young woman didn't look like much, but she had a mighty bellow. She shuffled toward a monitor in the center of the room.

Apollo stood up straight. "I'm sorry."

Hera waved her arm gracefully toward the telescope. "Please, look through the telescope."

I looked back at Lucifer and Dennis, who motioned me forward. I walked across the room and peered into the eye piece of the great telescope at a dead point in space.

"Do you see it?" Hera asked.

"I see nothingness and…nothingness."

"Keep watching. Apollo. Now!"

Apollo snapped his fingers and the solar system, my solar system, appeared out of nowhere, as if it never left. "That is proof that we can do what we say." Apollo snapped his fingers again and the solar system vanished again. "Do you see what we can do?"

I looked closely into the telescope for several seconds. "I mean, it looks interesting, but how do I know that's Earth? How do I know it's not like, a mirage?"

Hera sighed. "Urania. Increase the magnification. Apollo. Do it again."

Another snap of Apollo's fingers and Earth came back into our universe. I didn't let him snap again. I pulled the sword out of my hilt and in one swift motion, cut his hand off at the wrist. He roared in pain and I swiftly wound up and cut off the other one. The great god dropped to the ground, screaming in pain, writhing on the floor.

"What have you done to me?" Apollo wailed.

"Not as much as I'd like to, believe me."

I stepped toward Hera, who had backed onto her chair until she cowered from me. "I've thought over your proposal, my queen, and I have a better one."

Meanwhile, on Earth...

Rebecca Lobdell sat around in a circle with the other
survivors. Just a few hours before, they had been the best of
friends. Now they ate in suspicious silence under the watchful
eye of Rhea.

"We...can't do this," Rebecca finally said. "It's not right.
We can't just send somebody to their death, can we?"

An older, bespectacled man spoke up. "We've already
seen so much death, and Rhea has done so much for us. I find
it a small sacrifice to give back to her."

"Does that mean you volunteer?" Rebecca gave him a
withering look.

The man gulped loudly, then went back to his meal in
silence. Rebecca sneered at the group. "Are any of you
volunteering? Because if this is such a great deal, then
somebody just volunteer."

"Nobody wants to die," a mother responded, clutching her
child.

"Of course, nobody wants to die, and that's the thing, isn't
it? Nobody thinks they're going to die. You all think it's
going to be somebody else, don't you? But when that finger
points at you, I'm sure you'll be singing another tune."

Nobody looked at Rebecca as she pointed her finger
around at the group. "And of course, this isn't the end of it.
Rhea will get hungry again, and we will dwindle until we all
die. It's—"

A deafening screech from the sky made her drop
instinctively to the ground. Opening her eyes, she watched the
clouds swirl in a familiar chaotic pattern. It was the pull of the
black hole, and it was tugging at the meadow.

Rebecca breathed. Fear filled every inch of her as she felt
it reaching for her.

In an instant, it was over. Rebecca looked up and saw not
bats, but stars. Stars like the ones she remembered. There, to
the north, the Big Dipper. The moon popped into view, and

the black hole reformed into the sun. She was home. She couldn't believe it, but she was home.

In a single fit of elation, everybody jumped for joy. They hugged each other and screamed out. And then, the screeching started again, the skies shifted, and when it all stopped they were once again in front of Rhea.

"You dare try to leave me!" Rhea said. "I will destroy you all!"

The great Titan reached out to grab Rebecca, but her fingers closed on nothing but air. The screech began in earnest, the void disappeared again, and Rebecca Lobdell was home...again. Just like before, she watched the stars, the moon, and finally the sun pop back into view. She smiled an uneasy smile and drank it in, knowing at any instant, the void could reopen and swallow her.

Chapter 15

After we'd captured Apollo, Hera went down without a fight. Lucifer and Dennis tied them up while I traveled down the labyrinth of cells to find Bacchus. The unceasing moans overwhelmed me. Minotaurs, demons, Cyclopes, and other monsters who worked in the prison ogled me as I passed. They wanted to fight, but word traveled fast that I'd destroyed Apollo in less than thirty seconds. Their loyalty didn't extend to death.

There must have been a million or so trapped gods and monsters in those dungeons, and the cells went on forever. It was an impressive feat of engineering when it came down to it. To predict you could fill a million cells was a ballsy move. To do it, even more so.

I wondered if Hephaestus balked when Zeus and Hera told him to build a million cells. I mean, it sounded crazy, right? That's way too many cells to imagine, and yet Heph created this place, even knowing how crazy the numbers were, because he's a good foot soldier.

They kept Bacchus in cell block 74,321 with a thousand other gods and immortals. None of them had any way to use their powers. They had no way to do anything, except contemplate a death that would never come.

Bacchus cowered in the back of his cell with his knees curled up in his face. His white beard had turned a dark shade of gray to match his sullied toga. The regal and joyous god was replaced with a wretched, miserable one.

"Hello again, Bacchus," I said, walking up to his cell.

"Katrina, Katrina!" Bacchus ran to the bars of the prison and pressed his face against them. "You came! Let me out...oh, please let me out."

I watched him for a moment. His sniveling disgusted me. "I could do that. I have this nifty key that Hades gave me. It can open any cell in this place."

He marveled at the key. "Yes, please. Please do it."

"I've been thinking though, Bacchus, about whether you deserve to be let out." I took a few slow, thoughtful steps. "I mean, it was not cool what Apollo did to Earth, but was he wrong to arrest you? Let's face it, you're a crappy god, my friend. You messed up *everything*. The gods left you with a paradise and you turned it into a literal Hell on Earth."

Bacchus rubbed the snot from his nose. "Was it really a paradise, Katrina? When the gods lived there, they micromanaged every single moment of you humans' lives. They tricked you. They overpowered you. You might have had paradise, but you didn't have choice. Is that better?"

"You are asking if I would rather be manipulated and happy or Hell on Earth? I'll take option one."

"You think you would, but you're quite the free spirit, Katrina. You would have grown tired of it over time. Yet, with my world, honestly, I didn't care what you guys did, so long as you stayed out of my kingdom. War, famine, pestilence, torture—whatever you wanted to do—I was cool with it. You could have chosen the righteous path and lived in harmony, but you chose to devolve into warlike beings who fought over meaningless tracts of land. That wasn't me. That was all you."

"But you forced us to worship you. You built churches and mosques and synagogues, and watched people fight and die over you. Didn't you think even once about stepping in?"

"Aside from the time I came down to Earth and you crucified me and then bastardized my teachings?"

"Yes, aside from that," Katrina said, taken aback a bit by his honesty.

Bacchus shook his head. "No. Not one time. I just didn't care enough."

I turned away from him. "Well, maybe you need some more time to think about it, then."

"Wait, Katrina…no no no no no no no, Katrina! Let me out!"

I didn't respond to his pleas. I just walked out on him. All of this, everything I had done, was to save Bacchus, and Earth in the process. Yet, I saved it by myself, without him. We didn't need a god to save us. We didn't need anything.

*

I strolled back into the throne room, where Lucifer and Dennis stood guard over Hera and Apollo. The two gods both looked worthless though, huddled there, cowering in fear.

Hera hadn't stopped crying since I left her. "What have you done to him?" she sobbed. "He was perfect, and you destroyed him."

She was right. I looked over at Apollo, who was crouched in the fetal position. Since I'd used the Sword of Damocles to cut off his hands, he couldn't regenerate them, just like Hephaestus said. The smell of charred god flesh permeated the whole castle.

I knelt next to Hera. "That's the only thing you care about? Well, I can promise you that his imperfections won't last long. Cronus will eat him and then there will be nothing for you to worry about."

"No!"

I handed Lucifer the key and scroll Hephaestus gave me. "Do you know what to do?"

"Yes, ma'am. Wait for Zeus. Urania called out to him using every known channel. He will come, and I will tell him where to find you."

I placed my hand on his shoulder. "He might kill you."

"I know."

"I hope he doesn't."

"Me too."

It wasn't a good idea to piss off Zeus, the most powerful god in the universe, but I didn't much care anymore. I had saved my world, and my people. There was only one thing left to do: keep my promise to Connie and save her life.

I turned to Dennis. "Are you ready?"

Dennis picked up Hera and Apollo. "As I'll ever be."

I grabbed the sword and swung, cutting a hole in the universe. I could see Cronus asleep in his cave, and Connie sitting next to him. "Let's go."

*

I rolled out onto the dirt floor of Cronus's cave. Dennis caught Connie in a tight and passionate embrace. Cronus's eyes turned from them to me, and then they narrowed on the gods in front of me.

"These…are not Zeus, Katrina. I appreciate the meal, but none of this was part of the deal."

"I always overdeliver, Cronus. You can count on that." I kicked Apollo over to him. "This one you can have now. Hera, I need for the time being."

"This one is damaged," Cronus said, looking him over, crinkling his rocky brow. "I do not like damaged goods."

"Then don't eat him, you snob. I don't care what you do with him."

"No, no..." He gave a martyr's sigh. "I shall eat him. I need the sustenance."

I kicked Apollo toward Cronus again. He rolled closer as he struggled against his constraints. "Stop this! I am a god! You cannot do this!"

Apollo didn't say another word before Cronus opened his mouth and swallowed him whole. His screams echoed through the Titan's stomach for a moment before they disappeared.

"Apollo! No!" Hera cried, big, wet tears streaming down her beautiful face.

"Do I get her, too?" Cronus asked.

I shook my head. "Not yet. I need her…for now."

Cronus grumbled. "But, I am hungry."

"Deal with it," I replied. "I have a question. What happens when I kill a god?"

Cronus shrugged "It's no different than killing a man, really."

"Aren't gods immortal, though?"

"Only compared to humans, but they are nothing compared to me." Cronus chuckled and waved his stony fingers dismissively. "Have you ever had a dog, Katrina?"

"No, but she's killed a lot of demon dogs," Connie said from the corner, still embracing Dennis.

"Shut up, Connie."

"A dog lives for fifteen years or so," Cronus said. "While a human lives for seventy-five. To them, you are immortal. You never seem to age over their whole lives. And to the fruit fly, that lives a month, you are a god. It's no different with gods, humans, and Titans. It's only a matter of perspective."

"So, if I lop off Hera's head, I won't trigger some cataclysm."

I heard a whimper come from Hera and Cronus laughed. "No. Gods like to believe they are more important than they really are. The truth is, many worlds have life despite Zeus's silly decree about a planet requiring a god."

"That's good to know. Now, I need a favor."

"You always need a favor."

"It is to help you gain your vengeance," I said. "I need Connie to make my plan work."

"That was not part of the deal. You bring me Zeus, you can have Connie."

"Have I not proven myself a woman who gets things done? I brought you even more than you bargained for—*two* of the most powerful gods. I brought my world back from extinction, and now I'm going to get Zeus. But, I'll need Connie to help me."

"I'm sorry, Katrina, but an agreement is an agreement."

"Fine. Then I need something else."

He chuckled. "Of course, you do."

"Make me a god."

"Like it's that easy."

"We both know it is that easy. If you want Zeus, I need to match his power."

"So that you can match him, and then defeat me?"

"You can take it away as easily as you gave it. Just, give me the power, alright? We're so close."

"Very well."

Cronus closed his eyes and his lips parted. A wisp of golden energy spiraled out of his rocky gorge mouth and spun in the air. Then, like a lightning bolt, it shot into me. I toppled backwards into the rock wall behind me. When I opened my eyes again, a new power surged through my limbs.

"There," he said. "Don't disappoint me."

"Does this make us enemies now?"

Cronus shook his head. "I hold no ill will toward you. I granted you the strength of a god for destroying my enemies. You are every bit Zeus's equal now, if not his better. You have proven a friend to me, don't make me regret this."

I looked back at Connie and Dennis. They were no longer locked in embrace, but poised and ready to fight. "You're the last line of defense, okay? If Zeus gets into this room, it means he beat me and you have to stop him."

Chapter 16

I dragged Hera by her hair out of the cave that had once sent me into the throes of insanity. This time, they didn't stop me for even a second. My brain was so tightly wound, my thoughts racing thirteen steps forward and three to the side, that the caves didn't affect me. They couldn't keep up with me. I watched them affect Hera, though. Her mouth frothed, and her eyes rolled back in her head. She went limp and didn't regain her composure until we were outside listening to the water crash against the island's cliff face.

The rain poured heavily outside the cave as I leaned Hera against the wall and set myself up at the entrance.

"He won't come, you know," Hera said. "He doesn't really care about me."

"I know he doesn't, but he does care about his pride, and his pride is what I wounded by taking you. I don't know Zeus, but I know powerful men. He'll come."

"Powerful men like Cronus? Do you know what kind of evil he is?"

I nodded. "Yes. I've known my share of evil in my day."

"No. You haven't. You've known simple evil. You've known cute evil. You've never known real evil. Cronus is real evil. He has no conscience. All he wants is what he wants, and he will do anything to get it."

"So, exactly like you, then."

"I admit, we gods have lost our way, but our goal is a peaceful universe. We have always worked for the greater good."

"Is that what you call destroying whole solar systems?"

"Yes, when it means the rest of the universe lives. Do you not prune plants so that they have the best chance of surviving? This is no different."

"It's no different unless you're the leaf that gets pruned. How many worlds have you destroyed in your quest for goodness?"

"I don't know. A fair few."

"More than a few. There were thousands of gods in those dungeons, and I'll wager all of them governed habitable worlds."

"Most, yes."

"And they all had billions of souls they cared for, which means you've butchered trillions of souls."

"For the benefit of a million times that number! Would you not kill one percent of the universe to save the other 99 percent? Are you truly that blind? Do you really have that little sympathy for our plight?"

"I could never do that."

"That is weakness. You put the whole universe in jeopardy because of your vendetta. You would destroy everything to save one solar system—*your* solar system. You are no better than us."

A lightning bolt exploded into the ground, exploding sand and rocks in all directions. A dark figure emerged from the cloud cover: Zeus. The rain bounced off him as he made his way toward us. His shimmering toga and beard glowed white with electricity.

"It's time," I said, gripping my sword.

Zeus descended from the sky. "You have offended the gods, Katrina of Earth. I shall deal with you as I dealt with your minion." He tossed Lucifer's charred body at the foot of the cave entrance. The old angel gasped for breath.

"I'm sorry," I said to him through the tears welling in my eyes.

"It's not the first time you've killed me," Lucifer choked out.

Hera broke from her chains and ran across the rain toward Zeus. "My love. You have come to save me."

Zeus's eyes twitched, and a great lightning bolt sprung from them, exploding Hera backward. The heat melted her into the rock face. "No. I have come to defend your honor. There is a difference."

"You just killed your *wife*," I shouted. I'd heard they had a rocky marriage, but knowing a couple is arguing is a lot different from witnessing them kill each other.

"She will live, and she will learn the price of weakness. Now, it is your turn."

Zeus threw a lightning bolt at me. I watched it slow as it neared me, *Matrix*-style. The rain parted like a curtain as the bolt inched forward. I witnessed the world progress in only a nanosecond at a time. I grabbed the lightning bolt in midair and flung it back at him. The bolt careened off his shoulder and disappeared into the ocean.

"You are stronger than I expected, Katrina, but you are no match for me."

Zeus parted the clouds and sent a barrage of lightning at me. The bolts rained down and there were too many; I couldn't catch them all. I grabbed Lucifer and jumped back into the cave while they crashed all over the island.

Inside the cave, I tried to catch my breath and focus. I needed to come up with a plan. If I didn't move, I was done for, but I couldn't go back outside the cave. Zeus was waiting there, and he was too powerful. There was nothing left to do except retreat deeper toward Cronus's lair, where I would be a sitting duck. This is when I remembered it's important to talk junk. "Is that all you got?"

"Do you think I can't find you in there?" he shouted. "I designed this cave myself to detain my most dangerous prisoner ever. Do you not believe that it can keep you, too? And then what do you think will happen when Cronus gets hungry again? Let me tell you, an eternity inside Cronus's digestive tract is not a fun time. You will be devoured slowly over eons, every moment a torture."

"Just like this conversation!" I shouted back, pulling Lucifer through the cave with me.

Two lightning bolts grazed across my chest and exploded into the cave behind me. One of the walls collapsed just as I retreated into Cronus's lair. Dennis and Connie jumped back, while Cronus screamed out, indignant.

"What are you doing to my home?"

"It's not your home, it's your prison, and I'm destroying it!" I threw Lucifer on the ground of Cronus's cavern. He was fading fast. "Come on, buddy. Come on."

Connie looked up from the bottom of the pit, holding Artemis's bow and ready to strike. "What happened?"

"Just get ready to fight!" I shot back. "Zeus is right behind me."

"We're ready."

I placed my hands on Lucifer's chest and closed my eyes. Light radiated from every orifice and cascaded down his body before shooting out of his mouth in a huge beam. When I took my hands away, the old archangel was alive, his charred body replaced with a fresh one.

"What was that?" Lucifer asked.

"I guess I'm a god now," I replied.

The top of the cave exploded, spewing dust and stones all over us. The sandy, dusty floor beneath our feet turned to mud from the rain pouring down and we all looked like drowned, muddy rats. Zeus flew above us all, firing lightning down on every surface.

"Enough!" I shouted. "This ends now!"

Zeus sent a lightning bolt down on Connie. Jumping in front of the bolt, I used my sword to absorb the blow, then swung it around and sent the lightning back on Zeus. He dodged it effortlessly.

"You must do better than that, Katrina."

I turned to Connie and pointed at Artemis's bow. "You know how to use that bow?"

She shook her head. "How hard can it be? Pull and release, right?"

Connie pulled back the bow and let an arrow fly. It whizzed past Zeus's electrified body and disappeared into the cloud cover.

Meanwhile, Dennis and Lucifer flew through the storm at breakneck speeds to distract Zeus. They dipped and dodged every bolt he threw at them, but they couldn't take on the god directly.

"He has to come down here!" I shouted. "We'll never catch him."

"No, he doesn't." Lucifer said. "You're a god now! Fly!"

I willed my feet to levitate off the ground, and they did. I was even greater than I thought—and I thought I was pretty great. I flew into the air with my sword, but Zeus pulled out a flaming sword of his own and parried my strikes. He was too strong. Even as a god, I could not compete with Zeus's power. Nothing could…except maybe a Titan.

That's when I saw the massive chains that bound Cronus to the cave. "Connie! Give me some cover!"

Connie fired a string of arrows into the air. Zeus dodged them, losing his focus on me for a moment. That's when I flew down and cut the chains that bound Cronus to the earth.

"No!" Zeus shouted, but it was too late.

The Mad Titan burst forth from his prison, crushing what was left of the cave. He stood a hundred feet tall, towering over everything in sight.

"What have you done, fool?" Zeus shouted to me.

"What I had to."

Zeus struck Cronus with lightning, but the craggy, rock-faced behemoth didn't budge. Zeus was like a fly to Cronus, who swatted him down with his terrible, huge hands.

"You have corrupted my power for too long, Zeus," Cronus said, picking him up by the feet. "Now the time for vengeance is mine."

Cronus opened his mouth and swallowed Zeus whole. He sucked up the whole of the rain, too, and with a great belch, it was over.

*

Cronus shook off the last of his rocky prison before he sat down next to me, chomping on a dessert of Hera. The Titan peeled her burnt form off the side of the rock wall, and she screamed as she disappeared down his thick gullet. He now looked like a human, though his eyes were too small for his head, and his forehead too large for it. Otherwise, he was pretty much just a really big human.

A beautiful rainbow crowned the island. There was no longer a cave; there was only us on a shallow atoll, listening to the unforgiving ocean lap against the island. Connie,

275 Russell Nohelty 275

Dennis, and Lucifer sat around, looking off at the ocean or up at the sky, but Cronus fixated on me.

"You are a woman of your word. I release your friend from her debt."

"Thank god," Connie said, throwing her arms in the air.

Cronus grumbled. "The gods had nothing to do with it."

"What will you do now?" I asked him.

"There are many others, equal Zeus and Hera, who have defiled my way of life."

"Will you destroy them?"

Cronus smiled. The craggy rocks on his face cracked as the edges of his mouth curled up. "I feel vindicated in my world now, Katrina. I did not lie that my interest in this universe has waned, but I see now that there are things in it worth saving."

"You aren't going to blink it out of existence, then?"

Cronus smiled. "I will not. Now, my goal is to find my beloved Rhea. I thought of her much for these past millennia, and only want to be with her again."

"What do I do now?" I asked. "There's no god to rule over Earth. Eventually, we're going to get our comeuppance for that."

"Earth never needed a god, Katrina. But if you really want to stay on the level, then, well—I believe you are a god now, aren't you?"

"I am, huh?"

"I think you would make a good ruler."

And with that, Cronus stood up and grew a thousand feet tall. The tides quaked under him, as if the island he called home ached from his presence. The water rose violently, and the waves pounded the shoreline as Cronus took a step off the planet and vanished somewhere into the universe. Once he was gone, the water calmed, and the world stopped its restless tantrum. I turned to Dennis, Connie, and Lucifer.

"If I take on this gig on Earth, I suppose I'm going to need a new ruler for Hell."

"I'm not doing it," Lucifer said. "Just drop me off at the nearest bar and leave me be. I am out."

"I wasn't going to ask you. You're a horrible ruler." I turned to Connie. "You up for the challenge?"

She made a face. "That sounds horrible."

I shrugged. "It's actually not so bad, as long as you can get over the sulfur smell, but if you hate it, you can always trick some sap into taking your place."

"There is no way I'm moving to Hell," Dennis said. "And I'm not leaving Connie. Not again. Not ever."

I shook my head. "You wouldn't have to move, Dennis. Connie would have full access to Heaven whenever she wanted it." I looked Connie dead in the eye. "There's a new day dawning, and I want you to be part of it. I'm implementing my system, so people can earn their way out of Hell, and I want you to help me with it."

Lucifer leaned an elbow on my shoulder. "I thought Hades told you that everybody needed to return to the Source."

"Screw Hades. That's his version of Hell and he can keep it. We live on Earth. We will never bow to the gods again."

And with that, I cut open the rift, sighing as I saw Heaven illuminated off in the distance: My new home, as god of my people. I hoped I would be a good ruler, a fair ruler, and a just one. One that cared more for them than my own glory.

Book 3

Katrina Hates the Universe

Prologue

Ten thousand years ago, the world went through the end of times, the Apocalypse, and there was nothing we could do about it. God raptured all the good boys and girls up to some giant orgy in the sky. The rest of us were left on Earth, wondering "why not me?"

A rift opened in the desert. Demons, zombies, and all manner of Hellbeast poured out and roamed the land. They ripped apart everybody they could find and tortured us to the brink of extinction. Then one day they got bored and opted for a quiet life in the suburbs.

They squatted in the homes of the people they brutally murdered, stole our jobs, ate our food, and made our lives a living Hell. We thought the rampant destruction was bad, but that was nothing compared to the torture of listening to a demon play his guitar poorly all night.

They took everything from us, and left us quivering in the shadows, shells of our former selves. Two years of that was more than I could take. Living with monsters, working with them, and killing them was too much for my psyche, and I snapped. I realized the only person who could fix my plight and give me back my life was the Devil, so I set out to kill him.

I brought my best frenemy Connie and we traveled across the desert to the Hell rift. Along the way, we met up with the demon-jackass Thomas, who convinced me to join his rebellion against the Devil. Bad idea.

Before long, we came face to face with ole Lucifer himself, and I stabbed him through the heart. His death didn't change anything though. In fact, it made things so much worse, as it turned out Thomas was just using me to take the power of Hell for himself.

With Hell under his control, Thomas stormed Heaven and tried to take it over. The Hellspawn would have won, too, if God hadn't called me up to his aid. He gave me a big ass flaming sword and sent me off to kill Thomas, which I did.

What he didn't tell me is that Thomas's death left a void in the role of devil, a role which passed to me. For the next ten thousand years, I took care of Hell and did a fine job of it. I annexed Pluto as a colony for Hell's overflow. Then, a decade ago, the god of my world, Bacchus, was arrested and Apollo threw Earth into a black hole until Zeus resolved his trial.

That wasn't good enough for me, so I traveled across the galaxy to defeat Zeus and get him back. Along the way, I fought Hercules, beat Apollo, and set Cronus free from his rocky prison. After the dust settled, Earth was freed from its black hole, Cronus made me a god, and now I control the whole the solar system from Mercury to Pluto.

It's a lot to take in. I know.

TL;DR…

I went from a mortal to a god in a little over ten thousand years. Now, I am responsible for Heaven and Earth.

Chapter 1

Being a god really isn't that hard at the end of the day. I can see why it appealed to Bacchus. He was a sluggish waste of space during the eons Zeus assigned him to rule over Heaven and Earth on behalf of the gods, and now I knew why.

It was a tedious job, being a ruler, but it wasn't hard. The people on Earth were too busy rebuilding their civilization to cause problems, and once they died, they feared my wrath too much to step out of line even an inch. I can't believe Bacchus messed it up so bad.

He was better known as God, Yahweh, or Jehovah. Yes, that god. He's kind of a big deal in the three major religions of Earth, but he's not the only god. Not by a long shot. There are millions of gods across the universe. The pagans were right all along. Gods really did live among us, work with us, care for us, and trick us into screwing them…for a while, at least.

Gods only stayed on one planet long enough to make sure it could sustain itself. Then, they left to start a new civilization across the galaxy, leaving one god to rule over each habitable planet, as a regent.

In Earth's case, that regent was Bacchus. And boy, did he mess up.

Regents are supposed to look after habitable planets on behalf of all the gods and make sure their memory lived on, but Bacchus was so vain that he decided to convince people he was the only god in the cosmos, as if only one god could create everything. He was sloppy, and he got cocky, which is hardly surprising, considering he was the god of wine and debauchery. The gods ousted him, and I became the ruler of Heaven in his place.

So, how does a girl from Overbrook, Oregon, go from becoming a devil to ruling in Heaven? Slowly, and over the course of about ten thousand years. For the first thirty years of my existence, I lived as a human. For the next ten thousand years I was below them as the Devil, and for the last decade I've been above them, as a god.

This means my perspective on humanity changed over the years—quite literally. For a long time, I didn't believe that humanity had any redeeming qualities. After the Apocalypse, I saw nothing but weak-willed men and cowards. What I learned over the past few thousand years was that humans had the capability to be better, even if they lacked the desire. There was still death, destruction, and murder, but there was also great generosity. The world seemed a better place since I became a god, and my life was better, too.

Every morning I met my mother on the edge of a lake I'd built in the middle of Heaven. We sat for hours, sometimes, dangling our feet in the water, watching it cascade over the falls. It was the same every morning, no matter what else I had to get done, and I loved it. Today was no different.

"Mom," I asked. "Are you happy?"

She smiled. "Course I'm happy, kiddo. This is Heaven. Your dad's at home reading the paper. You're sitting by my side. What's not to be happy about?"

My dad was supposed to stay in Hell, having been turned into a hideous zombie before he died. Monsters weren't allowed into Heaven, but since I was a god, I bent the rules to let him through the pearly gates. Who was going to argue with me?

"I don't know."

"Do you know how painful it was to regrow my body?" She swirled her legs in the water. "Very. It was the most painful thing I've ever done by a factor of a thousand. I never thought I would forget that horrible time. But now, I can kick my legs into the water on the most beautiful lake I've ever seen, with my daughter." She smiled and nudged me. "If that can't breed happiness, what can?"

She was right, of course, but I just couldn't see it. I struggled with happiness, even as a god. I understood why I wasn't happy on Earth, and in Hell, but I really thought Heaven would bring about happiness, or at least serenity. It didn't.

I wanted to know how she found her happiness, but I decided not to push her further. It was a question I asked often, and while her answers changed over time, they never satisfied me. She was happy, though, and so I would feign happiness for her sake. I looked out into the water, hoping that happiness would wash over me, but like every other day, it eluded me.

It was still eluding me when a great black vortex ripped a hole in the sky. The vortex popped Heaven like a bubble and sucked everything—from the clouds to the lake to my mother—towards it.

"Mom! Run!" I shouted to her, but there was nowhere for her to go. She pumped her legs but couldn't move. We were stuck in place. I felt this before, when Apollo popped our sun and turned it into a black hole. Except now I was without the sword that allowed me to traverse the universe. I would be sucked through the vortex with my people, and we would all be doomed.

For one moment, then another, we fought helplessly against the vacuum. Through the dark vortex, a figure emerged. Faint at first, then gathering mass until it fell out of the hole and landed at my feet. I had no time to recognize the mass before two more of them fell out from the rift.

The last figure, with a weak, breathless voice waved an arm at the sky. "Close."

The rift closed on itself and vanished, as if it never existed in the first place. Heaven fell calm once more.

I grabbed my mother. "Are you okay?"

"I'm fine."

"Stay here." I ran over to the figures that fell from the rift. "Who are you?"

Weakly, the first body turned over. "Katrina…"

I recognized him immediately. It was Hephaestus, blacksmith of the Gods. His brawny form slumped over a pile of heavenly clouds, his beard singed black and smoking. He moved between his workshop in the depth of a mighty volcano where he made his most powerful weapons, and another on Aphrodite's planet where he worked on the front lines outfitting angels and gods with more standard fare. Now, he lay battered and bruised in front of me.

"My friend," I said. "What happened to you?"

"I will survive. Help the others."

I turned over the bloody toga next to him and found Aphrodite, goddess of love and ruler of the last planet Zeus created before I killed him. There was no more perfect being in all the galaxy when we first met. Now, she looked like a raw slab of meat. The left side of her face hung lower than her right, and a jagged gash ran from her forehead to her chin. She struggled to breath out of her mangled nose.

"Oh my gods...Angels! To me!"

Two angels flew up and grabbed onto Aphrodite. "Take her to my mansion. Tend to her."

"Yes, ma'am."

The last figure stumbled to her feet and I recognized her immediately as Velaska. She was the god of the underworld before Lucifer, who was Devil before me. Vain and cruel, she enjoyed playing games with people, offering them their heart's desire and then twisting their words. I did not like her, but it brought me no joy to see her struggling to walk toward me.

"They are coming," she said. "They will destroy us all."

Chapter 2

I tried to carry Hephaestus and Velaska to my mansion but struggled against their awkward weight. I called more angels, who flew them to my quarters as I followed behind. Unlike Bacchus, I preferred living indoors, near my subjects. He preferred to be out in front of them, aggrandizing for his own benefit.

I had constructed a small mansion in the middle of Heaven's Elysian Fields. It wasn't much, but it was enough for my needs. My mother and father lived in a small guest house behind the mansion, not because they had to—they could live anywhere in Heaven—but they liked being close to me.

My mansion was inspired by the Playboy mansion I'd watched on reruns of *The Girls Next Door*. Say what you will about the old perv, but Heff knew how to construct an edifice; a massive pool with grotto in the back, plenty of room so that you didn't have to see anybody you didn't want, and a slick, silk robe so you could hide your junk until it was time to knock boots. I look forward to the day he gets out of Hell and we can talk about it. It won't be for a while, though. He was disgusting.

The angels laid Hephaestus down in my best guest room, with pillows and mattress made of the softest clouds I could muster. He was, after all, my favorite of all the gods. Even on his best day, he didn't say much, but what he spoke made sense to me. He spoke of the land, and the iron, and the fire. He laughed about the past, admired the present, and spoke wistfully about the future.

I sat at the foot of his bed. "Hephaestus, what happened?"

"The Horde are coming."

"What are the Horde? When will they come?"

"They were too quick for us."

That was the last he spoke before drifting off into a fitful sleep. I watched him for a moment before I pulled up the

covers and let him rest. There would be time for questions
later.

*

My angels worked on Aphrodite to fix her mangled face, but
they could only do so much. Gods had immense power, that
was for sure, but they could not reconstruct their own faces.
Only time could do that.

I sat by her bedside while she cried. She was the strongest
god left in the pantheon with Zeus gone, but underneath the
regal facade, she didn't care about much more than idle
gossip. She often came to Earth to titter about the other gods
and tell tales of the past. Her favorites were love stories, and
stories that complimented her beauty.

"Did you know, Katrina dear, that I once had an affair
with Hercules?"

"Did I tell you, Katrina dear, that I just witnessed a cherub
and a siren fall in love?"

"Can I tell you, Katrina dear, how droll it is to be the most
beautiful person in all the land?"

It would be lying to say I didn't enjoy her nonsensical
rambling. I never cared for love, or beauty, or any of that
nonsense. Sex was utilitarian for me. I had an urge, I fixed the
urge. I certainly couldn't put up with somebody long enough
to fall in love with them.

Aphrodite on the other hand, fell in love with everybody.
Through her tears the only thing she managed to say was,
"How will somebody love me now that I am hideous?"

I didn't have an answer for her, nor could I deal with her
another minute longer. Looking at her made me want to emote
all over the place.

*

I gave Velaska the worst room in my mansion, the one that
was reserved for guests that pissed me off. It was the smallest
room, under the stairs so you heard clomping all day and
night. I got the idea from Harry Potter.

I didn't owe her any favors. After all, Velaska was the
reason Lucifer became the Devil, and since I took over for

him, I blamed her for my plight—and felt that blame was completely justified.

"Could you possibly find a lumpier mattress?" Velaska was terrorizing one of my angels when I entered the room. "Have you heard of memory foam? Of course not. This simply will not do."

"We can send you back through the portal if you want," I said. "I would really, really like that."

Velaska cleared her throat. "No, no. This will be fine."

The angel asked sheepishly if I needed anything else. I shook my head and sent him away with a polite smile.

Velaska scoffed. "I didn't know you could smile."

"I didn't know you could look so ragged."

"It was unintentional, I assure you. It's not like I planned to come through that portal, you know. It took the last of my remaining energy. I'm lucky I remembered the spell."

"I didn't know there was a spell for that. Lucifer seemed to believe the only way to cut through the universe was with the Sword of Damocles."

"Of course, he did. He doesn't know everything. He is old, but I am ancient. A spell is the quickest way. There is much magic in the world if you remember the old ways."

"Why did you come here?"

"Because we had no choice. As much as I hate this place, it is one of the few coordinates I remembered by heart. When the Horde came for the throne room, well …it was the only place we could go."

"Who are the Horde?"

Velaska shuddered. "Horrible creatures. A swarm of the biggest bugs you've ever seen, and completely heartless. They wear huge blasters attached to giant packs on their backs. The lasers they fired…they evaporated everything, including gods."

"That's impossible. I've only seen three weapons that could take down a god, and one of them is my sword, planted on the platform at the center of Heaven."

"And where is the others?"

"The Dagger of Obsolescence was fished from the lake of fire and rests on Pluto. But Artemis's bow? I don't know. After Cronus we…just left it. But nobody could find it on that planet. It's like finding a needle in a haystack."

"I've seen their technology, honey. They found something, and they brought a thousand ships to lay waste to Mount Olympus." She choked back her emotions. "They slaughtered everybody, Katrina. Everybody. Like it was nothing. Ten million became ten thousand in a matter of hours."

"What about Hercules and the others?"

"I do not know what fate awaits Hercules. We made a last stand on Mount Olympus, but…"

"How did they get to Mount Olympus? I thought you needed permission from a god for entrance?"

Velaska's face went white. "This was the most advanced race I've ever seen, Katrina. They did things I never thought possible. They wiped out gods like they were children. They destroyed towns like they were toys. Whole civilizations— civilizations that stood for hundreds, thousands of years— gone, in a matter of hours. I thought we would be safe on Mount Olympus, but they came for us, and it didn't go well. The Horde attacked in wave after wave, overwhelming our forces with their sheer numbers. Every time we took one out, three more would take its place.

"By the end, the three of us and Hercules were the only ones left. Hercules fought them off while I opened the portal. Once it was open, he kept the battle going while we disappeared. I hoped he got out, but no, I can't imagine he lived. Hundreds of other gods and angels, Katrina, I watched them just…evaporate."

I stood up. "Sounds like it's time to kick some ass. Let's get the gang back together and go—"

She shook her head. "There is no need. They will come for us here. They were already on their way. You can only wait to be destroyed, as I will."

I didn't make a habit of feeling sorry for Velaska, but something about the way she stared, dejected, at the floor, told me I should leave her alone for the moment. "Get some sleep. We'll make a plan soon."

*

I walked outside and sat down on my porch steps, looking up at the stars. They were more beautiful here in Heaven than anywhere else I'd ever seen them, and I often looked at them for comfort. Now, I looked at them with fear; fear for my people, fear for my planet, fear for myself.

I felt a hand on my shoulder. I hoped it was my mother, but it was Aphrodite.

"May I sit?" Her words slurred through her scarred lips.

I nodded and scooched over a bit. "You can speak. And well."

Aphrodite gathered her robes and placed herself beside me. A scar traveled from the tip of her chin, through the left side of her lip, through her left eye, and up into her scalp. The left side of her face drooped lower than the right, and yet, she still managed to make my porch steps look regal. "Yes, your angels truly are miracle workers."

"They are. I'm sorry they couldn't do more."

"Me too, but scars heal in time. We gods have an incredible capacity for regeneration."

"Not all of them."

Aphrodite bowed her head. "No. Not all of them. Too many died on my planet. And for that I will never be able to forgive myself."

"It wasn't your fault."

"That's the thing with leadership, Katrina. Everything is your glory, and everything is your fault. You should know that."

"I do."

"And you also know that this travesty will be visited on you soon, and there is nothing you can do to stop it."

"I do."

"And that all your people—all these people—they will be murdered." Aphrodite parted her arms and opened a hole in the floor of Heaven. Hundreds of children played and laughed on a playground down on Earth. "They will all die too. And they will blame you, and they will be right to blame you."

"What can I do?"

"There is nothing to be done. The Horde will be here soon. They are too powerful. I've never seen anything like them."

"But at the end of the day…they are mortal, right? They can be killed."

"Anything can be killed, even us gods." Aphrodite held her hands out in front of her, helpless. "They want us dead, all of us. They want everything we stand for dead. We used the last of our power to open the portal to get here. I'm sure they can trace it with whatever technology they've developed. There is nothing you can do but know that you will deal with it for the rest of your life."

I stood up. "I don't accept that."

"You can prepare for battle, but it is one you won't win."

I levitated off the ground and soared toward the barracks where the archangels kept residence. No horde of oversized bugs was going to destroy Earth on my watch. I'd saved it from the Apocalypse. I'd saved it from a black hole. I could save it from some alien bugs, too. Aphrodite may be a great lover, but she didn't know anything about war.

I wasn't halfway to the barracks when the sky opened again, quaking through Heaven and jangling the stars like windchimes. A black portal the size of seven suns swirled like a spiral above me and blotted out the stars. Black, gnarled spaceships swarmed out of the portal by the thousands and encircled Earth.

Michael and Dennis barreled up to me, concern etched on their faces. Michael led my archangels in their battles across the universe. Dennis, one of my oldest friends, died during the Apocalypse and became an archangel after helping me end it. They were my two greatest soldiers.

"What do we do?" Dennis said.

There wasn't time to skip a beat. "Round up the rest of the archangels, equip everybody you can. Heaven is at war."

Michael flew away, leaving Dennis to stare blankly. Dennis was good in a fight, but not always in a pinch. "Should I call her?"

"Yeah, you'd better. We're going to need her up here if we're going to survive this."

Dennis flicked his fingers and in an instant Connie appeared with Lucifer by her side, the two of them mid-conversation. "And we're going to—What the hell?"

Connie and I had been best friends until I watched her brother die—twice. After that, we became enemies. Still, she'd helped me topple the Apocalypse, earning her way into Heaven. After our last adventure, she agreed to take over for me as the Devil. She was very good at it, but now I needed her by my side in battle.

Connie turned to Dennis. "Baby! *Baby!* Give me some sugar!"

Connie and Dennis wrapped in an embrace. Soulmates, they'd met before the Apocalypse in my little town of Overbrook and stayed together through literally Heaven and Hell. Dennis pushed himself back a little and chuckled. "Sweetheart, you smell like sulfur."

"Well you smell like candy, but you don't hear me complaining!"

I turned to Lucifer, who had been the Devil before me and Bacchus's best soldier. He was on a diplomatic mission to oversee a new construction program in Dis, the biggest city in Hell. "We are at war, Lucifer."

Lucifer looked up at the ships pouring out of the vortex. "I see that. What can we do?"

"There are many troops in Hell, who are battle tested."

"You can't mean—"

I didn't let him finish. I turned to Connie, still caught in Dennis's embrace. "Alright, Connie, Dennis. That's enough of that. We need you. Look at what's happening."

Connie craned her neck to the sky. "What is this?"

"The Horde. Aphrodite and Velaska says they are the most technologically advanced race they have ever seen, and they are here to destroy us. They'll destroy me, and Heaven, and Hell as well. They're going to squish us if we don't squish them first."

Connie turned to me. "What do we do?"

"Something that only the two of us can bring forth."

"Hell on Earth?"

That's why I loved Connie. She was right in step with me.

"I don't see any other way. If they're as bad as the gods say, it will take everything we've got, which means combining our forces."

Connie used a sing-song voice. "It's not going to make the gods happy."

"*Pfft.* The gods live to be offended. Besides, if we don't stop the Horde here, there might not be any more gods left to care."

"Then let's do it."

The two of us shook hands, the ruler of Heaven and the ruler of Hell. Blue and red flames exploded around us and engulfed every corner of Heaven, Earth, and Hell. When I opened the floor of Heaven for a view, Connie and I watched the Earth crack open for the second time in our lives, Hell beasts pouring onto the land. This time, at least, I'd opened the rift by my own hand.

Then again, after all the junk I'd talked about Bacchus letting Hell reign on Earth, here I was doing the same thing. And it only took me a decade to do what he held off doing for thousands of years. If he was a bad god, what did that make me?

I gave Connie an eyebrow. "Don't let them go crazy. This isn't a free-for-all. Tell them to take their aggression out on the Horde."

She nodded. "I will do my best."

Velaska ran out of the mansion with Aphrodite and Hephaestus in tow. "What have you done?"

"We can't win this battle alone. We'll need all the help we can get. And now I need something from you."

"Of course, you do," Velaska said.

"You know the enemy. I need you to work with Michael and find out how to win this battle. Got it?"

"I do."

The ground quaked underneath us again. A massive ship emerged from the portal, which closed behind it. The ship was the size of the moon, except it was no moon, it was a battle station.

"The Planet Killer," Velaska said.

Connie gave her a withering look. "Come on, man. You can give it a better name than that."

"That thing is how they destroy planets so quickly. They can release a thousand ships from it at once. It holds a million soldiers with ease, and they can teleport down to anywhere on the planet in an instant. Poseidon and Ares defeated half the ships in their fleet, but the planet killer took them both out with one blast from their main cannon. Gods that have been around since time immortal, gone in a flash. If you cannot defeat that planet killer, you have no chance in beating the Horde, though even with it gone, I doubt anything can stop them."

In front of us materialized what could only be described as a giant fly dressed in a long robe and golden headdress. Two red eyes, segmented into a thousand hexagons, stared at all of us at once while six hairy arms twitched in every direction. Gold leaf coated its thorax and waxy wings.

"Find Michael, and the two of you *go!*" I hissed at Velaska. She snapped her fingers and was gone.

Around the fly, a half dozen human-sized bugs materialized, an assortment of overgrown millipedes, ants, and pill bugs. All of them were dressed in metal exoskeletons that glowed green and, just like Velaska said, all of them wore back packs dotted with green lights, connected to the blasters they carried in their scaly arms.

"I have come far to find you, god killer." The fly's guttural voice came through a long, sinewy mouth.

"What do you want?"

"First, to thank you. My race has long stood in fear of the gods. But you've shown us they can be killed."

My mind was racing, trying to take in this new information. I'd taught them what? I swallowed hard before croaking in response, "That's impossible."

"It is very possible." The fly snapped its fingers, and a holographic image of Artemis's bow appeared in front of us. "We have advanced. We have studied your signatures and your weapons. And now, we have the power to kill gods and humans alike. Every one of us."

"That's too much power. You don't know what you are doing."

The fly shook its bristled head. "No. Nothing is too powerful. We have the capacity for life. We have the capacity for death. I have united all the insect and arachnid clans under one civilization. Now, we will end yours. Witness."

The fly raised its arm. A speck of green light traveled across Heaven and up the side of my mansion.

"Don't do this."

"We have long been killed by your kind, god killer." The fly snapped its legs together and the light grew until it engulfed the whole house. "And we shall show you what it is like to be on the run. This is the end of humanity. It is the end of the gods. It is the end of everything."

My house exploded in front of me. The fires erupted twenty feet into the air. Hundreds of green lights illuminated the ground, and then Heaven exploded around us. We should have stayed and fought, but I knew there was no chance of survival, so we flew away like cowards.

I soared across the Elysian Fields, Aphrodite, Connie, Lucifer, Dennis, and Hephaestus in tow. So many centuries ago, I fought to save Heaven from a madman. Now I flew for my very existence. In front of me, thousands of insects descended on Heaven with massive blasters. There were pill bugs, flies, millipedes, and spiders. Each of them carried a mechanical pack with a metallic gun attached to it, bearing the insignia of a great infinity symbol.

"We are all one," they shouted, firing at us.

With every blast, residents of Heaven vanished from existence. A trail of green steam was all that remained, and the blasters sucked it up with gusto. As they did, the lights on their packs glowed brighter.

In the back of the battle, great ships collapsed into spiders with great red and green eyes. They crawled along the clouds of Heaven, squashing whole squadrons of angels with ease and cleaning up the rest with long blasts of cannon fire.

We needed help, and there was only one way off the planet. The Sword of Damocles could get us wherever we needed to go in the universe, and it rested on top of God's platform, the platform Bacchus used to rule over Heaven for so long.

"I am L'l'itoh. There is no escape," the fly pharaoh shouted behind us. "We will leave none alive that have the mark of the gods."

"What is that thing talking about?" I shouted to Hephaestus.

"When Zeus created life, unintended life would sometimes spring up out of the muck from the residual energy—he did his best to quash the byproduct..."

"Yes, yes. He made humans to look like gods, but Zeus also made us." L'l'itoh was following us, chiming in on our conversation like a bad dinner guest. A bad dinner guest who blew up your home planet. "We are his castoffs. We are the children he never wanted. All we wanted was to live in peace, but he destroyed that peace over and over, always favoring you."

The explosions intensified as even more ships descended on Heaven, firing blasters everywhere and burning away the floor of Heaven itself. From space, I watched as the planet killer launched a brutal attack on Earth, with laser blasts so enormous I could feel their heat even millions of miles away.

L'l'itoh's voice gave off a frightening echo against the explosions and blaster fire. "Now, we have the power," it shrieked. "Thanks to you, we are the ultimate power in the universe."

Ships were landing in front of Bacchus's platform as we approached, training their massive guns on us. Thousands of soldiers streamed out.

"This is crazy!" Connie said. "We're sitting ducks here!"

"We can't stay here," Lucifer agreed.

They were right. I looked around at the incoming Horde, then back at my friends.

Connie was watching me. "What are you going to do?"

"I'm going to get help. You guys need to get out of here! Remember, Connie, you have the power of a Devil. Find a way to fight back!" I snapped my fingers and Connie disappeared with Dennis and Lucifer, back to Hell. I hoped she could find a way to protect Earth until I came back.

"What's your plan, here?" Aphrodite could even make hollering a stately, refined act.

I ran to the middle of the platform. The Sword of Damocles sat in its rock holder, where I placed it a decade ago after returning from my journey around the universe. The Sword of Damocles could slice through a god and prevent them from regenerating, and it could cut a rift through the universe. The bugs had encircled the platform. It would be over in a moment.

I grabbed onto the hilt and lifted the sword into the air. "You ready?"

Hephaestus and Aphrodite nodded.

The sword had the power to cut open a rift to anywhere in the galaxy. We couldn't beat the monsters by ourselves, that much I knew. Somewhere out there, there was help, and I was going to find it.

I closed my eyes and thought of the only coordinates I remembered. The ones from Aphrodite's home world. Then, I swung the sword, making a tear in the sky. "Let's go."

Chapter 3

This was the second time I'd floated through the vacuum of space as Earth collapsed into disaster behind me. It had happened before when Apollo threw Earth into a black hole, and I felt like a coward then. This time, I openly wept. As the void closed behind us, the Horde's lasers unleashed a lethal barrage on Heaven. In my bones, I knew the only way to save my people was to get help, but that didn't ease my stomach. I just hoped I could find it before these stupid bugs destroyed everything.

I turned my attention forward, into the ever-expanding mystical power of space. The planets whizzed by like pebbles, and I wondered how many of them had been destroyed by the Horde. From there, my mind slipped to my parents. We'd only had a decade together after reuniting in Heaven, and it was a good decade. I pictured them looking up at the sky while their daughter abandoned them, their final thoughts lingering on my betrayal as the Horde blinked them out of existence.

I hoped they understood, this was the only way to save everything I've ever known. Odds were, my parents would be dead before I ever saw them again, but that was a thought I couldn't process right now. I had to focus on the mission at hand: Save Earth.

*

We were nearing the other side of the rift the sword had made. I watched Aphrodite and Hephaestus fade into its light just before the three of us rolled out into a warzone. I kicked myself for only being able to remember the coordinates to the world they'd only just narrowly escaped. Part of me had assumed—hoped—that the Horde would have dissipated and moved on to Earth, but I was wrong. Bugs of all types blasted through the love goddess's planet like something from a bad sci-fi movie.

A massive cockroach landed in front of me, aiming its blaster. I jumped away just as it fired a green blast, cratering the ground where I stood.

"Why...*why* would you come back *here?*" Aphrodite shouted.

"I figured it would be safe here with the Horde now on Earth!"

"Why would I jump away from here if it was safe?"

"Well, I didn't think of that! And it's a little late now, don't you think? Maybe next time, *you* can operate the—"

"Ladies," Hephaestus barked. "Maybe we can save this for another time, when we're not being blown up!"

"Yeah?" Aphrodite hollered over the sound of blasters. "And when is that going to be?"

The cockroach turned away from us and turned toward the battlefield, where it sprayed its blaster, incinerating the humans in its path. The telltale green mist rose into the sky and the cockroach greedily sucked it up into its backpack. As the bug came closer and opened fire again, we jumped out of the laser's way one more time.

I heard Aphrodite and Hephaestus yelling when I leapt over the small marble wall and rushed the cockroach. "I'll be right back!" I called back to them. The nasty little bug fired three beams at me, and I dodged each one until I was right in its face. I white-knuckled my sword and sliced the blade through its torso. The cockroach's thorax slid from its legs as it let out a final gasp.

"You can come out now!"

But it wasn't safe. The blaster ticked louder and louder under my feet. I knew from movies that meant something was going to explode. I rushed away from the blaster as a guttural boom shot me forward. The white heat from the explosion seared my face and I fell into a chasm where the burst washed over me.

It was over in a second, and then I looked up. For a moment the sky was clear, but then the lasers started again, and in greater numbers. The Horde troops blotted out the clear sky in an instant, turned it black with the sheer number of their troops.

"Now what, Katrina?" Aphrodite asked.

"I'm doing the best I can," I said. "I'm taking suggestions, though."

A thousand bugs surrounded us, some crawling on six legs, others hovering in the air. They fired beams from every direction, the blasters kicking up hot dirt and rocks around us.

"Well," Hephaestus said. "At least we get to die at home."

I didn't welcome death, but I certainly didn't fear it like some people, and certainly less than other gods. People were born with the knowledge they would eventually die, but a god was supposed to be immortal. I don't know. Basically, dying sucked, no matter how you sliced it.

"I just want to say," I said. "I hate that I'm going to die next to you."

"YOU WON'T. NOT TODAY!" a voice shouted from beyond the Horde's fire.

The voice was familiar. One I hadn't heard in a while. Sure enough, out of the sky jumped Hercules, clad in golden armor and wielding a broad sword. With one swift cut, he felled two pill bugs and a beetle, chopping them in half along with their weapons. "DUCK!"

Hercules jumped into the crater with us, and the two bugs he'd just sliced through exploded. Those explosions caused another blaster to explode, which caused another to explode, and another, and another. Soon, blasts stopped and the battlefield was silent. Dead Horde soldiers lined the battlefield.

Hercules turned to us, a triumphant smile on his face. "Friends! Welcome home!" He hugged Aphrodite tightly, then Hephaestus. When he reached for me, I turned away.

"No offense, but you're caked in sweat."

He laughed. "It is the sweat of battle. There is no more noble stench."

"Yeah...I'm still gonna pass."

I peeked my head over the top of the trench. The Horde army lay wasted on the battlefield. Still, in the distance, a black sea approached.

"How did you survive?" Aphrodite asked.

"It is a long and harrowing story," Hercules responded. He drew in a deep breath and opened his mouth to embark on what I was sure would be a highly embellished and completely obnoxious tale of his heroics, so I had to step in.

"I'm sure it is," I said. "Can we talk about it somewhere less…deadly?"

"But of course."

*

Hercules led us across the battlefield. I could see hundreds of Horde ships in the distance as they ravaged the land, destroying any semblance of humanity. Walking metal bugs skittered across the horizon, firing their cannons and vaporizing swaths of humans in an instant. I'd call it a massacre, but the word hardly does it justice.

Unlike Earth, Aphrodite's people had never migrated out of the Bronze Age, so they had no access to high-powered weapons. Even though Earth had been destroyed traveling through the black hole, they had caches of weapons all over the planet. Aphrodite's planet was literally fighting guns with swords and javelins. It wasn't going well. Humanity fought valiantly, but ineffectively.

"Shouldn't we be helping them?" I asked.

"We will," Hercules responded. "Now that you are here, we will."

Hercules stopped in front of a torn down building. It reminded me of Velaska's temple from the last time I visited, except the ornate columns and statues were nothing except rubble strewn about the ground.

"I built this hospital myself, with my bare hands. They destroyed it in less than a minute."

He reached down under the debris and pulled up a latch. A dozen children huddled together, squinting at the light flooding in. "Don't be afraid, little ones. I have found help."

He turned to us. "They are very scared. Be gentle. They have seen much."

Aphrodite walked forward first. "Children. I am Aphrodite. I wish only to protect you."

The children came out of the hovel and huddled around Aphrodite. They whispered to themselves as the goddess stood, still and magnanimous. Her smile cracked under her wounded lip, but she never wavered. "I went to find you aide, and I have come back with hope and help for all."

I grumbled under my breath at Aphrodite's lie. She didn't come back with help. She was as petrified as the rest of us, and wanted to leave, but I couldn't just say that and ruin any hope her people had of a real rescue.

"Let's get farther in there," I said to Hercules. "Before they find us."

Hercules nodded as he ducked into the dark corridor, followed by the children he protected. When he was gone, I turned to Aphrodite.

"That was quite a stunt you pulled back there, what with the lying and all."

Aphrodite smiled. "That is one thing you've never understood about ruling, Katrina. You must lie when it is in their best interest. Look at them. They are without hope. What good would it do to tell them we came back by accident? None. But, give them hope, and who knows what they can do."

I walked into the basement. "If you give them false hope, they will die in vain."

*

Underground, the deserted surface of the hospital gave way to a vibrant community of men, women, and children bustling to make food, sew clothes, and manufacture swords, maces, and lances.

"How can you stack up without guns?" I asked Hercules.

"We find a way. You can cut through their weapons with a sharp sword and shoot the bugs through the head with a sharp arrow. Just like anything else, they die."

"Even gods," I pointed out.

"Yes, even gods."

"Is this something you learned after we left?" Aphrodite asked.

"Yes, ma'am. There I was, in the throne room, serving as a diversion." Hercules puffed his chest with pride. "I swiped at them with my sword. I killed a couple that way. It was slow going, until I accidentally chopped one of their guns in half. Barely got away before they blew themselves up—along with half your castle I'm afraid to say, m'lady."

"A castle is just an edifice," Aphrodite said. "They can be rebuilt. It's the people that concern me. Did you learn anything else?"

"One more thing. The bugs are controlled from a safe distance by field generals, who move them around the battlefield like pawns. That is how they are so ruthless and precise, as if they share one mind. It's because they do. If you kill the generals, the rest of the bugs scatter. They return, and in bigger numbers, but the respite is welcomed."

"These weapons are weak!" Hephaestus yelled, bending a sword in his hand. "How could you use them on powerful weapons like those the Horde possess?"

"That's a good question, buddy," Hercules said. "The truth is we can't. The most effective weapons are ones that you created. Nothing else stands a chance. We work in small groups to take out the generals when we can, but even that is only a temporary relief."

"If it's so futile, then why even try?" Hephaestus smashed one fist into the other, frustrated.

"Because that is what we do, is it not?"

I walked between them. "Hephaestus, do you think you could help them build better weapons?"

"Possible, but I would need my forge on Olympus and the metal contained within it. If I could get them, and have a safe space to work, there's a chance."

I turned to Aphrodite. "Can you help us? We need to get up to Mt Olympus. I know you have the power."

"It's suicide."

"So is doing nothing. You don't have to come with us. I just need you to get us there."

Aphrodite scanned the crowd before her; her long-suffering people, looking to her for hope and comfort. "I will come with you. It is the job of a god to protect her people in any way she can."

Hercules placed a knife into Aphrodite's hand. "It was pretty nasty up there before the Horde destroyed it. I don't know what you will see up there."

She nodded. "Then we will find out together."

Aphrodite placed her hand on his shoulder and a blue light came for us. It tasted like warm, blueberry pie, just like it did the first time Aphrodite had taken me to Mount Olympus.

*

An instant later, we reappeared in front of Hephaestus's shop. Mount Olympus no longer burned. It was serene and peaceful, like I remembered. Dozens of bugs roamed around without their weapons drawn, as if they were having a pleasant stroll in the park.

It didn't last long, though. Two big millipedes landed on either side of us wearing their mechanical suits and sent a screeching signal into the air. Suddenly, every bug within a thousand feet turned to us and descended on Hephaestus's shop. They pulled their weapons and began to fire.

"Spread out!" Hercules gave a hearty bellow as he rushed forward and immediately sliced through two weapons. I swung my sword and cut three others in half. Aphrodite twisted her knife and cut into the exoskeleton of a spider. It fell twitching and screaming, and she daintily removed the blade.

Hephaestus hefted his sword in front of him. "Forward!"

We ran into the forge as the bugs closed around us. They didn't work in unison, as there was no general controlling them. Their blasts were haphazard and inaccurate.

"Grab everything you can!" Hephaestus was gathering tools and gesturing wildly to the metallurgy around him.

"There's no time!" I shouted. "Aphrodite, bring it all."

"I can't do that! It's too much!"

"Either do it or we die."

The bugs' blasters powered up. Aphrodite closed her eyes and—*poof*! The blaster streams passed right through us as we vanished from view, hitting other bugs in the crossfire.

*

We rematerialized with a loud crash on Aphrodite's world, just above the shelter Hercules had shown us. The entire forge appeared with us. Hephaestus and Hercules shook themselves off and stood up. I looked over at Aphrodite. Blood dripped from her eyes as she fell onto the ground.

"Aphrodite!" I scooped her up in my arms. "Come on... Come on."

In another moment, her eyes fluttered open. She coughed and shook her head meekly. "Don't make me do that again."

I smiled. "Don't tell me what to do."

Aphrodite touched my forehead. "I grant you access to Mount Olympus. Should you ever need it again, it will open for you."

"Why are you doing this?"

She smiled. "Because I never want to do that again."

"Fair enough."

She rose to her knees. "Did it work?"

I nodded. "You did it—but the Horde will be on us any second, I'm sure."

"Let them come," Hephaestus said. "I will be ready for them."

"Get going then," Hercules said. "We need more of your steel. Katrina, may I speak with you a moment?"

Hercules led me away from the prying ears of the gods, into another abandoned building destroyed by the Horde. "Even with his steel, there is not enough to win this fight. You know this to be true."

I nodded slowly. "Humans are resilient, but there aren't enough of them to wield Hephaestus's swords."

"They are not fast enough, either." He pounded his fist into his hand. "We need more gods. Now that we know how to defeat them, and we have access to better weapons, more gods on our side would assure us victory. I know it."

I folded my arms across my chest and stared at him. "You know where there are more gods? If the Horde hasn't gotten there first, then there are likely millions still in Hera's dungeon."

Hercules considered this, frowning. "But will they fight?"

"I don't know, honestly, but they're our only chance. They have every reason to fight. If the Horde hasn't come for them yet, it will. Some of them might deny us, sure, but enough will fight. Then, we can win here and take the fight back to Earth." I faltered for a moment, thinking about the gods I'd seen imprisoned in Hera's palace. "They're not going to listen to me."

Aphrodite stepped forward from the shadows. "I will go with you."

I turned to her, then gestured out at the destroyed planet. "These are your people. You can't leave them."

"And I will do anything to help them, including leave them. That is what being a leader is, as you know...you've left your own, have you not?"

I looked at Hercules. "How long can you last with just Hephaestus?"

"We have survived this long with less, but hurry."

"Do you know the coordinates?" I handed the sword to Aphrodite.

"Yes, Poseidon gave them to me before his last battle. Gods rest his soul." She closed her eyes and cut open the hole through space-time. "Let us go."

I fell into the hole, and watched Aphrodite fall behind me.

Chapter 4

You know, when you do something once, it's wonderful, but after a few times even the most amazing experiences become rote. I hate myself for saying it, but all I could think to myself as I tumbled through the universe was "When is this going to be over?"

You can't really converse in the vacuum of space, and the current just carries you forward. All I could do during the trip was think, and it wasn't the time for thinking. It was the time for action.

Earth was being destroyed by the Horde right now because of something I did, all because I killed Zeus. Who knew that defeating the big, bad evil would release an even bigger, badder evil on the universe?

I should have just done my bid in Hell and followed humanity, back when Earth was swallowed by that black hole. While humanity would have suffered with Rhea eating them, at least they would have been killed off slowly, and there'd be more chance of a fight. They wouldn't be instantaneously evaporated out of existence by enormous blasters.

What happened when you evaporated out of existence? Do you just stop…being? Are you reincarnated into the world as something else? Hades once told me that all matter returned to the source, to be reused by the spark of creation, and that we were just stewards for a soul's cleansing, so it could return pure and clean. The puke-green mist the Horde sucked up into their backpacks certainly didn't look clean to me.

I didn't have time to finish contemplating the fate of being evaporated into a green mist before the portal spat me out and I crash-landed on Hera's planet. It had been desolate when I visited once before, and the ensuing years hadn't done it any favors. It was still a barren wasteland devoid of hope.

The only building visible was Hera's immense castle, crumbling around the edges. Previously, thousands of monster guards patrolled the castle walls, but they were all gone now.

Only the vast expanse of the desert remained, expanding in every direction into the horizon.

I walked straight up to the drawbridge without a hassle. The mighty minotaur guard's post was deserted. Hera's world was eerily quiet. Aside from my own footsteps crunching on the dry sand of the desert, the only sound was the low moaning of prisoners inside the palace walls.

"I remember coming here for Hera's coronation," Aphrodite said. "Gods lined the streets. It was a paradise."

"I remember it being a shithole, just like this, except full of monsters."

The drawbridge laid on the ground in front of the castle, its wood bleached from the blazing sun. The beams creaked as we walked across, as if they hadn't felt pressure in years. Rust sprinkled from the metal chains while they rattled with our movement.

"It's a shame that Hera's palace fell into such disrepair," Aphrodite said.

"I don't know if I would say 'shame.'" I shrugged. "She was kind of a jerk."

"Yeah, that will happen when your husband hates you."

I considered that as I rubbed my hand across the flaking wall. Aphrodite had more sympathy in a hangnail than I had in my whole body, that was for sure. "It doesn't look like the Horde came through here."

"Even if they did, what would there be to destroy? This is the only structure on this planet, and it looks like it hasn't seen a caring hand in many moons."

"Yeah, well let's just hope that the prisoners inside can be useful."

Every step on the dry, scattered debris inside the prison felt like walking across a field of extra crunchy potato chips. Prisoners moaned and lay despondent, no longer struggling to free themselves. They laid in their cages wishing for death.

Death had come for some of the monsters, at least. The smell of their rotten corpses permeated the cells as we walked through. Aphrodite vomited again and again until there was nothing left to vomit, and then resorted to dry heaving.

"How can you not be retching?" she asked me.

"You've never been to Hell, have you?"

"Not for a long time."

"Well, I was the Devil for ten thousand years. And this isn't that bad by comparison."

"What was it like? Hell?"

"It's everything Heaven isn't. It's hot. It's loud. It's full of suffering people who would do anything to end their torment for even a moment. And it smells. Bad. You never get the smell off your clothes."

"I'll bet they will be happy to be blinked out of existence by the Horde."

"They might be, actually." It was something I hadn't thought of until now, but there was the chance that the Hellspawn would choose the Horde's side, as it's the one that led to the wanton destruction of their captors. The dead souls might just welcome the end of the world instead of enduring an eternity of pain.

From behind us, we heard the crunch of feet. I turned to see two emaciated demons standing there, in tattered armor.

"Your presence is requested," one said.

"With whom?" Aphrodite said.

"With she who runs this planet."

I gave a snort, looking around. "Somebody actually runs this place?"

"It's run by those of us that still care," the other said. "As best we can."

I gripped the handle of my great sword. "I can kill you with one slice. Do you know that?"

They nodded in unison, and the uglier one spoke. "We do, but that is one less sword stroke that you don't have to take if you come with us." He twitched for a moment, as if swallowing something gross. "She has also requested me to say, 'please.'"

"That is very kind of her," Aphrodite said. "I welcome her invitation."

I loosened my grip on the sword. "Lead the way, I guess."

*

The demons couldn't walk without the help of their lances, which they used as canes to inch forward one small step at a time. We passed other demons and minotaur guards, shuffling past each other in a daze as they tried their best to stay upright.

"Who did you get to take over for Hera after I fed her to Cronus?" I asked.

The slightly-less-ugly demon shrugged, disinterested. "You will see."

We stopped in front of the gilded gate that separated the prison from the palace. Last time I was here it took only one of them to open the door, and in just a few minutes. This time it took more than half an hour, waiting awkwardly while two emaciated cyclops struggled with all their might to open the immense doors. Eventually we walked through them and down the long, ornately adorned corridors of Hera's palace.

Except they weren't ornate any more. The pictures remained, but a dull film coated everything in the palace. Cobwebs and dust gathered on the gilded pillars and wafted off the once shimmering armor that lined the halls. My feet echoed against the marble walls, which had once been buffed shiny enough to reflect your face. Now they were coated with years of grime and neglect.

"Is that them?" a high-pitched voice shouted through the castle. "Bring them here."

"At once, madam."

The demon pushed me forward, and I grabbed his staff. "You are only still alive because I will it so. Touch me again and I will cut you into pieces."

The demon silenced himself the rest of the way to the throne room, which stood at the end of the hallway. All hallways in Hera's castle dead-ended at the throne room, like great spokes of a wheel in which Hera's throne was the hub.

On top of the dilapidated throne sat a meek, small woman with ill-fitting robes. She shifted in her seat as we approached. She tried to remain regal, but sucked at it, looking like a little girl playing dress-up in her mom's too-big high heels. I recognized her from my last visit to Hera's castle. She was the meek woman who worked with the telescopes.

Aphrodite, however, knew how to play the role of royalty. "What ho, good queen. Thank you for keeping Hera's in order."

The woman smiled and bowed. She looked genuinely flattered as she rose. "And you, good princess Aphrodite. What news do you bring?"

Aphrodite returned the bow. "I bring good tidings to you and yours. What news have you of my mother's kingdom?"

"I have kept it running quite expertly since she was taken from us."

"And I am ever grateful."

"As I am to you, for gracing us with your presence."

"Enough!" I shouted. "Who are you?"

Aphrodite elbowed me in the stomach. "Manners!"

"I don't have any of those. I have a unique set of skills, and manners aren't included."

"No," the woman said, walking down from her throne. "God killing. That is in your skill set, though, yes?"

"And you were the girl that helped set the telescope last time I was here. Uranus, right? The one who looked at all the stars."

"Urania," she snarled. "And yes—though I've had to take on the role of protector as of late."

"It looks like you have done well protecting yourself."

She scoffed. "I should think so. I spent years cleaning up after your last stunt. Most of Hera's guards abandoned the palace when you took her. Only the most loyal remained."

"Is that why the place looks like—"

"A dump? Yes. Because of you, there was no place left for gardeners or housekeepers in the castle. Most every warm body became a guard. They have just one mission: keep the prison safe. Keep everybody locked up. That was Hera's wish."

"That's funny, because we're here to—"

Another elbow from Aphrodite. "Let me handle this." She took a few graceful steps toward Urania. "My lady, have you heard of the Horde?"

The awkward goddess shook her head. "I have caught glimpses through the stars."

"They are a wicked race," Aphrodite's voice boomed. "They are committed on destroying all of the gods."

Urania's head wobbled on her skinny neck as she nodded in agreement. She was falling under the spell of Aphrodite's beauty. "That's horrible."

"Yes, it is. And worse…they are winning. They have decimated our ranks and killed hundreds of gods. Myself, Hephaestus, and Velaska were the only three to make it off my home world alive. Luckily, our travels connected us with Hercules as well."

"All my kin, murdered at the hands of the Horde?" Urania's voice was small as she digested this information.

"That's right. It's why we are here, to ask for your help. To beg for your aid."

The small goddess grew a few sizes as she settled into the role of someone running with the big dogs. "I will do anything I can. Ask of me what you will."

"I hoped you would say that. We need more men." Aphrodite looked at Urania pointedly. "We need you to release the gods and monsters from their cells and let them fight with us."

"That…that is heresy! It goes against my queen's wishes."

"I know," Aphrodite sighed. But then she took a step closer, and lowered her voice conspiratorially, "…but you are the queen now."

Urania thought for a moment. "Give me until the evening. Meanwhile, you will be brought to quarters."

*

I paced back and forth inside the dingy room where Urania's men had taken us. They had once been ornate and beautiful, I'm sure, before the marble statues and canopy bed fell into disrepair like the rest of the castle. "I hate this. Can't we just fight our way through these men and release the prisoners ourselves?"

Aphrodite smiled. "Yes. We could, but we are already low on men. Is destroying another planet prudent?"

"Is waiting? Every second we wait is a second that we aren't fighting. What are these lives compared to millions of my people?"

"They are lives. That is enough."

"Is it? Is it, Aphrodite? Cuz where I'm standing my people mean a lot more than these ones."

"I know," she sighed. "Something I learned early in my rule is that all people, no matter where they're from, have value, and if I value these people, I will value all people."

"That's stupid."

"It has led me to rule my people with love and kindness."

"And yet, all of our people suffer right now."

"Yes, they do. They hold steady with the faith that I work to save their suffering."

The double doors to our room swung open and Urania walked in. "I have a proposition for you," she announced without offering any sort of greeting. "I am aware that, if you desired, you could storm through our castle and release these men yourselves."

"At least you acknowledge it," I said under my breath.

"Therefore, I have an offer. I will give half my men to fight for you, along with every single prisoner you can convince to lay down their lives for you, if you do something for me."

Aphrodite scoffed. "And what is that, good Urania?"

"Take me to Cronus, so that I might get my queen back."

"That's crazy!" I shouted. "We're fighting a war here!"

"Yes, it seems like it, but for a brief moment in time I have something of value to you." Urania gestured to Aphrodite. "You, Katrina, are friends with Aphrodite, and she knows that any battle with me would be long and protracted. She doesn't have that kind of time. Her people suffer, and that weighs on her. Even if you do win, you will kill many of my men, men you desperately need right now." She folded her arms across her chest. "So that is my offer. You can easily ignore my wishes and take this castle by force, but I hope you do not. I offer all the men in this castle you can muster…and all I ask is you take me to Cronus."

"We need these men *now*," Aphrodite said.

Urania nodded emphatically, as if she'd anticipated this response. "And you will have them, as long as I have your word."

Aphrodite looked at me as she responded. "You have our word."

Urania smiled. "I appreciate that, but I'm afraid I really must hear it from both of you."

I figured she'd been giving herself pep talks in the mirror. She was bolder and more resolute than she'd been in the throne room. I sighed. "Very well. You have my word. I will take you to Cronus."

Urania clapped her hands together, nodding. She looked like she was trying to hide her relief that I hadn't dug my heels in. "Then you will have your men, if you can convince them to come with you. While they might not have a good life here, at least they are not at war."

"*Yet*," I corrected.

"Yes, quite."

*

We reached cell block 74,321, which held Bacchus, along with several hundred other gods from our sector of the galaxy. His face was gaunt, and clothes ragged. The years in a cage had not been kind to him. He looked like any tortured soul I'd ever found in Hell. Those in Hell long enough all wound up looking like Jesus on the cross, pale and emaciated. Except for the gluttons, of course. They were forced to stuff food into their fat faces until they exploded, then demons sewed them up and they did it again. It was one of my favorite punishments to watch, because they were just so pitiful and sad.

"You are just as pathetic as last time I saw you, Bacchus."

He squeezed his knees into his chest. "Have you come back to gloat? To see what I have become without you?"

I shook my head. "No. I've come to set you free."

"That is a very generous offer, but I don't believe you. You left me here to rot once before, after all."

"That's true, but today I have brought a friend."

Aphrodite stepped forward. "Hello, brother."

Bacchus gasped at the sight of Aphrodite's deformed face. "Good sister. What have they done to you? What has *she* done to you?"

Aphrodite held up her hand to quiet him. "Nothing, good brother. Sit. This is due to a great evil that ravages our kind. Do you remember what happened when father made new planets?"

"Of course," Bacchus nodded. "I loved to watch him create new life from nothing."

Aphrodite gave him a warm smile. "I always enjoyed that as well. But you know that while Zeus created great life, he was not perfect."

"He was the best of us."

"No. Only the most powerful. He's dead now, Bacchus. You do not have to fear him."

Bacchus dropped to his knees. "Dead? How?"

"I killed him," I blurted out. "Or more specifically Cronus ate him."

"You?" His eyes bulged, and he looked at Aphrodite, gesturing towards me. "And sister, you work with her?"

Aphrodite snapped her fingers. "Brother. You must listen. Grieve on your own time. Do you remember the castoffs?"

Bacchus thought for a moment. "The sparks of life that landed on other planets?"

"Yes. They traveled around the galaxy, and those sparks of life created new life. Unsupervised life. Evil life. Without us to mold it, that life grew in all sorts of ways. Plants, bugs, and monsters of all types."

"Father spent many lifetimes snuffing them out."

"He did his best, but even he is not infallible. After he died those monsters rose up and started killing us. They swept across the galaxy, Bacchus, and now they are on your doorstep. Earth's doorstep."

"I have to help them!" Bacchus shouted, hoarsely.

Aphrodite put her hand on his. "I hoped you would say that. You are our last hope. All of you prisoners are our last hope. You are the gods the Horde never knew about, and if we can bring you on our side, we have a chance."

Bacchus bowed his head. "I will help you sister, to avenge father. Once this is over though, I will destroy Katrina." He raised his eyes and glared at me.

I scoffed. "You can try. I'm a god now, and I pretty much beat the whole pantheon on my own without any powers. Imagine what I can do now."

"Katrina," Aphrodite said. "Shut up." She turned back to Bacchus. "If you help us, we will release you from this prison."

"What do you need of me?" he asked.

"You must help us recruit the others. They will listen to you, as you are one of them. Then, you must fight with us as a warrior. If you turn and run, you will be back here in an instant."

"And what of my world?"

"I've spoken to Katrina about this. If you help us defeat the Horde, we will give you back rule of Earth."

Bacchus leaned back slowly, considering this. "That is interesting."

I stepped forward, snarling. "But know, if you mess it up again, I will find you and kill you. No trial. No nothing. I am very good at killing gods."

"Understood."

"Do we have an accord, brother?" Aphrodite asked.

He nodded. "We have an accord."

*

With Bacchus's help we raised an army of fifteen thousand gods and lesser deities. We supplemented that with six thousand demons and lesser imps from Urania's army, along with one hundred thousand cyclops, zombies, and imprisoned monsters of all types scattered around the dungeon.

Still, that only made up a fraction of the prison. The rest decided they would rather rot away like cowards than face death like warriors, and all because they valued their eternal life. It was stupid to have an eternity of loneliness and boredom just because it was an eternity. What good is life if you're not living it?

Aphrodite organized the prisoners outside of the castle. Thousands of them stood shoulder to shoulder, god and demon alike.

"My kin, demi-gods, demons, devils, monsters of all types. We are at a great crossroads now. I have watched my planet decimated by violence. I have witnessed the Horde kill everything it touches. Now, you are our last hope. I know you are tired. I know you are hungry. But know this: With your victory over the Horde, you will be free!"

They cheered Aphrodite and I walked up to her. "I have to admit, you know how to rile up a crowd."

She surprised me with a girlish snicker. "It's not so hard. I've been training for this my whole existence." Her face changed once she'd absorbed the compliment, and she was serious again. "Once Hercules pushes the Horde back and we destroy the planet killer on my world, we will come for Earth."

"Sounds like a plan. I'll see you there."

I used my sword to cut a hole in space-time. Aphrodite nodded to me and jumped inside. I held the sword in place as the rest of her army streamed in after her. When the last of them had passed through, I turned to Urania. "Alright. I don't suppose you know where to start looking for Cronus, do you?

She didn't miss a beat. "I have an idea."

Chapter 5

Urania led me back into the castle and through the dungeon. As the chorus of moans carried through the prison, I couldn't shake the feeling that we simply didn't get enough recruits to win this fight. If we had done better, if Bacchus had been more convincing, then there wouldn't be any moans. Those gods would all be fighting for our cause.

"Of course, we monitored Cronus's world very closely. Did you know that?" she asked, walking through the golden doors to Hera's palace.

"I figured you might keep tabs on your greatest enemy. That how Artemis found us?"

"Of course. I delivered the news to Hera herself."

"I guess I have you to thank then."

Urania walked me through the throne room and down a long hallway lined with dusty portraits and disheveled medieval armor statues, then opened a circular blue door adorned with a smiling sun and led me into an observatory where dozens of demons bustled back and forth. Unlike the rest of the castle, this room was pristine.

"I thought everybody was on guard duty," I said to her.

"I said most everybody. Some things are more important than smelly prisoners. Helen! Come here."

A squat girl with long, red hair shuffled up to her, awaiting instructions.

"Can you pull the files on one hundred and twenty-three dot four hundred and twenty-one dot forty-six?"

Helen nodded her head and shambled away. Urania walked towards an enormous telescope set up in the middle of the room. "We followed Cronus for a while after the incident. He went on quite the killing spree after you set him free, eating several thousand civilizations."

"I thought you only had a passing knowledge of him?" I said.

"I don't have to tell you everything."

"Where is he now?" I asked.

"Beyond the void."

"What's… 'the void?'"

"Yes, well we couldn't just have a giant Titan roaming free, now could we? So, we sent him through a black hole. That seemed like the prudent thing to do."

Helen delivered a folder to Urania. "Here you go, ma'am."

Urania studied its contents for a moment. "Ah yes."

"How did you send him through a black hole?"

"Well, I studied Apollo, of course. I took his hands after you cut them off. See?"

Urania gestured to a large, glass tube which contained two golden hands suspended in a clear, liquid bath, pouring light into the room. "They were filled with power, and we discovered how to use that power to create a black hole."

"Fascinating, but why would you need to do that?"

"Because we must keep the universe in balance, and sometimes that means sending Mad Titans through black holes."

Urania sat in a chair and swiveled it toward a keyboard. She typed a few hundred keystrokes and the great observatory began to creak beneath our feet as it spun slowly. "It's really quite fascinating stuff. Do you want to read it?"

I shook my head. "I'm good."

"Suit yourself." The observatory stopped rotating and settled into silence. "There we go. That is the black hole we must go through to find Cronus."

"Cool. If you know all this, then why do you need me?"

"Simple. I'm a scientist, Katrina. You've met the Mad Titan. You befriended him. You are the reason he is free, after my people bound him."

I stared at her blankly, trying to figure out how she'd gone from talking about being a scientist to her people imprisoning Cronus.

"I need you to introduce me, so he doesn't eat me. Don't you see?"

"Ah, I do see." Why hadn't she just said that?

She pointed to my sword. "Plus, I don't have one of those thingies. That hole is a very, very long way away. I do love Hera, but not enough to spend a million years getting to her." She tapped a button on her keyboard and printed an image, then pointed at the coordinates on the sheet. "We need to go here. Can you handle that?"

Simple and direct. She was finally speaking my language. I swung the sword through the air and cut a hole into time-space. "Yeah. I can handle that."

*

We exited the portal in deep space, and immediately our bodies twisted and stretched, contorted by the black hole we'd entered. Every molecule of my body burned and ached as massive pressure weighed against me. I felt like I was in a wine press and on a medieval rack at the same time. It wasn't entirely comfortable.

We were traveling faster than I thought possible. This wasn't like the sword's portal—that was like floating. Being sucked into a black hole felt like taking LSD at a heavy metal concert and jumping into the middle of a mosh pit while robots pulled you like taffy.

High-pitched shrieks bombarded my ears, like a thousand million voices crying out at once. Vivid colors whizzed by in every combination and thousands of needles pricked every inch of my body like a constant full-body tattoo with needles made for elephants. I died a million times a second and was reborn into the cocoon of the black hole.

Then it was over, and I floated inside of nothing. Alone. Before it all went black.

*

I woke to Urania shaking me forcefully in the middle of black space. Or I assumed it was Urania. I couldn't see anything. There was no light. There was no sound. There was only shaking. A slap stung my face, and it brought me the rest of the way back into consciousness.

I grabbed onto Urania until she stopped shaking me. I was trying to tell her to stop but no sound was coming from me. I noticed her mouth was moving, too. We couldn't communicate in the void. There was no sound, nothing to see or feel. It was impossible to catch my bearings.

As I craned my neck around, a speck of light appeared in the darkness. I swam toward it, but it never got closer. I pedaled and kicked my feet helplessly. Finally, I pulled out my sword. The light from its flame illuminated Urania's blue face, frozen cold from the darkness of space. I pointed at the sword, then at her, then at the faint light in front of us. She nodded faintly and grabbed onto me.

I swung a wide stroke and fired a blast that propelled us toward the light. I didn't know what we would find there, whether it would be friend or foe. And if we did find Cronus, I didn't know whether he would eat us on sight, but we had to move forward.

Urania closed her eyes as we flew. I pitied her. She was the goddess of astronomy, and there were no stars here. She had nothing wondrous to fill her gaze. Everything she loved about the world was taken away except a bunch of tiny specks of light bobbing in the distance.

I didn't mind looking out into the void. I spent a lot of time alone in my long life, living in the darkness, even if I didn't live *for* it. It was a friend to me. We were simpatico.

*

It took hours to reach the light, and we didn't like what we saw when we got there. Giant lantern-carrying bats flew around a sunless planet. The flapping of their wings made a haunting, rhythmic melody. It lulled you to a false sense of calm, until the deep guttural screech from the bats' throats snapped you back to reality.

I maneuvered around the disgusting bats hovering high above the planet and headed for a landing. Water dominated the surface, even though it was frozen. Small pockets of land punctuated the ice. Lights speckled the planet, too faint for a city but too bright to be a mistake. I chose one at random and flew toward it.

Admittedly, I'm not the best flyer. I've only been a god for a decade, and I don't have much occasion to leave Heaven, or fly places, like, ever. So, trying to land gracefully

from a thousand feet in the air didn't go so well. While I
intended to slow myself carefully and touch down lightly, we
ended up crash-landing with a loud explosion half a mile from
the light of a small town, in a deep crater of my own making.

"Are you okay?" I asked Urania now that we could speak.

Groggily, Urania nodded. "I'm fine."

"That was quite the landing, huh?"

Urania brushed herself off. "Worst I can remember, but
you haven't been a god long. I suppose you'll get better with
time."

"I hope so. Now, I guess we just gotta find out if this
place is inhabited and whether they've seen a giant Titan,
right?"

Urania shrugged, palms up. "You are the one taking *me* to
Cronus, remember?"

I looked up above the crater ridge created by my crash
entry. Shadows blotted out what little light there was. "We
have company."

A low, male voice shouted, "Are you okay?"

Oh great, I thought, *that means the planet is inhabited.*

If the chatter around Earth meant anything, then the odds
were that they had met Rhea, Cronus's wife and powerful
Titan in her own right. They had certainly survived traveling
through a black hole as well, and their god still didn't come
for them. Unlike Earth, nobody had come to save this lot,
which meant they probably didn't have the best opinion of the
gods. I needed to be on my best behavior.

"Yes," I said casually. "We're alright. We're fine here."

I grabbed Urania and flew out of the hole, landing among
a group of twenty men, women, and children grouped around
the crater, some of them peering in.

"What are you?" the man said. "That you survive such a
fall?"

"That's not really your concern. Have you seen Cronus?
Do you know what a Cronus is?"

"I know of Cronus, yes. He is the destroyer of worlds,
eater of my people, and a blight to humanity."

"Where is he now?"

"Not here." He looked up sharply. "We must be careful. The bats are ever watchful. They will not miss a chance to feed."

Sure enough, I looked up to see the bat's lanterns shone brighter as they descended onto the planet. The sound from their wings overwhelmed my ears as they flew lower, and then, they attacked.

With one talon they held their lanterns, and with the other they swooped down and grabbed at the group. One bat caught a blond boy. I pulled out my sword and struck the monster before it flew away. Urania grabbed the boy and shuffled the townspeople into the crater for protection.

One by one, the bats attacked, and one by one, I fended them off. Eventually, they tired of attacking alone, and a colony of them attacked at the same time.

"Get back!" I shouted as I swung my sword.

A bat grabbed the hilt of my sword and dragged me into the air. The other monsters swooped toward the group of humans. Urania tried to fend them off, but let's face it, she was weak for a god.

The bat flew me into the air, higher and higher. I kicked and screamed, but the bat kept rising into the air. That's when I remembered that I could fly. Like I said, it's not a power I've had for a long time, and the thought seriously slipped my mind.

I pressed my legs on the chest of the bat and heaved with all my might. I broke free of the monster and sailed down to Earth. The bat came for me, but this time I was ready. I stuck my sword into its gut when it came close. Blood and entrails splattered onto me and the bat let out a disgusting squawk before it fell to the Earth.

I grabbed onto the bat and flung it towards its friends like a bowling ball. It knocked several of its cohorts away from the crater. I turned my sword downward and cut through another bat before landing inside the crater again.

"I killed two of your friends and can easily get more. Leave now, before you are destroyed!"

The bats seemed to understand me. They muddled around for a moment, then started toward the sky again, slowly. They sent glares in my direction during their retreat, waiting for me to falter, but I never did.

"I am Katrina, and I protect these people. If you hurt them, you will answer to me. Understand this and tremble before my might!" I'd picked up a little godspeak from hanging around with Aphrodite, apparently.

I leapt out of the crater and stood at its lip. Urania handed me one human after another and I pulled them to safety. Once they were all up on the cliff, the man spoke to me.

"Thank you, it has been a long time since we had a protector. My name is Ezekiel, but people call me Zeke."

"Tell me something," I said to him. "What do you know about Cronus?"

"In a moment, I will tell you everything. But first, let us get back to protection. Follow me."

*

The planet was, quite literally, a shit hole. Every four feet was a massive pile of white, foul-smelling feces. "That's from the bats," the man told me. "You don't get a lot of it anymore since they don't feed very often, but back when we were a few billion people, they had their fill."

"How many are you now?" Urania asked.

"Oh, it's hard to say since communication is down, but there's a few thousand in town, and I can't imagine it's different anywhere else on the planet."

"Is it the bats that are killing you?" Urania sidestepped a pile of mega-guano.

"Sometimes, ma'am. But also, all the old-fashioned ways. Taking too many sleeping pills, jumping off a building, shooting yourself with a gun."

A deep chill of understanding sank into my bones. "So, suicide."

"Yes, ma'am. Not a lot of hope left to hold onto anymore."

I saw the desolation myself then. The town Zeke spoke of looked like Syria after years of bombings, filled with broken buildings, broken people, and broken lives. Zeke stopped in front of a derelict building. Gold leaf pillars covered the ground in front of him.

"This was once the crowning achievement of our world. Now, it is a shell of its former self. Please, come inside."

I exchanged a look with Urania, and we followed the old man inside the building. He seemed trustworthy enough. It wasn't like we had anything better to do.

"It was a few years ago…" Zeke began.

"Technically, it was ten years ago, but who's counting," Urania said. I kind of wanted to punch her in the head.

Zeke nodded his head. "Forgive me. There isn't a whole lot of light around here, and the power is on the fritz most of the time. Time is hard to track without the stars. We try to account for it the best way we can here."

"Of course," Urania said. "I'm sorry."

"We weren't the most powerful race in the galaxy, but we were happy enough. We figured out how to get power from the sun. We earned enough to eat and had robots to do the stuff we didn't want to do. We didn't bother with space travel or any of that, but we didn't need to. We were pretty happy on Earth."

"That's going to be very confusing," I said with a dry chuckle. I really wanted to lighten the mood. "Earth is my planet."

His response was deadpan. "Well, I'm sorry, ma'am, but that's what we call it."

I didn't think anyone could take me more literally than ol' Zeke had, and then Urania chimed in. "Technically, that's what everybody calls their home worlds, at least human-like planets," she frowned. "Though I don't know what the Horde calls theirs."

"The Horde, you say?" Zeke looked up. "I know of them."

"You do? You've seen them?" I asked, glad we were getting somewhere.

"Of course. They are conquerors, but we were peaceful. Luckily, our god fended them off for us. Gods bless Hermes."

"*Hermes* was your god?"

"Yes, ma'am. He was righteous and true. Led us to salvation. It's a shame what Cronus done to him."

"What was that?" I asked.

"It was ten years ago, or so, as the nice lady pointed out."

"Urania. My name is Urania."

"Nice to meet you, ma'am. We heard from other planets that the Mad Titan was loose again and causing a ruckus across the whole universe. He was eating up everything in sight, trying to make up for a million years of not eating anything at all. His hunger was voracious. I heard he ate planets whole."

"He did," Urania said. "We watched it happen."

"Hermes tried to rally other gods to his cause, but they wouldn't come. Nobody would come. He could have left, but he didn't abandon us. He stayed and fought—fought bravely, too. Held out a while, but eventually the Mad Titan swallowed him whole."

"That's when it happened. Everything shifted. The world fell into oblivion. The screams of millions filled my ears and eyes, and suddenly, we were here."

"Did Rhea come?" I asked. "My people tell tales of Rhea coming and devouring civilizations. Was she here?"

Zeke nodded. "Yes. She left us with these bats for light. She thought about eating us, but then she saw Cronus and forgot about us. She went off with him, leaving us to fend for ourselves. War broke out over the few remaining resources, before they dried up. Then you came."

Urania placed her hand on Zeke's hand. "I'm sorry for your loss."

Zeke smiled. "That's very kind of you, ma'am, but it's not my place to complain. It's just, when I saw you two, I got a moment of hope again like I haven't had in a long time."

A spry woman ran up to Zeke. "We got another cougar in the hen house, boss."

"Sorry, ma'am," he said. "I gotta leave you now and deal with this. Whatever is mine is yours. Make yourselves at home."

He went away with the woman and left us alone in in the burnt-out hovel that was once a pillar of Zeke's world. We adjourned to a small corner of the building.

"I'm going to be honest with you," I said. "I have no clue what to do now." I started pacing, trying to walk out my thought process.

Urania stood still, following me with her eyes. "I know."

"There is nothing out there, but, well, nothing. Even if I knew where Cronus was, I would have no idea how to track him down."

"I know."

"You're the expert on the universe. Do you have any ideas?"

She shook her head. "No. Even if I had a telescope, I couldn't see anything in this dark."

I stopped short. "Or could you?"

Urania frowned, wondering what I was thinking. "No, I couldn't."

"There were enormous telescopes back on my Earth. We pointed them into the darkness and they would come back with incredible pictures. Couldn't we do that here?"

"Not unless we knew where to point. Do you have any idea how long it would take to get a picture like that from nothing? We could be here a billion years and not cover a sliver of the sky."

"But what if we knew where Cronus was going?"

Urania thought for a second. "That could work, but that assumes he traveled in a straight line."

I thought about this for a few seconds before giving a shrug. "It's the best lead we have."

We found Zeke heading back towards the building. He carried the hide of a cougar on his back. A dozen men walked with him, bruised and bloody.

"Zeke!" I shouted to him.

He turned. "What is it?"

"What's the biggest telescope you have on this planet?"

"Functional?" He set the cougar down like a sack of potatoes. "Shoot, I don't know."

"Okay, well, what's the largest one you remember?"

He thought for a moment, tapping his fingers on the cougar's head. "There was one in Grilmia, right around the southern pole. It was strong enough to see the furthest stars in the galaxy. We often joked that we could see our sister planets waving at us."

"Could you lead us there?" Urania asked.

He shook his head. "No. I am too old—and I'm too important here to leave everyone, but I can give you a map."

I smiled. "That'll do."

Chapter 6

Flying over the canyons and chasms of Zeke's Earth, I couldn't help but see my own planet reflected in its crevices. The gods really had no imagination. They designed this Earth almost exactly like mine, with five oceans, seven continents, and seven seas, all broken up, so you couldn't easily access all of it without boats.

"Why did you guys do that?" I asked Urania, who flew next to me. "Make everything the same?"

"I think the gods got a sense of what works and what doesn't. When you succeed, you chase that success again and again. It's human nature."

"Don't you mean 'god nature?'"

"They are one and the same, since humans were all created in our image."

"That's pretty boring, you know."

Urania shot me a look. "Don't blame me. I don't make the rules. I couldn't tell you why all these planets look the same. It's above my pay grade, I guess."

"Except for Hera's."

"And Cronus's, but they are ancient, and created for a specific purpose. They weren't meant to harness life, they were to contain it. This Earth, we created it to propagate life."

"Like a virus."

"Viruses are simple life. Humans are more complex, but you all evolved from the same thing."

"Like the Horde."

"Even though they aren't *approved* life, they are still living beings, so they follow the same rules: Breed, multiply, and expand. They're more pissed off than humans ever were, to be sure, and they also don't have the light of the gods to show them the way."

I rolled my eyes and laughed. "You really are full of yourselves, aren't you?"

"What?"

"You gods, you created life, and you fostered it, sure, but you also caused almost every war. Bacchus had more death carried out his name than anything else in human history combined."

"Bacchus isn't one of our best."

I looked down at my map. "I think we're here."

In front of me was a massive telescope. Even at this altitude, I could make out the gigantic observatory resting atop their world's highest peak, which, according to the map, they called Mount Tilab.

"Let's go."

*

Unlike Zeke's city, the façade of the observatory was well-maintained. It didn't have any battle scars like the rest of the planet. It seemed to survive being transported through the black hole without a scratch on it. It was a shame that the rest of the planet wasn't constructed as soundly.

"Should we knock?" I asked Urania.

"I am the goddess of astronomers. I'm relatively sure I'm invited anywhere there's a telescope. Besides, I doubt there's anybody inside."

She pushed open the door. It moaned and creaked, like it hadn't been opened in years. Inside, it was preserved beautifully. Much like Urania's observatory, this one was set up in a circle, with desks around a large telescope in the middle. Monitors speckled the room, and all showed the blackness of space.

A head popped up from behind one of the desks and scared the crap out of us; crazed hair and thick glasses bobbed as a woman skittered toward us. "You can't be in here!"

"Excuse me?" I said.

"You can't be in here," she repeated.

"I'm sorry, but we didn't expect anybody—"

"Of course, you wouldn't. Why would you expect somebody to do their job in these conditions? But, there is work to be done and I'm doing it, okay? I told them all I would do it and I'm doing it."

"What work?" I asked.

"*The* work. The only work that matters. Plotting the stars to find out where we are."

"Um, are you aware there are no stars?"

She carried loads of papers in her hand as she whisked from one desk to another. "Of course, I'm aware of that, but just because I can't see stars doesn't mean they don't exist. I just have to look harder, and you can't be in here disturbing my work."

"Are you alone here?" Urania asked, looking around the room.

The woman glanced up from her papers and nodded slowly. "Everybody else left or died. Very sad. Very sad. But I stayed, because that was the deal. I stay and figure it out. I have been talking to myself for…um…thirteen years, three months, seven days, and fourteen minutes. Give or take."

"And what have you figured out?"

"Oh, wouldn't you like to know? That's just the kind of thing you would like to know."

"Well…I *am* the goddess of astronomers, after all."

"Oh yes. That would be a thing you are, and I am the mountain of potatoes. You must think I'm pretty dumb, pretty dumb indeed."

Urania snapped her fingers, and a small orb glowed in her hands. It pulsated in the light as it rose into the sky. "I promise you, I'm telling the truth."

I raised my eyebrows, impressed. "I didn't know you could do that."

Urania smiled. "I haven't done it in a long time. Creating stars was always my favorite thing to supervise. So complex. So beautiful. Not much need for it anymore. Laborious work, too."

The star nestled in front of the woman, who stared at it slack jawed. "It just can't be. It's not possible."

Urania snapped her fingers again and the star vanished. "I promise you, anything is possible."

"Should I kneel then?" the woman asked.

Urania shook her head. "I'm not that kind of god. We do need your help though."

"Yes, yes, yes. That sounds like something you would need. I'm afraid I have no time, though. I have so much work to do."

"You did hear the part where I said I was a god, right?"

The woman whipped around. "I have to find out where we are, and where we are going. I think that is more pressing than your needs."

Urania smiled. "But we already know where we are."

"Do we?" She stared over her glasses. "Do we really? I once knew where we were in correlation to the rest of the stars. Now, I don't know. Look at this." She spun in a chair and opened a drawer. She held up picture after picture of blackness. "I've stared into the sky for years and the most I've ever seen is one ray of light. Otherwise, blackness. It doesn't matter how long I keep my telescope trained. It's blackness, after blackness, after blackness."

Urania held up the images. "Have you tried opening the iris full?"

"You think I don't know how to calibrate my own telescope?"

"That's not what I'm saying. I'm just saying that I do know a thing or two about telescopes. Being the god of astronomy and all. Perhaps we can work together?"

The woman nodded. "Perhaps. I am Sarah."

*

Urania and Sarah got along like old friends almost immediately. They spoke in words and phrases that I knew was language but couldn't comprehend. While they worked, Sarah told stories of her life. They were the only thing I understood.

"The last of my friends, they left many years ago on a trek down the mountain. I never heard from them again."

"That must be sad for you," Urania said.

"Can I just tell you that it's quite upsetting?" Sarah said. "Sometimes I think I drove them all away because, well, I like to talk. I like to talk to people, and I can talk for a long time about a good many things. Sometimes, people don't like that, especially other astronomers. They're a little bit...well, shy I guess, and I never was. I like people. Kind of a weird profession to go into if you like people, huh?"

Urania smiled. "A bit, but it's a welcome change of pace."

*

I felt out of place inside the observatory, so I went for a walk. Outside the air was crisp, and in the absence of stars, the night was darker than I'd ever known it. I gathered some kindling and lit it with my arm. I had forgotten about my devilish powers, but they were still active, bubbling just below the surface. The fire felt good against my skin. Some days, I missed Hell. The beauty of Heaven was nice, but the fires of Hell reminded me that I was alive.

Above Hell, I missed Earth more and more with each passing second and every inch we traveled away from it, and more than anything I missed being a human. Humans had it so easy and they didn't even realize it. All they had to do was screw, eat, and sleep. Their problems were so trivial compared to those of a god.

It's funny, with all my power, I felt more useless now than I did during the Apocalypse. At least then I had purpose. I had goals. My goal was simply survival, but at least it was a goal. But now my personal survival was no longer my main prerogative; I was a god and would survive long into the future.

It was my job to protect my people, and I had no idea how to do it. It came so easy to Aphrodite; she was born to rule. That same ability eluded me. Put me up against a monster and I could beat it, no problem, but these problems, these massive issues that affect the whole universe? I am completely lost facing them.

Urania burst outside, giddy with excitement, looking all around for me. "Katrina, we have something." She led me inside and pointed to a large, black monitor bolted to the ceiling at the center of the room. "Look up at that monitor."

I looked up into the screen. "I see nothing."

"Look closer."

I squinted and realized there was a dot of white in the middle of the blackness. "It's a white patch."

"It's the only light in the entire sky. That's where we have to go. I'm sure of it."

"Awesome." I clapped my hands together, trying to rev myself up for another journey through the portal. "Then let's saddle up."

Urania held her finger up and rooted through some papers on the desk with her other hand. "Not so fast. We already knew that part. We have no idea how far that dot is from us. It could be a single light year or a million. We needed another data point to make our calculations."

I couldn't hold back a groan. She was going to start nerding out again. "Bring it back around to why this is exciting."

"I looked through all of Sarah's old photos and found this set from the only patch of whiteness in the whole universe." Her fingers clicked across the keyboard. "Keep looking at it."

The slide changed, and it was the same dot. "What am I looking at?"

"Look closer. Do you see it? That little speck of black on the white?"

"I see a lot of black—wait." I moved closer to the screen. Sure enough, there was a black dot in the center of the whiteness. "Oh yeah."

"That's a way to do it, one way. It's how we used to find planets, by tracking as they pass in front of a star. Any planet worth its salt is going to pass in front of a star at some point, now isn't it?" Sarah said.

"It's primitive technology, but effective," Urania said without taking her eyes from the monitor.

"What does it mean?"

"It means there's a planet in front of that big white space, and if there's a planet, then all we have to do is calculate how far it is, and then we can jump there." Urania nodded to herself, satisfied. "It's the best plan we have."

"It's the only plan we have," Sarah corrected.

"And what makes that planet better than this one?" I asked. "Besides that it's closer to a big, white light?"

"Trust me," Sarah said. "Any planet is better than this one."

"Is it though?" I asked.

"To answer your questions," Urania interrupted. "I calculated that there is a 97.2 percent likelihood that the white light will lead us to Cronus, so if we get closer to that light, we get closer to Cronus. Is that good enough for you?"

"It's as good a plan as any, but this plan is pretty terrible. Let's do it."

*

It took Sarah and Urania several hours to calculate the path of the planet, and another couple to get the coordinates right, but eventually they had determined where we needed to go.

"How sure about this are you?" I asked.

"On what scale?" Urania asked.

"The 'are we going to die' scale."

"Oh, we won't die."

"That's encouraging."

"You're much more likely to be stranded out in the darkness forever," Sarah said, helpfully.

"Right. After all, we are gods."

"I'll bet that's nice."

"We won't die. I'm sure of it." Urania nudged me with a smile.

She could nudge me all she wanted. I wasn't convinced. "How do you know?"

"You made me a deal," Urania said. "And we haven't reached Cronus yet. You seem like the kind of woman who keeps her word."

I sighed. "Fair enough."

I memorized the coordinates and took out my sword. With one swoop, I cut open a hole in this new universe, then held out a polite hand to Urania. I didn't know whether it would work the same as it did as in our original universe, but I hoped that it would. "Get in."

"Thank you," Urania said. "You have made this god very happy."

"I wish you both well! That's a thing you wish, right?" Sarah said.

I'm pretty sure she was still talking long after Urania and I disappeared into the tear I made with the Sword of Damocles. I had no idea whether this portal would work the same way in this new universe as it did in my own universe, but I was glad to get away from Sarah, who for all her niceness and intelligence, never stopped talking.

Chapter 7

When we were in our original universe, the one with Hera's dungeon, Aphrodite's Earth, and my own, the sword's portal between worlds was filled with colors. Nebulas, galaxies, stars, and planets seemed to twinkle in every possible shape— and some shapes that seemed impossible. Some galaxies swirled like a Spirograph, while others clumped together like old gum. Still others spidered their tendrils across the universe.

And the colors, holy crap the colors. Every color you can imagine and some you've only dreamed of, mixed together in mind-blowing arrangements. That was what it was like back in our original universe, before we leapt through a black hole and ended up here.

But we were not in that universe any more. We were in a new universe; a universe filled with...nothing. Here, there was only darkness. There was no way to tell when the portal started or ended. Inside the portal, we couldn't even see each other. I knew Urania was there because she was holding my hand, but I couldn't see her.

I wanted to see her. I liked Urania, in a weird way. She wasn't like the other gods. She wasn't cocky or brash, she didn't talk down to people. She was excited for things, and wanted to work with humanity, not subjugate it. I'd never known a god like that.

They were usually ridiculously self-involved, and their fancies were banal and pedantic. Freakin' Aphrodite, talking down to everybody all the time, like she's better than them. And I mean, she is. For the gods' sake, she's a *god*, and a planetary regent to boot, but that doesn't mean she has to act so self-righteous all the time.

The gods—all of them—demanded constant, unwavering love, respect, and submission. Not Urania. She didn't demand anything. Not once in our time at the observatory did she talk down to Sarah. I liked that about her.

The Sword of Damocles's portal spat us out onto a new world, one we knew nothing about except that it was closer to the only bright light in this new universe than we were before.

And she was right. In fact, the bright light Urania saw in Sarah's observatory was right on top of us. Immediately upon exiting the portal, light washed over me. It blinded me but gave no warmth; it was like it existed outside of heat.

Imagine staring into the high beams of a Humvee from three inches away. The light wouldn't burn you, but the intense brightness would fill every inch of your sight with unyielding whiteness. Now, imagine that brightness followed you wherever your eyes turned. That's how this light consumed everything around it.

I fumbled around for Urania's hand, and thought I found it for a moment. However, it didn't squeeze me back. It didn't move at all, and it was cold to the touch. I held on a moment longer until I realized the thing in my hand was hairy and it had long, sharp talons at the end. I tossed it aside and wiped my hands on my pants. That was gross.

"Katrina!" Urania shouted. I couldn't see her, but I could hear her.

I crawled toward her voice. With every step, I passed over squishy bodies. I stepped over dozens of pointed snouts and teeth. One body felt like lizard monsters from *Land of the Lost* must have felt. The next body I crawled over had a ridged thorax and hairy arms—six of them. Its antennae bristled against my leg.

"Katrina!" Urania shouted again.

"I'm here!" I shouted back.

My eyes barely made out the contours of her body through the light. This planet had to be about the unluckiest I'd ever encountered. I couldn't imagine lasting a day with such a galling brightness showering down on me. I would go mad, even as a god. How the beings of this world survived, I could not imagine.

Urania flailed her arms through the air as she struggled to find her bearings. "Where are you?"

"I got you!" I said, grabbing her arm.

She spun around and latched onto my neck. "Don't let me go."

It was nice, for once, to not hate the feeling of an embrace. Her heart pulsed as I held her tight. She was scared, and so was I. We were in a foreign land, surrounded by death, hardly able to see a thing.

"Do you think this is where Cronus is hiding?" Urania asked. Her voice was close to my ear. Really close.

"I don't know. I really don't know much about him. We only met a couple times, and only briefly when we did."

"You knew him for longer than anybody else, except for Zeus."

"Maybe, but that doesn't mean I *know* him. You've known me longer than almost anybody else in the universe, and you barely know me."

"I know you well enough."

"That isn't even remotely true."

*

There was nothing we could do until we regained our sight except crawl around this new planet and hope nothing killed us. I was confident everything on this planet was dead, at least. Otherwise, something would have come to clean up the mass of carcasses lining every inch of the ground.

I held Urania's hand as we made our way through the piles of corpses littering every corner of the street, looking for a clean place to sit and hoping to adjust to the brightness shining down on the planet from above the atmosphere.

"Why are there so many dead bodies everywhere?" I asked her.

"I have a theory, but it's not fleshed out or anything. Did you know that if you are exposed to light for too long," Urania asked, "it could kill you?"

I squeezed Urania's hand tighter. "That doesn't sound right."

"Sure. Think about it. Most beings are used to sleeping when its dark out, right? And when it's light all the time it throws your body out of whack, and if things don't sleep, then they'll die, right?"

I found a hard surface that felt like asphalt, without any hairy legs or arms about, and pulled Urania close to me. "I seem to remember needing sleep some thousands of years ago."

"Of course, not us gods or anything, but most beings need sleep," Urania said. I felt her arm slide closer to me. "I think that whatever inhabited this planet…went crazy after being next to that light for too long, and eventually their sleep deprivation drove them mad, and eventually killed them."

"That still doesn't sound right."

"Well, it's a working theory, Katrina," Urania scoffed. "It's not like I'm an expert in hairy, weird things, or any sort of biology really. Maybe their bodies couldn't handle the pressure of coming through a black hole, or maybe they all drank some sort of potion. I don't know. I'm just killing time, alright?"

I laughed. "Easy, killer. I guess it's as good a theory as any. I mean, maybe not any theory, but any theory I have about what happened here."

Urania closed her hand inside of mine. "What do you think happened?"

I pushed my hair out of my face and looked at the street around me. "I don't know, maybe they just fought to the death in a Battle Royale. Or maybe it was a war. Or a nuclear attack."

"You would think of war, wouldn't you?"

"I'm good at fighting, so that's where my mind goes. Just keep talking. I like when you talk."

"About what?"

I leaned my head against Urania's shoulder. "Anything. I don't care."

"Uhm…did you know I am personally three million years old?" she asked. "Give or take a few hundred thousand years."

"I did not know that. My mother taught me never to ask a woman her age. You look good.'"

"Thank you. I always wondered how you humans got anything done in just a few decades. I could live another billion and not see one tenth of the stars in the sky."

"I think it's good," I replied. "To live a short life. I've been alive a long time and it drones on and on after a while. I don't know how many more years I can stand Heaven, and that's the best place on Earth."

"Oh, well I don't have that problem. I'm never on Hera's planet."

"Did you miss the part where you're ruling there in Hera's stead?"

"Yes. That is true, physically, but in my mind, I am all over the universe, from the smallest worlds to the biggest."

"So, this must freak you out then," I said, gesturing to the air around us. "Just having a big white void, surrounded by nothing except a dead planet."

"It's not ideal, not for me. Nothing brings me more joy than looking out on the night sky and seeing infinity. Did you know that they let me name all the constellations?"

I raised my eyebrows. "They do?"

"They're different everywhere in the universe, and I have to name them one at a time. It's very hard work." She was clearly excited just to talk about it. It was the sort of thing she geeked out over, but I didn't really get it.

"I've seen some of your work. I don't know how you can get a bull from a straight line."

Urania sounded exasperated. "That's because you have no imagination, Katrina."

"I've been told that before, but come on, it's literally a bent line that's supposed to represent a ram?"

"It didn't only represent a ram, though. It also represented a folded hand, and a fish, and about a hundred different things. Every time a new culture sprang up, I got to name the constellations again. The most fun part was seeing which constellations they chose as important to them."

My eyes had regained their focus, and yet I still didn't want to leave Urania's embrace. I studied her for a moment. "You actually like humanity, don't you?"

"Of course. Don't you?"

"No. They suck. Sometimes, a person is okay, but as a whole they are the worst."

"I never found that. Certainly, they often do foolish things, but they are also capable of such wonder."

"You haven't been around them for long."

Urania gave me an annoyed look before saying flatly, "I've helped create a thousand civilizations."

I pulled my arms away from her and shrugged. "Sure, but did you live among them or above them?"

"Usually the latter."

"It's a lot different when you're stuck right alongside them." I stood up to have a look around. "How are your eyes?"

Urania blinked. "They are better. I can see. Not that I want to."

Thousands of bug carcasses, each as big as me, littered every street corner, rotting in the bright light. I looked up toward their buildings, which were built like domed caves carved out of hills. They rose into the sky like giant ant hills, standing a hundred feet into the air.

"Do you recognize this place, Urania?"

"No." She shook her head and squinted in disbelief. "It doesn't look like any world I've ever seen."

"Do you think it belonged to the Horde?"

Urania shrugged, stepping over the carcass of a pill bug as it stared upward with dead eyes. "I don't know. All I can say for sure is that it's nothing like any planet I've ever seen. However, if I had to guess, I would say yes."

I bent down to pick up something like a piece of paper covered in some unintelligible scrawl. It was a language I had never seen before. Since I had become a god, I learned several different languages—Greek, Roman, Egyptian, Mali, Indian…okay, every language in the universe. I could read them all, instinctively. Everything I touched became English to me.

And yet, I didn't recognize this one. It was mostly squiggly lines, like trying to read Russian cyrillic, the hardest language in the world for me to understand by several factors. "I don't think this is going to help us. Can you read it?"

I handed the letter to Urania. She squinted at it. "I can't."

"Then I suppose we are at an impasse."

Urania smiled. "Not completely. Do you think they have observatories on this planet?"

I shrugged. "Probably. Why?"

"The stars look the same no matter your language. If we can find a map of the stars, I can tell you where they were from, and maybe even what happened to them."

"That doesn't sound...probable, Urania."

"There are only so many types of telescopes in the universe, and no matter what, you still need a really long lens to see into the stars. They had to start there, at least, which means there would be some mark of it on the planet. Unless the Horde didn't care about the stars at all, but of course, that's crazy."

"Why?"

"Because they're out there. They're in the stars, and that curiosity had to start somewhere. Sometime."

I couldn't argue with her.

*

One time, I went to Sunriver Observatory, just south of Bend, Oregon, with my parents while we were on a trip to see my cousin Cassandra. It was in the middle of a mountain range. Same with the observatory on Zeke's planet, and the one on the Horde's planet, as well.

It stood to reason that no matter how different our cultures were, science functioned the same anywhere. We needed to put our observatories high in the sky to be closest to the stars, and so did the Horde.

I don't know what the observatory was called except for "bunch of squiggles," but inside, it didn't look much different than the observatory we just left on Zeke's Earth. It was set up in a circle and surrounded by monitors. The monitors had a dozen different types of what I guessed were keyboards— though they were made for crazy bug hands—from small and compact to massive. Some were even baked into a wall.

"I found something," Urania shouted out.

There were no dead bodies in the observatory, which was a nice change of pace from the rest of the planet. We had flown over millions of corpses as we traveled across the planet. But since there were no live bodies either, the place had fallen into disrepair. The floors creaked, and the roof had long ago collapsed upon itself.

"What is it?" I said.

Urania stood in front of a large map of the stars. She pointed to a large cluster of stars. "This here is the section of stars where your Earth resides."

She traced her hand along the map from the bottom left toward the top right. "I recognize some of these star patterns." She stopped in the middle right of the poster and pointed emphatically. "There. That's it. I know where they are from!"

"Great," I shouted. "Where is that?"

She didn't speak for a moment. I heard her gasp softly and mutter, "Oh, great gods…it cannot be…" but she didn't complete the thought. She just sighed and lowered her eyes. Tears filled them. "I have to tell you a story."

"You can tell me anything."

"You know the gods can display…unsavory behavior, right?"

I nodded slowly, wondering what she was getting at. "It hasn't been lost on me."

"I just want you to remember that I'm not as bad as they are when I tell you this." She was still staring at her feet, and she barely whispered this last.

"Come on, Urania." I waved a hand dismissively, trying to put her at ease. "I'm a jerk. You're a jerk. We're all jerks. Out with it."

She stared past me, at nothing. "Right after you killed Zeus…that's when I started studying Apollo's hands. They could level entire stars and turn them into black holes. With Apollo gone, I had to find a way to harness his power. I tried for months, but I didn't make any headway. Those hands mocked me. They taunted me."

"They gave you the finger."

"Ha! I'm going to use that." Urania chuckled for a moment before she comported herself again. "But one day, I figured it out. I figured out a way to use the hands to collapse a black hole."

Tears swelled in her eyes. "I tested it, Katrina. I tested it over and over again. I tested it on stars without planets. I tested it on stars with planets. I tested it with stars…with stars I knew were…habitable."

I gasped, and Urania flinched. "You tested it on people!"

"Of course not." She threw me a glare. "We wouldn't do that."

"Apollo sent billions of my people through a black hole. Of course, you would do that."

"Fine. They would—*I* wouldn't. No. I wouldn't test it on…on *humans*."

Realization sank in and I leaned back against the wall. I placed my hand to my mouth on instinct. My voice lowered, and the breath left my lungs. "You tested it on the Horde."

She nodded. "I tested it on the Horde." Urania started crying. She slid down the map-wall onto the floor, sobbing big, messy tears. "I caused all of this. I pissed off the Horde and got them hunting us."

I kneeled next to her, placing a firm hand on her shoulder. "Hey, hey, hey. It's not you. It's not you. I know for a fact it wasn't you."

"Don't lie to me!"

I cupped her face in my hands. "It's true…it's true. L'l'itoh, whatever that crazy Bug-Hotep was called, told me. They hated Zeus and when I killed him, it showed them that gods could be killed. This is all because of me, all of it."

I choked up for a moment. "I…I am the one. Not you, goddamn it. Not you."

Her eyes were swollen and red, as were her cheeks. Still, she smiled at me. I reached up and wiped a big tear drop from her face.

And that's when I kissed her.

I didn't stop kissing her until she stopped crying.

*

I've had a lot of sex in my day. A lot. At least a thousand peoples' worth of sex. When I got bored, I often screwed the best guys and girls in Heaven, and when I got bored with them, I screwed the ones in Hell.

A lot of guys and girls, but I didn't do a lot of kissing—not without it leading to sex, anyway. But with Urania, we just kissed. For a long time. Then, we stopped and sat looking out at the bright, white light on the screen in silence.

"That was a thing we did," I said, finally.

"It was, and we did it because we both believe we're the worst person in the universe."

"Objectively, we are not people."

"Fine. The worst...*beings* in the universe. Whatever you want to believe. I don't think that's healthy."

I shook my head. "It's definitely not healthy. I am not healthy, though."

She leaned her head against the wall. The map crunched against the weight of her head. We were both quiet for a moment and then she said, "It's funny that they look up to us, isn't it?"

"Do they look up to us? Or do they fear us because we are so powerful?"

"Is there a difference?"

"Yes. I looked up to my mother, but I fear Cronus. I fear him because he could destroy me. I looked up to my father because he never would, even though he could."

Urania lifted an eyebrow. "That sounds like a semantic argument to me."

I pointed at her face. "Yes, I see in your eyes that you fear Cronus. When I said his name, your breath jumped."

"Yes, I fear him."

"He is a vengeful being, but is your desire to save Hera greater than your desire to face him? Because that's what it comes down to in the end—whether your desire to do something is greater than your desire to do nothing."

"Is that how you do things? Is that how you defeated Zeus?"

I laughed and weighed my hands in front of me. "Yes. I wanted my world back more than I feared the repercussions, more than I even thought of the repercussions. If I'd known what would happen though, I don't know if I would've done it."

"Yes, you would have."

She hadn't even skipped a beat to disagree with me on that one, and it made me smile. "Yes, I would have." I looked over at her then. "Are you ready to face him?"

Urania shook her head. "No. But it's better than doing nothing."

Chapter 8

It took us an hour of flying, propelled by my sword once the atmosphere fell away, to reach the white light. It was as if somebody took an eraser to a piece of the galaxy and wiped it from existence. I gripped Urania's hand, not lovingly, like she'd done with me, but with the force of a mother protecting her child.

"I'm going to protect you," I told her.

"I trust you."

We flew into the white light together. A warmth filled from my toes and fingers into my arms and finally into my heart. Urania vanished next to me, and then I faded as well. I tasted pancakes with warm, maple syrup. I hadn't had pancakes in eons.

The first thing I noticed when I rematerialized was the absolute overwhelming whiteness of everything around me. A beautiful white halo illuminated Urania; everything from her hair to her clothing glistened white. Pure white. She had never looked more like a god than that moment.

Wherever we were, everything was pure white, as if nobody had stepped foot in it ever before. There were no fingerprints, no smudge marks. Nothing except a beautiful and complete whiteness as far as my eyes could see.

"How are you feeling?" I asked.

"I'm fine," Urania said. "A little lightheaded is all."

We walked forward into the bright nothingness. Our feet clapped against the ground, but they didn't make any sound. In fact, nothing made a sound outside of our voices, not even the clicking of my knees or the rubbing of my fingers. Here in the nothingness I didn't hear anything except Urania's breath.

"I don't think we're in the right place," Urania said. "I don't see how anyone could live here."

"I do," I said. "It's quiet and lonely and there's no drama."

"I guess that's true," Urania conceded.

I spun around in every direction, but all I found was endless white space in every direction. We were beyond lost, and it scared me. Although I don't know if lost was the right word, because in order to be lost you needed to know where you were going. Usually when you're lost there's a way to find your way out. Here, there was nothing. It was only Urania and me.

It wasn't the worst thought that I'd ever had. In fact, it was kind of pleasant. If I didn't have the human race to save, a galaxy to save, staying in the nothing with Urania for the rest of time could have been kind of fun.

Of course, that's easy to say in the throes of new love—no, love is way too strong a word. Puppy dog infatuation. That's much more accurate. After all, if I learned nothing else from Keanu Reeves it's that relationships made from high stress situations never last.

"I don't like this," Urania said. "I really don't like this."

"Well that's a shame," I replied. "because I think we're stuck here."

"That can't be true. There has to be a way out."

"Oh, I'm sure there is. I've been stuck in a lot of places in my life. I've been stuck in Earth, Heaven, Hell, and now here. I've gotten out of all three of those places and I'm sure we'll get out of this one, too."

"That's good to hear."

"Just so we're clear, though, it took me ten thousand years to get out of Hell. So, while I'm sure we'll get home at some point, I'm not sure it will be before the universe ends, and I'm definitely not sure we'll get there before our worlds are destroyed."

"That's less good to hear."

"Yes, I didn't think you'd like that one. The good news is I'm not known for giving up."

Urania flopped over onto the ground. "I'm just going to lie here for a few hundred years."

"That's not a great idea. Your legs will atrophy."

"I don't care. No offense to you, but I'm not that excited to be stuck here without a way out, and no idea how long I'll be here. So, I'm just gonna wallow for a while."

"It won't be that bad. I'm very entertaining."

"You could be the most hilarious person on the planet, but you would still need new material eventually." She threw her arms into the air wildly. "Maybe not today, maybe not tomorrow, but some day you will need new stories and," she gestured to the pillowy, blank space around us, "where the *hell* are you going to get them here?"

"That's the first time I've ever heard you curse."

"You haven't known me that long. It seems like this situation deserves one."

I flopped down next to Urania. "You're cute when you curse."

Urania laughed despite herself. I liked her laugh. She wasn't trying to be cute. She wasn't trying to contain herself. She was full-body heaving with laughter, complete with snorts and convulsions.

"What if we never get out of here?" Urania asked after the laughter died. "What will happen to the universe?"

"The universe will survive, Urania. You should know that better than anybody. The universe will keep going. It doesn't really care about us, at least not as much as we care about it."

"That's comforting, in a weird way."

*

I don't know how long I laid there listening to Urania breathe, but she was right, eventually it got tiring. It's amazing how tiring it is to do nothing. I hadn't felt so exhausted in ages. I'd traipsed around the galaxy, fought gods, even traveled to other dimensions, yet I had never been so tired.

Neither of us said anything for a long time. We both stared into various places in the middle distance, our eyes unable to land on anything solid. There wasn't anything solid there. Just a wall of white. "Can I ask you a question?"

"You can ask anything, though I reserve the right not to answer it."

"Back in that observatory. You created that star out of nothing. How? I thought only Cronus could create life."

Urania chuckled. "That's an old parlor trick Apollo taught me—rearranging a couple molecules and igniting them. It's not really creation. It's nothing more than a cheap illusion."

"Well, it worked."

She smiled sweetly at me. "Sure, but lots of tricks work on people that don't know any better. At the end of the day, they are just illusions."

I watched her brush the hair from her eyes and take a deep breath. I wanted to listen to her talk more, but even more so, I wanted to watch her exist. I could have watched her forever, but in the silence of that perfect moment I heard something. It was faint. It was the sounds of laughter echoing in the distance.

"Do you hear that?" I asked.

Urania sat up. "I do!"

We rocketed to our feet and flew towards the sound. We didn't care if it was our doom or our salvation. We just knew that it was something—anything—and anything was better than nothing.

We lost the voice again and again and again, but eventually it stopped, and started booming in front of us. Another voice joined it, this one deeper and gruffer than the other. It wasn't just a laugh we heard then. It was talking—well, more like mumbling really, followed by the distinct sound of orgasmic moaning.

Eventually, the light titter of the voice became a voluminous roar of moans and groans, punctuated by a massive climax that thundered down the whiteness. By that time, we were within sight of two figures lying on their backs and laughing.

"Are you hungry, my dear?" the male said. I immediately recognized Cronus, no longer covered in rocks, but smooth as a baby's bottom and naked as a jay bird.

"Yes, my dear. Quite famished actually," the other voice said. It must be Rhea. I had heard of her wicked, tree-like veneer from many millions of my subjects, but now she lay naked and smooth, like Cronus.

Cronus sat up and snapped his fingers. A minotaur appeared in front of Rhea. "Oh," she said. "No, I'm not in the mood for bull."

Cronus gobbled it up. "How about fish?" He snapped his fingers together, and a mermaid appeared in front of her. Rhea tossed the mermaid up in the air and bit down hard on its shoulders, slurping the rest of it into her mouth.

"This is good, but I would love it to be more human."

"Well, we have a massive supply of humans. Any preference?"

"How about just a sampler?"

Cronus smiled and snapped his fingers. A dozen humans of all races and sizes fell onto the ground. They tried to scream, but their mouths didn't work. They tried to run, but their feet couldn't move them. They could only watch as they were eaten one at a time and pray that their ends were swift.

I moved toward Cronus, but Urania held me back. "Wait. They are hungry. They might eat us."

"And when they're done, who's to say they're going to stick around? It has to be now."

Urania nodded. I grabbed her hand and she hunkered behind me a bit as we walked forward. "What ho, good Cronus?"

He cocked his head to the side, confused, and then plastered a big smile on his face. "Why, if it isn't Katrina, scourge of the gods and Apocalypses alike. What ho, indeed?"

"Oh, you know. Just taking a stroll through the nothingness."

Cronus picked up a human and gnawed on his legs. "Of course. And what brings you beyond the universe?"

"It seemed like the place to be."

"Who is this, dear?" Rhea asked, peering curiously at us. I stood with my shoulders back, feet planted squarely, while Urania tried hard not to look like she was cowering behind me, peeking over my shoulder.

"Why, this is the woman we have to thank for releasing me." Cronus paused and cast a glance at me. "Oh, I'm sorry. Do you prefer 'woman' or 'god?'"

"How about just Katrina?" I said.

"A god, you say?" Rhea licked her lips. "It's been a long time since I've had god. Is she on the menu?"

Cronus smiled. "I'm afraid she's not, my dear. I like her too well. But her friend here is a different story." He looked Urania up and down in a way that sickened me. "She has the light of a god about her."

"This is Urania. She is the goddess of astronomy. And she is not on the menu either."

Rhea's eyes flashed. "I decide what's on the menu!"

"Of course, good Rhea. I meant no disrespect. It's just that..." I honestly didn't know exactly how to say what I was trying to say, but this was no time to be at a loss for words. And so I just wrapped my fingers around Urania's hand.

Cronus instantly made the connection. "Of course, young Katrina. We all have our needs. As a courtesy, we will not eat your...friend."

I nodded. "Much appreciated."

Rhea sat back in a huff but seemed willing to not eat Urania for the time being. It's the small victories.

"So, tell me, what is going on in the universe these days?" Cronus rested his chin on his hand and leaned forward like a girl at a sleepover. I never thought I'd mentally compare a god-eating Titan to a teenage girl.

I took a few steps forward, though Urania stayed put. "The Horde. They're destroying everything the gods hold dear. They've already destroyed at least one planet and now they've turned their sights on Earth."

"Good! Brat gods had it coming." Cronus laughed. "It's the least they deserve for imprisoning me! I hope they suffer greatly and get themselves wiped from the universe."

Urania stepped forward then, too. "You think it's funny that we're suffering?"

Cronus guffawed. "Of course. It's always funny when people get what they deserve."

"Our universe is burning," Urania scoffed. "Your children and grandchildren are being slaughtered alive, and you don't care at all, do you?"

"I will be honest. I hadn't thought about your pathetic, puny universe for eons before you showed up here. We are having too much fun here." He wrapped his arms around Rhea. "Aren't we, my love?"

Rhea smiled. "Oh yes. That universe is a fickle place. Always on the edge of collapse, needing this thing or that thing repaired. It's a nightmare. I wouldn't wish it on my worst enemy."

"Better to be in the nothingness, where everything is simple," Cronus added. "However, now that you are here I have a feeling the complexity of my life will resume in earnest, yes?"

"I'm afraid so, my friend," I said. "Urania and I have come a long way to ask you a question, and I'm afraid you're not going to like it."

Cronus leaned back on his haunches. "Then why say it at all, if it will offend me?"

Urania sighed. "Because it must be asked."

"Then ask it, impetuous one."

There was only a brief moment's hesitation before Urania swallowed hard and unleashed what sounded like a well-practiced request. She'd been giving herself pep talks again. "I would like for you to let Hera go. She is my queen, and my lord, and she did nothing to you. She is not Zeus."

Cronus studied her, cocking his head. "No, my child. She is not Zeus. She did not imprison me inside that tomb, or send my love into a black hole of nothingness, did she?"

"No. She did not."

Rhea leaned forward with a sneer. "But she did not help us, either. Did she?"

"She couldn't. She didn't—"

"You are a sweet child to come all this way," Cronus said. "Let me ask, would she have done the same for you?"

"Of course not! She is a queen. It is my duty to protect my queen. It is her duty to rule, and she does it with grace and fairness in horrible conditions. She has sacrificed everything to protect the gods' justice, and she deserves better than to waste away in your stomach."

Cronus scoffed. "Rule for you or rule over you, my child? It seems you might have developed a sickening attachment to this god you love so."

Rhea pointed at her hand, still wrapped in mine. "Maybe you have a fascination with powerful women. Did you know that I, too, am a powerful woman?" She wiggled her shoulders back and forth and inched closer to us, her lips twisted into a mocking pout.

Urania gripped my hand with all her strength. "I love my queen because she is wise and just, not because of any infatuation."

Cronus turned to me. "And what think you, Katrina, of this madness? To petition a Titan for the return of a god, a god that helped imprison him?"

"It is not my place to judge," I said. "The Horde is obliterating planets in my universe. I need an army to get rid of them. Urania can help but wanted me to take her to Hera, so I did. I tend not to think too hard about these things."

Cronus smiled. "That is why I like you, Katrina. You think with your gut, not with your head. But you have lived around these gods for a short time now. What do you think of them? Do you think they are worthy of redemption?"

"Honestly, Cronus. I don't know. They are petty, mean, impetuous, stubborn…and whatever else is in the thesaurus for 'asshole.' They're so much like humans it's impossible to tell them apart." I looked over at Urania. "But, like humans, they are also sweet, and kind. I love humans as much as I hate them. I figure that's the way I feel about the gods, too."

"I will contemplate for a while. You have given me much to consider." The Titan studied me closely. "Your friend wishes for her queen's release. Is there anything else you would ask of me?"

I nodded. "There is. Now that I'm here I realize that there is only one being in the galaxy who can help me on my quest to destroy the Horde."

Cronus smiled. "I appreciate it, but I will not go back to your universe, or any universe. I am quite happy here, outside of time and space."

"I understand that, my friend. I was, however, talking about Zeus. I would very much like to speak with him."

He twisted his face into a snarl. "You ask much, Katrina."

"Hey, you invited me to ask. It's simple, really. I can't think of anything I need more than to save my planet, and Zeus is best suited to do that." I cocked my head at him. "And you are the only one who can deliver Zeus."

"Very well. Leave me to think."

"Where should we go? It's kind of sparse here."

Cronus snapped his fingers, and we were gone in a blink.

Chapter 9

I don't know if Cronus meant to send us to the most horrific place imaginable, but if so, then mission accomplished, buddy. Urania and I materialized in a factory. Millions of humans lined its walls, dangling from meat hooks, kicking, screaming, waiting to die. They were born in suffering, and they would die suffering, which is the human condition, but here it was played out to the ultimate degree. And after ruling in Hell, I know about suffering. I'd never imagined there was a fate worse than Hell, that's for sure, but Cronus seemed to have perfected the formula.

"Cronus really doesn't care about humans, does he?" Urania asked, looking over the railing.

"He doesn't care about anything. To him, we are all his playthings. This is his place. He cares about us as much as we care about Barbie dolls or G. I. Joe."

"What's a Barbie doll?" Urania said, walking toward the stairs at the edge of the ledge.

I smiled at the memory. "It's a silly, little toy they push on girls. He cares about us, as much as you care about your telescope."

Urania inhaled sharply and frowned defensively. "I love my telescopes."

"Sure, but it's a tool to you." I shrugged. "What happens if it breaks in half?"

Here was the pause I was waiting for. We walked down a flight of metal stairs to the factory floor while Urania considered my question. She finally admitted, "I would get another one."

"Exactly. Do you mourn the loss of it? Do you weep for it? Of course not. You fix it or buy another one. That telescope is an object. It was designed for a specific use and is easily, maybe endlessly, replaceable. It's the same for him with us. We are just objects to him."

Urania frowned. "Hera always told me Cronus was a monster. I believed her, and now I know she was right."

We passed a giant, metal machine and watched as some robots fed some weird, mutton-like substance into it. A conveyor belt carried it through the machine and to the other side, where a fully formed human plopped out. Not a baby human either. This one was a fully formed adult male. They were every color and shape under the sun, but none of them were female. There were so many wieners.

"I don't think he's a monster. I used to destroy Barbie dolls and toy trucks as a child for fun. I burned them for kicks. I wasn't a monster. I was just playing with my toys, and toys don't have feelings, no matter what Pixar wants you to believe."

"If he doesn't care about us, then why is he even entertaining our requests?"

"I don't know. Maybe, just maybe, he's bored. I mean, you said it yourself. A white space for eternity is kind of dull. I know we bring the drama and that's a pain in the ass, but at least we aren't boring."

Urania's mouth was forming her response when she turned from solid to translucent, to a white blur, and then she was gone. She faded from my sight, leaving me clutching at a patch of whiteness where she had been.

"Urania! Urania!"

But it was too late. Cronus had sent for her. He would either grant her request to rescue Hera or destroy her for sport. It was a fifty-fifty proposition.

There were no human workers in the factory, only robots. Back when I was lord of Hell, I'd thought about automating things down there, but that would have displaced far too many monsters and left them with no place to go. It was easier to just keep doing things the old way, and keep the demons moderately happy, than to modernize and make Hell worse for most and better for some.

While I looked up at the dangling penises, in disturbed, disgusted awe of Cronus's warehouse, I too began to feel my molecules pulling apart; I was fading from the scenery. I smiled as I tasted pancakes, happy to be gone from such a horrible place.

*

I rematerialized in front of Cronus. At his feet, Urania wept and cradled a broken, bruised Hera in her arms.

"She's alive," Cronus said.

"I don't really care," I replied.

"I know, which is what I like most about you."

"Funny, it's what I hate most about me."

Cronus shook his head. "You are above this world, Katrina, and this universe. You understand that this is all meaningless, and yet you struggle against it. I find that beautiful."

"I don't really care about that, either."

"But therein lies the rub, doesn't it?" Rhea said from over Cronus's shoulder. "Because if you don't care at all, then he doesn't have to let you speak with Zeus."

"Very good point, my dear," Cronus added. "In fact, I don't have to give you anything you asked for, and you won't care."

I twitched for a moment. "I don't care."

He smiled. "You are a very good liar, Katrina. Has anybody else told you that?"

I nodded. "Once or twice. The secret is in lying to yourself."

"Very true," Rhea responded. "A good god must also be a good liar, feeding their subjects lies and deceptions for their own good."

"I'm starting to see why Zeus wanted all you Titans dead."

"Ah yes, Zeus," Cronus said. "The bane of my existence. And you wish to speak with him. Is that right? Do you believe he wants to speak with you, after what you did to him?"

I shook my head. "No. I don't think he ever wants to speak with me again. He's too happy in there to want to escape your belly, even for just a few seconds."

"You are much less respectful than your friend," Rhea stated, shaking her head with disappointment. "Did you know that?"

"I am less respectful than most people."

"She came to me with deference," Cronus said. "You come to me with sarcasm."

"And yet only one of us released you from your prison and allowed you to reconnect with Rhea."

"That's not fair, using guilt against me," Cronus said.

"It doesn't have to be fair. It is a statement of fact. The guilt is yours. Now get this straight. Whether you help me or not, I will go back and defeat the Horde, because that's what I do. I defeat things."

Cronus laughed. "You know, that is funny. Very, very funny. Alright, Katrina. I will bid you see Zeus."

*

It looked like it was going to take a while for Cronus to vomit up Zeus, so I helped Urania look after Hera. The queen goddess was scalded badly on the left side of her body. Her eyes were wide with horror and she muttered under her breath, but her words were incoherent and impossible to understand.

"My queen, my queen, my queen," Urania cooed over and over again. "Look at me."

Urania hadn't stopped crying since I'd first seen her here. She didn't even mind the mucus and saliva puddle she sat in, or the thick goop coating Hera's body.

When Zeus came out, he was covered in the same membrane as Hera, and initially sported the same look of terror. However, he soon comported himself and turned to Cronus.

"Vicious Titan!" he shouted. "Why have you brought me back out of your body? To show me mercy only to send me back into peril again?"

"Actually," Cronus said. "That isn't the reason, though I must say it is an excellent ancillary benefit."

Zeus looked over at Hera. "And my wife, too. Look at what you have done to her. What sort of trickery is this?"

"No trickery. I have let Hera go because a brave soul came and asked for her release. Another brave soul came for you. That is why you are here."

Zeus finally saw me. "You!"

He rushed toward me but collapsed immediately. His wobbly legs were burned badly by the acid in Cronus's stomach. His arms were eaten through to the bone, and only a thin tendon held his jaw together.

"What could you want with me?" he asked. "To gloat in my face once more?"

I knelt next to him. "I am a bitter woman, but even I'm not that bitter."

"What, then, do you want?"

"I need your help. My people. Your people. Our people. They are being destroyed by the Horde."

"Why should I help your people? They are bastards and criminals, all of them. I protected you for eons, and for my kindness I was repaid with eternal torture. I say let the Horde have their way with you. I dealt with them for a million years. You can fight them now."

"It's not the same as last time. They can kill gods now."

Zeus held his jaw as he laughed. "Of course they can. I held them in check for eons with my immortality. I threatened their obliteration. They feared me so and that kept them compliant."

"Yes, until I defeated you."

"And once you did, they knew I was lying about being immortal. How long has it been, child, since you killed me?"

"A decade."

"They are quick to seek their revenge."

"They have already destroyed Aphrodite's world, and they are coming for mine. Hundreds of gods are dead. Billions, maybe trillions of humans. I need your help. What do you know that can help me defeat them?"

He shook his head. "Nothing you don't already know, I'm sure. The Horde is strong, but their strength is in their technology. Destroy their technology and they are nothing. The planet killer bases are the seat of their power. Defeat those, and all their technology will cease working, and they will just be bugs to squash."

"How? We don't have enough people. We've lost so many."

Zeus leaned in toward me and spoke in a hushed tone. "There is a secret in the stars. Did you know that?"

"What secret?"

"These black holes. They hold souls. In each one there are billions of people who have died and never found peace. If you can reverse what Apollo did and turn those black holes back into stars, then you will release those souls. With them, you have a chance. Use these souls against them."

"You are being awfully cooperative, Zeus."

"Yes. You have given me a great gift, this time away from my torture. Even if only a moment. Can you do me one small favor in return?"

"If it's within my power."

"Take me to her. My love."

I honestly wasn't sure who he was talking about. I scanned the faces of Urania and Rhea, but neither one of them were really paying attention. When I looked back at him, he had one half-melted arm raised, pointing towards Hera. The last time I'd seen them together, he'd lightning-bolted her to a rock wall, but I wasn't going to ask any questions. I scooped him off the ground and carried him over to Hera, his wife. He kneeled next to her and cupped her hands.

"My wife, I often dreamt you would suffer greatly. Now that I see it, the sight brings me no joy."

Hera's eyes focused on him. "And you look as terrible as I always imagined in my mind. Unlike you, seeing your misery brings me great satisfaction. A fitting end to a terrible man."

Zeus kneeled next to her. "How did it get so bad between us, wife?" He squeezed Hera's hand tightly. "We were in such love, once. I never thought anything could tear us apart."

Hera clasped her gooey hand over Zeus's. "What has become of us?"

"That is a question I have asked for a million years, well before Cronus had his way with us."

Hera grinned. "That was almost an apology."

He smiled back at her, but in that smile, Cronus snatched him up and tossed him into his mouth. Zeus's bones crunched as the Titan ground him in his teeth, and his screams curdled my blood as he struggled against the oppressively strong teeth inside Cronus's mouth. I could see the glee in Cronus's eyes as he crushed Zeus's spine. Then it was silent, aside from the sound of Hera's dovelike weeping.

"What are you doing?" I shouted at Cronus as he swallowed.

"You told me you wanted to speak to Zeus, not that they should speak with each other."

Hera's face went white and then her whole body seized. She was tweaking and twitching and although Urania tried to calm her, it was no use. She couldn't stop.

"Katrina!" Urania pleaded. "Do something!"

I turned to Cronus. "Fix her!"

"I can't. I only promised to return her to you, which I've done. Now, if there is nothing else, I will take my leave."

"Wait!" I shouted. "There is something else."

"Katrina!" Urania's head snapped up. "What are you doing?"

"What I have to do," I responded, turning back to Cronus. "Zeus said something. He said that you can close a black hole and return the people inside it back into the world. Is that true?"

Cronus gave a disinterested shrug. "I must say, on this, Zeus knows more than I. There was never any reason for me to open other dimensions. That's a god thing."

I stepped forward. "Then I need another favor."

"You are pushing it, Katrina."

"I know, but I must have Apollo back. He is the only one who can reclaim the stars."

"I can't help you there, Katrina," Cronus sighed. "I've already freed one god. I cannot free another. That would be a bad look."

"What do you care about looks?" I scoffed.

Cronus chuckled. "You are right, I don't care. I was trying to be polite. I just don't want to do it, okay?"

Hera shot up. Her eyes focused. "I volunteer! I volunteer!"

"What do you volunteer for?" Urania asked.

"I volunteer to take his place. My dear Apollo. I will trade for him."

"Hera, no!" Urania shouted. "I have done so much to free you."

Hera looked toward Urania, but not at her. She looked through her. "I will always be grateful for that, but I cannot spend eternity imagining a world where I had a chance to save my beloved Apollo and did not take it. This physical agony is bearable compared to the guilt of making him suffer."

"Yes, my queen."

She put a hand on Urania's face. "I love you. In a way."

Cronus gulped down Hera right out of Urania's hands. "That is acceptable," he said, with a full mouth.

*

"I can't believe you," Urania spat at me as we waited for Apollo to make his way up the Titan's esophagus. Cronus wretched over and over, heaving up more and more bile as we waited.

My mouth fell open. "Whoa now, what did *I* do?"

"You were willing to trade Hera for Apollo!"

"Um...did we see the same thing? Hera did that. Not me."

"But you let it happen." Urania looked like a toddler, using her sleeve to brush tears from her face.

I held out my hands in disbelief. Why was I always getting blamed for things? "As much as I would love to take credit for everything, I can't just make people do things. Hera made her choice."

"Then it was all for nothing."

"At least we get Apollo."

Urania grunted. "I wouldn't walk to the end of the hall to save Apollo." She crossed her arms and looked over to where Cronus was hunched over like a cat retching a hairball. "Besides, we don't even need him. We have his hands."

I was done with this argument before it even started, and now it had jumped the shark and landed in a pool of pure stupidity. "No offense, Urania, but have you ever collapsed a black hole back into a star?"

"No."

"Ever done it a few thousand times?"

"No."

"Does anybody but Apollo and Apollo alone have that power?"

"No."

"And that's why we need him. Cuz you can't do it."

Urania uncrossed her arms and wheeled on me. "Well, did you know that you're a real asshole?"

She must have been really pissed to whip out vocabulary like that, but I wouldn't give her the satisfaction of seeing it sting. I gave a wry smile. "I've been told, once or twice."

"Alright," Cronus shouted. "It's done! Shut up. I can't take your bickering anymore." We looked over and found a moist Apollo, drenched with saliva. His once beautiful locks were burned off and his scalp was covered in patchy burns. His arms were seared to a crisp and cut off at the wrist.

I forgot Urania and knelt next to him. "Do you remember me, Apollo?"

He looked up at me. "I remember everything. I remember you cutting off my hands, feeding me to Cronus, and I remember every excruciating second being in his stomach. Never have I felt such agony."

"Well, good news, buddy. You're out now, and you're gonna help us save the universe."

"I will do no such thing."

I smiled. "Well, you can help us save the universe or go back into his belly. I don't have time to mess around anymore."

He thought for a moment. "I suppose, given those choices, I will help you."

"I thought you would."

"But I won't like it."

"I don't care."

"Enough!" Cronus roared. "Will you leave me now! Your incessant prattling on has given me a headache."

"I'm sorry, great Cronus," Urania said. "I understand your pl—"

"Hush, little one," Rhea said, turning to her husband. "I'm bored—and hungry. How long must we listen to them go on and on about nothing?"

"You are right, wife. I do not wish to hear any more from this lot." Cronus turned to me. "Be gone with you."

Rhea ran her fingers up Cronus's chest. "You know they will come back, though, don't you?"

Cronus leaned toward me. "Is this true? Will you keep interrupting my peace with your favors again and again, Katrina?"

I shook my head and held my hands up helplessly. "I don't know. I don't really want to ever come back here, but I'm not gonna say that it'll never happen. And as far as other people coming, it seems unlikely, but who knows? I'm not the keeper of the universe."

Cronus nodded. "I appreciate your honesty. Unfortunately, I cannot take that chance. Your universe is too cumbersome and annoying to deal with for one more moment. I have no choice but to wipe it from existence."

"Whoa!" I shouted. "That's a little excessive, don't you think?"

"Actually, I think I've been too lenient for too long. I should have destroyed your universe eons ago."

"Chill out," I said. "We're leaving."

"Then others will come, like you said. And others. And others. Look, it's just too much. I should have ended your universe right when I found Rhea."

"What?" I shouted. "One annoyance is too much for you to deal with?"

"Well, yes," Cronus responded, snapping his fingers. "I suggest you get your affairs in order. The creeping whiteness will spread across Rhea's prison universe first, then invade every other dimension and universe in existence, until there is nothing left except peace and quiet, forever."

"This is a really drastic step to a simple problem. Couldn't you just, make a door or something?"

"Hmmm...I suppose I could...but what's done is done."

Apollo rose to his feet, leaning his mangled body against my shoulder. He collapsed in a heap, his eyes rolling back in his head. I tried to grab his hand but remembered that he didn't have any. I looked over at Urania, and suddenly, I had an idea.

"What if we cut off our universe from yours, preventing anybody from finding you again?" I asked him. "If we could reverse every black hole and create no way for anything to bother you, what then? Will you leave our universe alone?"

"I don't know," Cronus said. "You can try it and see. I suppose it could work, as long as you sealed it tight."

Then, with a snap of Cronus's fingers, we were gone into the ether. My taste for pancakes died in that moment.

Chapter 10

In a blink, we appeared on the Horde home world, looking up at the whiteness encroaching around us, spidering out from Cronus's universe and into this one and growing with each passing second.

I looked to my left and saw Urania, still bawling ugly tears. On the other side floated Apollo, handless, bruised, and gaunt.

"This is not the universe I remember," Apollo said.

"That's because this isn't our universe. This is a whole different—you know what. It's gonna take time to explain that we just don't have right now. Let's go."

I grabbed Apollo's shoulder and turned to Urania. "I know you are hurting, but I need you. I need you to tell me where we need to go. Otherwise, we're going to end up stuck here in the middle of space-time for the rest of eternity."

Urania sniffled and looked over to me. "Why do I care about that now? My mission is a failure."

I nodded. "Well, yeah, but we have a new mission now. We have to make sure the universe isn't destroyed. That's a pretty big one, wouldn't you agree?"

Urania wiped her eyes. "Yes, I would."

"Do you mind filling me in?" Apollo said.

"You're on a need-to-know basis, and right now you don't need to know anything, unless you can get us back to our universe."

"I guess I just need to be quiet, then."

I gave him a little shove, just for good measure. "That would be wise."

"I don't know why you spit so much venom at me, Katrina. I haven't done anything to you."

"You sent my world into a black hole and scarred billions of people for life."

"True, but that was my sworn duty. Do you not have a sworn duty?"

I shook my head. "No. I pretty much do whatever I want whenever I want to do it."

"That might have been true once, but I see it in your eyes. You have a duty to your people, much like I had a duty to carry out Zeus's bidding. It just so happened our duties were at odds with each other. Not unlike two countries at war. Their people might be friends, or even family, but their duties make them enemies for a time."

"So, we are not enemies now?"

Apollo shook his head. "It would seem like our interests are very much aligned. I'm interested in not seeing our universe end. I very much enjoyed living in it."

"Well, at least we agree on that much."

"See, isn't that better?"

"Not really," I said. "But it'll have to do. How do we do this then, Urania?"

"I don't know." She rubbed her chin thoughtfully. "I can go back to the observatory and try to plot a course to a black hole, but it's not likely I'll find anything in the blackness of this universe."

"So, we're stuck here?" I said, throwing my hands in the air.

"Do you realize I can feel them?" Apollo said.

"Feel what?"

"I feel the black holes, every one of them. They are my creations. They cry out in pain and anguish, and I feel them all." Apollo closed his eyes and took a deep breath. "Yes, even now I can feel them."

"Okay, where is the closest one?" I asked. "Can you find it for me?"

"Yes," Apollo nodded. "I have it in my mind's eye now."

"Hold out your stumps."

Apollo stretched out his arms, sighing piteously at the stubs where his hands should be. I placed the blade of my sword between them. "Think hard. Really hard."

I slashed the Sword of Damocles downwards and a rift opened. On the other side, I saw a black hole swirling in front of me.

"Let's go."

I pushed Apollo into the portal, then followed Urania through it. Inside, I watched in horror as the whiteness of Cronus's universe ate the darkness of this one. If I didn't find a black hole and get back to my universe soon, this creeping whiteness would invade Aphrodite's planet and my own, slowly unraveling the fabric of our universe and wiping it from existence.

This was bad. Really bad. I wanted to save my world, and I ended up damning the universe. I only had one idea to save everything, and it meant trusting that Apollo really did want the universe to exist. That wasn't a guarantee, but for all his yammering on, he had never lied in any of my interactions with him. He was a mass murderer, but never a liar, at least not to me.

I popped out of the portal as the whiteness encroached on everything behind us. In its wake, thousands of planets lit up against the white sky. Each one with thousands, or millions, or even billion of people on it, all doomed, and each brought into this universe by a black hole.

However, black holes weren't one-way streets. You could use a black hole to enter a universe and to leave it as well, which meant that Cronus's creeping whiteness could use those black holes to enter our universe and destroy everything.

But…if I could reverse the black holes, and turn them back into stars, thus closing all the doors to this universe, I would be able to keep Cronus's whiteness bound to this universe, like a giant dam.

I took one last look at this universe before I felt the pull of the black hole behind me. I turned around just in time to see my hands stretch into long tendrils and dissolve into the black hole.

I passed through the horrible screams and outreached arms of the souls trapped inside its vortex. If my plan worked, I could save them and my universe at the same time. If I failed, I would doom us all. It wouldn't matter if we won the battle against the Horde. Cronus's whims would wipe us out of existence before we could ever enjoy it.

*

The black hole shot us out at a million miles an hour. My face flapped like those old *Ren and Stimpy* cartoons. I forced my arm forward and tugged Apollo and Urania close to me. Then, I swung my sword and created a blast that slowed our speed to a manageable sailing one, using my powers of flight to slow us even more.

Once we stopped completely, I caught my breath and looked over at Urania. "Are you okay?"

"I'm fine," she said, puffy eyed. "Better than I look."

Apollo nodded. "I'm fine, too, not that it matters."

"I suppose it's time," I said, "to let you both in on the plan."

"That would be nice," Urania said.

"How many black holes did you create during your time as a god?"

"I don't know. A few thousand...maybe ten thousand?"

"And with each one, you sent them to that universe, right? The one we just came from, with the darkness and the big growing, white light that's going to doom us all?"

"I only know one way to create a black hole," Apollo said slowly. "So yes, I would assume that's the case. Why?"

"I think all those black holes are how Cronus's creeping whiteness is going to make its way into our universe. If we can close those black holes, then I think we can stop the creeping whiteness in its tracks before it invades our universe."

"You think, or you know?" Urania asked.

"I think. That's the best I got. I'm going off the cuff here. I don't have answers. I just have a theory that we have just enough time to try before this whole universe is doomed. Can we please get on the same page?"

Urania looked down. "I'm sorry."

"It's fine," I said, even though I only half meant it. "Now, Zeus said there are millions of souls are trapped in those black holes, right?"

"That's right," Urania said.

"Then we can kill two birds with one stone by turning those black holes back into suns."

"But we can't do that," Urania said. "I only know how to turn suns into black holes."

"That's true." I turned to Apollo. "You only know how to turn suns into black holes, but Apollo here knows how to do both, don't you?"

He nodded. "I've been known to make them go both ways, but it has been many moons. I've never done it on such a large scale before, and I would need my hands."

"Good news then. Urania has kept them in a jar for you all these years."

Apollo made a face. "That's gross, and a little morbid."

I nodded. "I agree. But she used them to build a machine to turn suns into black holes from millions of miles away."

"That's child's play. I've done that before."

"Yeah, but have you done it a couple million times at once?" Oh, the ego. There's no better way to manipulate someone than by insulting their ego. Even in his decrepit, singed state, I could see Apollo bristling.

"I have not. I've always done it one at a time. Doing thousands at one time, that's impossible."

"For you alone but imagine what you could do with your power and Urania's machine. You could magnify your powers by a million times or more, easily."

"I like the sound of that," Apollo said.

"I don't!" Urania shouted. "What's to stop him from turning every sun into a black hole, or taking control of the whole universe, with power like that?"

"It's simple," I said to Urania. "He loves the universe. He said it himself. He doesn't want to see it destroyed."

"That's right," Apollo said. "It is my fatal flaw."

"Mine too." I turned to Urania. "Do you know the way home?"

She nodded. "I do."

"Good, because the first stop is your planet. We will use the observatory to amplify Apollo's powers, and once we've closed all the black holes, we'll bring the rest of your troops to Aphrodite's world to finish the Horde for good."

Urania smiled. "That sounds like a plan."

I handed her the sword. "Think really hard in your mind's eye. Believe that's where you are going, and then swipe up in one smooth motion."

Urania took a deep breath and closed her eyes. She thought for a moment. Then, she swiped. The portal opened, and we jumped inside.

*

I didn't realize how much I missed my own universe until I entered Urania's portal. The vivid colors of the stars exploded underneath me as we zipped forward. The nebulas crashed upon each other in epic splendor, sending cosmic sparks into the surrounding galaxies.

After the dark nothingness of the other universe, my wide-eyed love of the stars grew tenfold.

Judging from the look of wonder on Urania's face, the absence of stars had weighed on her soul, even if she hadn't known it. I watched the reflection of the stars in her eyes as she silently greeted each one like an old friend.

Feeling the energy of the universe around me, I threw out my arms and floated through the stars. It had never occurred to me to fly through the stars before, but right then it was everything I ever wanted. I felt the dainty hand of Urania wrap around mine, and we flew together.

I knew we had a lot of work to do, but for a few moments, I was free.

Chapter 11

The feeling of freedom I had falling through the chasm of space and time didn't last long. The minute we hit the ground on Hera's planet, we were in the middle of a hellfire storm. The Horde's ships rained fire on the castle and bug troopers armed with blasters stormed the walls. Massive walkers crawled up the sides and destroyed what remained of Urania's troops.

"Oh no," I muttered, pulling Apollo behind the corner of the castle, where Urania was already hidden.

"What are we gonna do? What are we gonna do?" She was panicking.

"Pull yourself together," I said. "How well do you know this castle?"

"I know it better than the back of my hand."

Apollo grumbled. "Or my hand."

"Chill out, Apollo!" I snapped. "Urania, can you get us to the observatory?"

"From the outside? Right around the corner from here, you'll see the telescope poking out of the dome."

"Show me."

Urania led us around the castle. The Horde shot at the castle above us. Huge chunks of wall nearly crushed us as they crashed from hundreds of feet above. We'd made our way around another corner when I saw a huge closed dome on top of a back wall.

"Alright," Urania said. "Behind that wall is the telescope."

"There's probably a million Horde troops inside, waiting for any resistance."

Urania shook her head. "I don't think so. I ordered my men to unlock all the cages and let the prisoners go, in case of attack. They'll hold off the Horde for a while."

"Are these still the same prisoners who wouldn't fight the Horde before?"

Urania nodded. "Yes, but they have a reason to fight. Now the Horde are attacking them personally."

"Hang on," I said. "What makes you think they won't be hailed as liberators?"

"Simple. The Horde aren't liberating them, they're killing them."

It sounded like solid logic to me. "Fine. Then let's go."

I flew up to the wall behind the castle. It was one of the few unmolested walls in the whole castle. The Horde focused their attacks on the prison, probably because most of the gods were in there. Meanwhile, it allowed us to sneak onto the observatory unnoticed.

"This is going to take a delicate touch," I said, pulling my sword out of its sheath.

"Are you sure you can do delicate?" Urania said.

"If I'm honest, no."

The flaming sword sliced into the stone easily enough, and with all the deftness I could manage, I cut a hole into the wall. I pushed the rubble into the observatory and led the others inside.

"That was impressive," Urania told me.

"I know. I'm very impressive. Often, even to myself. Now get to work."

I led Apollo over to Urania where his hands were encased in glass at its base. They still gave off a golden shimmer that illuminated the room. Apollo stared at them for a moment, a long moment, before he started to cry.

"These hands…they are dead. They can never work."

Urania pulled him up. "They aren't dead, or at least not dead to magic. I don't know how or why, but they still work. They will respond to you."

Apollo pulled open the glass case and touched the hands with his forearms. A shiny glow washed over him as he closed his eyes for a moment in deep thought.

The moment we opened the telescope, it was going to draw the entire Horde army to our position. We would have no more than a couple minutes to fix the entire universe before the Horde descended on us.

"Are you almost ready? We don't have much time here, Apollo."

"I can't rush this. Cronus's creeping white will invade this universe and destroy us all if I miss even one black hole, right? If I forget even one, this universe is over, isn't it?"

I nodded. "Yes."

"Then I need to be precise. We only have one shot at this."

"I appreciate your attention to detail, but you know we aren't made of time, right?"

He wrapped his arms around the jar that held his hands. He wept once more that his hands were lost forever. "I'm ready."

"What do you need me to do?" Urania asked him.

"Nothing. Just flip the switch when I tell you and be prepared to fight."

"I've never fought before, for even one second, in my entire life."

Apollo smiled gently. "This is a good time to start."

I stood by the door with my sword drawn. Beyond the observatory doors, we could hear the distant destruction of the prison, the fighting and dying of gods and monsters alike in the throne room.

"Just stay behind me," I told Urania. "and you'll be fine."

"If there is one thing you have in spades, Katrina," Apollo said. "it's confidence."

"It's because I always win. It's easy to have confidence if you always win."

"That is true, but inner peace comes from continuing on after you lose."

"Yes, well I don't have any of that. Just confidence."

Apollo smiled again as he turned his eyes to Urania. "It is time. Turn on the machine."

With a flurry of keystrokes into the main console, Urania moved the telescope into position. It rocked and rattled for a moment, then a high-pitched screech came from inside it. The outer doors on the observatory opened and the telescope stretched into the sky, its core turning from white to yellow to red and finally to blue before a beam shot through it like a cannon and split a thousand ways.

The Horde stopped firing immediately. The ships turned in midair and the bugs rushed toward us. It was only moments before the firing erupted on our position.

"We won't have long!" I shouted at Apollo. He didn't respond. Every ounce of his power channeled into the beam.

I heard the bugs pattering down the hallway toward us. I braced myself against the door but knew it wouldn't hold. The observatory wasn't made for battle. I needed to buy us more time. If the bugs got into this room, it was all over for us. I would have to lead them away and take as many of them down with me as I could.

I pulled open the door to the observatory. The bugs rushed toward me a hundred deep. Their blasters shot at me. I ran out the doorway and sliced through the guns of four caterpillars. Their guns exploded, which caused a chain reaction down the hall, killing bees, ants, flies, and all sorts of giant, misshapen insects.

That didn't stop the blasts for long though, and another wave of bugs fired their weapons at us. I slid down the hallway into the throne room and literally cut several of them off at the knees, then cut their weapons in half.

Demons and gods fought tooth and nail, with their fists and whatever powers they possessed, against the bugs that invaded the throne room.

"Cut the guns in half!" I screamed to them.

Those within earshot followed my instructions, and soon the explosions caused several garrisons of bug soldiers to fall backward. Others abandoned their guns and fought with their fists.

The ground quaked under me. I glanced up to see a dozen of the Horde's ships firing at the observatory. In just a few more seconds, the telescope would fall and everything we worked for would be ruined. I shouted at the guards and prisoners who fought alongside me. "Hold the line! Don't let them through!"

Leaping into the air, I flew through a blaster hole in the roof of Hera's throne room. I needed to keep the Horde's fire away from the telescope, which meant I had to cause a major distraction.

Luckily, a ship floated right above me. If I destroyed it, the explosion would grab the attention of the whole fleet.

I lit myself on fire, a trick held over from my old Devil days. My white-hot rage worked to help my flame burn brighter and more intense. I slammed into the ship's hull as a fiery ball of magma, and blew through the other side with ease.

The ship exploded in a sizzling hailstorm that sent shrapnel through the air. The other ships turned their attention toward me and opened fire. I swerved to avoid their blasts, and their errant shots blew up two of their spider walkers crawling across the roof toward the observatory.

A half-dozen other metal spiders remained and made their way toward the telescope, ready to dismantle it. I couldn't let that happen. As the ships fired, I weaved along the top of the castle. The ships' blasts blew chunks off the roof inches from my face as I zigged and zagged from one spider crawler to the next, growing hotter and hotter as I slammed through each walker until they all exploded behind me.

It only took a minute to destroy the walkers, but that was another minute that Urania and Apollo had to make our plan work. Next, I led the remaining eleven ships on a chase away from the castle and into the surrounding desert. I was much nimbler than they were, and it wasn't hard to avoid the blast of their weapons as they blew debris up from the ground around me.

I couldn't keep them away from the observatory forever, though. Not without leaving Urania and Apollo vulnerable to the Horde army fighting a tired army of beleaguered guards and emaciated prisoners, which meant I needed to go on the offensive.

Spinning around in midair and making a beeline toward the armada, I slammed my white-hot body through two ships on my first pass. They exploded gloriously, sending their burning wreckage down to the sand below us.

I quelled the fire surrounding my body and latched on to another ship. As the ship sped across the desert, it turned the blaster under its hull to get a better shot at me. I ripped it off the hull with my free arm and fired, sending bullets through its bow. I fell away from the ship as it exploded into a thousand pieces.

Eight more ships buzzed around me. I turned the blaster on them and let out a barrage of gunfire which destroyed the rest of them. I left the pile of smoldering wreckage there in the desert and flew back to the castle. The gods and monsters were doing their best to halt the Horde's advance, but there was no stopping them. There were too many.

"How much more time did you need?" I shouted to Urania, who was clinging tightly to Apollo's quivering body.

"Who knows? More."

Every muscle in Apollo's body locked up at once. He no longer quivered, but instead let out a low, guttural moan.

And that's when I heard a low rumble from across the galaxy. I looked up and saw it, a sea of red fire rushed in from the sky, crashing into Apollo again and again. It came on like a wave, a wave of countless, damned souls. They surged forward until they disappeared into Apollo, leaving an ocean of Horde dead in their wake.

When Apollo had finally absorbed all of the souls into his body, he let out a shriek. A red beam shot out of him like a flame thrower, hitting the planet killer ship that hovered above Hera's world.

The ship smoked and caught fire, then erupted into a million, brilliant pieces. A shockwave from the beam blew through the sky and every ship in the Horde's fleet exploded. The castle fell silent. Apollo fell over, spent, and the threat of the Horde vanished.

For a moment, we were safe.

Chapter 12

Urania tended Apollo as he laid on the ground in the throne room. We moved him there after the fighting calmed. We wanted to get him to a bed but feared he would die if we carried him any further. His eyes bled from the tremendous power he unleashed. He couldn't speak. There were burn marks on his face and mouth from the release of energy, and third-degree burns seared his body. His breathing was labored, and he struggled to stay alive.

Dozens of Urania's soldiers worked to bring Apollo back to health, but their methods were clunky at best. They weren't doctors. They were blunt instruments. Meanwhile, gods and monsters, freed from their bondage, shuffled around the throne room plotting their next move.

As Apollo recovered, I walked through the prison. Thousands upon thousands of prisoners laid slaughtered throughout the hallways, coupled with the guards who they died fighting alongside. The Horde laid next to them, weapons still in their hands. The looks of horror on their faces made my day. They died suffering, like they'd made us suffer.

I pulled the gun from one of the Horde worker bees, ripping it from the hose that connected it to the backpack. The lights on the side still glowed an ominous green. I pressed my finger on the trigger and fired a hole straight through the ceiling. *I could get used to this*, I said to myself with a smile.

After I'd ripped their hoses off, I brought a stack of the guns back to the throne room. A small group of demons huddled around. "Go pull these guns from all of the Horde soldiers you can find. Rip them off their hoses and bring them here."

The demons looked back at Urania, who nodded at them, before leaving the two of us together with a pained Apollo.

"You did good," I said to her. I resisted the urge to reach out and pat her on the back or hug her.

"I didn't do anything," Urania said in a small voice. "I just stood there."

"No," Apollo said. "You stayed by my side. That was everything."

"You all designed this telescope," I added. "And it gave us the first win ever against these sons of bitches."

"It doesn't feel that way."

"I agree," Apollo said. "I did the yeoman's share of the work. Why do you not heap praise on me?"

"Because I still don't like you." I brushed off some battle-dust from my pants. "I need to round up the remaining soldiers. We can use them in the fight to come. No use in staying here."

"More fighting," Urania said. "Can't we just enjoy this win?"

I shook my head. "The Horde are still out there, on Aphrodite's planet and on mine. We can't enjoy anything until we've beaten them back."

She nodded. "If you say so."

I walked over to a cadre of three dozen gods, broken and bruised, who were tending to themselves. They were beaten and weary, but they had survived, and that meant something.

"Do you know who I am?" I asked.

A large, white-bearded god stood up. Wings protruded from his brow and framed his face. "I do. You are Katrina, the god killer."

I nodded. "I'll take that name. And you have seen the Horde and lived. What is your name?"

"Hypnos," the god said, bowing.

"I hope you know how uncommon it is to fight the Horde and live."

"We are not everybody," a tall god with long wings protruding out of her back said. "We have been hardened by the prison."

I could see that it was true as I studied the haggard faces of the deities. "Clearly. Which is why we need you."

"And we have been weakened by this world, too, Nike," Hypnos said. The other gods muttered in agreement.

"But I see the strength in you, Hypnos. Look around. The Horde is gone from this world, but it still rampages across the universe, destroying worlds like my own."

"Like Apollo destroyed our planets?" A short goddess in a tattered green dress shouted.

"Demeter is right!" Nike shouted. "Why should we trust a god who works with a traitor like Apollo when he took our planets and locked us up here!"

I nodded again. "It is true that he did all those things, and I hate him for them. Apollo also sent my world beyond our universe and I hated him so much that I traveled across space to bring it back. I lopped off his hands, and fed him to Cronus myself, and yet I work with him now…because he is our best chance of beating the Horde."

"Who cares about the Horde," Hypnos said. "Let them destroy your worlds."

I nodded. "That's one thought, but Apollo just brought your planets back from the other universe—"

"Shells of their former greatness, I'm sure," Demeter scoffed.

"This is true. They are surely not the same as before, but your planets do exist, and I give them back to you, as a gesture of goodwill."

"What is your price?" Nike asked.

I shook my head at the gods as they scowled at me. "No price. They are yours, with the hope that you want to defend them as much as I want to defend my home. Because if you return to your planets without winning this fight then the Horde will come for you, and they will defeat you. Trust me, whatever horror your planets experienced, it is nothing compared to what the Horde will bring. So, I ask, what would you do for your planets?"

"We would defend them with our lives," Demeter shouted.

"That's good to hear, because it will come to that. The Horde are more vicious than anything I've ever seen before. They have technology so advanced it can vaporize a god in a second. They are currently attacking two worlds that I know of; Aphrodite's planet, and my own."

I summoned the demons forward, who tossed down a pile of the Horde's blasters on the ground between me and the prisoner gods. "I need you to help me retake both planets. Together, we make a stand right now."

Hypnos stepped forward and picked up a weapon. "I could use this to destroy you right now and take control of this planet."

"You could, but it wouldn't change anything that's happened. It will only net you a crappy planet and one less god in the fight against the Horde."

The wing-faced god turned to the other gods, rag tag and feeble as they were. Their eyes, for the first time in ages, filled with hope. They all had planets again, and that was enough to buoy their spirits. After a long moment tracking across the faces of the other gods, he turned back to me.

"Then I fight."

I smiled. One by one the gods came forward and pledged their loyalty to me. Their chants rumbled through the hall.

*

"I need to know how you did that," I said to Apollo after giving him a moment to regain his faculties.

Apollo shook his head. "I don't know. It's as if I was a magnet. I just stood there as the souls came to me. I felt them come, but I don't know how I called them."

"I need you to figure it out because I need you to come with us and do it again."

"I...can't."

Urania grabbed his shoulder. "You can. You must."

"I have another question," I said. "Did you get them all? Did you close all of the holes?"

Apollo looked down at his feet. "I don't know. I think so. I got as many as I felt, but who knows if that is every single one in the universe."

"You do. I need you to know."

"I just can't."

"You realize that if even one of those black holes stayed open, the entire universe is screwed, right?"

He looked up at his hands encased inside the glass case on the telescope. They no longer gave off the faint golden glow they once did; they were withered and black. "I've done all I can. I feel no black holes swirling around. My soul is at rest and my beautiful hands are now useless."

"Your hands did not do this, Apollo," Urania said. "You did. I've never seen anything so powerful."

"Perhaps."

I looked at Urania. "What about you? Do you think he's closed everything?"

Urania looked at me. "As far as I know. I can't scan every inch of the universe. I'm good, but even a god has limits."

"And do you think he can do it again?"

"I don't know, honestly. He's very weak. I'm not a god specialist. I deal in star things."

"Do what you can. We need him."

Urania grabbed my hand, but I pulled away. I couldn't deal with her right now. I ignored her wounded look. We were about to go to war, and if I cared about anybody they would be a liability. Right now, I needed to think straight.

I walked out of the observatory into the throne room. Five dozen gods and a hundred monsters milled around the room, readying themselves for war. They were old, weak, and feeble. They had been starved for millennia, and now deep chasms in their eyes belied their noble birth. But they were all I had, and so they were going to have to work. I hopped up onto a chair.

"Listen up. These weapons we've taken—they shatter if they're cut, and then explode. If your weapon gets cut, don't think—just throw that sucker as far away from you as possible. When we reach Aphrodite's home world, we're going to get more weapons from Hephaestus, if he's still alive."

I drew my sword just for the dramatic flair. Gods were into that sort of thing. "First to Aphrodite's world, and then onto mine to destroy the Horde forever! This is the last stand of the gods. And you are gods. You may not look it now, but you are mighty and fierce. The Horde kills you because they fear you…and they *should* fear you. Without you, they will march across the galaxy, unstoppable. But you will not let that happen. You will destroy them!"

Thunderous applause arose from the crowd. They had spent a long time living without hope, and it came flooding back onto them with great relish.

Urania walked into the throne room with her arms folded. She was the only one not screaming deliriously. She gave me an eye as I cut open the portal to Aphrodite's world and watched the gods rush through it.

I hoped I wasn't leading them to their deaths, but a large part of me didn't care. I just wanted to get back home and win this battle. Everything else would fall into place if I could just get that done.

*

It was an impressive sight, dozens of armed gods flying through the portal, free for the first time since who knows when, and ready to fight. Urania and I held up the rear. I didn't hold hands with her or float in wonder at the stars. I just readied myself for battle.

The portal took us to the same warzone we'd left a few days before. I tumbled out and came to a ready stance, but there were no gunshots. There were no bullets at all. It was silent.

"Katrina!" I didn't know people could be gregarious in a war zone, but if anybody could, it would be Hercules.

He stepped out of the shadows with Hephaestus, both covered in dust and bruises. Hephaestus accidentally wiped some of his blood on me when he wrapped me in a big bear hug. "It's good to see you."

"And you brought friends," Hercules added.

"Yes. I hope it is enough."

"We shall see. We've driven the Horde back into their ship and we are preparing for the final assault on their planet killer now. Once that is finished, we will bring the fight to your world."

"You guys are really kicking butt, then."

Hephaestus puffed out his chest a bit. "The hundreds of monsters and gods Aphrodite brought back turned the tides of battle."

"Yeah, we kicked ass on Hera's planet, too."

"These are the remaining troops, I see."

I nodded. Hercules looked behind me, where Urania was holding Apollo up. The journey had been hard on him. "And is that the great Apollo? How tragic an end."

"Don't count him out so quickly. He brought down the planet killer." I gave Apollo a smart pat on the back and he winced.

"How?" Hercules asked.

"I don't know exactly, but maybe he can do it again."

"Let's bring you to the boss, then."

Hercules snapped his fingers, and we were gone. Immediately I tasted blueberry pie. I didn't realize how much I'd missed it.

*

We reappeared in front of Aphrodite's castle. The whole edifice was blown into rubble. One entire wall lay crumbled on the ground, though dozens of Aphrodite's cherubs worked to repair it. Hercules led us through the front gates, where hundreds of gods and demons crowded into the throne room. One of those gods happened to be Bacchus.

"I'm happy to see you made it through the battle," I said to him.

"Yes, whereas I am unhappy that you survived this long. I thought I would be able to take back over my world in peace, without any objections from you. However, if not, I am willing to fight for it."

I sighed and gave a dry chuckle. "Once this is over, you will have your world back without a fight. I promise you that."

"Katrina!" Hercules shouted. "Don't dawdle."

I caught up to Hercules as he walked up to the throne. Far from the opulent throne I remembered, this throne was simply a fold-up chair, like the one you would take to a bar-b-que.

"That chair's quite the downgrade," I said.

"The chair doesn't make the ruler," Aphrodite said. "The ruler makes the chair." She was right: she still managed to look regal sitting on it. Her face had healed nicely. The scar was almost faded completely, and her lip no longer hung low on one side.

"I have news."

"And more troops, I hear."

"Many. Along with Hera's favorite god, Apollo."

Apollo stepped forward meekly. He could barely stand. His gaunt bones rattled as he took a knee. The goddess stared at him for a few moments before saying, "You look worse for wear."

He nodded. "As do you."

"War has taken a toll on us all."

"Apollo destroyed the planet killer," I said. "I know you plan to use your remaining troops to take it down, but I propose another way."

Aphrodite leaned forward. "I'm listening."

"I will leave Apollo with you to take down the planet killer. Meanwhile, I will take most of your troops to my planet. Once Apollo takes down the planet killer, you join us."

"And what if he is unable to perform?"

"I will leave you Urania to be sure you succeed."

Urania's jaw dropped and the way her robes shuffled, I wondered if she had stomped her foot. "I want to go with you!"

I turned to her. "We all want a lot of things. I need you to stay here."

Aphrodite cleared her throat. "I do not like this plan. However, you have done as much for this planet as anyone. The troops you sent us turned the tide of war. If you say it will work, I will accept your request. I hope, for all of us, that this works."

I nodded. "Urania will get the equipment you'll need."

"Very good."

I kneeled next to Apollo. "I need you to make magic again."

Apollo shook his head. "I…can't…I can't…I—"

"Listen to me." I held his head up so I could look him in the face. "Yes, you can. You have to."

He groaned and sighed from deep, deep down, and managed a sighing nod. It was the most confirmation I was going to get out of him.

I walked toward the great doors at the end of the throne room. Urania caught up to me. "Hey! So, what? Are you trying to abandon me?"

I shook my head. "No. It makes more sense for you to stay here, that's all."

"I will not. I'll be most valuable by your side."

"How? You can't fight. You can't shoot. You are frightened of battle. How are you anything but a liability to me?"

Urania couldn't speak. She just cried the big, wet tears which had become her staple. I'd seen them too often for them to sway my resolve.

I shook my head. "That's exactly what I mean. You can help this fight. You just can't help me. Not anymore."

"You really are heartless."

I left Urania to cry and walked toward my troops. "Gather around!"

My voice boomed through the halls. "You have fought valiantly, and I know you want to bask in your glory, but my world needs your help to stop the Horde. If we stop them on my planet, then they can never harm yours. If we defeat them, we can save the universe forever! Are you with me?"

A hushed moment, then Bacchus shouted through the silence. "To victory!"

The rest of the gods shouted in kind. Whipped into a fury, I opened the portal to my world and watched them lumber through. For the first time since the Horde attacked, I was going home. This time, to victory.

Chapter 13

I thought the guilt festering in my belly would subside the moment I opened the portal to head back home, but it didn't. The guilt followed me across the universe, into another one, and back again, pooling in my gut with every step I took away from Earth, but now that I was coming home it still festered, and I didn't know why.

I was returning to save my people. I should be proud. The Horde made me flee my home. Now I had built an army capable of kicking the Horde in the ass and sending them to the furthest ends of the galaxy. We'd already kicked them off two worlds.

Yet, it overwhelmed me, the guilt I felt for abandoning my people. I was about to see my world for the first time since the Horde invaded, and I feared it was too late. Earth would already be destroyed because I spent too much time helping others, at the expense of my people. I spent too much time making googly eyes at Urania to make a difference.

Perhaps Dennis, Connie, and Velaska did their jobs, and held off the invasion. I didn't know how that was possible, when the Horde had wiped out nearly the entire pantheon of gods without much fuss, but I remembered how strong Earth stayed in the face of the Apocalypse, and in rebuilding after being sucked into a black hole. That hadn't been easy, even for me. But they'd done it.

I often counted them out, I admit. It was easy to count them out after nuclear war, and after famine wiped out half their kind, and after global warming required them to hide in small areas of habitable land for generations and forced them to build those cities into the sky. They never stopped, though. They never gave up. That was the amazing thing about humanity.

This would be the last battle, not only for myself, but for the gods and humans, too. If we failed here, there was no telling what would happen. Humans were not advanced enough to defeat them without us. They didn't have the

each other to kill the last remaining Horde soldiers left on the battlefield.

The fighting continued for another hour as we mopped up the last remnants of the Horde army in Heaven. We didn't allow surrender. Every Horde soldier we found was butchered in front of my eyes. They took no prisoners, and neither would we.

Once we'd finished slaughtering the vanquished, the Hellspawn gathered the Horde dead into a pile in the center of Heaven and I jettisoned them into space. No ceremony for them. Once they were a safe distance, my gods vaporized them with their guns.

Well, most of my gods. There was one missing. Bacchus. I found him on the platform where he'd lived on for so long. He was celebrating his victory on a comfortable chair, drinking a bottle of mead.

"This is a familiar sight, Bacchus," I said to him.

"Katrina, Katrina, Katrina. Forgive an old god. I couldn't resist a drink to celebrate. It has been so long since I felt the cold taste of mead on my lips."

I pulled up a chair next to him and took a swig from the bottle. "Did you like it? Being god of this world?"

He laughed. "No. It was a relentless pain. So much responsibility."

I took another swig of mead before passing it to him. "Yeah, it's a lot of people to manage."

"I never wanted responsibility, and I didn't take to it well." He took a long drink.

"I think it's safe to say you were terrible. You set about the Apocalypse, after all."

"Yes, but in all fairness, so did you." He cupped a hand to his ear. "Are those zombies I hear...?"

I nodded. "Yes, and it only took me a decade to unleash Hell on Earth. It turns out that it's not as easy to be God as I thought."

"I suppose we are both terrible gods, then."

"That we are," I said. "I am happy to fight alongside a god as terrible as yourself."

"The same to you." He sat back with a heavy sigh. "After sitting in this chair again, I realize that it ill suits me, governing this world. I don't want it."

"What will you do when this is done, then, without a planet to govern?"

"This is a big universe, Katrina, and for a very long time I have seen far too little of it. I plan to roam far and wide. Of course," he paused to take another sip. "that's assuming I live through this battle."

"That is a big assumption."

We drank in silence until the mead was gone. He never asked me why I left him to rot in that cell, and I never asked him what it was like to lose all hope of rescue. There were so many questions I had, but they would have to remain unsaid until the end of time, which could be sooner rather than later.

After the bottle was done, he stumbled off, and Connie stumbled in to take his place. I hadn't seen her in a long time. The first thing I did was give her a massive hug. I wasn't known for my affection, and Devils weren't known for theirs, but we fell into each other like old friends.

"It's good to see you, Connie," I whispered in her ear.

"I'm glad you're not dead," she said.

We chuckled together as I released her. "How's the battle on the front lines?"

She held her head. "You don't want to know."

"No, really. I want to know everything."

"The planet killer killed half the population in a couple hours, and half of those remaining died in the fighting since you left. My armies are helping a little, but we're getting our asses handed to us."

"And Velaska?"

As if on cue, a blue light zapped in front of me and Velaska appeared, not a hair out of place and a cunning smile on her flawless face. "Did I hear my name?"

Connie grunted. "She hasn't been any help."

"That's not true," Velaska said. "I've been working a different angle than you, is all."

"Your angle is sitting very far away from the battle and eating grapes all day while cavorting with the Horde."

"No," Velaska shook her head. "It's making in-roads with certain, nefarious factions, who will help me gather the most important thing in the world—information, and you don't gather information by killing people."

"No, but it's a great way to end a war."

"Piffle," Velaska said, waving her arm. "Brute force is a stupid way to fight. Wars are won by finding a weakness in the enemy and exploiting it, which is what I've been working on."

"Our people are dying!" Connie shouted. "While you dine on caviar!"

Velaska yawned. "In my defense, they aren't really my people. They haven't been my people for a long time."

Fire shot out my nose. "Alright! Enough!" Connie and Velaska fell silent. "Velaska, did you find anything useful or not?"

Velaska pulled a schematic from her pocket. "I did, in fact. One of my spies learned that the planet killers are powered by the sun. If you take out the sun, you'll take out their power."

I blinked. "That's going to be a little hard to do."

"Can't we just pop that sun into a black hole and suck out all the bug's power?" Connie asked.

I shook my head. "No. That would be a very bad idea." The truth is, it would be a great option, if it didn't mean inciting Cronus's wrath and causing the end of the universe. I didn't want to tell them about that possible course of events, and hoped my tone conveyed the dire consequences of enacting that option. "Connie, how is the army of Hell holding up?"

"Usually, innumerable battle deaths would mean more recruits to my side. Except when people die from those stupid bug zapper things, they disappear into the ether instead of joining my army." Connie exhaled and rubbed her forehead. "We're holding right now, and with your men on the lines we can fight them back for a while longer, but we need to do something *big* and *soon*."

"Don't worry. I have a secret weapon. Once Apollo and Urania are done on Aphrodite's world, they're heading our way."

"I don't know if we have that long." Connie raised her eyebrows, shaking her head. "We need to take out that planet killer now or there won't be enough of us left."

"I need you to keep them busy a little while longer. Take my men. Distribute them as you see fit. I have a plan, but it means you are in charge here. Can you handle that?"

Connie nodded. "We've handled it this far."

"One more question. My parents…" I faltered.

Velaska and Connie looked at each other. Connie sighed a long, sad sigh. "Your father…was vaporized in the first attack. I'm so sorry. Their pharaoh, L'l'itoh, took your mother. We have no idea what happened to her."

Velaska stepped forward. "The last I heard she was on the planet killer."

I balled my fist. "Then we don't destroy it 'til we get her back."

"What if she's already dead?"

"Until I see it for myself, she's alive. There is no time to waste. I wanted to give Aphrodite time to destroy the planet killer on her world, but I need those troops now." I sighed loudly. "I know it's a big deal to ask you to keep up the fight without me again. It breaks my heart to leave, but I swear I'll be back with a way to win this war for good."

With that, I cut open a portal to the universe. "Keep the fight going. Don't take down that planet killer until I get back."

Chapter 14

It saddened me to see the planet killer still hovering over Aphrodite's world, but at least there was no more battling. The people of her world guided bugs into holding cells and shot the ones that didn't fit. I wondered if they had families back on their home planet. It seemed like the Horde were a lot like us on their own world, except that they brutally murdered humans, and we just wanted to be left alone to murder ourselves.

A brief taste of blueberry pie and I was in front of Aphrodite's castle. The power to come and go from Mount Olympus was not granted lightly, and I appreciated Aphrodite's gesture. Inside the castle, Urania was setting up the telescope from her observatory inside the throne room. There was nobody inside except for her, Aphrodite, and Apollo, standing in a circle around the telescope.

"What ho, Aphrodite. I have good news and bad news."

Aphrodite looked over her shoulder. "Before you ask, we can't get the telescope to work again and Apollo is too weak to call forth the ghosts. However, we have been able to neutralize most of the threat. The planet killer still shoots at our heavily populated towns, but they don't seem to be able to mount enough of a threat to take us down. Aside from the laser in the planet killer, the Horde seem to be neutralized."

"I actually had something in mind to help with that," I said, kneeling in front of Apollo. "I know that you can turn a sun into a black hole, but can you do anything else with it?"

"I can do anything to it, but obviously we risk ending the universe if we're not careful..." He gave me a look.

"Can you put out a sun?" I asked.

"Like a candle?" He shook his head. "Matter can't be created or destroyed, Katrina. Even gods have to deal with that."

"And yet, the weapons of the Horde don't. They put people out of existence. Isn't that weird?"

"There is a reason, even if I don't know what it is. All energy goes somewhere, and when a sun goes out, it explodes." He frowned. "And even if a sun was moved, something would have to take its place or the planets around it would lose their orbit and collapse upon each other."

"Fine. Can you move a sun somewhere else, temporarily?"

"I suppose," Apollo said, and then thought for a moment. "If there was a planet of equal size and mass to that of the star, they could swap positions. However, this is not my department, I'm afraid. I'm only good at stars. Urania is the whiz at moving planets."

"I didn't know you could do that," I said, turning to Urania. Her lips were pursed.

"Yes. I suppose there is a lot we don't know about each other."

I decided to actively avoid that comment. "So, is it possible?"

Urania sighed. "I haven't tried since I was a child, but I suppose it's possible."

"Is there something that could match the size and weight of this sun?"

"I believe I know of a planet like that. What are you—"

"Is there one that can match the size and mass of my Earth's sun?"

Urania furrowed her brow. "What do you have in mind?"

"The planet killer is powered by the sun. So, I want to exchange a planet for a sun, replacing the mass of the sun with a planet's. If it goes well, we can stop the planet killer from giving off energy long enough to destroy it from the inside."

"Why can't you just blow it up?" Aphrodite asked. "We were just going to blow it up."

I gave her a look. "Since when are you all about blowing things up?" She shrugged. "Well, we can't 'just blow it up' because my mom is inside of the one on my Earth."

"Oh...and you're sure she's still alive?"

I scowled at her. "Can you do it or not?"

She gave Apollo a glance. "His body is badly damaged, but I think if we work together, then yes, we can do it."

"We have been working on an idea, actually." Urania walked over and offered Apollo her arm. "Apollo's power was not locked in his hands. It courses through his whole body. His hands were only the conduit." Urania grabbed the nub of Apollo's arm. "I can be the conduit."

"Are you sure?"

"No. I've never been used as a conduit before."

Apollo balanced himself on her elbow and gave a smile reminiscent of his former, cocky self. "It's easier than it looks, manipulating the universe."

Urania just shook her head. "I'll take your word for it."

"Trust me. In a few moments, you'll see just how easy it is. Close your eyes." Apollo and Urania both closed their eyes, and Apollo took in a deep breath. "Okay now, think about the planet. Think about it hard. Do you have it in your mind's eye?"

"Yes. Yes, I have it."

"Okay. On the count of three, we are going to switch them. Okay?"

"Okay."

"1… 2… 3… *Now!*"

A shockwave exploded above us as the sun vanished from space and the sky fell to darkness. We looked out to see the star no longer existed, and in its place was a massive planet. Ten times bigger than any I've ever seen.

"You did it!" I shouted to Urania, gathering her up in my arms. For a moment I forgot myself, and very nearly kissed her, but I quickly put her down and collected myself. "Sorry."

She nodded, avoiding my eyes. "I'm glad we were successful. Now to destroy the Planet Killer once and for all."

"Yes," Aphrodite said. "Assuming what you say is true, we should be able to overtake the planet killer with no problems. That is a big if, though. How are you sure this will work?"

"I have it on good authority," I replied.

"Whose?" She studied me up and down for a moment before saying slowly, "Please tell me it's not Velaska."

My silence said everything to her. She didn't furrow her brow, though; she only chuckled. "I hope she has more sense now than she did then."

"I hope so, too. To give her credit, she has helped sustain our troops, and she helped keep my world alive. I have to trust her."

Aphrodite nodded. "I will send my troops into the planet killer to destroy it. If it is as you say, this is a great day for our people."

I turned to Urania. "Can you do it again, even from really far away?"

She hesitated. "I think so."

Apollo patted her on the back with the nub of his hand. "Are you kidding? She was fantastic. She could move every planet in the galaxy if she wanted."

I smiled. "I have no doubt. I'm heading back to Earth to prepare the final assault on the planet killer. I need you to wait for two hours, and then switch my sun with another planet. Can you do that?"

Urania gave me a level stare. "I can, but I won't."

"What do you mean you won't?" My voice was ice.

"I mean I won't do it unless I come with you."

"That's impossible. Aphrodite needs you."

Aphrodite made a face and shrugged. "I am perfectly capable of leading my troops without an invalid and his assistant hanging around me."

"What if this plan fails?" I asked her.

"Then there is nothing they can do for me. Now, take these two off my hands."

*

I didn't like the idea of bringing Urania to an active war zone, but as Aphrodite reminded me, the hills of Heaven were no less safe than her own. We were both dealing with a fight against the Horde, and Aphrodite's world could be attacked at any time by new forces. Anything can happen in war. If she were attacked, then Urania and Apollo would surely be destroyed. At least with me, there were soldiers to protect them.

When we got back to Heaven, I brought Urania to see Velaska. She was watching the battles down on Earth with near manic glee. "Oh, this is so delicious."

"You're sick," I said. "Did you know that?"

She laughed at me. "Please, you humans love your violent television. This is no different."

"Whatever." I did not have the time to deal with an idiotic conversation. "Listen. Are you sure that darkness will destroy the planet killer? Because if not, I just sent Aphrodite on a suicide mission."

"I don't know what powers those blasters, but that planet killer is powered by the sun as sure as I have ever been a god, and that planet killer powers all the other ships."

"That's what I wanted to hear. Gather Connie, Michael, and Dennis. It's time to end this once and for all."

*

The plan was simple. Once Urania and Apollo swapped the planet for the sun, we would go in hard against the ships that encircled Earth, destroying them in one brutal attack as they powered down. I didn't want any chance they'd come back online and keep fighting after we took down the planet killer from the inside. Then, while the humans and demons held down the fight on Earth, gods and angels would take the fight to the planet killer itself. I only had one request, that my mother would be rescued before we blew up the planet killer for good.

Once I'd finished explaining everything, I looked to each of their faces. There was Connie, Dennis, and Michael, who had helped me overtake Heaven once, long ago; there was Apollo and Urania, the cosmic star-summoning duo, and my advisors Hercules and Velaska. "Is everybody okay with that plan?"

Michael raised his hand. "How many points of entry on the planet killer?"

"As many as we can muster. Far as we can tell from recon on Hera's home world, there are thousands of entry points.

The middle of the planet killer houses the control center and the core."

"So, it will be an all-out blitz?" Dennis asked.

Connie chimed in. "That thing is crazy guarded. Let's get at it from all angles so maybe *one* of us will get in there"

"Right," I nodded, thinking through a few details. "We split up into two-person teams and gang rush the middle— Hercules, you're with me. We'll put Hephaestus with Bacchus, and so on."

"That sounds dangerous," Dennis said.

"It is, and don't forget that planet killer probably has some sort of battery, so it's not going to shut down immediately. We don't know what we're gonna find inside, so be careful."

*

And so, it came to pass that I stood in front of an army of gods and angels, flanked by Velaska, Connie, and Dennis, staring at a planet killer base almost as big as Earth itself.

"Do I have to go?" Velaska asked me.

"Ha! Please, you'll complain the whole time. You led us this far. If we fail, you'll be the only one left to destroy the Horde."

"Thank god," she said.

I winked. "You're welcome." Turning to Urania and Apollo, I said, "It's time."

Urania nodded to me then grabbed Apollo by the forearm. They muttered together under their breath, searching the cosmos for the right planet. Her eyes bobbed back and forth under her lids. Apollo's did the same. Eventually, their eyes popped open and they looked at each other.

"Ready?" Apollo asked.

"Ready."

Urania looked up at me. "Good luck."

My eyes lingered on her for a long moment before I said anything else. I wanted to tell her so much, but my lips couldn't form the words. "You too," was all I said.

And with that, Urania closed her eyes again and clasped Apollo's forearm tighter. "1... 2... 3..."

A sonic boom exploded through the solar system as our sun faded away and was replaced by a planet of equal size and mass. Heaven, once a beacon of light, was now shrouded in darkness. The planet killer itself went dark, too, illuminated only by the light reflecting off of the stars. I watched as the lights from the base dimmed, and then shut completely, before popping back online.

"They're on backup power," I shouted. "Go now. Go! Now!"

Hundreds of angels and gods flew toward the planet killer. Immediately its launch bays opened, and hundreds of ships streamed out of it, coming at us like a swarm of locusts. "Get in any way you can!"

I shot through the air toward the ship. Blasters whizzed by my face as I neared the base, evaporating the angels around me, but I kept on. The laser-light guided my way.

"Gunners! Fire!"

The gods fired their blasters at the ships, but that did little to scare them off. The weapons of the Horde that we were using couldn't penetrate their own ships. At least, I thought to myself, not the handguns. I flew up to one of the ships and ripped the gun off its wing before flinging it into another ship to explode.

I held the gun I just ripped off the ship in front of me and fired. Just like that, half a dozen ships blew up. "Take the weapons from the ships and use them!"

An army of angels flew toward the ships and ripped the guns off their wings just like I had done. They fired shots, clearing a path for us to get to the planet killer. We were in the fight again.

As we closed in, the planet killer cannons replaced the lasers from the warships. They were bigger, stronger, and more devastating. They fired the width of a football field and three times as far. The beams from the planet killer were a sea of green in front of us.

Luckily, the weapons were as slow as they were powerful, and we easily dodged them. On the surface of the planet killer, more turrets fired at us.

"Cover me!" I shouted to Hercules as I cut into the hull.

Hercules flew forward and stuck his fist through a turret in front of us. The shock of his fist's impact caused the turret to explode and created a hole for him to disappear into. I finished cutting my own hole through the planet killer's surface and jumped in, leaving the angels to finish off the other Horde ships.

Chapter 15

The inside of the ship's guts looked like the Borg ship from *Star Trek*, mixed with some of the most horrific parts of *Alien*. Green goop coated everything and gave a dull glow. Clear tubes carried the goop through the cramped hallways and underneath the metal grates of the floor. The tubes gave off an unnatural heat that made the hallways damp and sticky, like a swamp in the summer.

"Hercules!" I shouted down one of the hallways.

A moment later, he shot of out a closet covered in goop and wires. "Here, Katrina. I apologize for the tardiness."

Three pill bugs and an ant skittered around the corner firing lasers. I swung my sword, but it banged against the wall. I couldn't get a good angle.

"That's not going to work." Hercules pulled two daggers out of his boot and flung them at the bugs, cutting their blasters in half. He took another dagger out and passed it to me as the blasters exploded and quaked the ship. "Use this. It will help navigate these tight hallways."

I bent over the ant and found a working blaster. "No thanks. I think this will work just fine."

I don't really like guns. I always preferred to get my hands dirty, but there is something to be said for the ruthless efficiency of a good blaster by your side in a tight corridor. I used it to make quick work of several throngs of bugs that swarmed after us, and four turrets trying to bring us down, on our way through the hallway.

A screech blew through the planet killer as we moved through the ship and the Horde was alerted to our presence, but with hundreds of gods making their way through the corridors, hopefully there wasn't enough bug power to stop us all.

I assumed that the spherical shape of the planet killer would funnel us toward the center of it, but that didn't end up being the case. It seemed like every path led to nowhere. Four times in the first thirty minutes of our invasion, I ran into another team of gods pinned down by a pack of bugs. Once the dust cleared, we were a group of six instead of two, including Bacchus, who was fascinated by the green goop in the tubes above us.

"Did you know," Bacchus said, "that all these tubes are flowing in the same direction?"

"No. I didn't."

"I'll bet if we follow them, they'll take us to somewhere important."

"It's as good a plan as any." Hercules nodded. "We should do that."

So, we did. Lo and behold, they led us into the repository of tubes, a massive glowing hole at the center of the planet killer. The green goop drained into it like a waterfall and moved all around the base. Hovering above the goop vat was a large console and a dozen bugs working on a massive control panel. Across from them was L'l'itoh, the pharaoh fly. It sat silently on its throne and stared at the goop, mesmerized.

"Okay, there's the fly thing," I said. "This has to be the place. Let's get to my mother and get out of here."

"Where is she?" Hercules said.

I shrugged. "I dunno. There has to some sort of weird prison system in here somewhere…"

"Is that you, Katrina?" a voice echoed from one of the tubes down the hall. I turned in time to see Michael and Dennis hopped out of it, battered and bruised. Michael saw me and motioned me to follow him.

"Katrina, you gotta see this," Michael said.

They led me down a path to a large array of what could most accurately be called televisions, except they were circular and only glowed red and green, like Christmas.

"We found these on our raid. Most have shut down. It looks like the power down is happening from the edges of the ship to the center but look at this one."

Dennis pointed to a monitor that showed L'l'itoh staring at the green goop. It was dressed as ornately as when I saw it before, like the most lavish pharaoh in the universe. The monitor changed, and I saw L'l'itoh from another position.

Next to it, with her head dropped low, my mother sat bound and gagged.

"Son of a bitch."

"Daughter of a bitch," Hercules corrected.

"What's she doing there?" I asked Connie.

"I don't know," she responded. "I'm not the Horde. It seems like they need her for something, though, even if it's just protection against you."

"Alright, if that's the case, how do we get my mother out without hurting her?"

After a long moment, Dennis answered first, his palms turned up in a helpless gesture. "I don't know, Katrina."

"Yes, you do," I grumbled back at him. "You know exactly what you think we should do."

Bacchus stepped forward. "You're right, Katrina. We do. It's one life weighed against millions. Billions even."

"That's crazy. The one parameter of this mission was—"

"Our mission is to stop the Horde," Michael said. "To do that, we must destroy this planet killer. Or is that not what you want?"

"Of course, it is!"

"Then we have a chance to do that now. Yes, your mother is in danger, but so is the entire human race. So are all our races. Is your mother's life really worth more than that?"

I shook with rage. "Yes!"

Hercules put his hand on my shoulder. "You are compromised, Katrina. Your feelings are getting in the way of your judgment. We should go in hard and take them all out now."

I slapped him across the face. Big, soggy tears streamed out of my eyes. "Fine. Let's take it down. But do not open fire until you have a clear shot. I will not have my mother's life be in vain."

I jumped over the balcony in the lead. The others followed a distance behind me. We floated down slowly and quietly. The descent was at least three hundred feet, and we had to be silent the whole time to avoid startling L'l'itoh, who sat poised at the edge of the vat.

Thousands of locusts lined the walls around the vat, feeding off the heat of the green goop. All at once they opened their eyes. They didn't have guns, but their sheer numbers scared me.

"I wouldn't fire if I were you," L'l'itoh shouted from its throne at the bottom of the shaft. Its voice echoed off the walls and caused the locusts to notice us. "This is very explosive, as reactors go. One false move and we will be blown away. You, me, and your mother."

L'l'itoh snapped its fingers and two locusts picked my mother up off the floor and hovered her over the vat of green ooze. She kicked at the air, fighting to free herself.

"Let go of me!" she shouted, but it was no use.

"You are very smart, Katrina. I really didn't think about transferring planets and stars to neutralize my ship. There are only two gods in the whole cosmos who could pull that off, and you found them. It was quite an ingenious plot. Our ship will lose power in a matter of hours."

L'l'itoh rubbed its hairy front legs together and the locusts tensed up. "It's already happening. Power is concentrated here, at the core, to enact my plan. Had I known, I could have siphoned the power from the stars into our reserves, but your attack caught us by surprise. I used too much power destroying your precious world. I have none left to keep this ship going for long. I suppose that means I will have to move faster than I intended."

L'l'itoh snapped its legs together again. The locusts flew off the wall and formed a shield between me and the other gods. I turned back, but only saw a thick, black shield of darkness.

The fly chuckled. "That will distract them long enough. You gods are so pitifully few, and you multiply so very seldom. It's almost as if you wanted to go extinct. Of course, that is why you needed a god to look over your pathetic planet, isn't it? To protect you? To coddle you? Because you couldn't evolve on your own? That is the trick of it, Katie—"

I glared. "Don't call me that."

"You seem fierce now, but the truth is that your species is weak. The gods knew it, which is why they had to nurse every planet you inhabit, like you were babies. Without them, you would never even exist."

"Is this what it's all about? You weren't loved enough as a kid? Does it just piss you off that the gods loved us more than they loved you?"

Mom chewed through her gag. She whimpered at me. "Sweetheart! Get away from here!"

"I won't go anywhere. Not without you." I turned to L'l'itoh. "Is that why you kidnapped my mother?"

L'l'itoh chuckled. "No. She had nothing to do with my plan. Kidnapping your mother and watching her suffer is just a delicious bonus."

"So, what is your plan then?"

L'l'itoh smiled. "Did you know there is a little piece of god inside every human, Katrina?"

"I've heard that once or twice."

"When you kill a lot of humans that equals a lot of pieces of god."

"I don't think it works that way. The particles disappear into the ether."

The fly shook its head. "No. Matter cannot be created or destroyed any more by me than by Zeus. No. All those guns…they fed back into backpacks, which fed into this vat. Human essence, distilled down into its purest form. A million sparks from a millions gods, all at my feet. It is my greatest invention. It will ensure my people never go without protection again. *I* will become their god."

"You're crazy."

L'l'itoh stood. Its cape flew off, and it placed its crown and jewels on the throne, until it was naked. "I will give you a choice, Katrina. You can kill me still, but if you do so, your mother will vanish into this vat and add her soul to those I've collected. Or, you can save her, and I will fall into the vat, assume my destiny, and ascend into godhood."

L'l'itoh snapped its legs together and the locusts dropped my mother. At the same time, L'l'itoh fell into the green goop. I only had time to either kill L'l'itoh or save my mother, not both, and I knew my choice before it was given to me.

I had to save my mother, even if it meant the end of everything.

Chapter 16

I caught my mother right before she landed in the green goop. I don't know if I'd ever flown that fast before and worried I would snap her neck with the force of my catch, but she opened her eyes and smiled at me. I wrapped her in my arms and placed her on L'l'itoh's throne.

"You shouldn't have saved me," she told me.

I smiled. "I know, but there are some things that you do even though you aren't supposed to."

I was so stupid. This was the exact reason that I didn't want Urania to come, because I knew she would compromise my judgment, and it had happened anyway. I should have killed L'l'itoh, but in the heat of the moment I made a rash choice. I chose my mother over the fate of the universe—all of them. Now, I had no choice but to wait until the Bug Pharaoh emerged from the goop. And I had no idea what to expect.

I stared down, waiting, and explosions lit the core about me. Dennis, Connie, Michael, and the other gods burst through the wall of locusts. They floated in the air around me as I watched for L'l'itoh to reappear.

"What happened?" Hercules gasped.

"L'l'itoh went into the goop," I replied.

"Great. Then let's blow it up and get out of here," Dennis said.

"What if it comes out a god?" I asked.

"Who cares?" Bacchus said. "Then at least the planet killer is dead. We'll deal with L'l'itoh when and if it's still alive after the explosion."

"I agree with the drunkard," Hercules said.

"Yeah, Katrina," Dennis said. "We came here to destroy the planet killer, and now we can."

I looked up at them. "You're right. Blow it."

I grabbed my mother's hand and wrapped it around my shoulder. Hercules gathered our guns together and stacked them in front of us. With my free hand, I pulled out my sword and sliced the guns down the center before kicking them into the goop.

We flew to safety. Above us, a long shaft led to the top of the planet killer. Had we used it the first time we would have been in the main core in moments, instead of hours.

Bacchus and the other gods followed me out of the core and into space. Just a few moments later, I heard the first explosions from inside. Immediately, the ship began to teeter.

"Fall back!" I shouted.

We beelined for the other side of Earth as the shockwave from the planet killer's explosion cast shrapnel for thousands of miles. The remnants would shower down on Earth for at least a generation.

"There's no way anything survived," Hercules said to me. "That explosion could have destroyed a million gods at once."

"So, it's over?" my mother asked. "It's really over?"

"No," I said. "That was too easy."

"Easy!" Bacchus shouted. "It took out who knows how many gods and probably killed millions of people, and it almost killed us as well. I wouldn't call any of it easy. Well-deserved is more like it."

I pulled out my sword. "Just watch. Take my mother away and watch." I turned to the rest of the gods. "All of you. Go back to Heaven and watch. I will risk no more gods today."

"Katrina," Hercules said. "This is madness!"

"I know what I'm doing."

"Then you must know it is foolish."

"And I am a fool. Do you trust this fool?"

Hercules nodded. "I do."

"Then take everybody back to Heaven. Tell Urania and Apollo to switch the planets back. I want some light again."

Hercules didn't say another word. He took my mother and flew back to Heaven, along with all the others. I set off toward the planet killer. Shrapnel from the base coated the whole sky with metal and debris and made it hard to move. I pushed through slowly in the darkness, not knowing what I would find.

The light came quickly. With another sonic boom, our sun was back in the sky around Earth. Now I could see all the shrapnel at once. At its center was an orb of blackness twinkling against the light from the sun.

I moved toward it and it pulsated at my movement, vibrating forward and back with pure energy, and emitted a low hiss. I sliced at it with my sword, but the blade went through the matter like water. I touched the orb and it gave to my hand.

I pushed a little further, and my arm disappeared into sludge. It wasn't sticky or wet. My arm only felt a tight pressure. I pushed my other arm inside, and it vanished along with the first. Slowly, I made my way inside the orb. At the center sat a small, green, pulsating figure.

When I moved toward it, its eyes popped open. It couldn't speak, but I felt its words burrow into my brain.

"You cannot kill me, Katrina. Not anymore."

I dared not open my mouth lest I inhale the dangerous sludge, so I thought my words. "Anything can be killed, L'l'itoh. You have proven that."

"I have ascended beyond mortality, beyond the gods. Zeus needed Cronus's power to create life," L'l'itoh said, looking down at its hands, "But I have that gift inside me. I am the alpha and the omega; the most powerful being in the galaxy."

"You are wrong. I have seen Cronus. He controls the horizontal and the vertical. He is the beginning and the end. No matter how powerful you are, you will never be as powerful as him."

"I am as powerful! Powerful enough to destroy this whole universe with a single thought."

"Then you will have destroyed us all, including your own people. In that case, you'll be no better than Zeus."

"I am better, but the destruction of the universe will be worth it to see your kind suffer."

"I thought you became a god to protect your kind."

"I have none left to care for."

"There are others, I am sure. I saw them on my travels. There were even monsters that survived in the other dimension."

L'l'itoh paused. "You have seen them? Where?"

I showed it the pictures in my mind, recounting my whole journey—the bug world, Cronus, everything up until the moment I stepped foot into the goop.

"Cronus created all of this. He created the gods. He created the universe. He created Zeus, and he keeps Zeus in his stomach."

L'l'itoh twitched at the mere mention of Zeus. "Wait," it said breathlessly. "Zeus is alive?"

I nodded. "He has suffered for years in the belly of Cronus. I had no idea how much he made your kind suffer before you came to my planet, no idea how much the gods made you suffer for simply existing. Believe that. My people, they knew nothing. Your quarrel is not with us. It's with Zeus."

L'l'itoh stayed silent for a long moment. Its long, hairy legs rubbed together. It let out a long sigh, followed by another, as it considered what I had said. Finally, it looked me in the eyes. "Very well, Katrina. You make a compelling point. How do I get to them?"

"Let me help you."

"What is the catch?"

"You will probably die. Cronus does not take kindly to gods. Treat him with deference. Your quarrel is not with him, but with Zeus."

"Understood, Katrina. Now, let me go." There was a long moment of silence. "I would like to meet my maker."

And then, in an instant, the entire orb shattered. L'l'itoh's glowing eyes took up a third of its head, and it stood three dozen feet tall, pulsating with power.

Meanwhile, I was covered in green goop.

*

It was weird to willingly allow L'l'itoh into Heaven after spending so much energy and time fighting it, and after so many deaths. There were grumbles across all of Heaven, but it was my house, and I made the rules. I stood on Heaven's platform with Urania, Apollo, Bacchus, and the pantheon of remaining gods. So many had died to create the life force that transformed L'l'itoh into what it was now, and there was nothing we could do to bring them back.

"Where will I go?" L'l'itoh asked.

"We will send you beyond our universe. Once you are there, you can never come back. Do you understand?"

"I understand that you do not comprehend a way for me to come back yet. I, however, know anything is possible."

I turned to Urania and Apollo. "Urania, do you think you can hold the planets in line while Apollo opens the black hole?"

"That is the most dangerous thing I've ever heard anybody doing. Ever," Urania responded. "What about Cronus's creeping whiteness? If even a drop of it comes through, it will spread across the universe and destroy us all."

"I understand it is a risk, Urania, but I can only deal with one problem at a time. I'm banking it'll take a second for that whiteness to sneak through, so let's close it quick, okay?"

"You realize this is what I told you to do before, right?" Connie said.

I gave her a look. "I fully acknowledge that, but I'm taking credit for it, now. That's the benefit of being a god."

"Fair enough." Connie rolled her eyes. "As long as you know it was my idea."

"I'll make sure to blame you if it fails," I said with a coy smile.

"We should just fight it," Apollo said.

"Maybe, but it almost slaughtered all of us before it became a hulking god. We won't last an instant against it now."

"She is correct, Apollo," L'l'itoh said. "It is best to deal with me this way. The whiteness might destroy you, but if you do not grant my wish, then I most certainly will."

"We are going to risk the whole universe, so we won't die?" Aphrodite asked.

"Well," I said. "That's pretty much what we've been doing this whole time."

"Fine," Urania conceded. "Let's just get it over with." She closed her eyes and shook. The Earth shook with her, and then Heaven quaked, too. "Hurry."

I gave L'l'itoh a half-hearted salute. "Are you ready?"

L'l'itoh nodded. "As I ever was."

"Fly to the sun. We'll create the black hole when you get close enough."

"You will not trick me, will you?"

"Of course not. That's not my bag."

L'l'itoh stood, giving me an appraising look. "I believe you." The bug god flew away faster than I had ever seen anything fly before. I watched its trail streak across Venus, and finally to Mercury.

"Now!" I shouted to Apollo.

At once, the sun became a black hole and sucked in anything that moved. Urania did all she could to hold the planets in place. Her hands shook, and her nose bled. I watched as L'l'itoh's streak fell into the black hole and disappeared.

"Close it!" I shouted.

And like that, the portal was closed. Heaven stopped shaking and Urania fell to her knees. I dropped beside her. "You did it," I said, kissing her cheek. "You did it."

"Is it over?" She was panting.

"It's over." I turned to Apollo. "It's over, right?"

"As far as I know…it's over."

"Until Cronus gets a visit from a fly god," Urania said. "And then we may have to deal with him again."

I chuckled. "We'll deal with that when it comes." I cupped her hand in mine. "Right now, can we just enjoy the win?"

Urania looked up at me and smiled. Her hands cradled my face. It was nice.

*

We monitored the skies for another week to make sure that none of the whiteness leaked into our universe. We would never be sure of course, but it seemed like we were safe.

Meanwhile, Aphrodite took Hercules, Hephaestus, and the other gods back to her world. Bacchus, true to his word, left Earth and went to travel the universe. The gods wanted me to lead them, but I was a wartime general at best. Aphrodite was more likely to lead them in a time of peace. Besides, I didn't want to be around any of them for longer than necessary.

All except Urania. She stayed with me. For the first time in ten thousand years, I was at peace. I cared about her as much as I cared about my own mother.

She says I'm a mama's girl. I guess that's fair, since I risked the lives of everyone in the universe to save the old lady. I know, it's a bit of a problem. We're working on it.

My mother still lives with us, except she lives inside our new castle, instead of in the guest house. Without my father, there was no reason for her to live by herself.

Connie and I also agreed to let the demons roam Earth for a while, as thanks for fighting against the Horde. They helped clear out the remaining enclaves of Horde soldiers and burned the dead for good measure.

Humans grew accustomed to fighting alongside the Hellspawn and a weird bond grew between them. We brought the most vicious beasts back down to Hell, but those that could survive living around humans did very well. Who knows, maybe one day they'll even make it into Heaven?

I don't know what's gonna happen on Earth in the future, and for now that's okay. I'm more about living in the moment anyway.

*

You just finished *And Death Followed Behind Her*. If you liked this book, make sure to check out the *And Doom Followed Behind Her*.

And Doom Followed Behind Her tell the rest of the story from the perspective of Rebecca Lobdell, who went through Hell on Earth during *And Death Followed Behind Her*.

See more of her story story by picking up *And Doom Followed Behind Her* today, which combines the first three books in the Lobdell Chronicles; *Every Planet Has a Godschurch, There's Every Reason to Fear,* and *The End Tastes Like Pancakes.*

*

Here's a preview of the book.

And Doom Followed Behind Her

By:
Russell Nohelty

Edited by:
Leah Lederman

Proofread by:
Katrina Roets

Cover by:
Paramita Bhattacharjee

Chapter 1

I woke up with a vicious hangover, rolled over in my bed, and popped two aspirin. There was a finite supply of aspirin left in the city, and I hoarded as much as I could. When a new shipment came to the hospital, I made sure the orderlies held back a crate just for me.

Most of the thieves went for the morphine or other addictive drugs they could flip on the streets, but not me. I didn't need the money. I got paid a lot for doing my job, and so I was happy with bags of saline, clean needles, and aspirin, which all went to cure my daily hangovers.

I trudged across the room and hung a bag of saline from the coat rack, right next to the floor-length leather coat which had become my calling card after the war. The needle stuck in its familiar place on my arm and the saline did its job rehydrating me.

Back in my old life, things were simpler. Back then, I might've complained about living in a crappy apartment above a dive bar, but if the last twenty years have taught me nothing else, it's to never take anything for granted, and I never do; not anymore. I've rolled with the punches and they've come hard and fast enough to knock out everybody I ever loved, leaving me alone in this world, living in a derelict apartment in the slums.

People left me alone in the slums. That's why I lived here. In the better parts of the city there were way too many rules. In the slums, nobody cared what anyone did, and as long as you could take care of yourself, nobody messed with you.

The problem with living here is that the water wasn't clean. Brown liquid belched out of every sink, so I made sure to keep lots of clean, natural water around, boiled and purified for my drinking pleasure. There was a guy named Jack down at the water treatment plant, and in return for a screw every now and then, he delivered me more water than I ever needed.

Yes, we still screwed, even in the worst of times. It was about the only thing we did for fun, but we had to choose our partners carefully. You couldn't just screw anything that moved. Some of the demons got into the prostitutes, and if those prostitutes screwed one of your lays, you could get a series of diseases that—well, let's just say you didn't want. That's why I vetted my men carefully before letting them lay the pipe to me.

*

After the saline drip finished, I turned on the purified water filter for a shower. I stripped off my clothes and caught a quick glimpse of my naked body in the mirror. Dark jagged scars cut up and down my torso, and a wide gash slit across my face, a constant reminder of the time a demon saved my life from the Horde, only to be vaporized in the process.

Twenty years ago, the Horde descended upon us. They were a race of disgusting bugs of all types—ants, millipedes, spiders, flies, and more. If you could name it, they existed in the ranks of the Horde. Armed with blasters that could disintegrate a person in an instant, they set out to destroy us. It was a nightmare.

Within hours of their arrival, they leveled most of our major cities with lasers from their massive spaceship stationed above the atmosphere. Before they even touched down on Earth, we'd lost billions of people. Then they released their invasion force, which blotted out the sky and turned day into night, and by the end, we lost a few billion more.

Every inch of me was the memory of the great battles from that war, the scars of which reminded me I was still alive when so many other people—better people—died. I lost one of my eyes in the war and had it replaced with a mechanical red one whose wires spread across the left side of my face and caused my cheek to involuntarily spasm. It wasn't pretty, but it gave me two eyes and depth perception, which was important in the new normal. Some might even say it's why I can be so accurate with a gun, because I have a cyborg's eyesight. I think it's because I practiced for a long-ass time.

*

Every day in Thebos started out the same. I walked down to the bar under my apartment and waited for orders to come. One of Piggy's disgusting lieutenants came to the bar under my apartment by around eight am and gave me a list of chores for the day.

The chores changed daily, but they all involved using violence in some way or another. They might be collecting money, offing somebody, or sending a message with my fists. It didn't matter what it was, I was supposed to do it, and I did, every day, crossing off my missions as I accomplished them.

Sometimes it took an hour. Sometimes jobs went late into the night. It all depended on the day. It didn't matter to me. It all paid the same, whether I had ten tasks or two. Once I crossed them all off my list, I ended up at Matt's bar again to drink it off.

I heard everything that went on down there through the floorboards, which is how I knew that Matt was up, cleaning the bar from last night. After I was dressed, I walked down the creaky stairs.

"Morning," I said, walking through the door.

It was the only place in Piggy's quadrant that didn't pay protection money to him. That's because I personally protected the bar from hooligans and in exchange, they let me drink for free. Honestly, with as much as I drank, they would have made out better paying for protection.

"We're not open yet," Matt replied, brushing dirt across the floor with an old broom.

I sat down at the bar. "That's what you always say. Whiskey, neat."

"I'm serious this time. We ain't open."

I spun around on my bar stool, making sure he knew I didn't care. "I don't want to pull rank on you, Matt, but this was the deal."

He didn't bother looking at me. "You aren't worth it. You're drinking me out of business."

"I don't see anybody messing with you. That's more than I could say for most of the businesses in this town, so I think I'm plenty worth it. Of course, if you don't think so, I could stop protecting this place altogether and see what happens. I don't like your odds though."

Matt stopped his sweeping with a sigh. He couldn't argue with me. He also knew a threat when he heard one. "Fine. One drink."

"No, as many drinks as I damn well please."

Matt walked over to the bar and poured me a glass of whiskey, straight up, no ice. Whiskey was the one drink still readily available in Thebos and everybody left chugged the stuff like water. It was the only drink you could guarantee wasn't contaminated, the bonuses being that it made you forget your problems, and if you drank enough, you'd die, which was always a plus.

"Here you go," Matt said.

I knocked back the drink in one shot. I didn't taste the bitterness of the alcohol, but then I couldn't taste anything. A gun backfire during the war made sure of that.

Matt leaned himself against the bar and rubbed his finger on my hand. "Did you know we've never had sex before?"

I smiled at him. He heard me having sex with other people—those floorboards worked both ways—and it always stuck like a craw in Matt's side, but I was adamant that I couldn't protect his bar and sleep with him at the same time. Since I didn't want to find a new bar, we couldn't bang. I moved my hand. "Did you know I've killed people for less?"

He leaned in closer. "Please. You don't have the stomach to kill me."

My jacket flew open and, in a flash, my pistol dug into Matt's forehead. "You have no idea what my stomach is capable of, my friend."

After a second of tension, we both laughed. In a different life, decent people wouldn't have laughed at a legitimate death threat. But we've all learned something in the past few years; laughing about it is the only way to survive.

I holstered the gun, still chuckling. "Next time I pull my gun on you, I'm gonna shoot you with it."

Matt wiped the tears out of his eyes. "That'll be the day."

The bell chimed over the door and a fat, oafish demon walked into the bar. The only demon up before ten am was my handler, Odahai. He was disgusting, with a face like an ogre and breath ten times worse. Yes, I said demon. They lived among us. It's part of what made life such a miserable experience for all of us.

We weren't ready for the Horde War. When they came from the sky, we didn't know what to do. I still have nightmares of their unyielding forces. Earth quickly became a nightmarish Hellscape—and I mean Hellscape in the most literal way possible. When the Horde attacked, it triggered an Apocalypse.

Yes, a biblical one.

I know it sounded crazy, but that doesn't make it any less true.

Rifts to Hell opened all around the world, and monsters of every type entered our world. Demons, ghosts, dragons, orcs, and more rose from Hell and scattered along the Earth. I heard stories about Hell on Earth eons ago but seeing it with my own eyes was wholly unbelievable.

Even more unbelievable . . . it turned out they were on our side. The army of the damned took up arms alongside us to drive back the forces of the Horde. The Horde's forces were endless, but so were those of the undead. Together, we held off the armies of the Horde and drove them back—and eventually we won.

After the Horde Wars, nothing was the same. People who once clung tightly onto their last shred of hope abandoned it and stared dead eyed into the ether, waiting for the sweet call of death. We had all been through so much, and somehow survived. We lost our loved ones, our souls, and our reasons for living.

Yet, we were still very alive, and we dared not take that for granted. So many of us didn't make it out of the fight that killing ourselves, well, it felt downright selfish. So, we plowed along. This was the new normal, and we were determined to get along, even after we'd lost everything.

On top of the shit burger that was our lives, some genius decided it was be a good idea to let the demons stay on Earth if they wanted. I guess I kind of understood it, in theory. After all, humanity would have been wiped out without them. Whoever made that decision really screwed us though, because demons like Odahai didn't play nice.

Odahai's knuckles dragged behind him as he hobbled into the bar toward me. He was broad enough that all but the widest doors forced him to enter at an angle. He reached into his pocket and handed me a slip of paper.

I unfolded it and looked over the note quickly. It only had three tasks on it. "Is this it?"

Odahai chuckled to himself like I'd made a joke. "That's it."

"What's so funny?"

But he didn't have to answer. I scrolled my eyes down the list and my stomach dropped when I got to the last item.

Goddamn it. Sometimes my job really sucked.

Chapter 2

Ten years before the Horde descended on us, Earth was pulled into a black hole. It happened in an instant. We were minding our own business, living a pretty decent life, when the sun collapsed upon itself, creating a black hole and sucking Earth through it. We called it the "Sun Incident."

It sucked. My head felt like it split right down the center. A million screams bellow from the edges of your brain while every color in the rainbow tries to flay you alive.

Every one of us prayed for death in that moment, and most people had their prayers answered. Eighty percent of the human race died—eight billion people. Dead. In an instant. I can't even imagine that many people.

Those of us that survived wondered what made us special, but we knew in our hearts the answer was nothing. We just got lucky.

Somehow, I survived that ordeal.

Eventually, Earth was pulled back into our universe as fast as it was sent away. The sun returned to normal and the world kept spinning, as if nothing ever happened. Scientists studied the phenomenon for years with no results, until they threw up their hands and shrugged, chalking it up to a thing that happened sometimes. There were rumors that Apollo himself sent us into oblivion and pulled us back out again. I don't know if that's true, but it wasn't the craziest thing I'd ever heard. Not even close.

I trudged through the streets of Thebos, dreading everything I had to do that day. There wasn't a lot of time for dread in my life, and certainly not for pain, but some tasks managed to pierce through my thick outer shell. I had never failed to deliver on anything Piggy asked of me, and I wasn't going to start now. Some of his errands truly tested my patience, though, like the last one on my list. Every task I accomplished moved me closer to it. Usually I didn't mind working for demons, but today I loathed it.

It was hell, trying to live with them. No matter how much humanity wanted to work together and rebuild ourselves, the demons had their own ideas. They lived for the chaos. During the war, the demons had a purpose—something to slaughter. They directed their overblown sense of rage toward the Horde and were both effective and efficient on the battlefield. Their bravery and zeal for winning could not be overstated.

When the battling stopped, their anger had nowhere to go except toward us. Demons were already used to taking their aggression out on humanity, since it's what they did down in Hell. They were our torturers and our wardens. After the Horde Wars, they decided to do what came naturally, and lord over us again.

Once they beat us down, the demons battled each other for control of a world that wasn't much worth fighting over. They developed their little fiefdoms all over the world. Eventually, those fiefdoms turned into kingdoms, and we had no choice but to serve our war lords, unless we wanted to pay the ultimate price.

*

The first job on my list was to pick up protection money from a bodega in Little Kenya. A group of African refugees were stranded in Thebos after the Horde War and set up a community together. Up until two weeks ago, they used Piggy's men for protection, just like everybody else, but that changed. They thought it would be a good idea to use their own people as protection. Piggy had a problem with that—a big problem.

If one community could get away with protecting themselves, then more would surely follow, and the need for Piggy's services would vanish. It was my job to show them the error of their ways, starting with one shop and working my way up to burning the whole town to the ground if necessary.

It was a charming store, with colorfully painted walls and little statues carved into the wood lining the counter. The smell of turmeric and ginger filled the air as I walked through the aisles. I found the owner filleting a chicken behind a glass case full of exotic meats.

Piggy could have picked any store on the block to teach a lesson, but this time it was this guy's store. He had no idea what was coming for him. They never did. The fickle finger of fate pointed to him, though, just like it pointed to everybody at some point in their lives. For the unlucky ones, it pointed their way again and again. Life was heartless and cruel. Most days, you escaped the odds, but some days, some days you rolled snake eyes and crapped out.

"Mr. Mwangi?" I said with a warm smile. A smile was disarming. It made people take down their guard, and it worked with him, too. Mwangi turned from his work with none of the tenseness that would have been appropriate, based on my appearance—and my reputation. Instead, he showed a bright smile that showed off a nice set of teeth.

"Yes," he said, cheerfully. "How may I help you?"

"Well," I said, gesturing at the shop around me. "This is a lovely store you have here. It smells, so alive, you know. Most stores I go into smell a little like death, if they smell like anything at all. But this one? It's almost overpowering, honestly. Almost like an old-time marketplace."

He puffed out his chest with pride. "Well, thank you. I try to keep it pleasant and inviting, like home. Most of my customers don't have a good memory of home any more, and I like to think this is like going into a little slice of Kenya."

It didn't matter where you were, people loved to be complimented. Compliment somebody enough and you would surely get into their good graces. That was a guarantee.

"A little slice of Kenya." I ran my finger across the deli window. "Damn if that isn't beautiful. How long you had this place?"

"Next month will be my fifth year," he said, placing his hands on the counter.

"That's not bad. Most of these businesses, they rise and fall overnight. But not you. You lasted five years. That's quite an accomplishment."

"And hopefully another five more."

"Hmm," I said, looking down at a picture of Mr. Mwangi surrounded by seven children. "Well, that's where things get interesting. See, Mr. Mwangi, I would love it if you could last another five years. I really would, but it's dangerous out there. Thebos is full of thieves and scoundrels."

His eyes were wide, and he nodded solemnly. "Oh, I know. I have been very lucky."

"Lucky. That's one way to put it, Mr. Mwangi. But I think you have a guardian angel looking out for you. Yes, I do, because nobody is that lucky. At least, not in my experience."

The smile on his face faltered. "What do you want?"

I put my hands in the air, pretending to be nonchalant. "I'm just trying to have a conversation. You have kids, Mr. Mwangi?"

Mwangi pointed at me with his meat cleaver. "I think you should leave."

"Whoa," I said. "That's not very nice, Mr. Mwangi. I'm just trying to be pleasant. Don't you want to be pleasant? Just answer me, do you have any children?"

Mwangi folded his arms across his chest. "Two children."

I picked up the picture of him with his children. "This picture here shows seven kids. Let me guess, the other five died in the war?"

"You should leave." His voice fell hollow.

I placed the picture back down carefully. "I get it. I lost people in the war, too. A lot of them. Every person I ever cared about, actually. It's good you have two kids left, Mr. Mwangi. It really is. Most people, they have no attachment to this world. It's good you still have some left."

"Get. Out."

"In a minute, Mr. Mwangi," I said. "I see it in your eyes, you just want me to get to the point. Well, here it is. I have a favor to ask you."

"I know your face. I recognize you. Your eye gives you away." Mwangi laid his hands on the glass case. "Tell your pig boss I will not pay."

I strolled toward him, shaking my head. "That's not very nice. He doesn't call you names, Mr. Mwangi. And he could, since you haven't paid him his money for the last two weeks."

"And I won't."

I chuckled. "That's where you are wrong, Mr. Mwangi."

I grabbed a metal rack that held a collection of spices and thrust it to the ground. My steel-toed black boots were perfect for inflicting damage on glass without breaking my foot. I used them to round-house through his meat rack.

Mwangi jumped back. "What are you doing?"

"I'm showing you that life is dangerous!" I shouted. "We can all use protection, Mr. Mwangi."

"I can handle you myself!" Mwangi said, lurching forward with his meat cleaver.

I held up a warning finger. "This is not funny, Mr. Mwangi. I have no time for your nonsense. You will pay my boss today or I will burn this shop to the ground."

Mwangi rushed around the counter and swung at me. The trick to fighting somebody that owes you money is hurting them badly enough that they bow to your superior strength without fatally injuring them. You don't want to kill them. Heck, that would make it easy. It's much harder to wound somebody than to outright kill them.

Mwangi swung again. I shot up my arm to block and clasped my hand onto his wrist. I spun him around to the floor and he dropped his knife, whimpering in pain.

"Mr. Mwangi, that is not nice."

"Please!" he said. "Please stop."

"I didn't want to start with you, Mr. Mwangi, but you left me no choice. Now, you will pay me what you owe, and you will tell every other shop owner on this block that the only protection in this town comes from me, or I will take everyone you ever loved, and you will watch them bleed out in your arms. Do you understand?"

Having loved ones is a liability. I used it as a bargaining chip every chance I got. Our own lives don't hold much value, but when you love somebody, you put a value on their soul. And that cripples you. If this poor shop owner had no loved ones, losing his shop and his life would mean nothing, but once I threatened to take away the things he loved, he became putty in my hand.

"Fine!" he shouted. "I will pay! I will pay!"

I let go of his wrist. "I knew you would, Mr. Mwangi. I knew you would."

Chapter 3

I left Mr. Mwangi's store with all the money in his register. He whined about not being able to make rent that month, and that his children would starve. I didn't care. Starvation was a far better fate than getting their throats slit. Besides, it wasn't my fault he still had loved ones. That was just bad planning on his part.

"Hey!" I heard a young man shout to me as I rounded the corner away from Mr. Mwangi's store. "Hey! I'm talking to you!"

I turned around to see a dark-skinned, young man pointing a gun at my face. Behind him, four others pounded crowbars and baseball bats into their palms. They tried their best to seem intimidating, but they clearly didn't have any clue what horrors I'd seen. Nothing they did could frighten me.

"I'll be takin' that money, ya see?" The boy with the gun waved it in my face.

I placed the wad of money in my coat pocket. "No, you won't."

"Dis is our neighborhood, ya see?" the boy with the gun said. "We protect it, and we profit from it. Ain't nobody gonna pay if we just let ya walk."

"Yeah," I said, taking a step forward. "That's the point."

The young man wobbled as he backtracked a step. His stance was all wrong. He didn't know what he was doing. "Don't cha take another step."

I lunged forward as the young man's bullets whizzed past me. I grabbed his arm and slammed his face into my knee. The gun slipped onto the ground when I broke his trigger finger.

"You broke my hand!" he whimpered.

I kicked the gun away and pulled out two revolvers from the gun belt under my coat. "Now, listen here. This isn't your neighborhood. It's Gliporg's. Leave, forget this ever happened, and he'll let you live whatever miserable life you have left."

"Get her, boys!" the young boy screamed just before I put a bullet between his eyes. The four others charged forward. I ducked the first crowbar and fired a bullet into its owner's belly. His friend reared back to strike me, so I spun on my heels and shot him through the neck.

Two gang members left, and I had my two guns trained on them. "Don't make me kill you."

The boys looked at each other, then rushed toward me as if I couldn't shoot them both at once. They were wrong. I blew a hole in both their chests and watched as each one flew backwards, dead before they even hit the ground. One of them bounced off a parked car.

Mwangi ran outside his shop, visibly shaken, and I turned my guns toward him. "This is why you need me for protection, Mr. Mwangi. There are hooligans about. You're lucky they didn't land a blow on me. Otherwise, I would have no choice but to follow through with my threat to burn down your shop."

"I'll see you next week, Mr. Mwangi." I kicked the boy's gun into the gutter. "This town is very dangerous. I think the price of your protection just doubled."

Mwangi had no choice but to nod as he watched the blood of five young boys bleed into the sewer in front of his store.

*

I crossed the first item off my list as I waited on the roof of a dilapidated, tenement high-rise pointing a M-2400 sniper rifle at the mansion across the street. The building used to be two hundred stories tall, but now it sat, a pathetic, dilapidated structure. I climbed up four stories of rotten, wooden stairwell and found a perfect sniper perch. Nothing but a ruin, really. An ideal place to lay in wait.

The mansion I aimed my gun at belonged to Piggy's biggest rival—a demon named Ctumiti—who ran the southwest quadrant of the city. We all called him "Itty" behind his back. He was self-conscious about the fact that he was the runt of the warlords, but what he lacked in size he made up for in viciousness.

Ul'brem had forced an uneasy ceasefire between Itty and Piggy for the last year, but last night one of Piggy's best lieutenants, Ylgur, defected to Itty's band of mercenaries and Piggy didn't like that one bit. Piggy demanded loyalty and paid top dollar for it. If one of his own crossed him, they had to die.

I'll be honest, I wished that I had more trouble working for demons, but I just—don't. At all. I've had a lot of horrible bosses over the years, and demons weren't the worst of them. I worked for whoever paid the most. When there was still a government to speak of, they needed help disposing of despots. After the Horde War, it was demon warlords who controlled huge tracts of land and fought each other bitterly for more.

The thing is . . . they were both equally bad, but the demons paid more and paid faster. It truly didn't matter who I worked for, murder was murder. I was always good at rolling with the punches. Psychologists would call it moral ambiguity, but I don't care for big words or headshrinkers. I just know I'm a survivor.

Before the war, I was a naïve, little girl who loved creature comforts. It didn't take long for me to figure out that if I wanted to live, I needed to be ruthless and cunning, tough as stone and sharp as a razor's edge. I spent all of my waking hours training my body to fight like a champion and my mind to abandon all emotion. I also took the time to develop a unique set of skills which kept me in high demand long after the war was over.

I became a sniper. I could fight well enough, but my real gift was sitting in dark crevices, planting, and waiting for bugs to pop their heads up so I could eliminate them one at a time. I preferred the elegance of a long-range kill over the brutality of a close one. It was less taxing on the muscles if you didn't mind extreme boredom, which I didn't. The life of a sniper was boring, but I enjoyed the tedium of sitting in wait. It gave me time to clear my head and think. I was a prodigy, really, and after the war, demons enlisted my services to kill each other.

I was a deadly accurate shot and a compassionless killer, two traits highly sought in the chaotic aftermath of the war. Business was good in Thebos, until things settled and Ul'brem emerged as its king. After that, snipers weren't as much in demand. Still, I enjoyed jobs like these that gave me the chance to dust off my skills.

After an hour of waiting, a long, black Humvee limousine pulled up in front of the house. Out stepped two of Itty's guards, followed by the traitor, Ylgur, a demon dressed in a three-piece pinstripe suit and decked out in gold chains. He always was a flashy one. It made my job easy.

I steadied my breath and peered through the sight. I couldn't use a laser for guidance. Not with so many guards around. The wind blew from the southeast, but the demon charges fired straight and true even in a tornado. I only had one shot. If I wasn't perfect, Ylgur would scurry underground and never emerge again.

I took one more breath and held it. Then I slowly squeezed the trigger until the sound of the demon hunter whizzed through the air and blew Ylgur's head into a hundred pieces. I pulled the gun down from the ledge and crossed number two off my list.

Only one item left and that's when my dread kicked into high gear.

*

If you liked this preview, make sure to pick up *And Doom Followed Behind Her* today.

ALSO BY
RUSSELL NOHELTY

THE GODVERSE CHRONICLES
And Death Followed Behind Her
And Doom Followed Behind Her
And Ruin Followed Behind Her
And Hell Followed Behind Her
Katrina Hates the Dead
Pixie Dust

OTHER NOVEL WORK
My Father Didn't Kill Himself
Sorry for Existing
Gumshoes: The Case of Madison's Father
The Invasion Saga
The Vessel
Worst Thing in the Universe

OTHER ILLUSTRATED WORK
The Little Bird and the Little Worm
Ichabod Jones: Monster Hunter
Gherkin Boy

www.russellnohelty.com

www.wannabepress.com

CPSIA information can be obtained
at www.ICGtesting.com
Printed in the USA
FSHW020220290121
78110FS